P

# Playing the Field

Zoë Foster Blake enjoys writing her biography because she can write things like, 'The literary world was shocked when Foster Blake was controversially awarded the Man Booker prize for the third time', despite the fact that this is patently untrue.

Things that *are* true include a decade of journalism writing for titles such as *Cosmopolitan*, *Harper's BAZAAR* and *Sunday Style*, as well as being the founder of all-natural Australian skin care line, Go-To.

Zoë has written four novels, *Air Kisses*, *Playing the Field*, *The Younger Man* and *The Wrong Girl*; a dating and relationship book, *Textbook Romance*, written in conjunction with Hamish Blake; and *Amazinger Face*, a collection of her best beauty tips and tricks.

She lives in Springfield with her husband, Homer, and her three children, Maggie, Lisa and Bart.

# BOOKS BY ZOË FOSTER BLAKE

*Air Kisses*

*Playing the Field*

*The Younger Man*

*Textbook Romance*
(with Hamish Blake)

*Amazinger Face*

*The Wrong Girl*

# Playing the Field

# ZOË FOSTER BLAKE

PENGUIN BOOKS

PENGUIN BOOKS

UK | USA | Canada | Ireland | Australia
India | New Zealand | South Africa | China

Penguin Books is part of the Penguin Random House group of companies
whose addresses can be found at global.penguinrandomhouse.com.

Penguin
Random House
Australia

Cover design by Laura Thomas © Penguin Group (Australia)
Text design by Kirby Armstrong © Penguin Group (Australia)
Cover photography: Legs: DreamPictures/Getty Images; Grass: lazybuffy/Shutterstock
Author photograph by Paul Suesse
Typeset in Fairfield by Post Pre-press Group, Brisbane, Queensland
Printed and bound in Australia by McPherson's Printing Group, Maryborough, Victoria

National Library of Australia
Cataloguing-in-Publication data:

Foster Blake, Zoë.
Playing the field / Zoë Foster Blake.
9780143204244 (pbk.)
Previously published: Michael Joseph, 2010.

A823.4

penguin.com.au

# ROUND 1
## Spilled Drinks vs Providence Inc.

I turned from the bar and prepared to navigate my way through the mass of heaving, loud, beautiful people to our seats in the courtyard. I was doing a brilliant job, nursing the drinks to my chest and caving my shoulders to protect them, until I was knocked from behind. Half of each drink went flying onto the back of the guy unlucky enough to be standing in front of me.

'Oh, shit, shit, sorry, *shit!*' I said, trying to grip the now-slimy glasses.

He turned slowly around. With my hands full and covered in vodka, I was unable to do anything but offer what I hoped was a sincere apology via my eyes. His mouth was open and his fingers were pulling his shirt out from his substantially wet back. And somewhere high above, God was high-fiving someone on his incredible handiwork.

Deep blue sparkling eyes set against an olive backdrop, and a warm, mischievous smile housing a set of fluorescent white teeth. Quite tall with dark, dark brown hair, longish and floppy and tucked behind his ears in that sexy, European Underweary Model way. A rugged growth around his mouth and cheeks – the kind you don't notice unless you're forced to write a description of it in a book. In short, a twenty-first-century Adonis.

He raised an eyebrow and his smile widened. We locked eyes, and for a few charged seconds the music, the floor and the pulsing liquor-friends surrounding us went out of focus, leaving only him, and me, and 4000 kilowatts of electricity. I couldn't lift my feet, shift my eyes away from his, or mute the chorus of one thousand visually stimulated brain cells collectively applauding in my head.

'That's one way to offer me a drink,' he said good-naturedly, shaking his shirt out but not taking his eyes off me.

'I'm so sorry. I . . . I was pushed,' I said, wincing at how wet he was. At the same moment, I was jolted again from behind, and launched forward from the waist up.

'Noted and forgiven,' he said, smiling cheekily.

'Okay, uh, sorry again about your shirt . . . ' I offered a weak smile and made to move away.

'Could I buy you a replacement?' he said quickly, a verbal hand on the wrist to stop me walking away.

'Well, that makes *no* sense,' I said, laughing and shaking my head. He was staring at me with his eyebrows up and a smile no one with a pulse could resist. 'But thank you.' I smiled sweetly, blushing, and turned to walk.

'It makes sense in that you wouldn't be getting away so fast,' he said in a singsong voice with his palms outstretched, as if to say: *Am I right, or am I right?*

'Really, it's fine,' I said, my brain throwing a spanner at my vocal chords for passing up the opportunity. I flashed him another dazzly smile and disappeared mysteriously into the crowd.

'Hey, wait – I didn't catch your name,' I heard him shout, but I kept walking. We'd need new drinks soon, and I'd be sure to walk past him again. Until then, he could wonder. Well played, Sergeant Seductive, well played.

'You should take longer next time,' Colette said when I finally plonked down next to her. 'What, you get thirsty on the way?' she continued, surveying the half-empty glasses.

'No, some dickhead pushed me and I spilled them all over probably the *best*-looking man in the universe! Ohmygod, Col. He had this smile . . . it was weird, we just stared at each other, like we had some instant connection. I know, I *know*, shut up.'

'Mills! *Boon!* Come quick! We've got the beginnings of a great story-line,' she said, laughing.

'He even offered to buy replacements, when it was so not his fault . . .'

'Look at you, Jay – all smitten over some random in a bar!' she said, digging me in the ribs. As my older sister, it was in her job description to rib me, physically and figuratively, every time I showed any hint of liking a guy, ever.

'Did you give him your number?'

'Oh, yeah, in the three seconds we spent together.'

'Well, what are you doing? You gonna go give it to him, or sit out here like a loser?'

'I'm staying here. But I may walk past him and make him ask me for it when I get the next round.'

'Maybe just write it on your forehead, or scribble it across your tits,' Col offered, raising her glass to her lips.

'You mean, show him from the outset the kind of classy bird I am?'

She ignored me, instead making a loud slurping noise. 'There's actually nothing left in this,' she said, peering into her drink.

I leaped up. 'Leave it to me,' I said, giddy with excitement, already turning to walk inside.

'Actually, know what? I really can't be arsed waiting another twenty minutes. I think we should roll. I'm beat.'

No! *No go home!* I screamed on the inside.

'Ohh, come on, just one more?' I said aloud, fidgeting to get inside and see Adonis again. 'You promised one drink and, technically, that was not even half of one . . .'

3

Dramatic sigh.

'Okay then. But don't take so bloody long this time. If you see Fabio, give him your number then keep walking. Treat 'em mean and all that shit.'

I grabbed my gloss out of my handbag and applied a fresh layer before prancing gaily inside, heading back over in His direction, my heart racing.

When I got to the scene of the spill, Adonis had vanished. I held my breath and looked around, to the left, to the right, trying to keep it all on the low-low. But he was nowhere to be seen. I put my head down and slowly made my way over to the stairs so that I could inconspicuously scan the entire room, which seemed to have tripled in volume and people since I was here four minutes ago.

I looked, and I looked. And I looked. But he was gone. My heart, unaccustomed to such intense feelings within such condensed time-frames, plummeted through my body to the floor, where it mocked me quietly for getting my hopes up over a guy whose eyes drilled through mine because he'd put away fourteen rum and Cokes, not because he thought I was The One.

You *fool*, Jean. Why didn't you give him your name when he asked? And your number and email and blood type, too? Now he's gone and you'll never see him again.

I turned and walked back outside, my shoulders slumped, my tone deflated.

'He's gone, Col.'

Colette stood up and put her black patent studded bag on her shoulder.

'Oh, Jay. If it's meant to be, then you'll run into him again . . .' She scrunched up her face sympathetically and led the way inside. I followed, my eyes combing the sea of heads for Adonis, but he hadn't just gone to the bathroom, and he hadn't just slipped off to the ATM. He'd gone.

# ROUND 2
## The Size Eights vs The Size Fourteens

She was not a slim woman. But 'overweight' wasn't accurate, either. The phrase 'average weight' would've felt cheated, embarrassed to be associated with her. Yet 'fat' seemed cruel.

All frazzled blonde hair and frosted watermelon lipstick, with diamanté-encrusted sunglasses jammed on her head, she was that unique shape one earns by enjoying soft cheeses, crisp sauv blanc, and coffee 'n' cake with The Girls. There was nothing wrong with any of this, of course, except that she was violently disillusioned by her shape, clothing size and age. Which is how she had found herself standing before me, one toe pointed, as though about to launch into a small solo from *Swan Lake*. Her hands smoothed the fabric of the dress over her thighs as she surveyed her frame in the mirror, head tilted to one side.

'Ooooh, and I could wear that pretty coral necklace Gary bought me for my birthday. It would set off the aqua so nice.'

'Lovely,' I said, nodding, smiling, speaking slowly and reassuringly. I cleared my throat. 'Tell me, does it feel . . . restrictive at all?'

She raised her eyebrows, darting her small, kohl-saturated eyes towards me. I knew this look. It was a blend of fear, surprise and wounded self-defence. It said: Why? Do you think I look fat? *Is there something you'd like to tell me?*

'No. Why? Does it look it?'

She twirled quickly to look at her bum, which had been flattened and widened and squished so that pockets of cellulite peeked through the satin, and the material cut in at the hips.

'No, no, no . . . (Clever-shop-assistant rule #1: Never, ever answer a question like this in the affirmative). I mean, you could *try* the size up (#2: Never mention size numbers) and see if it feels more comfortable (#3: Never refer to a garment looking better, only *feeling* better). You see, this design is a small make (#4: Always describe any ill-fitting garment as being a small make to ensure customer knows it's not them, it's the design). We've found a lot of customers have had to move up in size (#5: Always refer to Other Customers so that customer thinks they are normal and not even remotely optimistic in their sizing choice). So how about we try it, just in case?' (#6: Smile and nod, pretending this is merely a congenial suggestion, as opposed to a sly avenue for implementing a size up.)

'Well, okay, but . . . I like what it's doing for my bust. A size up might not give me so much *oomph*.'

The *oomph* she spoke of, and now fondly handled, reminded me of two deflated water balloons taped onto a wall, and then gaffer-taped around the bottom third in an attempt to push some of the water up into the top third. It was a sad vision of a woman clutching onto the days when her breasts were perky and firm and allowed to roam under spaghetti-strapped dresses and fine-cotton T-shirts without the assistance or restriction of a bra.

Ingrid, my boss, said that I wasted too much time and energy styling ungrateful cows, but I couldn't understand why she wouldn't want a rash of thrilled, confident women flitting around town, attributing their wonderful new understanding of clothing – and magnetism for compliments – to our little store.

A few minutes later, as I passed back her receipt (she bought the size up), Ingrid walked in holding a tray of coffees. She raised her eyebrows and folded down her bottom lip in a 'Well *done*' manner. I smiled smugly. Impressing Ingrid was akin to impressing a toddler using nothing but a head of broccoli. She wasn't so much critical as prematurely disappointed in what I was bound to ruin.

'Now, here's your dress,' I said to the customer. 'You have a won-derful night. And promise me you'll wear a bra?'

'Oooh now, I can't promise that! Thanks for everything, love.' She turned, pink clamshell mobile to her ear, tale of the Amazing New Dress ready to explode.

'What'd your new best friend buy?' Ingrid asked as soon as Blondie was out the door. She tucked her short black hair behind her ear as she waited for my answer. She was wearing all black, as always: a particularly well-cut pencil skirt with a black frilly blouse and towering black peep-toe heels. A flaming red mouth of lipstick with black-winged eyeliner completed her ode to the 1940s.

'A $400 dress and a new reputation.'

'Sorry, I'm afraid I didn't catch your name – was it Trinny, or Susannah?' she smirked.

'That's it, tease me for making you money.'

'Oh, settle down, doll.' Ingrid called everyone 'doll'.

'I'm nearly at my target, you know.'

'Mmm . . .'

Ingrid wasn't keen about letting a backyard designer into her high-fashion boutique, but I'd begged her to let me put some of my jewellery pieces on display, just to see if they'd sell. Being Ingrid, she'd set me a sales target to achieve before I was allowed to put my first 'collection' on the counter.

Part of Ingrid's issue, I sensed, was that my designs were decid-edly un-Ingrid. They were tribal, ethnic-inspired, antique, boho pieces using wood, brightly coloured stones and rocks, gold and silver, with animal, plant and tree motifs. I liked to wear stacks of intricate cuffs on my wrists, and layers of delicate gold necklaces around my neck; Ingrid preferred diamonds and an Omega.

But I was taking her promise seriously. I'd moved to Sydney from the Gold Coast three months ago for a number of reasons: 1) My best friend had just moved to London with her fancy new fiancé (boredom); 2) My sister was in a post-relationship mess and needed me (support); 3) I couldn't bear living with Mum and Godfrey a nanosecond longer, much as I adored them (insanity); and 4) I thought that maybe if I moved out of home and had no life and no friends, I would take my designing seriously, and perhaps even turn it into a proper money-making business (motivation). This last reason despite the fact that I'd had little training: jewellery-making at school and a one-year design course after I'd realised that my commerce degree was about as me as a handlebar moustache and a Harley, and had deferred indefinitely.

But for all my good intent, I was struggling. I had only seven finished pieces so far: three necklaces, two cuffs and two sets of earrings. For some reason, the last three pieces – Ingrid had requested ten – were coming along at the rate of soybean growth. It concerned me greatly. If I couldn't even complete a collection of ten, what hope did I have of ever being a true, certified designer?

'You look nice today,' I said, changing the topic.

'Justin is taking me out to dinner tonight.'

Justin was Ingrid's half-boyfriend. He was still officially married, but he was separated, and he felt that was good enough. Ingrid? Not so much. Though it wasn't that she was hanging out for a wedding – she'd been married once before, and didn't seem to be interested in kitting up in ivory again any time soon. But Justin screwed with her head in an atomic fashion; he was fifteen years her senior, Clooney-esque, wealthy and successful – and, I thought, excessively sleazy. I had no idea what Ingrid was doing, but had a feeling it had something to with the faint ticking noise emanating from her ovaries. Despite her prickly exterior I knew that some-where there was a woman who desperately wanted to be covered in a small human's spit and spew, and while I had no idea of her *actual* age, she had to be flirting with forty. Perhaps she saw Justin as her only chance of a ticket to the delivery room. Sure, maybe she was 'settling' with a pig who was still married to another woman, but maybe she was also smarter than I gave her credit for.

'Oh, that's nice.'

She was looking at emails on her BlackBerry.

'Tell me, have you finished off that invoice I asked you to do yesterday?'

Sale jubilation officially concluded.

# ROUND 3
## The Dates vs The Droughts

Col had combined a short grey singlet dress with tan leather sandals. A flimsy, elegant black waistcoat was slung over her shoulders, and her wrists were drowning in bangles, cuffs and random pieces of leather string – all of which, Hermès cuff aside, I'd made for her. It was a typical Colette outfit – seamlessly thrown together but looking as though it had been pondered over for hours.

On top of several kilos of metal, Col was also wearing an uncharacteristically large smile. She had left her natural honey curls alone, for once, and they framed her face perfectly, making her skin look more olive and her green eyes even prettier. I always told her she should wear her hair curly more often, but she preferred it straight. Made her feel 'groomed', she said, as opposed to 'some surfy wench'.

'Hi, Jay, hey, Ingrid.'

'Hi, Colette.' Ingrid looked up for less than a second, issued a brief smile and went back to the Karen Walker skirts that had just come in. She thought Col visited too often, distracting both me and the customers.

'You're in a good mood,' I said slowly. 'How come?'

'Oh, you know, sold my first house for Gerard.'

'Shut *up!*' I squealed. I ran around and hugged her, not caring what Ingrid thought. 'Oh, that is *the* best news. I'm so happy. Who, where, when?'

'This young guy, actually. Bought it with his brother. Not too bad a sort, either. Could do with some sun – was haunting the agency with his paleness – but funny as. Meeting him this arvo to —'

'Ohmygod, are you going on a *date?*'

Col didn't have dates. Well, she hadn't for months, anyway. She was in an anti-men phase after what had happened with Eric, who had been her fiancé until, well, he wasn't. She found out that he'd been having an affair with his ex-girlfriend – a scrawny rat of a woman who taught yoga to other equally scrawny rats – just five weeks after he'd proposed. She *swears* she wasn't snooping, but she'd 'found' an email from the woman in his Gmail account, and it was so explicit and so recent, and presented such a disgusting trail of to-and-fro from the both of them, that she'd called it off that day.

That was almost four months ago. He'd called and he'd sent obscenely large bouquets, but Colette was having none of it. She'd taken their dog, the blender, the espresso machine and all the best furniture, and moved out. Mum had tried to persuade her to move back up to the Gold Coast, but Col was about as keen on that as she was on getting 'Eric' tattooed on her right shoulder. Instead, she'd convinced me to come and live with her. Which, given how gutted she was, and that a move to Sydney had been on my radar anyway, was a relatively easy decision.

I was equally single, sans the simmering rage. I'd broken up with my last boyfriend, Jeremy, not long before. He was a sweet boy: an electrician with warm brown eyes and a talent for guitar rivalled only by his talent for building the perfect University Cigarette. But he also had a chronic pot addiction and an inclination towards alien conspiracy theories.

At first it had seemed so romantic and naughty, smoking a joint together after a night out, giggling and making Dorito sandwiches and dissecting *Futurama*. Then, when he refused to go anywhere without first inhaling some electric spinach, it became annoying. And finally, when I busted him smoking a joint before work, it became unbearable.

He told me he'd quit, that he'd never touch marijuana again, and that he loved me, but I couldn't seem to get past his bloodshot eyes during these declarations. He tried to call a few times, and even turned up at my place with some petrol-station flowers and a badly written poem, but my attraction to him had long gone. I wished him and his bong the best, and told him not to come round any more. In this sense, my move south came at the perfect time.

'No offence, Jay, but: *You're a moron*. He and his brother just have to sign some paperwork. And he's not my type – not even in the same postcode.'

She saw the quiet disappointment in my eyes.

'Don't worry, I'm not about to ship off to the Mad Island of Lesbos just yet.'

I laughed. 'Well, I'm thrilled for you. And I hope that commission means we can go for a yummy dinner . . . Hey, we still going to pick up those bedside tables this arvo?'

'Shit sticks! Totally forgot about that. Can you grab me from Lucio's at five?' She saw the blank look on my face. I was as confident finding my way around Sydney as I was negotiating foreign arms policies. 'It's that one we went to after the movie last week?'

'Oh yes, I remember the one.'

'Thanks, Jay.'

I hugged her again and kissed her on the cheek and tried not to think about the fact that if I had given my number to Adonis on Saturday, *I* could be off meeting a guy for coffee this afternoon.

# ROUND 4
## Fate United vs
## The Coincidences

I pulled up in front of Lucio's at ten past five in Mary, the little white Mazda who had been with me since Year 11 and had been my transport to Sydney, filled with clothes, shoes, jewels and all of my most beloved books, music and magazines. I called Col's mobile.

'Coming!' she answered. 'I see you out front.'

I hung up and started fiddling with my long brown hair, wondering whether I should get a fringe. I folded some back over itself and held it over my forehead in a high-tech simulation. Just then the passenger door opened and two sets of legs greeted me. Colette bent down.

'Hey, Jay . . . Nice hair, idiot.' I dropped the faux fringe quickly. 'This is Frank.' A second face bent down. It belonged to a man in his thirties who smiled and said, 'Sweet park.'

'Thanks!' I beamed back. I enjoyed being the cute little sister. It was my favourite role.

'So, Colette tells me you work at that posh dress joint on High Street, huh? Mum loves to throw Dad's money in there. She's probably already secured your Christmas bonus.'

I laughed. 'Tell her to say hi next time she comes in . . . So, uh, you ready, Col? We've got to get there before 5.30 . . .'

Another set of legs walked up to the car.

'Oh, and this is Frank's brother, Josh.'

A smiling, tanned face furnished with beautiful teeth and dark floppy hair leaned down. And somewhere in the area of my body that ensured I had oxygen travelling to my heart and brain, there was a malfunction. It was *Adonis*. Holygodamnfrickenshit, it was Adonis!

I caught his eyes for a flicker before blushing and dropping my head.

'Hey, do I . . . do I know you?' His voice wafted in slowly. *Shit.* Why couldn't this have happened when I was looking pretty? I didn't even have any makeup on. 'You're the girl from Balcony!' he exclaimed. 'You spilled your drinks on me. It *was* you, right?'

Before I could utter a response, Frank's voice had thieved the aural spotlight.

'So, make sure you have no plans on Wednesday, okay? 'Cos that's the day I'm going to ring out of the blue and suggest we do something completely spontaneous.'

Frank started walking backwards towards the BMW parked in the no-stopping zone up ahead. He stood at the passenger door and called to Josh, who was still looking at me in disbelief.

'It was you, wasn't it?' he said, smiling, his eyes shining brightly.

I looked at him and nodded, smiling shyly, my right hand running nervously through my hair.

'Josh! Activate the automated door opening mechanism at once!' Frank boomed.

I dropped my head so that Josh didn't feel inspired to make any further conversation. I was acutely aware that I was performing situational suicide: I had thought of nothing but this man for days, and here I was being all coy and insipid now that he had magically presented himself.

Frank blew Col a kiss and stepped into the car, and Josh, a look of surprise and amusement dancing across his face, bid Colette and me farewell with a wave and a smile, and stepped into the driver's seat.

'Wednesdaaaaaay!' Frank yelled as they pulled away.

'Too much, isn't he?' Colette said with finality, climbing into Mary.

'I think he's funny!' I wanted the topic of Frank to be over, so that

I could launch into the topic of Adonis.

'Thinks he's a comedian.'

'Well, that's not so bad. Even *you* managed a few laughs.'

'So, get this, Jay. Frank's brother, Josh – PS how stupidly hot is he? – is some big football star, right, and he was one of the people who came and looked at that massive penthouse on River Parade. Must have some serious clams.'

Col had great difficulty understanding the confidentiality aspect of the real-estate agent's role.

'Frank works at News Limited as the publicity something-something. Reckons he can get us tickets to any event we want. You know, he'd have potential if he wasn't so full-on . . .'

I let her launch into her spiel on all the things Frank should change so that she could date him once before telling him she 'wasn't looking for anything just now'. As I half listened, my mind spun off to another dimension entirely: of all the siblings Col had sold a house to, and of all the days for me to pick her up, it was *him*. That shit simply doesn't happen unless you're meant to be together living on an island somewhere, deliriously in love, existing on coconuts and gently massaging SPF 30 onto each other's backs.

'Shame Josh has a girlfriend or we could've had a double date,' Col said as a verbal full stop to her soliloquy.

My fluttering, frenzied heart stopped cold.

'Really?' I said, trying to sound nonchalant.

'Mmm. Some model slashie TV bird. Been together for a couple of years, I think.'

Girlfriend. Model. Couple of years.

*Computer says no.*

'Ooh!' Col squealed. 'There's a park – quick! Good one.' She grabbed her handbag from the floor. 'The gods are smiling on us today, aren't they, Jay?'

No, I thought. Not really.

# ROUND 5
## Googling vs Ignorant Bliss

'Working hard, I see?'

I looked up from my magazine to see Frank standing in front of me.

'Hi, Frank! Yeah, uh, Tuesdays are usually pretty slow . . .'

He looked around at the empty store.

'Okay, *really* slow,' I confessed. We laughed.

'So, Jean Jeanie, I wanted to drop these off for you to give Colette, to show her the kind of no-expenses-spared romance-athon she's in for with the Frankonator. I would've taken them to her work, except I didn't want her workmates to get jealous and resent her.'

He pulled out a bunch of pathetic plastic flowers from behind his back.

'Why, they're just beautiful, Frank,' I gushed.

'Right you are. Now, I'd appreciate it if you put them in water – purified, of course – and the finest Venetian vase you have.' I laughed. He was as lacking in confidence as Donald Trump was money. And Col was nuttier than a Snickers: he *was* funny! And persistent! And romantic! And a funny, persistent, romantic guy was just what she needed.

'I'd better go. Josh and I are parked in a no-stopping.'

My heart began racing – Josh was nearby?

Suddenly a voice piped up from behind Frank.

'Found a dress for your big date yet, Frankie?'

And there he was, standing in front of me. Adonis. He was wearing a grey V-neck jumper, dark blue jeans and the kind of trendy white trainers that looked generic but were probably bought for several million dollars. His skin was glowing, his smile radiated; he emitted a kind of halo. He really was astonishingly handsome. Especially with his eyes twinkling like that. I blushed, dropped my head and looked down. When I looked back up, he caught my eye for the slightest second before looking back to Frank. I silently cursed the hair gods for failing to warn me to do something with my hair this morning. It was filthy and cowlicky and messily braided.

'No, I've decided I'll just borrow that pink one of yours. As you can imagine, Jean, we're often mistaken for identical twins.' The joke lay in the fact that Frank was at least three inches shorter, ten kilos lighter and roughly a fifth as handsome as his brother.

'Hey Jean,' Josh said, now standing next to Frank, close enough for me to be able to reach out and touch.

'Hi,' I managed weakly, still smiling at Frank's self-deprecation. I could feel the prickly heat that inferred my face was now the colour usually reserved for the deeply sunburned.

'We've gotta stop running into each other like this.' Josh gave me a mischievous smile, his blue eyes searing into mine.

'You two know each other?' Frank asked.

'I —'

'We —'

We both stopped. I laughed nervously.

'Jean threw a drink at me once.'

'No no, it was an acciden—'

'I'm kidding, I'm kidding.' Josh laughed. I shook my head, flushing further – if that were possible – with embarrassment.

Frank looked at me, then at Josh, then back at me. A knowing smile spread over his face. 'I see.'

I cleared my throat. 'So, um, Frank, I'll see that your flowers get to Colette and I'll tell her you stopped by.'

'Muchos grassyass. Well, we'll let you get back to your . . . work,' he said, glancing at my magazine. 'Just don't exert yourself, okay? Could put your back out.' He turned and walked out of the shop, jingling his keys.

I giggled and tucked some hair behind my ear – #82 in my alphabetised catalogue of Annoying Nervous Tics.

'Later, Jean.' Josh smiled and drilled into me with those eyes again. As he turned and walked out of the shop, I exhaled a breath I didn't even know I was holding.

Once they had disappeared from sight, my hand flew to my mouth, half from shock, half from disbelief. What exactly was fate, that filthy little wench, up to? Suddenly, within the space of two weeks, I had seen Josh three times. And I'm sorry, but that was flirting he was doing just then. It *was*! And what of his beautiful girlfriend? I'm sure *she* wouldn't like to know he was asking some random girl if he could buy her drinks, and handing out his dizzying smile on a silver platter.

I wondered how serious they were . . . *Google!* Google would open the lid on Josh's relationship; after all, he was supposed to be some big-shot footballer, so there'd be plenty of dirt on him online. Why hadn't I thought of this before? *Loser.*

I tapped in his name on the work computer. Site after site came up. Whoa. Seems he *was* quite the star. Oooh, shirtless shots – right click, save. Aaaand – right click, save again. I wondered how I could have got this far in life without having heard of him. I put it down to living in another state. That and having roughly as much interest in football as a Muslim did in pork.

Most of the sites were sport-based and full of statistics or reviews of Josh's game. He was twenty-seven, an Aries, and liked *The Family Guy.* There was the occasional gay blogger waxing lyrical about his 'hot sizzly pecs' and 'eyes that were made for the bedroom!!' And then there were the women's magazine websites that cooed over his ridiculous physical beauty and featured more shirtless shots of him in his training gear. There was a story implying he'd had a tryst with a Playmate after judging her in a bikini competition, one linking him to Natalie Imbruglia, and one speculating on his fidelity, which was nestled cosily between several boozy shots of him with what looked to be some seriously loose women. Instantly a small bonfire of curiosity and jealousy flared up. But I pressed on bravely with my online stalking.

Right click, save.

And then I saw them: Josh Fox and Tess Clifton. They were captured midway up the red carpet at a film premiere two months back. He looked confident and smiley, wearing an olive green shirt and an open-necked black suit. She – all cascading toffee waves and feline green eyes – looked, well, kind of smug. She wore a bright yellow mini-dress which should've been garish but actually looked quite adorable on her perfectly slim and tanned frame. She was enormously TV-ready and very conventionally pretty. He had his arm around her waist, but I was pleased to see that there was definitely distance and a slight awkwardness between the two of them. They didn't look ready to announce a six-figure, six-page-spread engagement just yet.

I studied her. Was that the kind of girl he liked? My hair was that length – longer, even – but it was dark brown, not expensive Jennifer Aniston blonde. My eyes were brown and my skin was the brand of fair that repelled fake tan and violently opposed the sun. I looked terrible in yellow, and my bust was an optimistic B. I was screwed.

Nevertheless, I continued on, frenzied with curiosity. The first entry on their considerably well-documented romance was two years back. It was from the social pages of *The Times*, and reported that they had been spotted at a trendy beachside diner having breakfast. He was the 'handsome football star' and she was the 'gorgeous socialite' who just happened to be the daughter of the chairman of his football club, Henry Clifton.

Oh, Josh. What nous, dating the boss's daughter.

There was clearly no hope for me, despite his propensity for eye-locking and power-smiling. I wished them many genetically blessed babies and clicked off the Internet in defeat.

# ROUND 6
## Chemistry vs The Clowns

Frank and Colette were on their date, so I took Dave, Colette's neurotic little Maltese Terrier, for a walk to the park, where I felt chubby and guilty watching people close to vomiting throw their bodies around in a sadistic boot camp. As Dave sniffed around, trying to locate the tree fortunate enough to receive his stream of priceless yellow gold, I wondered when I might start making friends down here. I really only had Col, and while her friends were nice enough, they were all 29-ish like Col, and a bit rougher, and a bit not-my-friends. Or they were married with small children. Fun *as* for a single 24-year-old like me.

As always, following this realisation, I tried not to resent moving down, reminding myself of the 'give it six months' rule – I couldn't pack it in and run back to the beach yet. Anyway, I wasn't *hating* it down here; I was just lonely. All I really did was work, and pester Col to spend time with me on the weekends and show me around a city that she'd become disenchanted with years ago. I guess I was still enjoying the bigness of the city: being able to get dinner after 9.30 p.m., and being able to choose from a whole cast of decent clubs and bars, as opposed to three. I found the people a lot more inspiring for my work, too. When I went people-watching around Surry Hills and Kings Cross, and to the markets and all the crazy vintage stores and antique warehouses, I always felt compelled to create exotic, odd new pieces, using new stones and new styles and new metals. That's what I should be doing today: making some jewellery. Not watching TV and making excuses. I sighed, watching Dave allocate several urination millilitres to a large Moreton Bay Fig. I called him and set off home, filled with the obligation to create, which I knew translated to a twelve per cent chance of follow-through.

I heard the door slam just as I walked out of the bathroom, towelling my hair.

'Honey, I'm hooo-ome,' Col yelled down the hallway.

'Soooooo,' I asked, smiling through my words, 'how'd it go?'

She came into the hallway, still holding her keys, and leaned against the wall. Her face was a goo-free zone. Not good. I really, really wanted her to like Frank. She hadn't even torn through a rebound guy yet – surely that was due by now? Even though Frank was far too nice and funny to be miscast as the rebound guy.

She sighed.

'Meh. He took me to some silly Lebanese place where we smoked hookah and there were fat belly dancers jiggling their guts in my face as I was trying to eat my lamb. Zero chemistry.'

'*Really?* Col . . . are you maybe cutting him off a little prematurely?'

She stopped jangling her keys and considered my question for a few seconds.

'Yeah, probably. But d'you know what? I couldn't be fucked wasting energy on a relationship that isn't going anywhere. Don't look at me like that; I know what I need a little better than you and your fancy exposed nipples.'

I looked down and pulled my towel back up, smiling sheepishly.

She sighed. 'Okay. Case in point: he went in for the kiss and I gave him *my cheek*. So fucking awkward. I just can't picture myself *being* with him. Like, having sex with him would be kind of . . . kind of gross.'

I shook my head, smiling. 'You're a tough crowd, Coliflower.'

She walked to the kitchen and got herself a glass of water.

'Urgh, that hookah was foul. I feel like I've smoked a kilo of apple-flavoured ciggies.'

'As opposed to your usual Marlboro-flavoured ones, you mean?'

'I told you, I've quit.'

'Mm-hmmm . . .'

'Whatever. What'd you and Dave do tonight?'

'Nothing. Walk, then boring dinner. I was going to do some work, but I saw that you'd spread your tax shit all over the desk – which was the perfect excuse to watch *CSI*.' I grinned, walking towards my bedroom door. 'See you in the morning. ' I closed the door softly behind me.

If Col didn't want a relationship, then please at least let Frank be interested in a friendship with her, I quickly prayed to the fate fairies. That way I could see Josh again, even if I couldn't touch him.

The next morning, as I was getting ready to head to the shop, Mum called, wanting to know whether she'd need to bring sheets for her visit this weekend. She asked every time she came down, just in case we had been the victims of a vicious linen burglary since the last time she stayed.

Mum still lived on the Gold Coast with her second husband, my stepfather, Godfrey. They met at the 1999 Animals First Christmas party: Godfrey pointed out that she had some cat hair on her cropped cream bolero, and the rest is history. Now they were the Posh and Becks of the Queensland pet industry.

Mum's passion in life was exotic Persian cats. She bred kittens for weirdo cat-lovers and showed her queen – BillyJeanSkyBelle – all around the country. BillyJeanSkyBelle was a Best in Show super-cat, who, because of her perfect jaw line, correctly spaced facial arrangement, plum-sized eyes and dense black hair, lived a life of privilege. She slept on Mum's pillow at night and ate only fresh organic chicken, tuna or beef. She had her own seat in Mum's fire-engine-red Camry and a series of velour jumpers with 'BJSB' embroidered on the back. All of this was incredibly amusing to Col and me, but Mum failed to see the joke.

'She's earned me more than you two,' she'd say.

'Don't see *you* winning any competitions,' she'd say.

'Do *you* have your own website?' she'd say.

To me, cats were nothing more than attitude dressed in fur coats, but they were Mum's world. The obsession began with Wilbur, a two-toned Persian who'd made her lonely nights less so. When Dad had left, leaving Mum and us and his role as the local butcher for Mum's tacky hairdresser cousin, Suzy, a friend of Mum's had given her Wilbur.

We knew from Uncle Darren that Suzy and Dad had skipped town and were now living on an opal-mining farm in the arse-end of Australia. I had tried to contact him a few times when I was younger, but he had never made any attempt to get in touch with me, and the one time I actually spoke with him, he was awkward, impatient and got off the phone after a few minutes, citing a chook that had broken free from the pen. Years of birthdays spent hoping he'd call, and vivid, powerful dreams of him returning home (usually with a pony called Bucky as an apology gift) without fruition had led to a brand of deep-seated hatred and bitterness.

Godfrey, while more like a daggy uncle, filled the void nicely. He was the kind of guy who had worn a moustache since 1976, combed over his hair, and was still pulling out five-cent pieces from behind my ear and slipping a twenty-dollar note into birthday cards involving illustrations of purple tennis rackets. Col and I payed him out constantly, of course. But Godfrey didn't care. He knew his place in life, and it absolutely thrilled him.

I loved Mum and Godfrey's number-one-fan brand of love. Godfrey made Mum's cup of tea for her every single morning, and they went for a walk together after dinner every single evening. They had 'date night' the last Friday of every month, and sang karaoke at home for fun. Just the two of them. Sober. Their love and support for, and adoration of, each other gave me hope while simultaneously raising my relationship bar somewhere up near the ozone layer.

'So you'll be home when I arrive? To let me in?' Mum spoke fast, and while I wouldn't call her voice screechy, it was definitely in the higher octaves and had a distinct nasal quality.

'Yes, but only if you come armed with several sets of sheets.'

'Stop being smart, Jean. I'm just trying to lessen my burden on you.'

'Mum, you're never a burden. And stop with the "when I arrive" stuff: you know I'm going to pick you up from the airport.'

'Now Jean, that's not necces—'

'Shoosh. I'll be there at 5.15, 'kay? Will you have your mobile?'

'Of course I will. Jean, you are silly sometimes. Besides, I've just put the new kittens online and I've been getting calls from all over Australia. Even had a man from Melbourne call and offer to fly the little tortoiseshell down! Can you imagine?'

I laughed. 'Mum, I gotta go. See you tomorrow. Love to Godfrey.'

'What about towels? Do I need to bring a towel? I'm sure the last thing you girls need is baskets full of washi—'

'Mum, no towels, sheets, mattresses or floorboards are required. See you tomorrow.'

I walked out to the kitchen looking for my shoes, catching the tail end of Col's phone conversation as I did so.

'Okay, I promise. Yes. I realise that. Okay! *Jesus!* I'll speak to you tomorrow. Bye.' She hung up and rolled her eyes.

'What was all that about?' I asked with a smile.

25

She sighed. 'Frank invited us to watch Josh play tomorrow night' (my heart skipped a beat at his name) 'over at Ewan Stadium. Which would be a brilliant idea, save for one tiny flaw: it's stupid.'

I spoke immediately, forgetting to play it cool.

'Well, you know, I've never been to a game, and I'm pretty sure Mum hasn't either. Maybe it could be fun?' I stopped and thought for a second. 'Hang on, is this a date we're intruding on?'

Col picked up her bowl of muesli and spooned in a mouthful.

'Ha. I'd hardly call the *football* a date. Especially with you there. And Mum.'

'Riiiight,' I said, filling a glass with water and taking a gulp.

'Can you imagine Mum at the football?' Col laughed, scraping the sides of her bowl with her spoon.

'Oooh . . . what do you think her Sporting Event outfit will be?' I said with a glint in my eye. 'Something casual, probably – like her gold jumper and those knee-high purple boots.'

Col winced, shaking her head. Mum loved anything that sparkled, replicated a large predatory cat or showed off her boobs. She was violently out of style. It was like she'd got to 1987 and decided that the fashion at that minute was just so *her* that she'd stay right there, thank you very much, and the rest of us could go on ahead without her. Col and I, with our combined love of fashion, had tried for years to drag her wardrobe into something resembling that of a twenty-first-century woman in her fifties, but she was intractable. Finally we had accepted her for who she was – while doing up a button here, or blending out her blush there.

'No way. Reckon she'll go full WAG-style and wear tight jeans, those stripper shoes she's had since the nineties, and some wack cleavage-cruncher. You watch!'

'Oh shit, you're so right.' I suddenly panicked at the idea of Mum and her lace/frilled/crocheted-covered mams meeting Josh's mum, who was sure to be the kind of stunning, stylish woman who single-handedly kept Ralph Lauren in business. After all, she was a regular at the shop – Frank had said so.

'Whatever she wears, we'll just tell them she had a fancy-dress party to go to afterwards,' Col said conclusively. She paused. 'With a Bangles theme.'

We both burst into laughter.

I picked up my bag and keys. 'I gotta go.' I paused. 'Tell Frank we'll come. It'll be fun.'

'I'll think about it. Hey, wonder if we'll get to meet Josh's girl-friend,' she said, her back to me while she rinsed out her bowl.

'Mmm,' I said, praying she had some insight into her/them.

'Frank said she's a punish, actually. Says Josh's completely whipped.'

'Really?' I said, unable to disguise the interest in my voice.

She opened the dishwasher, then spun around and squinted at me. 'Jay, if I didn't know any better, I'd think you had a thing for little Josh.'

I thought about telling her he was Adonis from that night at Balcony. That he had completely consumed me ever since. That I dreamt of kissing him and that I wished Tess and her father would be transferred to Zimbabwe. But I didn't have the energy to endure her teasing, or risk Frank getting wind of it and telling Josh, so I kept my response to a dismissive 'Pfft' as I walked through the living room to the door.

# ROUND 7
## Denim vs Tracksuits

I got to work, nursing an enormous blueberry muffin and two skinny lattes, just as two women walked in. One veered over to the new-arrivals rack. The second, a pretty redhead with enormous blue eyes, came over to the counter, smiling, and asking whether she might finish paying off her lay-by, please. Ingrid smiled at me briefly and snapped into work mode; I placed the coffees behind the counter's mammoth floral arrangement – Ingrid insisted on fresh flowers every Monday – and strode over to her friend, telling her to let me know if she needed any help with sizes.

As I waited for her to try on a tight mini-dress that was completely starved of sexual subtlety, I wondered if I would see Josh after the football match. Nah, he'd go off with Tess to some uber-luxury penthouse and make love on a bearskin rug while sipping on Dom Pérignon, obviously. I cursed inwardly at the bittersweet taste of his proximity versus his unavailability.

A text buzzed in my pocket. I always kept my phone on me, even though Ingrid repeatedly told me not to.

wr on 4 game

I had a feeling Col had done that thing where she could sense I liked Josh and was now actively creating a situation where she could get more clues. She was not so much nosey as nasally fixated. I texted back.

What you gonna wear?

I'd decided that I'd take my cue from her, as I had no idea.

dunno who cares well b surrounded by yobs im not wasting good outfit on thm

Her total disregard for punctuation *killed* me. The more I nagged her about it, the lazier she was. She loved to annoy me, especially since I was so pedantic about text messages being like every other form of writing and, as such, deserving of capital letters, complete words and commas.

True. Better get out our best tracksuits.

frank mentioned after match party all laid on w family partners etc so maybe wear ur uggboots w the diamantes

I took in a sharp breath of air. I *would* be seeing Josh tomorrow night. My body performed a giddy little jump without my brain instructing it to do so. How adorable that my body and my brain felt the same way.

'Jean, are you even listening?' Ingrid stared at me.

'What? Sorry.' I quickly hid my phone.

'Did you definitely send that invoice to Romance? That Jamie woman went ballistic on the phone yesterday, saying it was overdue, and that her accounts were going to be all out of joint because of us, but I'm pretty sure we sent it last week with the Bluebird invoice?'

'Bloody Jamie . . .' I exhaled. 'I definitely sent it, I know I did.' Ingrid shook her head and opened up our email inbox, searching for the email. Spotting a dress on the ground – another of Ingrid's pet hates – I bent down and picked it up. It was a white dress with an enormous neckline that always slipped off the hanger. Just as I placed it back on, I heard a deep voice behind me.

'Mmmmladies, how are we?'

I turned to see Cameron standing at the door of the shop, one arm above his head, which was turned to one side with an eyebrow raised, the other hand on his hip. He sported a shaved head, three-day growth, a lurid green T-shirt, black jeans, and black-and-white chequered Vans. His brown, almond-shaped eyes flashed mischievously and his cheeky smile lit up his tanned face.

Cameron worked at Vinyl, the street-wear store next door. Since I'd started in the shop, he'd kept me sane on slow days with his stupid sense of humour and anecdotes from his second job as DJ Pink at local nightclub the Nursery. Ingrid, a woman who suffered fools in the same way a Venus flytrap suffers insects, oscillated between adoring him and wanting to sweep him out of the store with a large broom. They fought endlessly, in that back-and-forth TV sitcom way, each trying to outdo the other with insults. He was the only person who could get away with taunting and teasing her. I kept waiting for her to lose her shit at him but, amazingly, she never did. The most he got was scathing insults and door-slamming. I think it frustrated him.

I had grown to adore Cam in an I-never-had-a-brother-and-you'll-do-nicely-thank-you way. He reminded me of growing up at home, messing around, being a brat; having fun. He was easy to be around. He kept things light when I overanalysed or fretted over one of Ingrid's moods or toneless, scary texts.

'Wow, Cameron. Just think how sexy that pose would be if you actually had some muscles in your arms,' I said.

He snorted. 'Muscles are for losers. A real man relies on charm and knowing how to use Al Green appropriately.' He straightened up and hip-hop pimp-limped towards the counter, peeking into the brown bag housing what was left of my muffin.

'Didn't ask if I wanted one. Thanks, girls. I'll remember that next time you're hungry and you want a musk.' Cameron had an unhealthy – literally and figuratively – obsession with musk sticks. He was rarely without a small bag of baby-pink stems. Hence his DJ name. He leaned on the counter and gazed at Ingrid.

'So, how's the boyfriend, Ingrid?'

'How're the genital herpes, Cameron?'

'I see you're in your customary sunny mood.'

'I see you're going to be unsavoury, as usual.'

'But if I'm *un*savoury . . . wouldn't that imply that I'm sweet?'

Cameron spun to look at me for backup. I lifted my shoulders and eyebrows, pursing my lips.

'Can't help you, sorry.'

'Bor-ing. Come on Ingrid, spill – tell me all about him. Is he a good kisser? Do you go all a-flutter when his name comes up on your screen? Does he let you ride in the front of his milk-delivery truck?'

'Cameron, while you would *of course* be the first person I would reveal all of my romantic dealings to, I'm afraid I have nothing. Now piss off, I've got work to do. Don't you have cheap neon T-shirts to be selling or something?'

'Rather be selling them than piece after piece of overpriced lycra.' He turned to face me, holding up the muffin bag.

'You done with this?'

I nodded. 'You need the fat more than I do.'

He walked out of the store with his catch of the day, saluting us as he went. 'As always, girls, the pleasure is all yours.'

Ingrid shook her head. 'Honestly, if he wasn't so cute to look at . . .'

# ROUND 8
## Diamantés vs Linen

Mum was terribly flustered at the idea of going to the football. She was cranky at Colette for not telling her yesterday so that she could have brought the right outfit, and at me for not letting her wear her new 'Italian Design' floral diamanté-encrusted jeans. She kept running her hands through her short blonde-streaked hair and then cursing because she'd had it 'done' this morning and now it was all 'mucky'.

'We nearly ready, guys?' Col walked in, looking so cool, so pretty – all, of course, without having spent a second on her outfit. She wore tight black jeans, a white T-shirt with a bow tie printed on it, her leather jacket and black ankle boots. She had applied some mascara, black kohl, cheek crème and lip balm, jammed her hair in a messy topknot, and was effortlessly gorgeous. Despite my ability to dress others, and my desire to design, my outfits never came together like hers. In fact, I wouldn't even call what I wore an outfit; it was just clothes. And compared with hers, they always felt a bit mismatched or boring. That said, I felt good in my new black top, a rash of bracelets and bands that I'd made, tight dark jeans and heels. I'd taken a good two inches off the length of my hair before blow-drying it, but no one even noticed. As usual.

'Fuck me! Mum, what the hell are those things on your legs?'

Mum, who always took more notice of Col's opinion than mine, looked at her pants, and then, grumbling and huffing, removed them so that she was standing in her white lacy knickers.

'Colette, I don't know what you think is attractive about that gutter mouth.' She folded the offending pants and placed them back in her suitcase. 'There. Are you happy now? S'pose you'd prefer me to wear a ball gown, the way you carry on.'

'Mum, they're lovely. Honestly. It's just that, well, maybe some plain black pants would be more . . . suitable? Oh, and I have a good top you can wear!' Col took off down the hall to her bedroom while Mum begrudgingly pulled some black pants out of her suitcase and put them on.

I didn't realise they had stirrups.

Oh, and look – there are enormous gold zips on the front, too.

Part of me wanted to plant a bow in her hair, hand her a mic and let her be the eighties pop sensation she knew deep down she was meant to be.

We arrived at the stadium and were met by Frank, who ushered us up to the members area, where we were greeted with pies, fries (with tomato sauce and ketchup: Frank's rules) and red wine. His mum was running late, which was good, as it was all quite hectic getting settled before the starting siren blew.

I watched the cheerleaders with great interest; they all seemed to be exactly the same height and weight, and to patronise the same hairdresser. Their knee-high white boots and lycra midriff tops troubled me deeply: they looked better suited to a dimmed stage dotted with poles than to a football field.

'So, Janine, how long are you staying with your beautiful daughters?' Frank was playing Ultimate Guy in front of Mum.

'Oh, just the weekend, Frank. Have to be back Monday because Godfrey's not too good at minding the newborns.'

'I love your top, by the way. Colette told me you were a very snappy dresser and now I can see for myself.'

I rolled my eyes. Col snorted at his sycophancy. Mum put her hand on her chest and gasped.

'Oh, Frank, that's the thing! It's not even my top! I had a very smart pair of jeans that I wanted to wear but they insis—'

'Hello there!' An elegant, feminine voice piped up from behind, and a beautiful face framed by choppy salt-and-pepper hair, and punctuated with vibrant pinky-coral lipstick and kind dark blue eyes, appeared. She was wearing black man-style pants, a white blouse with its collar up, a large, glorious turquoise necklace and shiny, heavy-looking silver drop earrings. She was very, very chic.

'The *traffic*! Used to be able to get here in a spiffy twenty minutes, now it takes me almost an hour! Madness.'

She shook her head and placed a large brown leather handbag on the spare seat next to Frank. He kissed her on the cheek and passed her a glass of wine.

'Ladies, this is Kerrie; Kerrie this is Janine, Jean and the beautiful Colette.'

'Frank!' Colette blushed and held out her hand to Kerrie. 'Lovely to meet you, Kerrie.'

'And you. I've heard a lot about you in a very short space of time. Couldn't wait to meet you.' Her eyes sparkled mischievously. I immediately understood where Josh got it. She kissed Col on the cheek, taking her in approvingly, before shifting her blue eyes to Mum and me.

'Janine, *gorgeous* earrings. Look at them, would you? Jane, nice to meet you.' She nodded, enthusiastically moving her eyebrows up and down at each of us.

'It's *Jean*, Mum,' Frank said.

People always called me Jane. I'd tired of correcting people, and explaining I was named Jean because Mum had an obsession with France when she had me. Ditto Colette. Not surprisingly, our 'weird' French names provided the perfect fodder for schoolyard teasing in a place where everyone was called Jenny or Kim or Rebecca.

'Sorry, Jean, got the hearing of a wombat.' She smiled warmly, sincerely, and a surge of guilt tore through me for wishing Mum was as elegant, witty and stylish as Kerrie Fox.

Suddenly, Kerrie squealed. 'Oh, look! They're coming on!'

My eyes flew to the field. Sure enough, Josh's team were running on, only they were so small down there that I couldn't tell which one he was. Reading my mind, Col piped up.

'Frank, which number is Josh?'

'Number one,' Kerrie said proudly. 'He's the full-back, up under the goalpost there. Obviously the best player on the team. No bias whatsoever. Isn't that right, Frankie?'

Now that I knew who he was, I couldn't take my eyes off him: his legs, his back, his bum, his face when it came up on the big screen. He was the vision of athleticism, screaming up and down the field, catching high balls and even, at one point, scoring. My absence from the conversation wasn't noticed. Frank and Colette had swapped seats so Kerrie and Mum could chat; they barely even watched the game, they were so deep in conversation about pure-breds and Pomeranians and Persians.

I remained silent, watching the field as if I understood what was going on. Really I was just visually marking Josh, but no one seemed to notice, so I didn't need to pretend otherwise. Half-time came, and with it more wine. I downed mine so quickly, anxious about seeing Josh and meeting The Amazing Tess at the after-match party, that Mum gave me a 'look'.

'That's not very ladylike, Jean,' she said, pretending to whisper but actually speaking quite audibly.

The Bulls lost, which Frank kindly explained was the fault of someone called 'Bippo', and a complete tragedy. I watched him and Col as we gathered our things and set off for the function. I'd noticed that whenever he'd put his arm along the back of her seat, or said something adoring and patted her on the knee, she'd slowly but surely wriggled out of his affection zone. She wasn't into him. This would be the last time we ever saw him. Which meant this could be the last time I saw Josh. Bugger.

# ROUND 9
## Tess vs Any Other Female

The function room was ye olde style grand, with roof-to-floor blood-red curtains, sea-green and white patterned carpet, and gold fixtures galore. Furnishing the room were not very many chairs, lots of tables with infant-sized meat pies, the occasional cheese platter, bored-looking wait staff and what appeared to be around three billion attractive blonde women.

I took them in as fast as I could without staring. One gaggle had Bulls-jersey-clad children racing around them, smashing into their legs and demanding lemonade. The women carried on with their talking and wine, stopping only to tell the children to 'go *back* to the creche!', which appeared to be located at the far end of the room, behind a partition – or, at least, I guessed it was, as that's where children spilled from, like froth on boiling pasta.

I noticed a nectarine-sized rock on the finger of one woman – a tall, Nordic-looking girl who was breathtakingly beautiful in that disturbing, bad-for-your-self-confidence way. Make that two rings of the stone-fruit variety. Three. Okay, so these women would be the players' wives. Wow. From their incy-wincy bums and lusty-busty cleavage, it seemed impossible that some of them had actually grown small humans inside. Maybe they knew the doctor who delivered Victoria Beckham's babies. Via her ear.

Just to the right of the pram-pushers was a group of long-haired, loud, thickly glossed girls who appeared unburdened by large, heavy rings or three-year-olds. The girlfriends? One looked to be no older than twenty. She was pretty, so pretty. All chestnut hair and green eyes and ballet slippers. She was the exception. A few wore boots and dresses, and some wore jeans – but the denim was merely the bread in their outfit sandwiches, helpfully holding in place the same four-inch heels, lacquered nails, bust-drenched singlet tops and constellation of Tiffany jewellery favoured by the mums. It was a chilly autumn evening but this didn't inhibit bare legs and arms. Not all of them were housing merely tendons and bones, either; there were all shapes and sizes, just as there was a range of ages and flashy handbags amongst the group.

As a collective, these women were a sight to behold. No wonder they landed the country's most famous and successful sportsmen. It seemed most were the epitome of Hot Girl: everything about their appearance was finely constructed to make them as attractive as possible to the opposite sex, from long hair to skinny-leg jeans, terrifyingly spiky high heels and an emphasis on cleavage. I touched my brown hair, and considered my paltry B-cup and pale skin. I wouldn't last sixty seconds in that group, and if I did it would only be to do up someone's zipper or fetch them another drink. I took in their gesticulations, their long, square-tipped nails and their immaculate eye makeup. It looked a hard world to be a part of – like trying to fly nonchalantly into a beehive unnoticed when you're a fruit bat.

It occurred to me that I was being granted access to a secret world, a world that usually exists only for people in weekly magazines or page 9 gossip. This made it extremely difficult not to stare, like when someone says, 'Don't look now, but the hot guy behind you has taken his shirt off and is rubbing honey all over his chest.'

'The boys take forever in the sheds,' Kerrie said with a wave of her arm, interrupting my study session. 'Josh is usually last, doing his hair and putting on his makeup.' She winked at Mum and me.

I turned to check on Col, and saw her standing with Frank, who was on his phone, and a tall, genetically flawless blonde. A tall, genetically flawless blonde called Tess Clifton – I recognised her from my Internet research. Even from behind I could tell Tess was employing the kind of big hand gestures and laughter and dramatic hair-flicking that Col despises. And from the glazed look in Col's eyes, I could tell that her brain was slowly frying. She caught me looking and, using only a split-second widening of her eyes, issued an urgent SOS. I nodded towards Mum and shrugged, smiling smugly. Col ever so slightly snapped her head and pursed her lips: the non-vocal equivalent of Get The Fuck Over Here Now.

I didn't want to meet Tess. It would only depress me. But then, some part of me *needed* to meet her, wanted to study her, to know every morsel there was to know about her, so that I could figure out what made her so special. I looked to Mum, who was having a glorious time with Kerrie. She'd be fine without me.

'Tess, I want you to meet my sister, Jean.' As soon as I arrived, Col interrupted whatever long tangent Tess was on, to draw me into the conversation. I was dying to know why Col was so pained in Tess's presence. Was the girl stupid? Bad breath? Infuriatingly patronising?

One look at Tess's red, lazy eyes answered my question: she was pissed as a newt.

'Oh, hiiiiii,' she said, kissing me on the cheek. 'God, you two don't look anything alike – different dads?'

Ouch.

She backtracked in the way that implied she didn't need to, being her, but would for our sake.

'I mean, you're both *absolutely* stunning, dongetmewrong, but, just so different!' She giggled and swigged from her champagne. I smiled and tried to ignore Col aggressively pinching my arm.

I was amazed that despite the fact Tess had obviously polished off a small French region's worth of grapes, her presentation remained magnificent. Her Hitchcock-blonde hair was full, thick, long and impeccably blow-dried. I thought of my plain brown hair, and the blow-dry I thought was perfect until I saw hers. How did you get those flicks and waves? She was probably born with them. Same with the perfectly applied smoky-eye. And the engagement-ring-sized rocks in her ears.

'So, Jane, your sister tells me you design jewellery.' She flicked her hair to one side, all the better for showing off that outrageous lobe candy, and looked at me with her head tilted.

'It's *Jean*,' Col interrupted.

'Um, yes, well, I mean, a little bit, yes,' I smiled self-deprecatingly.

'Ohhh, that's so cute.'

Awesome. My career had just been reduced to one word, and it was the same word used to describe baby ducks. Tess looked back to Col.

'You have awesome style – very Nicole Richie. I just *love* it. Do you work in fashion at all? You must, with that style. Tell me *everything*.'

*Uh, no, Colette doesn't, but I just told you I did.* I took a deep breath and tried not to be offended. She knew naught about me, and her booze-saturated off-the-cuff remarks meant nothing. I was not to take it to heart, I quietly reassured my wilting confidence.

A tall, beautiful brunette with a long fringe, swishy hair and dark, heavily made-up eyes suddenly interrupted without so much as a look at Col or me. She was wearing a short black dress and black over-the-knee boots, and clutching a red wine and a shiny mobile phone in one hand, and a pack of Cartier cigarettes in the other.

'Ummmmm, so Morgan is *totes* drunk and can't remember where she put her new bag. Did you have it? She thinks someone took it from the box and she's looked everywhere and she's losing her shit 'cos she only bought it today.'

Tess rolled her eyes and sighed.

'Jesus, she's *always* doing this. I *told* her she shouldn't drink white wine. No, I didn't pick it up from the box. Tell her to chill, it'll show up.'

Fringey nodded and, giving Col and me a quick glance, turned and disappeared back into the crowd.

'So,' Col asked, clearing her throat, mountains of icing sugar coating her words, 'what did you say you do, Tess?'

Tess closed her eyes and smiled, 'Well.' Small pause. 'I actually want to be a TV host.' Eyes opened for effect. Dramatic pause (for the compliments and/or applause to roll in) . . .

Col folded her arms, smiling wickedly.

'Wow. You'd sure be great at that. Let me guess, you'd do a sports show! Why, it just makes sense, with your dad being the chairman of the club, and Josh and all . . . ' Oh, Col was evil when she was having fun with her prey.

Tess laughed, missing any derision.

'Oh *God*, no! There's way too much football in my life as it is. I always tell Josh he chose the wrong sport: far more money in Formula 1, not to mention all that travel . . . ' Her eyes drifted dreamily for a second before snapping back. 'No, I'm about to start as guest host on a kids' TV show on cable called *Betty's Place*, and Daddy's sure he can get me a full-time spot, what with all his contacts at the station and all.' She smiled as if we knew exactly what she was talking about. I nodded.

'You'd be super. You're just made for the camera – such pretty eyes,' Col said, sprinkling her comment with a brand of sarcasm only a sibling could pick up.

Suddenly Tess's eyes lit up.

'*Josh!*' she dumped her empty glass on the table to her right, hoicked her bag (enormous, gold and tan, Gucci) back up onto her shoulder, and pushed aggressively through the crowd to reach him. Frank, who was finishing his phone call, was one of her casualties, stepping back to let her fly past.

'She must have picked up on the scent of a platinum credit card,' he joked.

I tried not to snigger, but Col let out a loud, boisterous laugh.

'Sorry to leave you with that,' he said, jerking his thumb in the direction of Tess's trail. 'She's even worse when she's pissed, if it's possible.'

'Ohhh, come now, she's not *that* bad,' Col offered. Frank raised one eyebrow. She smiled. 'I don't mean to speak out of school, Frank, but how the fuck did she and Josh end up together? She's *torture*.'

'Oh, trust me, I struggle with it every time I'm forced to endure another story about how massively and totally incredibly famous and awesome she's about to be,' he said, shaking his head. 'She didn't used to be that bad,' he continued, looking around to make sure neither of the parties being discussed was in range. 'She's gotten worse the more famous Josh gets. So insecure. Overcompensates. And you know her dad is Josh's boss, right? Anyway. They've been on–off, on–off for years, but between you and me, I think Josh is about to pull out his get-out-of-jail-free card. I told him to prepare for a delivery of decapitated wildlife.'

'*Really?*' My mouth ejected the word with speed and with excitement but *without* permission. I immediately regretted it; it gave away too much. Frank looked at me, a slow smile spreading over his face.

'Why, Jeanie – fancy stepping in to take Tess's spot?' He poked me on the collarbone and made cooing noises before launching into a chant: 'Jeanie's got a cru-sh, Jeanie's got a *cru-sh* . . .'

'Frank, cut it out,' I said, blushing furiously.

'Who *doesn't* have a crush on Josh?' Col stepped in to protect me.

'Not you, I hope,' he said to Colette. 'You're meant to have a crush on me.'

She squirmed noticeably. Frank saw it.

'Did you just cringe? *You did!* You cringed!' he was pointing at Col and shaking his head, smiling incredulously. 'I can't believe you just cringed at having a crush on me.'

'Don't be a schmuck,' she said dismissively.

Frank looked over his shoulder, still shaking his head in apparent disbelief. 'Get ready, girls – the much better looking Fox is on his way over.'

I took a deep breath.

As Josh walked over to our little group, he was stopped by people every half-step. Tess stood by his side, smiling as though it were she who had played the game, and perhaps created Josh in a laboratory, too. Just as he neared us, Kerrie swooped in from stage left to give her boy a big kiss and a hug. I could just hear her telling him he had played a wonderful game, despite the result, and asking whether he was okay, and had they fed him, and what on earth was that bandage around his wrist.

He nodded, telling her he was okay, before dumping his enormous bag and rotating his shoulder a few times, wincing. Kerrie skittled off to get her star progeny a drink, and Tess immediately put her perfectly French-manicured fingers – they had to be acrylics, they were far too long and square – on his shoulder and gave it a small rub. He looked at her and smiled, and she kissed him on the lips. As he pulled his head away, he saw me watching them. I snapped my head down. Ooooh, that's not good. Creepy that he busted me watching them kiss. I kept my head down for a few seconds before slowly raising it to face Col; but my eyes remained locked in Josh's direction. He was looking at me, bemused, with those blue, blue eyes. I melted in the same way a front-row fan melts when Enrique Inglesias sings half a lyric in her direction, mid-concert: I knew it meant nothing, but I *so* wanted to believe it did.

'Hi, girls, how are you both? Enjoy the game?'

Despite Tess playing nurse behind him, pathetically, uselessly rubbing his shoulder while holding a conversation with a gorgeous brunette – definitely another Girlfriend – who had come out of nowhere, Josh had managed to shuffle forward into our circle.

'I loved the part where you kicked it out on the full,' Col said, with a big, confident smile. Frank dissolved into laughter; Josh shook his head.

'Colette, I'm afraid you've been framed; kicking out on the full is a very bad thing to do in a game.'

Her face fell. 'Oh, shit Josh, sorry, I had no idea . . . *Frank!*'

Frank was still laughing so hard he was unable to speak. And then Josh was looking at me again.

'Enjoy the game, Jean?' He smiled at me, warmly, expectantly, genuinely.

'Yes, thank you. Nice try you scored there.' Knowing absolutely nothing else about the game, I stopped. Hopefully that would be enough for him.

'Did Mum ensure you had a wine in your hand at all times?'

I felt uneasy chatting to him while Tess rubbed his shoulder. How fitting, I thought dryly; she literally had her claws stuck into him.

'Actually, she and my mum kept each other busy.'

'Your mum came? Where is she? Let's meet her! Mums love me.' He smiled convincingly. I saw Mum still chatting to a woman Kerrie had introduced her to earlier. I'm guessing felines were the topic, judging by Mum's wild gesticulations and excited eyes.

'She's over there with yours. She's the one with the tiny earrings and understated lipstick.' His eyes searched the crowd before settling on Mum. His face relaxed and broke into a big smile. He shook his head at me as if to say, 'Smartarse'.

'She looks busy, I'll get her later.'

'Get who later, babe?'

Tess had noticed that Josh and I had been talking for longer than the authorised limit and asserted herself by wrapping her arms around his waist and interrupting the conversation. Subtle as a semitrailer.

'Colette and Jean's mum. Hey, did you drive?'

She put on a sad face and that infuriating baby voice that some women mistakenly employ, somehow thinking men are attracted to the idea of conversing with an infant.

'Yes, baby, but I had a little, little bit to drink, so I think you might have to drive home . . .'

'Riiiiight.' His tone sharpened. 'Guess I'm not having a drink with the boys then.'

'Baby, I'm sorry, but the game was so boring, Melinda and I had nothing to do *but* drink.'

Josh's eyes flickered. 'Like I always say, you don't have to come to the games.' His tone was cold. 'Where's Mum with that drink?' He untangled himself from Tess, moving past Frank and Colette, who were laughing and carrying on, to find Kerrie. My eyes followed him. And Tess's eyes followed mine. She folded her arms and smiled wickedly.

'It's okay, sweetheart. I'm sure he'll be fine without you for a few minutes.' With that, she turned and stalked after him.

What was that? Was I that obvious? Had she sensed my feelings for him? Or was she just a complete bitch? Col saw me standing alone and walked over to me.

'She's onto you.'

I snapped my head to face my sister.

'What?'

'Are you honestly going to stand there and tell me you don't have a thing for Josh?' She smiled, her brows raised in disbelief.

'Jay, Josh told Frank he'd met you at Balcony that night we were there. He was that guy you spilled the drinks on and went all stupid over, wasn't he?' She put her hand on my shoulder. 'Why didn't you tell me it was him, once you'd made the connection?'

I shrugged her hand off, my mind awash with thoughts of fight or flight. I decided to go with the former. Less effort.

'Because I knew you'd only bag me out about it – like you are right now.'

'*Jaaaaay*,' Col's voice softened. 'I'm not bagging you out. I just thought you'd tell me something like that. The reason I'm bringing this up, if you'll stop losing your shit for a second, is because if you'd listened to what I said, Josh *offered* that information to Frank.' She paused, her eyes wide. 'Um, which means he's thinking about you?'

I looked away from her, my emotions unsure of which direction they were meant to be heading: anger or excitement. Could that be right? Surely not. Josh was property of one Tess Clifton, aspiring children's TV host and proud owner of ten acrylic tips.

Col tugged at my hair, smiling cheekily.

'Can you stop being shitty with me now, Angry Anderson?' Her voice sparkled with victory. 'If you *do*,' she continued in a singsong voice, 'I'll buy you shoes *just like Mu-um's*.'

Despite my best efforts at staying cranky, I smiled. I hated that she always had me at the end of her emotional thermometer, adjusting me as it suited her. She put her arm around my shoulder and whispered, 'He's ending it with her, you know.' The hairs on the back of my neck stood up; my hearing suddenly rivalling that of a small, hungry bat. 'Frank said so.'

I couldn't help it: I looked at her, my eyes screaming what my pride wouldn't allow me to ask, which was basically along the lines of, 'Really? Really *truly*?'

'And lucky for you I didn't end things with Frank yet, darling sister, because he's invited us to their cousin's engagement party next weekend. Both of us. And you're coming. Even though it's bound to be fucking diabolical.'

# ROUND 10
## The Optimists vs The Realists

I was fat for the engagement party. My boobs were sore and annoying, and my stomach had blown out. Everything I tried on accentuated my hormonally-whacked size and exacerbated my irritability.

'No, I won't allow it.' Col was shaking her head at my Final Fucking Choice, in which I stood – in the incorrect bra and undies – in my bedroom, which was littered with the corpses of Unsuitable Options. 'Empire-line makes you look even fatter, for starters. Plus, boys think you look pregnant in that style. And, if you recall, Jay, the idea of tonight is to blow Josh out of the water, not to make him think you retained all of it.'

I grunted. 'All very easy for you to say, Miss I-Don't-Get-PMS, but —'

'Tired of it. Shut up, and put that orange dress back on. It's cute, not too short, and it makes your skin and hair and eyes look pretty. There's no way he'll miss you in that.'

'I'll only wear it,' I said slowly, 'if I can wear your new Chloe shoes.' Col's new heels were dark brown, outrageously high and so, so perfect. At least I would feel good about one item I was wearing. She exhaled.

'You fat little slug. I was going to wear them, but I'm sure you had already figured that much out. All right, *fine*. Just hurry up and do something with your hair and face; Frank's picking us up in twenty minutes.'

I wished I'd washed my hair last night instead of this morning; it was all clean and fluffy and stupid and being very naughty indeed. I jammed it back in a high, loose bun – I thought it was very bed-head chic, actually, and it made me feel more streamlined. And as the dress had a high-ish neckline, hair up worked better. Hair dealt with, I could focus on my makeup.

Nerves fluttered delicately through me as I tried to pull off a sexy, smoky-eye effect with the one shadow palette I owned. But it was too much, I decided, and wiped off the majority. Instead, I added my usual fourteen laps of black kohl. A trio of thick gold and black bracelets served as the icing on my outfit.

I was dying to ask Col if Josh had dumped Tess yet, but didn't want to appear callous. The thing was, what if he hadn't? What if she was going to be there tonight? I couldn't bear the thought. Especially after her nasty 'sweetheart' comment last week at the football. I found that I could, however, spin her nastiness around: she wouldn't have said anything like that if she wasn't thinking Josh was paying me a little too much attention. I could live with that, I thought, almost smiling.


Frank arrived ten minutes late, and as Colette and I walked out to his car, I noticed Josh wasn't in it. Reading my thoughts, Frank waited till I'd climbed into the back before turning to look at me, his face swathed in cheekiness. 'S'alright Jeanie, he's still coming; he just got a ride with Mum and Dad.'

I blushed. He laughed.

'You're looking good, little Jay. As for your sister,' Frank turned to take her in, 'well, she could've put in some effort, if you know what I mean.'

Col shook her head, smiling. She got the joke. She'd had her hair coloured this morning, which meant it was all fancy and swishy and blow-dried, and she was wearing a gorgeous cream Roman-style dress that went to the floor, and around six kilos of my gold bracelets. She looked absolutely beautiful. I felt like a small, odour-releasing insect by comparison.

We arrived at the venue, situated directly on the harbour, which was glimmering beautifully in the autumn evening sun. Nothing had been said about Josh and Tess and whether they would be here together. Either way, I started to feel very, very anxious. I re-did my lip gloss for the fifth time since leaving home and thought about what I would say to Josh when I actually saw him. I wanted to stop being the bumbling and nervous girl I became within the bounds of his piercing eyes and dizzying aura, and start being the confident, fun-loving girl I was in Real Life. We walked in, being stopped every few metres by Frank's family and friends. 'These are my backup singers,' he said to our polite groans. 'I'll be doing the star perform-ance a little later.'

I excused myself and went to the bar to order three champagnes as Colette and Frank spoke to an old man in a chair, who looked to be a few birthdays behind the earth's crust. The waiter was excruci-atingly slow; I felt incredibly exposed at the bar by myself, especially in a dress that I now believed to be far too short for an engagement party, especially since most girls had opted for long and flowing and elegant over quirky and arse-skimming.

'Shit, that was hard work,' Col said, after extricating herself from Gramps. 'Wow, look at this. No expense spared, huh?'

'Mmm,' I absent-mindedly agreed, my eyes darting uncontrolla-bly around the room looking for Josh. 'Can you imagine what the wedding will be like?'

'They *can't* be serious,' Col said, gasping. 'There's a digital slide-show of the couple on every wall! Now I've seen it all.'

I laughed and followed her gaze, but my eyes looked only for a certain blonde head swanning through the crowd, its body latched onto a certain blue-eyed boy.

'Well, girls,' said Frank, who'd sidled up to Colette and whisked a champagne out of my hand, 'this is how I think Colette and I will be celebrating our engagement. Only we'll also get some marble busts made and some thrones on stage. What do you think, schnooky?'

'I think you forgot the dancing midgets and the baton twirlers.'

'I did too. Will you forgive me, my future wife?'

At that, Colette smiled and shook her head. 'Idiot.'

'Finally,' a voice – The Voice – said behind me. 'Real people.'

I held my breath.

'Jooooooosh,' cooed Col, her tone clearly for my benefit. 'How are you? You look *very* dapper. Nice tie.'

'What? What about *my* tie?' Frank interjected. Ignoring him, Josh stepped past to kiss Colette hello. Then he turned around completely to face me, and he looked at me, and he leaned in, and he kissed me on the cheek. He smelled of the ocean and fresh green leaves and clean laundry. I inhaled him as though I were ill, and to smell him were to be healed.

'Hi Jean. That's a great colour on you.' He looked me up and down as he said this, smiling his beautiful smile.

I looked down, nervously tucking some invisible hair behind my ear. As usual.

'Thank you, Josh,' I said, finally locating my vocal chords. You don't look so bad yourself, I wanted to say. Violent understatement. In his jet-black suit with his dark grey tie and his light grey shirt, he looked gobsmackingly, traffic-stoppingly, Giorgio Armani advertisementy handsome. He stepped back to make the four of us into a circle, still smiling at me.

'No Tess?' Frank asked Josh brashly – rather inappropriately, I thought, but I was glad he had.

Josh squirmed ever so slightly. I noticed this because I was watching every square inch of his body for some sign that yes, they had broken up, and she had been shipped off to Dubai to film a reality TV show, never to return to Australia.

'Uh, she couldn't make it.'

Frank, either not sensing or not caring about Josh's obvious discomfort, ploughed ahead in his tact tractor.

'You did it last night, didn't you? Broke up with her?'

My heart started pumping excessive amounts of blood to my brain. Had he done it? Was it true? Had he actually broken free of Tess's plastic claws?

'Are you *right* there?' Col reproached Frank, shaking her head. 'I'm pretty sure Josh doesn't want to talk about that right now.'

I watched Josh straighten out his tie and gather himself. 'Girls, please excuse my brother. He was born without many vital organs, most notably a brain. Now, can I get either of you a drink?'

Col smiled, holding up her champagne. 'We're good thanks, Josh.'

'Good. Excuse me, then.' He stepped back and walked briskly towards the bar. Col slapped Frank with her clutch.

'Frank, I can't believe you said that! Whether he's broken up with Tess or not, he doesn't want you speaking about it in front of us!'

Frank let out a dramatic, exasperated sigh.

'Girls, girls, girls. If you knew half the shit Josh's been through with her . . . They've broken up maybe six billion times before. Last time she even threatened to tell her dad to drop him to reserve grade if he dumped her. She's all class.'

Col was looking at me, smiling, so many things being said in her eyes.

'So she's that bad, huh?'

'No. Double it and square it, and then you're getting close.'

'And you think they've really broken up this time?'

'If they hadn't, she'd be here. There's nothing the Wicked Witch likes more than to dress up and parade her superstar boyfriend.'

'Hmmmm,' said Col, with a devilish glint in her eye. 'So that would make Josh single.'

'Indeed it would,' said Frank, understanding the game completely. 'Just like Jean, no?'

'Guys!' I whisper-shouted. 'He's just broken up with his girlfriend! Show some compassion, please.'

'Jean, *surely* you're not going to stand there and tell us you're not interested in being the next Miss Josh Fox?' Frank said with mock shock.

I took a long sip of my champagne and folded my arms. They were being complete morons and I wasn't standing for it. Besides, Josh would be back any second.

'Jay, settle down.' Col was using her Big Sis Knows Best voice. 'If you just admit that you like him, we can help orchestrate it.'

'Yeah Jean, we can have you in the gossip pages and topless on the cover of *FHM* within weeks!' Frank piped up.

'Guys, honestly, if you don't shut it, I'll —'

'Admit you like him, and we'll stop.' Col spoke and smiled as though she were offering fairy-dusted strawberries. It annoyed me. A lot. Nervous energy coupled with PMS irrationality meant I was not coping with her twisted brand of 'fun'.

'I barely even know him. How could I like him?'

'Methinks the lady doth protest too much,' said Frank in a snooty English accent.

'Frank,' I said, shaking my head and closing my eyes. 'Colette. Can you please stop?'

'Stop what?' Josh interjected, sidling up between Frank and me. He was drinking champagne, not beer, and I smiled inside. Masculine *and* refined . . .

'Stop telling her how great her legs are in that dress. She's getting all embarrassed.' Colette took a sip of her champagne to wash down the lie. 'Come on, Frank, weren't you going to introduce me to your dad?' She grabbed Frank's elbow and steered him away, smiling over her shoulder at us as they were sucked into the crowd.

I laughed a breathy, nervous laugh.

'Should I be worried about my suit and that glass of champagne?'

I turned to look up at him. The grey in his shirt and tie reflected the darker pigments of his irises, and his eyes looked even bluer than usual. They were locked onto mine: open, inviting, warm. He smiled. My heart did a triple somersault. His was a smile that involved so much more than just a widening of the lips and a crinkling of the eyes. It was the same smile that I'd seen on him that first night at Balcony, and it was tinged with intent, with possibilities. It was the kind of smile that I knew would ruin me, and turn my life inside out, and cause me to have sleepless nights, and make me watch my phone every minute of the day, and think about nothing else but the man attached to it.

Bring it on.

'Nah,' I said mischievously, returning his look with double the intent and a side of lasciviousness. 'Think you're safe for tonight.'

He suddenly winced and started rubbing his ankle.

'Do you mind if we sit down? I've got tendonitis and can't stand for too long. I know I may *look* young, but I'm an old man underneath.'

'Of course, Grampa. Lead the way.'

We made our way to the second, and far less busy, bar and sat on two clear resin stools – very hip. Conscious of my upper thighs, I perched on the furthest edge of my stool, gripping strongly onto the leg bar with my heels while trying to look completely normal.

'So, Colette says you design jewellery – is that right?'

'Yes,' I said, beaming. How thoughtful of him to bring this up.

'I've never met a designer before. What's the name of your label?'

'Um, I don't really have one yet . . . '

'And you just taught yourself how to make this stuff?'

'No, I've done courses, but, well, I suppose . . . I dunno, I guess it's a bit like golf – once you know how to hit the ball correctly, you keep improving and improving each time you play.' Did I really just use a golf metaphor? What was I, a fifty-year-old man trying to teach his son the ways of the world?

'You play golf?' His eyebrows shot up.

'Um, sometimes, yeah. Badly. Godfrey – that's my stepdad – he taught Mum, Col and me years back. It's this daggy family thing we do. We even – and I can't believe I'm admitting this – we even have *matching vests.*'

Josh dropped his head back and laughed a deep, hearty laugh. It was a glorious, infectious guffaw, the kind that made you congratulate yourself for saying something funny enough to be rewarded with its splendour.

'Pink?'

'Frosted lemon, thank you.'

He laughed again. I took a sip of my champagne with such carelessness that it splashed onto my chin. *Whoa.* How many glasses had I had already? Three? Four? Combined with heavy paracetamol for my period pain. Clever girl. No wonder I was being so 'hilarious'. I put the glass down so that I could discretely wipe my chin, and noticed Josh watching me, smiling.

Realising he'd been caught, Josh cleared his throat and took a sip of his beer. (He could only handle one champagne, he'd revealed, and that was usually for appearances. Knew he was too perfect.)

'So, um, Tess not able to come tonight?' I ventured cheekily, fuelled by a heady mix of alcohol, painkillers and flirting bravado.

Between Frank's, well, *frank* description of Tess and Josh's current state and the fact that Josh had spent the last hour with me, laughing and smiling, even a pot plant could see that something was amiss. He sighed, scrunching his mouth to one side. And then to the other. And finally, back to the first. He ran his fingers through his hair and looked out at the sea of people, talking, drinking, mingling, congratulating.

'It's okay, you don't need to say anything,' I reassured him quickly.

It really was none of my business, after all.

'No, no, you're right. I mean, I can't, well, it wouldn't be — ' He stopped and looked me straight in the eyes. 'I wouldn't be sitting here with you if things were right with Tess, put it that way.'

I felt as though someone had just placed a large woollen blanket around my heart.

A voice boomed over the PA, cutting through the music and my precious, important little moment like a knife. '*Ladies and gentleman, if we could have your attention, please? If you could all gather around the centre of the room, the groom-to-be would like to propose a toast to his beautiful wife-to-be.*'

Please no, don't let this conversation end here, I beseeched the Universe, God, Buddha, Oprah. Anyone.

'Hey, Jean,' Josh said, standing up and looking at me shyly. 'I realise how inappropriate this may seem, but could we maybe have a coffee sometime? Only if you want to – it's fine if not, I'll totally understand . . .'

I swallowed, looking at his smiling face.

'Yes. I'd love that.'

He offered his arm to help me down, and I took it, my insides melting and my spirits even higher than my blood alcohol level.

# ROUND 11
## The No-dials vs The Noodles

Sunday I awoke filled with hope and dreams of three-hour conversations and verbal foreplay, loosely centred around a twin-set of skim lattes.

No call from Josh.

I put it down to him not wanting to appear too keen.

As Monday skipped in, I was wary of too much build-up, but secretly convinced that today was The Day he'd call to set up that coffee. By the time Tuesday slunk over, despondent and dreary and dripping with a muted form of anger, I was almost certain Tess had wrangled her way back in, or that I was a chump.

To compound things, the weather had morphed from beautiful crisp autumn into miserable, wet winter. Which meant the shop was dead, because what woman wanted to buy herself a pretty frock when she couldn't manage to get from her front door to her car without ruining her new suede boots and losing her perfectly ghd-straight hair to sixty drops of frizz-inducing curl?

I was re-dressing the windows for the third time when a duo of tanned, heeled, very attractive, very loud women walked in. There was something immediately familiar about them. Were they off a TV show? I knew I'd seen their faces somewhere before. The first – a tall, slim brunette with dark CD-sized sunglasses, a caramel skivvy and what appeared to be leggings mistakenly worn as Real Life pants tucked into chocolate knee-high boots – rifled angrily through our clothes as she spoke.

'It's a goddamn joke. Mark forgot to call the builders, or just doesn't see it as a priority, but they won't listen to *me*, so the kitchen looks like a bomb has hit it, and I'm trying to cook some dinner for the kids in the fuckin' *bathroom*, and he has the hide – the fuckin' gall – to tell me to calm down when I arc up over it.'

The second woman, a short-haired blonde the size of a young teenager, had every spare vicinity littered with jewellery, including an engagement ring that was big enough to act as a beacon for extra-terrestrial life. She was unfolding T-shirts and singlets and placing them against her body before roughly putting them back on the table, as though it were *their* fault Mark was being such an arsehole.

'It makes me *sick* the way they're mollycoddled,' she chimed in across the shop, apparently unconcerned that I couldn't help but hear. 'I mean, *we're* the ones who have to support the boys when they lose, and cook for them, and clean up after them. I'm basically raising the girls alone because of *football*. Football is *always* first, and then they're like, "Oh, by the way, we're going away for a week," with no notice whatsoever. I mean, just 'cos the coach wants to get away from *his* missus, why should we all suffer?'

ZING! I should have known where I'd seen them before. The oversized wedding candy was a dead giveaway; they were WAGs I'd seen after the Bulls match.

'*We're* the ones who deserve a week off,' said leggings, yanking out a long white dress and holding it up against herself in the mirror. She sighed and jammed it back on the rack, pulling out her phone and checking it.

'Kel, I've gotta go get Hunter from judo. You gonna stay or —'

'I'd better go too. Hopefully, Audi have the car finished by now – Rosie and April will be doing Mum's head in.' She sighed dramatically.

'I'll have to try and find a dress next week, I suppose. Probably on the bloody day of the ball, like last year. Tell you what, it didn't used to be like this; I used to have bloody weeks to tart myself up for a ball: the hair, the paraffin pedicures . . .'

They walked out, hissing and bitching like a couple of old men flirting with dementia, and the clothes and I issued a collective sigh of relief. Wow. Being a footballer's wife sounded like a real fun time.

As they walked out, Col walked in. She'd been away in the Gold Coast hinterland since Sunday, visiting a girlfriend who'd just had a baby. Of course she *would* be away when: 1) Ingrid was out of town at some fashion buyers' conference; 2) The shop was as lively as a log; and 3) I needed to know stuff about Josh, like whether he was still in possession of a pulse.

Col glanced at the duo as they walked off down the street and raised her eyebrows.

'You got a nightclub out the back I don't know about?'

'I think,' I whispered, 'I recognise them from the after-match thingy the other night.'

'WAGS! Paddock partners! Think you're right. Geeeeez, who else would dress up for High Street?'

'How was Brooke? What'd they call the baby? Is he cute?'

'She's good. Utterly sleep-deprived, but happy. They called him – wait for it – Jason. But spelled J–A–C–E–N.'

I covered my smiling mouth with my hand.

'Oh well, as long as he's healthy and she's healthy, that's all that counts, right?'

She held up a T-shirt, looking at her reflection in the mirror on the wall.

'Ohmygod!' she suddenly exclaimed, turning to face me. 'Did Josh call? Did you see him? I've been dying to know. Having no service was killing me!'

I shook my head. 'Nothin. Nada. Nix.'

She squinted in confusion.

'Well, that makes no sense. Frank said he didn't shut up about you after the engagement party. Maybe I'll call him and get the juice —'

'No! No don't, Col. So he didn't call – no big deal.'

She put one hand on her hip and gave me her 'Are you for real?' face.

'As *if* he won't call. *Pl-ease*. He didn't move more than a metre away from you at that party. Even though you were all fat and bitchy.' She grinned. I rolled my eyes.

Her phone rang. She looked at its face, swore and answered it with her office voice.

'Noodle box? Hokkien? Oyster sauce?' Cameron stood at the doorway, a twenty-dollar note in his hand. 'It's my turn to pay, remember?' He was wearing a white shirt with a dark blue vest, red tie and black jeans. Terrifyingly cool, as usual.

I was starving and hadn't even thought about lunch yet. Perfect.

Cam spied Col on the far side of the shop.

'Colette, you look ravishing! How lovely of you to grace us with your presence.' It was my long-term consideration that Cameron was in love with Colette. (Then again, most men who met her were.) She and Ingrid both thought he was in love with me. It was an ongoing debate.

'She's on the phone. Can't hear you. I might have rice noodles with chicken and cashew nuts, actually. Just make sure there's no mushrooms, please.'

He put on A Voice.

'To most folk, she *looked* like a regular human being, but few knew the shocking truth: that if she was to consume one mushroom, just one little mushroom – even a champignon – her skin would fall off and her brain would implode.'

I clapped slowly, deliberately.

'What about her?' he said, his thumb jacked in Colette's direction.

'Col . . .' She looked at me. 'Lunch?' I mouthed. She shook her head irritably and covered her spare ear with her hand.

'Nope, just us. Need cash?'

'Please. I'm so moneyed, honey.'

I shook my head.

'Can you please get me a chai latte as well? Soy.'

'I've got a lazier suggestion: why don't you drink a real latte instead?'

'Pleeeeease?'

'Nooooo,' he whined. 'That means I have to go all the way down the other end of Lloyd street and then back up.'

'Pleeeeeease?' I smiled and batted my eyelids.

'Flirting again, huh? I've already told you: just because you want to take all my clothes off, right here on this shop floor, doesn't mean I do. Takes two to tango. Especially the way I tango.'

Before I could protest, he'd disappeared.

Col was still on the phone. I needed her to hurry up so we could discuss Josh again before Cameron came back. I cleared my throat loudly. She looked over and I made the wind-it-up signal. She frowned, waving me away with her hand. I went back to my merchandising.

Twenty minutes later, when Cameron sauntered into the shop, balancing noodle boxes and a tray of drinks, Colette was just hanging up.

'Did you get me anything?' Col asked, sighing with exhaustion.

Cameron's eyes widened. 'But I thought you didn't want anythi—'

'I'm fucking with you, Cameron.' She smiled devilishly.

'You know, sometimes I forget how hilarious you are.' He placed the food on the counter and unloaded my noodles. 'Can we eat here? It's not like you've got any customers.'

Well, Ingrid *was* away . . .

'Just don't make a mess, you little grommet.'

Col pulled her keys out of her bag and walked to the door.

'Shit, almost forgot what I came for. Jay, I've got to put my car in to get the radiator fixed this arvo. Can you pick me up after work, please?'

I nodded.

'Enjoy your MSG, you two.'

With that, she was gone. Cameron looked after her, unapologetically checking out her arse. I pulled both stools to the counter and impatiently split my chopsticks to dive in. I smiled, thinking about Col's confidence that Josh would *definitely* be calling. And anyway, it had actually only been two and a half days.

'What's gotten into you?' Cameron asked, shovelling a huge tangle of noodles into his mouth.

'Oh, nothing,' I said, grinning like a loon, opening my noodle box.

'Shum umph, whaf iph ish?' he said as he chewed.

'Gross. Don't speak with food in your mouth.'

He rolled his eyes and chewed deliberately until it was all gone. 'There. Happy? Now. Who is he?'

I blushed. 'What? I don't know what you're talking about.'

'Whatever. Come on, spit it out. It's not that deadshit real-estate agent with the fivehead and the coke habit, is it?'

'Dean? God no! It's *so* not him.' Col had introduced me to Dean, proving that, on occasions, she still didn't know me at all. I sighed, delicately gathering a few strands of noodles and placing them neatly into my mouth. I hated eating in front of boys; it made me so self-conscious.

'Come on, tell me. I told you about Emoly.'

Her name was Emily, but we had changed it to reflect her angst-ridden, theatrical, heavy-eyelined Emo tendencies.

'Yeah, uh, because you *had* to. She was hanging 'round your shop every single day like a seagull hoping for chips.'

'She's not made of steel; I'm irresistible. Enough deflecting. Who is he?'

'He's no one.'

'Wrong! You've just admitted "he" exists, so he, in fact, isn't no one.'

'Cameron, it's nothing. We haven't even been on a date.'

'Oh, you're way too easy. You'd make a terrible suspect. So, what does he do?'

'Cameron, I don't *have* to tell you about my private life, you know. It's not a given.'

He pinched some of my noodles with his chopsticks.

'Fireman? Magician? Garbage collector?'

I smiled, wiping my mouth of invisible sauce.

'Multimillionaire? The guy who invented those vibrating condoms?'

'Why, Cameron, you have such high expectations of me.'

'Well, you kind of always date losers, so what do you expect?'

'Oh, and Chantelle the bead-necklace maker with the greasy hair wasn't? And let's not forget – what was her name? Jodie? Jordan? The girl who auditioned for not one, not two, but three reality TV shows?'

'Hey, she was good in the sack.'

I laughed. 'Whatever. Pot. Kettle. Black.'

'Just means I haven't found the right one yet. But this isn't about *me*, this is about you and your new boyfriend. Come on, I got you lunch.'

I shook my head. There was no way in hell I was telling him. He thought sportsmen – footballers, in particular – were lower than the magma surrounding the earth's core. I couldn't be bothered dealing with his jibes.

'If I start to actually date him, then maybe I'll tell. But I'm not gonna jinx it at this stage just 'cos you're being insufferable.'

'Oh come *on*. Who cares? What could he do that could possibly be worse than real estate? Oh, wait. Oh hohohoooo, this is *too good*. He's a used-car salesman, isn't he?'

I laughed.

'Last time I run around for your stupid chai farte.'

I shrugged my shoulders and smiled, closing my noodle box and sliding my chopsticks under the handle. 'Work beckons. Guess you'll just have to find out another time.'

I walked over to the door to lob my empty box into the bin outside. Just as I did, Col came careering back in, walking straight to the T-shirt table.

'Forgot my jacket.'

Cameron had a twinkle in his eye.

'Hey, Col,' he yelled, 'what do you think of Jean's new boyfriend?'

'Oh look, I hate footballers as much as the nex—'

'NO!' I screamed. But it was too late. Cameron's eyes flashed and his eyebrows shot up.

'A footballer? He's a *footballer*?'

'Col!'

She looked startled. 'What? What'd I do?'

'Your little sister was trying to keep her dark secret from me. But now I know.'

'Is that all?' she said irritably. 'Later, losers.'

I stood with my hands on my hips, waiting for his tirade.

'So, which one?'

'As *if* I'm telling you that.'

'As *if* I won't find out.'

I exhaled, looking to the side so I didn't have to see his expression.

'Josh Fox,' I said in a voice more suited to secret-agent-headpiece murmuring.

'Josh *Fox*? No, who really?'

'Cam, it's Josh.'

Cam looked baffled.

'Dude, he's got a girlfriend. Her hot little sister works as door bitch at the Nursery. She's always on about *Josh this*, *Josh that*. Brings as many of his thug team-mates in as often as she can and the manager gives her a bonus. Should be the other way round – keep them away and then get a fuckin' bonus. Do you know how many of them get busted with girls in the toilets? Do you? And do you know what they do in there with them? It ain't yoga, but it sure does involve some interesting positions . . .'

I snorted. 'Of course, of *all* the footballers in the world, you would have some random link to the one I like.'

'Don't worry, Jean,' he said sarcastically. 'I'm sure he's different from the rest. Intelligent, caring . . . and not at all a total fuckwit with a different groupie hanging off him every week.'

'Oh, piss off.' I wasn't interested in his flagrant, uninformed stereotyping.

'I'm going. And hey, good luck with the beefcake. Can't *wait* to hear how it all unfolds.' Smirking, he took his rubbish and his Coke and sauntered past me, out the door.

Fuck Cameron. What did he know.

# ROUND 12
## Fierce Anticipation vs The First Date

I woke the next morning with a start. Today had a Joshy flavour to it – I could feel it in my nose. I had spent the minutes before sleep the previous night visualising his name manifesting itself on my phone by the end of the day, and hated to think of my fierce disappointment should this effort fail to produce results.

I used Tess's shiny, long TV-ad hair as motive for blow-drying my hair properly today. I had a lot of time to come up with a motive: seventy minutes was a long time to spend doing your hair before so much as a whiff of caffeine or a banana. I tried not to tell myself it was because I would be seeing Josh, even though my hair and I both knew I was building myself up for one dramatic fall should I hear nothing from him today.

Col was at the gym, which was a blessing; she could be too much at 8 a.m. I ate my toast, made my tea, switched on the weather channel and flipped through *Harper's BAZAAR*. I ripped out a few pages of an eveningwear shoot. The adornments were incredible: all heavy metal cuffs, and layer upon layer of chains dripping with oversized charms. I was going to post them up on my inspiration board in the spare/sewing/computer room. Maybe I could make something like that next time I was in a makey mood. Hopefully this would be sometime before I hit menopause.

Feeling good in my black cigarette pants, peep-toe shoes and delicate ruffled blouse (courtesy of my forty per cent discount at the shop), I left for work, stopping to collect our mail from the post-office box on the way. Just as I was getting back into the car, I heard a horn tooting from the passing traffic. I smiled to myself. Excellent. All that wrestling with my hair dryer had been worth the effort. But the horn kept going, and I heard a voice yell, 'Jean!'

I snapped my head up. There was Josh in his black BMW, stationary so that I might see him, and holding up traffic in the process. The cars behind him began beeping furiously, so he sped off. I grinned from ear to ear. *Yes!* Yesyesyes! Not only had my hour-plus of heat-styling been worth it, but there was no *way* he couldn't call now. Perfect, perfect, *perfect!*

Just as I was about to pull out, his car came racing down the street towards me. He pulled up illegally in front and jumped out, jogging over to my window, which I wound down clumsily, as fast as Mary would allow.

'Jean!' He looked handsome, even in a ridiculous yellow silky tracksuit. How could that be? 'So glad I saw you! Hey, I'm sorry I haven't called – you must think I'm a total bastard. But we've been in lockdown since Monday, in a training camp down at Browns Beach, and I didn't get a chance to tell Frank, which I realised I should've 'cos then he could've told your sister why I'd disappeared . . .'

I smiled. 'Josh, it's fine.' No chance in hell he was going to see that he had pushed me into a cave mere centimetres from the cliffs of insanity.

He jammed his hands into his pockets and shook his head, smiling excitedly. 'Can't believe I saw you! We just got off the bus, like, ten minutes ago.'

'How funny,' I said, then went blank, enjoying the absence of my conversation skills as much as most people enjoy cutting themselves while chopping zucchini.

He looked down at me intently. 'Jean, do you think I could maybe take you to dinner tonight? That's if, you know, you don't already have plans . . .'

Thoughts of him and Tess sharing strands of spaghetti bolognaise in dimly lit restaurants reluctantly took their coats and left. I would cancel on Stevie Wonder to have dinner with Josh tonight.

'Sure, that'd be nice,' I said, trying to contain the excitement in my voice.

A horn blared to our right, and then: 'Bulls *suck*!'

I looked around, taken aback. Who would say such a thing?

Josh laughed. 'We kinda do suck at the moment. So, um, how about maybe you text me your address and I can pick you up around 7.30? Does that suit you?'

'Sure, no problem.'

'Well, I look forward to it.' He smiled warmly. 'See you tonight!'

With that he waved, smiled, trotted back to his shiny car, pulled out, honked twice (adorably), and was gone. Bless him and his silky, flared pants.

I smiled at how tortured I'd been, thinking that he wasn't calling me because he'd gone back to a girl with beautiful eyes, blonde, voluminous hair and a father who owned the club he played for. How very silly of me indeed, I thought. How perfectly outrageous. The smile swelled uncontrollably. I had hoped to hear from him today, but I certainly hadn't expected to see him *and* score a date all in one two-minute bubble of roadside coincidence. I needed to tell Col.

Someone has a date tonight . . .

Vibrate, chime, lights, action.

Is it tess clifton

Haha.

so u gonna do it on the 1st date

Oh yeah, totally. Best way to keep a guy interested.

Wonder wr thuggo footyhead will tk u . . . mcdnlds?

Hopefully. Can I wear your shoes again? Come on. Be nice.

well see. b home at 6 2 dress u in ur finest boob tb n nee highs – thts
wt wags wr, rite?

Who knew?

I was in a fantastic mood as I opened up the store. A homeless man
could've greeted me with urine-soaked pants and a c-word-soaked
tirade – it had happened before – and I still wouldn't have quit my
Disney Princess humming. I wanted a customer to style. I always
did a cracking job when I was in a good mood.

Come on, someone come in. *Anyone.*

No dice. Save for Ingrid, who stalked in twenty minutes later, by
which time I was groping and grabbing at the window mannequins,
changing their outfits to reflect not the weather or even the current
fashion, but my mood.

'Did you just put a tuxedo jacket over a hoodie?' she asked. She
never bothered with platitudes.

I looked at my plastic model. Yes, it appears I did. How about
that. 'I think it kind of works . . .' I said. 'How was your trip?'

'Well, I think you're high. No one will wear that; take it off, please,
Jean. I want dresses. It's racing time.'

I slumped and exhaled loudly.

'Oh, you will carry on, won't you, you stubborn little mule.

68

Tomorrow it comes down.'

'Thank you,' I said gaily, trying to yank – delicately – an embroidered miniskirt onto hoodie-tux girl without it looking inappropriate.

'So, how was the trip?'

'As exciting as you might imagine. Ran into vile Jackie Denison. I swear, she's single-handedly keeping Botox afloat.'

I giggled and busied myself with putting opaque tights on to my model.

'When you're finished manhandling that poor woman, would you grab me a coffee?'

'Of course. Toast?'

I always offered but she never wanted any. I rarely saw Ingrid eat; she seemed to exist on coffee and rogue particles of lipstick.

'Just coffee, thanks, Jean.'

There'd be no coffee for me. My heartbeat was already set to hummingbird pace, and if I were any more alert I would be accused of drug use.

# ROUND 13
## Nerves vs Italian Curves

Col was adamant I looked 'incredible' for the first date. I felt the term was subjective, and that some might in fact view what I was wearing as 'overdressed', or perhaps 'bridesmaid-appropriate', but she wasn't having it. I – or rather, Col – had settled on her beautiful peach-toned slip dress and some tan strappy heels. I had to admit I did feel pretty sexy. My hair swished and swirled around me as I walked down the steps of our terrace onto the street, where Josh's black beast was waiting silently, engine off, lights on. I wondered whether he was watching me walk down the stairs, and made sure to step carefully, lest I stack it – which was very likely in these shoes, and being me.

My little heart was pounding and my mouth was dry as I opened the passenger door. What if he was wearing jeans and a T-shirt? What if he thought I was completely over the top and trying to compete with Tess? That I was some stupid Queenslander who totally overdressed? I took a deep breath.

'Hi, Jean. You look beautiful. Very pretty dress.'

Several million hectopascals snuck out of my pores in relief and delight.

'Thank you,' I said, grateful for the darkness that hid my teenagey flush of embarrassment. I arranged myself daintily into the huge leather bucket seat and looked at Josh, who swiftly swooped in for a kiss on the cheek. He smelled like Man. Sexy Man. I took him in as he started the car. He was wearing a long-sleeved black V-neck, grey pants and cool black trainers that looked as though they had been sitting on a shop shelf until a few hours ago. He was freshly shaved and his skin was smooth and flawless. I couldn't believe I got to spend an entire evening with him.

He looked me directly in the eyes – this seemed to be his custom – as though I were someone far more engaging and beautiful than I actually was. Every time he did this something inside me lifted before returning gently back into place. Not sure what. Probably my pancreas.

'I know you'd rather I'd worn my yellow tracksuit, but I had to make do since it was in the wash. Next time, promise.'

I giggled like a Monty Python cast member in drag. Since when did guys make me this silly and shy? I was usually rather formidable on a date, cracking jokes and making them laugh and being quite entertaining in general. But Josh was different. Just his presence had me rattled. I wondered whether I would be the same if he were just Josh, and not Josh Fox. Perhaps, I reluctantly conceded, his fame was to blame for my unusual nervousness.

My phone beeped loudly. I got it out to switch it to vibrate so that it wouldn't sear through our evening again. It was Col.

hv fun sweet tits x yeeew!

I shook my head. Honestly.

We arrived at the restaurant, a tiny Italian place I'd never heard of in a district I'd never been to, and witnessed Josh greet his very own welcoming committee.

'Josh!' said a tall man with a comical moustache. 'Long time no see! When you gonna start putting some points on the board, huh? You boys are ruining my whole tipping comp!'

'Tony, I do apologise. This Sunday we'll set things straight, I promise.'

'If you can't beat the Vikings, you're in *real* trouble, boy! Now, who is this gorgeous young lady?'

I blushed.

'Allegra,' he yelled in the direction of the kitchen, 'some champagne!' And then to us, 'Now, over here, please.' He lowered his voice. 'I've saved you the best table in the house.'

As we walked past the other diners, I recognised a soapie actress and a brother–sister design duo whose clothes I adored. Who would've guessed such a tiny place in such a ghetto suburb would be host to all these famous people? Thank you, Col, for annoying me to the point of rage to dress up, I said silently.

We took our seats and I realised why it was the best table: we had views over the entire city, from an angle I didn't know existed.

'Woooooow,' I breathed. 'Josh, this view is amazing.'

'I know. I love it here. Tony always looks after me. Are you sure you're okay with Italian?'

It dawned on me that the last time he was here, he would have been with Tess. That made sense; she would've fitted in here. Me? I was just A Girl.

'Oh shit. You don't like Italian, do you, I should've ask—'

'No, no! I love it! Honestly.'

A slim, attractive Italian woman with her long hair tied back in a ponytail suddenly appeared with a bottle of Veuve. She had poured herself into a tight black dress and applied several kilos of lipstick to her already heavily made-up face. She had to be Allegra. No one that glamorous could have a name like Sharon or Debbie.

'Joooooosh,' she purred, planting a kiss on his cheek. 'So lovely to see you again. Have you been well?' She poured two glasses of champagne as she spoke, without lifting her gaze from Josh's eyes.

'I have, thank you, Allegra. And yourself?'

He was careful to look at her, but never for longer than a few seconds.

'You know, same same. Busy. We've missed you in here. Why don't you come see me any more? I see all the other boys around – mostly Lukey, of course – but never you!' She pouted. Wow. A Real Life woman pouting. This was priceless.

'I'm sure that after tonight's meal I'll be back again next week because I will have been reminded how good your father's cooking is.' Josh looked at me and smiled.

'Well, enjoy your meal.' Allegra held the bottle and smiled her big, pretty smile, her eyes drilling holes into Josh's. Then she turned and walked away. Gosh. I'd never experienced anything like it.

Josh grabbed his champagne flute and raised it. 'I propose a toast,' he said. 'To finally being able to buy you a drink.' I laughed and we each took a sip.

'So, how's Colette?'

'Oh, she's fine.'

'Have she and Frank been in touch? I haven't seen him for a while.'

'Um . . . not sure, actually. She's been away so I haven't spoken to her.' I hoped to steer Josh onto another topic but was too slow.

'Do you . . . do you think she likes him?' His eyes were full of hope.

Shit. What exactly do I say here? Earlier tonight, Col had confided to me that she wasn't going to pursue the Frank thing any more, on any level. Despite the fact that she'd told him she didn't want a relationship just now, he didn't seem to be willing to keep things on the friendship level. ('Only human,' she'd said, as she always did when a guy fell for her.) And now that Josh and I seemed to be working out, she was 'actioning the fade-out', she said. Both she and Frank had been out of town the past week, so it was kind of easy for her to do it.

'Um, well, I mean, I think they talk on the phone sometimes . . . '

I may as well have been describing the carpet.

73

'Uh-huuuuuh, but I didn't ask how often they spoke on the phone.'
I smiled. 'Okay, well, it's just that — Oh, I really shouldn't say.'

'What? Is she seeing another guy?'

'God, no.' I shook my head and slurped a big sip of champagne.
'No, see the thing is, she got hurt pretty badly by her ex-fiancé a
few months back. I think she's just – and this is nothing to do with
Frank – but I think she's just not ready for anything yet.'

'Whoa. Ex-*fiancé*? What'd he do to her? No, actually, that's none
of my business. Sorry, Jean. You don't have to tell me a thing.'

'He cheated on her. With his ex.'

'Ouch.'

'Mm-hmmm. I don't get it, you know. Why would you get engaged
if you still wanted to sleep around? Or if you still had feelings for
someone else? You're in a relationship because you want to be in a
relationship. 'Sjust stupid.'

'Col's awesome. Frank never shuts up about her.' He took a sip
of champagne.

'So!' I said brightly. 'Tell me about your camp. Did you have bon-
fires and play trust games and tell ghost stories?'

He threw his head back and laughed. Oh, I'd never tire of that
laugh.

'Noooo, nononono. It's not *that* kind of camp. It's only called
"camp" because we're away. It's just like training, only at night we
have, say, a motivational speaker, or fans come and eat dinner with
us, or we all watch a movie.'

'Sounds like camp to me.'

He smiled. 'It's not fun, trust me. We only ever go if we're playing
really, really badly, so they up the ante on everything: training, strat-
egy, preaching about attitude, you name it. It's like a boot camp, I
guess you could say.'

'So, have you decided which of my delicious treats you would like
to try yet?' asked Tony, who had snuck up on us from behind.

'Oh, Tony – we haven't even looked yet. Sorry.'

'Maybe I can decide for you? Some tasting plates of my finest dishes?'

Josh looked at me, his eyebrows raised. 'Would you be happy to do that, Jean?'

'Of course. I'm sure whatever you select will be lovely,' I said, snapping my menu shut.

'Wonderful! You won't regret it,' said Tony, as he dipped in and grabbed our menus. 'Now, some wine. Red? White? I have a beautiful pinot from the south of France you will love . . .'

More questioning eyebrow movements from Josh.

'Sounds perfect,' I said. Josh smiled warmly. I wondered if this was weird for him, to be dating a new girl so soon after breaking up with his long-term girlfriend. But he seemed to be at ease.

The truth is I don't like red wine, but I didn't want to look like hard work. I'd drink straight ouzo from a gumboot in order to appear the easy, non-fussed girl who could roll with whatever she was given; for whom nothing was a drama. Guys loved those girls.

'So, did you enjoy the game the other week? Tell me the truth. Between you and me, I find footy pretty boring.' I could feel my eyebrows lifting. 'I mean, when I'm *playing* it's not boring, but my team-mates – they all watch five or six games a weekend. I can't do it. I'd rather go for a ride. Hey, you ever been to Crow Mountain? It's amazing. I'll take you up there one day. It's a bitch of a walk, but it's worth it for the sunset . . .'

Oh, *stop it*. Seriously, cut it out. A handsome, smart football-hero guy who liked bike-riding and sunsets? Somebody was yanking my crank. Next he'll tell me he started a Fluffy Kitten Appreciation Facebook group.

'Sweetie, your wine . . .' The Italian was back, forcing her musky, woody fragrance and impressive mams onto Josh as she leaned over him, slowly pouring his wine.

'Thank you, Allegra.' He didn't take his eyes away from mine.

She poured mine in half the time, tipping from roughly a metre away.

'Just sing if you need me,' she cooed before jiggling away. She made Jessica Rabbit look like fuckin' Alice in Wonderland. I'd never had a woman openly come onto a guy I was with before. It would have been fascinating if it weren't so unsettling.

'Nice, huh?' he asked, placing his wine back on the table.

'Mmm, delicious,' I said, tasting nothing more than a motley blend of vinegar and redcurrants. 'What do you ride?' I asked, following up our pre-Allegra conversation.

'A mountain bike. I'm not that great – and I mean that, I'm not even being self-deprecating – but I love it. I ride when I can with two schoolmates, Aaron and Damon. We're planning a trip to the Andes next year. Wanna come?'

I laughed. 'No thanks.'

'You sure?' His eyes sparkled mischievously. 'If you're lucky, you might get frostbite . . .'

'As enticing as that sounds —'

' . . . lose a few fingers – maybe a whole foot?'

We laughed and sipped our wine, enjoying the giddiness and silliness of the newness of what I hoped was mutual attraction.

'So, Jean, you free Sunday?' he said, eyebrows sneaking towards his hairline. 'Would you maybe – that's if you're not busy, of course – want to come and see us get smashed by the comp front-runners? I can promise at least a 30-point flogging . . .'

'Shouldn't you be thinking positive? Visualising a win?'

He took a long sip of wine, then looked at me seriously.

'Maybe you're right. I mean, I thought about seeing you again after Balcony, and look what happened. Basically fell into my lap!' He grinned.

A lap already nursing a girlfriend, I thought.

'I'm not in your lap yet,' I said playfully, champagne mingling with red wine in my bloodstream, and both having a wonderful time.

He smiled mischievously. 'You said *yet*.'

# ROUND 14
## Optimism vs Deathly Silence

The next morning I afforded myself a ten-minute snooze to think about how perfect Josh was, in every – single – way. I turned on my phone, closing my eyes and hoping for the chime of a text . . . Nothing.

Well, *that's* not very nice. I'd sent *him* one after I'd got inside last night. After we'd sat in his car, and he'd leaned over, and he'd kissed me on the mouth, ever so graciously, before pulling back, his eyes shining, his smile wide and comforting, to tell me that he'd *really* enjoyed the evening. Part of me had been thrilled that he *hadn't* launched in for the full-on pash, as that would have implied that he probably tried it on with every girl who delicately arranged the length of her dress as she sank into his enormous passenger seat. But another part of me wished he'd cut sick.

Maybe my text had offended him, I thought suddenly, as I made my way down High Street to get my chai latte (soy; no sugar) that afternoon. What did I write again? I checked my sent items.

Thank you for a beautiful evening. The only improvement would've been if we'd gone to a pub and watched some footy. Kidding. Thanks again x

Totally innocuous. No way he couldn't see the joke. My brain suddenly flew from first to sixth gear, without so much as a tap on the clutch. I wondered whether maybe he'd thought again about Tess, after having been on a date and kissed another girl. Maybe he liked her more than he realised. Maybe he'd even decided he wanted to get back with her, so that when he went to places like Tony's, he had a Somebody, not a Nobody, on his arm.

I wasn't used to this kind of post-date paranoia and insecurity. I usually played the cool customer, letting the boy sweat on whether I'd had a good time. I realised this had been easy for me in the past because the kind of guys I'd been seeing had been, well, *nice*, but nothing too special. Nothing like Josh, basically. I hoped I could pump the brakes with this one; I was ready to see him for lunch today, and dinner too, and maybe a hot chocolate after that.

When I got back to the shop, my 'Back in seven-and-a-half minutes' sign had been removed. Ingrid was back. She'd been at some seminar for fashion retailers. I had no idea what went down at these things and didn't care. Presumably, they learned how to up-sell a belt with a dress, or how to bully people whose arse looked three times larger than was legally permitted in a dress to buy it anyway.

I walked in to find her chatting with Colette. That was the upside of working on the same strip as my sister: we could annoy each other not only at home, but at work, too. I'm not sure that Ingrid saw it in such a positive light.

Col looked up when she saw me. She looked kind of tired, or sad, or hung over.

'Hi, guys,' I said. 'How was the course, Ingrid?'

'Five hours of my life I'll never get back, put it that way.'

'Col, you okay? You look upset.'

'No, no, no,' she said quickly. 'Just tired. *So!* How was the date with the local hero?'

I offered a strained smile; I didn't want Ingrid to know about Josh. But Col was exceptionally talented at spilling – nay, throwing around – beans I'd prefer to have stayed inside the bowl.

'Yeah, it was nice.' I sensed my smile extend into a dreamy grin without my consent.

'Call the missing persons unit, Ingrid, she's *gone*.'

'You had a date, Jean?' Ingrid was wearing a bemused expression. I felt my face flush.

'Yeah, yeah. Last night, actually.'

'Did he go for the goodnight grope?'

'No, *Col*! Jesus. He's a gentleman. Just a kiss on the lips. But, you know, a lingering one. A good one . . .'

Ingrid and Colette made silly cooing noises as the colour of my face slid up the vegetable scale from tomato to beetroot.

'Where did he take you? Was he wearing jeans? Please say no!'

'No, he wore *pants*. He's actually got really nice style, you know, considering he's, well . . .'

'A thug?' Ingrid offered.

'An athlete. He's quite stylish. There's something very Beckham about him.'

'And that would make you, let me see, Posh?' Ingrid had a devious glint in her eye. 'I need coffee. Anyone like one?'

'No thanks,' Col and I said in unison, watching as she walked out before we continued the conversation.

'Anyway, so — '

'Your tits are bigger than hers,' Col said dismissively. 'And she *paid* for hers. That's saying something.'

Col was fascinated by Ingrid's boob job.

'*Anyway,*' I said loudly to shut her up, 'so we went to some little restaurant in a backstreet somewhere but it was this beautiful food, and there were all these celebrities in there — '

'Elton John? Madonna?'

'And we drank champagne and — '

'Look at you!' Col said with huge eyes. 'You're all loopy and retarded! You look like you used to after you and Jeremy had been smoking reefers.'

'I like him, Col,' I said, savouring the admission, twirling my hair around my finger. 'I *really* like him. He's smart, and he's funny, and he's ambitious, and he's gorgeous, and he's a total gentlema—'

'Clearly, you must be talking about me,' a voice said from behind.

Col's eyes rolled. 'Gee, Cameron, how we've missed you since, oooh, yesterday.'

'I didn't see you yesterday, thank you. I was off sick. Not that either of you sent me flowers, or brought me chicken soup, or so much as called to see if I was okay.'

'Well, you look fine to us,' Col said, folding her arms, not in the mood for the Cameron show. 'What do you want?'

'Man. Someone needs to tell that boyfriend of yours he needs to start satisfying his lady.'

'For the last fucking time, Cameron, he's not my fucking boyfriend. I – don't – have – a – fucking – boyfriend.'

Not even Col's scary not-in-the-mood tone could deter him.

'What about you, Jean? Do you have a fucking boyfriend? Not in the true sense of the word, of course. You're a lady, unlike the trollop beside you.' His arms were folded, and the look in his eyes was questioning, unkind.

'No,' I said, immediately blushing, which, in Cameron's eyes, read as a flashing neon sign bearing the word 'YES'.

'Really?' he asked slowly, leaning against the doorframe, a wicked smile etched on his face. 'So, who were you talking about just before?' His eyes penetrated me, daring me not to answer.

'Oh for God's sake, Cameron,' said Col. 'You don't have interrogation rights. Leave her alone. At least one of us has found someone they like enough to hang out with.' She started looking in her bag for her keys. 'I'm off, Jay. I'll get the full story tonight. Cameron – don't be an arsehole.' She walked out, wagging her finger at him.

Still Cameron's eyes didn't leave me.

'So, Jean, how *are* things with Mr Pigskin?' He smiled but there was no warmth to it.

'Know what, Cameron? Great, actually.'

He laughed a short, nasty laugh.

'Ohhhh, Jeany. I did give you more credit than that, but it seems you're not quite as smart as I thou—'

'What are you on about? What's this great hatred you have for footballers? What, did one of them pick on you at school or something? Is that it? Still nursing some scar tissue?'

He continued to smile that twisted smile, shaking his head in a way that infuriated me more than him actually saying something.

'Jean, you don't have a clue what you're getting yourself into. You've got no idea what kind of players and headfucks these guys are. How they treat women. How *many* women they treat. I've seen it first-hand, at pretty much every club and bar in this city. Girls present themselves, and footballers lap it up. Every weekend. Every team. So save your frothing until you get some clue. Then you'll be wishing you'd listened to me rather than —'

'Listened to you *what?* You've said nothing constructive, just that you have some intense aversion to footballers. And that is *such* a stereotype. You haven't even said why! Sounds to me like you're jealous of them, because they've got girls falling all over them, and money and fame, and you're . . . you're just a little retail whore!'

The pseudo smile finally faded, replaced by a stone-cold glare. I'd gone too far. Fuck it. He'd written me the permission slip for that.

I sighed. 'Cam, this is the first guy I've actually liked since I've been down here. Why can't you just let me enjoy it?'

'Whatevs, Jean.'

He turned his back and walked out the door. Good. What was his *problem*? Why was he being such a little bitch? Dammit, he made me so *angry* sometimes.

I checked my phone for something from the man I had just defended, even though, deep down, I had no idea yet whether he was even worth defending. He could turn out to be Majorus Prickus and I would have to go back to Cameron with my tail between my legs. I'd rather eat excrement soup than admit he was right.

Still nothing from Josh. Damn him, what was taking him so long? I took a sip of my scalding hot chai and burned my tongue. 'Fuck,' I cursed. Ingrid walked back in just as the word left my mouth.

'What's going on? Are you okay?'

'Just burned my tongue, that's all. And, well, to be honest, Cameron was here and he was being such a prick. I don't know what his problem is. He's never even met the guy!'

A knowing smile spread over her face.

'He doesn't need to have met him. The fact that he gets to go on dates with you is enough for Cam.'

'Urgh, he makes me so *cranky*!'

'So, have you heard from Beckham today? Is there a second date locked in?'

'No. But he said he had training all morning,' I said quickly. That's twice I'd defended him in five minutes. How interesting.

Saturday morning, having not heard a beep, peep or chime from Josh all of Friday night – a night spent pretending to enjoy dinner and a movie with Col while surreptitiously checking for messages every three minutes – I checked my phone with several metric tonnes of anticipation. No banana.

Well, I thought reassuringly, I *had* to hear from him today, because he had invited me to the game tomorrow, so he'd have to call today to organise tickets or something. With that appeasing thought, I got out of bed and walked to the bathroom for a shower. I had the day off; Ingrid's friend Victoria came and helped out at the shop every so often. I kind of wished I was working, though, as it would prevent me from psychotically waiting for my phone screen to light up with Josh's name. Instead, an overwhelmingly empty day loomed.

Standing in front of my wardrobe, I wondered what to do with my Saturday. Why couldn't Josh call and suggest lunch? Or even a coffee? I figured the ball was as much in my court as his, but I'd already texted him. Plus, it wasn't my style. I liked the boy to initiate things. It just felt more romantic that way. The fifties were severely underrated, to my mind.

I decided to go for my dark blue jeans, my trusty ballet slippers and a Breton. I wished I had a Burberry trench to throw over the top. And maybe some sexy black knee-high boots. These ballet slippers were so . . . cute. Cute was dull. I wanted to look sexy, grown up. Like a woman, not a girl. I sighed dramatically and threw my hair up into my usual bee's bum. Wow. How *glamorous*. I looked at myself in the mirror and decided I needed a new wardrobe and new hair. Like, a lot. Maybe I would go shopping, I thought. What I *should* be doing is making some jewellery; that would be the Right Way to spend the day. I screwed my mouth to one side and sat on my bed, contemplating . . . Nup. I was dressed; I was going out. I was going to walk along Will Street and look in all the boutiques for inspiration for some new pieces. Maybe I would even buy some new stones. Yes! That's what I would do. I'd be productive – or, at least, appear to be – and keep my mind busy and far, far away from my silent, blank phone.

# ROUND 15
## Arrivals vs Departures

Sunday morning there was an envelope on my phone screen with Josh's name attached to it. I almost deleted it in my furious race to open and read it. It came after an increasingly agitated morning, afternoon and evening of silence, and a sleepless, angry night, tossing and turning and getting obscenely, irrationally angry at Josh Fucking Fox, who asked me to go to his stupid game and then couldn't even be bothered following up with a call or a text even though I thought we'd had a pretty nice date and we kind of *maybe* liked each other.

I opened it, my heart thumping.

Hey Jean. I'm not sure how 2 say this but have decided 2 get back w Tess. Thought should b honest w u. So sorry to stuff u abt.

I re-read it.

I read it again.

No. No, this can't be. It has to be some sick joke. It was so brutal! So clinical! So final! How did he manage to break up with me before we'd even really started dating? It'd be impressive if it weren't so fucking diabolical.

I grabbed my phone, put on my dressing gown and stormed to Col's door, tapping on it in a semi-light fashion but in a way that she couldn't possibly ignore.

'Col? Co-oool?'

'Whaaaaat?'

I opened the door; she was splayed across the bed, nude as usual. She pulled the sheet up over her chest.

'What's happened?' she croaked, her eyes still closed.

'Josh is back with Tess,' I said, half whispering, which was stupid as we were the only two in the room, and we were both awake.

She sat up like a shot, her face screwed up, her eyes blinking open, trying to find focus. She jammed some of her curls behind an ear. '*What?*'

'I'll read it to you: Hey Jean. I'm not sure how 2 say this but have decided 2 get back w Tess. Thought should b honest w u. So sorry to stuff u abt.'

'Fuck *off.*'

'Yep.'

'Show me.' I handed her the phone and she read the offending message. 'Fuck, man. That's heavy.'

I sat on her bed, my eyes darting around the dark room, trying to keep pace with my thoughts. I took the phone back from her to read it again.

'What you gonna do?' Col's puffy eyes were struggling to stay open.

'Would "Good luck and I wish you both many sexually transmitted diseases" get the sentiment across, do you think?'

She smiled, sort of.

'Nah, don't even let him know you care.'

'So I write nothing?'

'You write nothing.'

'I just . . . how, why, *where* did that come from? It's weird more than anything. Doesn't even sound like him, you know? I mean, we had a nice date – and we *did* have a nice date, I'm not attributing more meaning to it than there was – and he invited me to his game today, and now this!'

'Total dog act.'

I sighed deeply. 'What are you doing today?'

She cleared her throat. 'Um, just . . . just heading over to Holly's place, actually. She's got a bit of a barbecue thing on.'

I slumped. I so wanted to hang with Col today. The idea of a whole day full of nothing was too much to contemplate, especially as it was originally meant to include outfit-trying-on, a game of football, WAG-watching, and possibly an after-match drink with Josh, but now held nothing except the foul stench of cowardice and rejection.

'Maybe I could come?'

She looked surprised, and then apologetic.

'Oh, Jay, I'd love you to but it's just, you know, a really tight group of us . . . just the Uni girls. How about we go for a drink at that new little wine bar round the corner when I get back? Five-ish?'

That was unlike Col; she usually invited me wherever she was going. And Holly liked me, I knew she did.

''Kay, cool.' I walked out and closed the door behind me, having no idea how I would fill the day. How quickly everything could change. Josh Fox? You are a dog.

# ROUND 16
## The Insane vs The Innocent

I was at the wine bar, one glass of rosé and half a cheese platter down, when Josh's name flashed up on my screen. It was such a shock it took a few vibrations for me to understand. I'd waited days for this moment and now that it was happening, it felt dreamlike.

'Col, Josh is calling! Shit, shit, shit, what do I *do?*'

'Let it ring out, Jay! *No way* are you answering it.' She put down her drink and shook her head emphatically.

I watched 'Josh' flash and flash until the screen went dead and the keypad locked itself. My eyes went up to Col's. 'Do think he'll leave a message?'

'Hmmmm,' she said, popping an olive thoughtfully into her mouth. 'Yes. Yes, I do. God knows what – I mean, there's not much you can follow up a text like that with.'

I watched my screen. Nothing. He wasn't leaving a message. Shit! I should've answered. Why didn't I answer? Reading my mind, Col spoke up.

'Jay, if you'd answered, it'd be like saying, "Oh, sure, you can kick me in the babymaker via text and I'll still happily answer your calls. No problem! And hey, while I've got you on the phone, is there anything else you'd like to say to smash my ego? Maybe you think my nose is big? My boobs too small?"'

I smiled despite myself. An envelope appeared on my phone, indicating a voicemail had been left. 'He left one!'

I dialled my mailbox, heart racing, eyes locked onto Col's as I began to listen to Josh's voice. The message was an epic and by the time I reached the end, I was shaking my head, a disbelieving smile on my face. When I finally hung up, Col was chomping her short painted nails in suspense.

'*What?* What did he *say*?'

'Okay, so *get this*. Man. Okay, so Tess came around to their house Friday night, a total mess and claiming she'd been contemplating self-harm, and demanding to see Josh. And he still lives at home, right, in this granny flat that's not really part of the house. So his mum lets her wait until he gets home, 'cos he's at a team dinner. Anyway, so he gets in the door, sees her, hears her out, and tries to be a gentleman about it, and after an hour or so, he drives her home, and then when he gets home, he realises she's stolen his mobile!'

Colette's brow was furrowed in confusion and disbelief.

'But it gets better! So he calls it, and it's off. So he goes over to Tess's – she still lives at home too. And he's panicking, thinking she's going though every number and message in that thing, and their maid – I know, can you believe people actually have maids – says she doesn't want any visitors. And he's like, "She's got my phone, I need it," but the maid is adamant: no, he can't come in. Then Tess's dad, Henry, walks past the door, and he's the chief of the board at the club, right? And he sees Josh there – you won't believe this part – and says, "Oh, I've been meaning to call you. Come in for a chat." And then he lays it on that he would really love it if Josh would reconsider his position with Tess, because she's so upset about it all, and they really do make a "sterling" couple! And of course Josh can't say what a mad-woman his daughter is, and that she is going through his phone right now, so he just leaves, and has to leave his phone there.'

'Fuck *off*. No way!' Col's eyes were the size of CDs.

'Yep, but it gets *even* better! So on Saturday he goes around again, only to find out she's gone down to Melbourne for the weekend. With his phone and —'

'She's *actually* insane. Like, clinically.'

'Oh, totally. And *she's* the one who sent that text to me late on Saturday night, pretending to be him!'

'Oh – my – fuckin' – God. You wouldn't read about it, would you?'

I could only shake my head.

'This calls for more wine. Excuse me, *excuse me*! Hi, yes, another two of the same, please? Thank you.'

I was relieved and shocked and freaked out all at once. I thought things like that only happened in movies or TV soaps, except that it would then transpire that Tess was actually possessed by the devil, or already under psychiatric watch for having ice-picked her last boyfriend. Maybe she had.

'Wonder why he didn't just cancel his number or something, once he knew she had his phone,' Col said, cutting some more brie and spreading it onto a cracker.

'Yeah, I thought that too . . .'

'So clearly he got it back somehow, to be calling you from it?'

'Yeah – this is the best bit. He skipped the after-game function today and drove to their place, mad as hell, 'cos the players always stay in a hotel the night before the game, so it was his first chance, and their maid had the phone waiting for him in an envelope. How weird is *that*? Like nothing had happened – it was just waiting for him, as though they'd been expecting him!'

'That is some fucked-up shit. Who *are* these people?'

'Frank *did* say she was psycho . . .'

'He did, didn't he? But that's like, you know, the whole family are in on it or something. Creepy. Reminds me of that *Twilight Zone* episode where the guy runs out of petrol and ends up in that place and the girl has no mouth.'

I laughed, still shaking my head. It had been shaking solidly for five minutes, as if I were one of those toys executives have on their desks.

'Well, at least it wasn't him who sent the text. That's some good news. And he obviously called you as soon as he got his phone back. Did he know she'd sent that text?'

'Yeah, she left it in sent items – what a fruitloop. I mean, you'd at least delete it, right?'

'Unless she *wanted* him to see it.'

'Where's the benefit in that?'

'Who knows, with Madam Bunny Boiler . . .'

'Anyway, he was very, very apologetic. And so embarrassed.'

'She's such a dipshit – thanks for that, just there, thanks – he'll never get back with her now, after she's pulled shit like this on him.' Col raised her fresh wine glass.

'He sounds pretty angry with her.'

'Makes you look like a saint. She's actually helped your cause, if you think about it. Seriously, she just took her chances with Josh out the back and shot them.'

A rush of excitement raced through me at this realisation. It was true: Tess had just made a monumental dick of herself. And I was the poor victim, for whom Josh now felt terrible. Poor little perfect, non-phone-stealing Jean.

'Will you call him back?'

'I should, shouldn't I? I mean, it wasn't his fault.'

'S'pose so. But later. Tell me again how she got the phone in the first place . . .'

# ROUND 17
## Explanations vs Forgiveness

'I'm *really* sorry.' Josh sat twisting his body to face me, his lovely big eyes searching for any hint of upset in mine. He'd come around as soon as I'd called him back, preferring to apologise in person, and now we were parked at a lookout more suited to making out than apologising about mentally unstable ex-girlfriends.

I smiled. 'Josh, I understand; it's not actually your fault. At all.'

'I know, but . . . well, no, it *is* my fault, because I could've got Colette's number off Frank and got the message through that way, so you didn't think I was a pig who said he'd call and then never did, and especially after last week's non-calling fiasco, and after I'd invited you to the game . . . That sounds like the work of a class-A arsehole.'

'Relax,' I said casually, trying hard to be the no-fuss, no-drama girl I thought Josh would like. In fact, I was thoroughly enjoying playing the Holy One. 'It's all good. So, you guys won today?'

He exhaled deeply. 'We did, actually. Finally.'

'And how did you play?'

'Not bad, to be honest. Two tries. Would've been three if you'd been in the stands.'

I blushed, despite myself.

'Shouldn't you be out having a drink with the boys? To celebrate?'

'Yeah, I guess. They'll be going all night, though; I might meet up with them later. This – seeing you, explaining everything – was important.' He looked me directly in the eyes and put his hand on mine, caressing it gently. His touch made my whole body stand to attention. I felt like a schoolgirl on the path to her first kiss.

I looked back into his eyes. I knew that look: it was the one that immediately preceded a ki— Josh leaned over and kissed me. His lips were soft, his breath sweet. He opened his mouth ever so slightly and I took my cue to kiss him back in a similar manner. We kissed slowly, our heads moving gently from side to side, both taking care not to make a tender moment into a first-base moment. He placed my hand in his and locked our fingers together, taking his other hand to the nape of my neck at the same time, carefully, softly caressing my head. Oh, he was good – very good – at this.

He moved forward in his seat, kissing me with more intensity. I mirrored him, leaning into him, taking one hand over and onto his chest, rubbing his muscles. We remained like this, our breathing getting faster, our kisses becoming hungrier, my hair becoming more and more rat's-nesty beneath his hand, until his phone blared with 'Eye of the Tiger'. We opened our eyes at the same moment, and laughed. I settled back into my seat, smoothing my hair as best I could, trying to steady my breathing as he fumbled for his phone. He looked at the screen and shook his head.

'It's Pilko.'

'Ahhh, Pilko,' I said. 'Pilkomatic. The Pilkster. How is he?'

Confusion flickered in Josh's eyes before he broke into a smile. 'Smartarse.'

'Let me guess. He's calling to say stop making out and come have a beer?'

'Something like that.' He smiled and leaned over to grab my hand. 'But I'd rather stay here with you, doing what we were just doing . . .'

I smoothed my jeans over my legs and gave him a coy smile.

'Well, you know, you're only human,' I said, giving Col's line a spin.

'You're not.' He came in close and kissed me on the lips, then looked me in the eyes. 'You're from another planet. You're too perfect.'

'That's —' he kissed me, 'so —' he kissed me, 'cheesy,' I mumbled as he kissed me.

He sat back and sighed. 'I really couldn't be arsed . . .'

'Cold beer waits for no man, Foxman.'

He laughed, shaking his head. 'That's what the boys call me.'

'Go on, go.'

'God, you're so laid-back! Tess – sorry to bring her up again, but she used to *hate* me going for drinks with the boys. She'd always kick up a massive stink. And you're basically telling me to piss off and start drinking. Funny thing is, that makes me want to go even less than I did before I saw you in that top.'

I looked down at my top; it was veeeery low-cut. My wearing it had not been an accident. I smiled, blushing.

We drove back silently the few blocks to my place, Josh's hand resting on my thigh. I wanted him to leave it there forever. Thank God for automatics.

'You know, you could come with me, if you wanted.'

I grabbed my handbag off the floor.

'Thank you, but no. I'm beat.' It was true. His antics, or rather Tess's, had exhausted me. My mind had been in the red zone for days. 'Have fun.'

'Jean, I'm so sorry and so embarrassed about this whole thing. Rest assured I'll be strapping my phone to my flesh from here on.'

Just then, 'Eye of the Tiger' kicked in again. We laughed.

'See ya.'

'Bye, Jeanie. I'll call you tomorrow. You have my word.'

He leaned over for a goodbye kiss. I made it a short one, pulling back just as he was beginning what could easily have turned into another session.

'Playing hardball, huh?'

'You know it.'

I winked and got out of the car, closed the door, and strutted up our steps in a way I hoped looked sexy. Did I just wink? Jesus. Where did that come from? Last time I'd tried to wink sexily at a guy, it was Jeremy and he'd thought I had something in my eye. And yet I'd just pulled it off with Josh. Josh the superstar footballer and town hero and phenomenal kisser and boy who would've preferred to stay in his car making out with me than go drinking with the boys.

As I unlocked the door I wondered why Tess had cared so much when he went out. So what? They'd won and they wanted a few beers, what was the big deal? She had some serious issues. A whole encyclopaedia of them.

I skipped into the living room, dumping my bag on the dining table. Josh liked me, Josh liiiiked me! And he wasn't back with Tess, and I was a winking, easygoing, fun-loving girl. And even if I wasn't, he thought I was.

My phone buzzed.

Perfect Jean, I forgot 2 ask, du want 2 come 2 charity ball 4 the club wed nite? Boring but wd love u 2 come. Want 2 show u off . . .

Actively ignoring the painful phonetic format, I focused on the content: Josh was inviting me to a ball. With all of the players and all of their wives and girlfriends and *maybe even Tess*. At the very least, a lot of people who knew Tess. And knew her to be Josh's girl. My heartbeat raced at the idea; I couldn't think of one thing that would be more terrifying, fatal earthquake aside. Nope. Nothing. What would I wear? And what the hell did 'ball' mean? Was it a gown situation, or was a cocktail dress all that was required? Ingrid would definitely be handing over the Best Dress in the Shop for this, whatever it took on my part.

I'll arrange for my horse and carriage to be free that night. Thank you for inviting me. Have a fun night.

Kiss? I'd given him one last time and that hadn't done me any favours. Nope, no kiss. I was playing the cool dream-girl too well to drop the ball, as it were, now. Immediately, my phone buzzed.

I'll b honoured 2 hv u by my side. See u then x

Ha! *He* did the kiss! I tilted back my head and laughed. And you know what? I *could* hold my own at this ball thing. I was Perfect Jean.

# ROUND 18
## Elegant vs Excessive

My insides had been taken hostage by a heaving swarm of frenzied, nausea-inducing nerves. There was as much chance of me being cool and calm at the ball as there was of a kiwifruit conducting a tax audit.

At least I had a dress sorted. Ingrid had said I could wear the Ultimate Cocktail Dress if I did all the paperwork by today. She was a bit of a cow like that, but the lure of wearing that dress – all black and slinky and bust-boosting and tight as a glove in all the right places before dropping elegantly to the floor, and thus being non-tight in all the right places too – was intoxicating. The explanation behind her generous sartorial permission slip was that if I looked good, and the WAGs noticed, they might slither into the shop and spend some of their partners' hard-earned cash. Simple kindness of heart would be too much to ask.

Thankfully for my twice-not-called, three-times-shy paranoia, Josh had called yesterday to confirm and to make sure I was still coming. He said he would pick me up at 6.30, and that he was looking forward to seeing me all dressed up. I had casually dropped into the conversation the fact that I was feeling a little nervous about meeting everyone. He guffawed and said that they'd love me, as though bringing a new girl to a big event were entirely quotidian.

I wasn't so sure. I figured they were probably all tight with Tess, and would heavily resent me and the electrifying pace at which I had sauntered onto the scene and thieved Josh away from her, even though I was a nobody, had only ever had a handful of professional blow-dries in my life, and there was an aggressive pimple beginning to mass in a very antisocial manner on my chin.

Josh was either blissfully ignorant of my anxiety, or else he was playing the role of Confident Guy beautifully, unprepared to let on that despite the fact he had just replaced his long-term girlfriend with a velocity usually reserved for small mating amphibians, everything was totally cool.

The more I allowed my thoughts to fester, the more jittery I became. Not only was I going to be walking onto Tess's turf, against a tide of acid-tongued, acrylic-taloned cronies, but at the very least I was attending a ball with a guy I barely knew, and no reliable intelligence of the fucking dress code. I was a little girl from Queensland – we wore thongs year-round, and believed that lycra made for an acceptable evening dress! I needed to calm down. I needed intravenous Valium. Fuck! Where was Col? Col would help.

'All ready for the ball, WAGarella?'

'Col, I'm starting to think I shouldn't go . . .'

'What? Are you *retarded*?'

'No, hang on. Think about it: these are *WAGs*. They're fucking perfect! You saw them at the game. They'll probably all take the day off to get spray tans and blow-dries, while I finish work an hour before I'm being picked up – and I had to fight Ingrid even for that. And my hair needs a colour, and I've got a spot, and Tess might be there, and even if she's not, all the girlfriends will be pro-Tess —'

'Okay, someone needs to put the crack pipe *down*.'

I took a deep breath in, releasing it slowly. My heart was racing.

'Now, listen to me. You are going to this ball. You are wearing a *hot dress*. Josh asked you because he wants your company and he wants to show you off, but I also think he's smarter than you're giving him credit for. I think he's making a statement by taking you so soon after he broke up with Tess; it shows he's not gonna pussyfoot around in the shadow of the Great Nutbag.'

'Do you think?' None of that had occurred to me. Especially the part about Josh orchestrating this as a kind of PR stunt.

'She stole his phone, for fuck's sake!'

'Hmmm. Guess you're right.'

'So, you're going to look hot, and smile at all the haters, and —'

'Did you just say "haters"?'

'And you're going to enjoy your evening knowing you deserve to be there just as much as any of them bitches.'

'You're so gangsta, Col.'

'I'll try to get home by six to help you get ready. Did you still need fashion tape?'

'Thanks Col. Oh and heeeey, who's the new dude, huh?'

'Whaddyamean?' Col's voice changed ever so slightly, taking on a hint of defence.

'Well, I saw some big guy's hoodie in your room this morning. Figured you must have worn it home from his place . . .'

'It's Holly's,' she said quickly. 'I was at hers on the weekend and it's her boyfriend's.' She sounded nervous. I had a hunch she was hiding something from me.

'When were you there?'

'Ummmm, Jay? What's with the fifty questions? If I was seeing a new guy, don't you think I'd tell you?'

'Okay, okay.'

She exhaled dramatically.

'See you tonight, loser.'

'Peace out, boy scout.'

I frowned, wondering why the conversation had spiked so violently at the end there. She was so highly strung sometimes. Why would she need to get so defensive about a hoodie? I didn't care if she was seeing someone. Maybe she thought I would tell Josh and that was slack to Frank. Yeah, that must be it.

Then I realised something. Holly didn't have a boyfriend.

# ROUND 19
## East Germany vs Colombia

'If I park here, is that too far for you in those shoes? I know – I'll drop you off and go park then come ba—'

Like *hizzell*. There was no way I was going to stand out the front like No-mates Nigel, watching everyone go in, while I waited anxiously for Josh. Uh-uh.

'No, no, I'm fine to walk.' (Lie.) 'Really.' (Double lie.) 'But thank you for offering.'

'Okay. Sorry, Jeanie, they should really get some valet going.'

'Or offer limousines . . .'

He smiled. 'I think you'll agree a Hummerzine would be the classier option.'

We grinned at each other. He looked incredible: a sharp, fitted black suit, a shirt of a fairyfloss-pink so subtle it might have been white before being washed with some red socks, and a lilac tie. I wondered if anyone styled him, or if he was intrinsically stylish. Either way: *bravo*. He'd give any gay man a run for his Prada trainers.

I clambered out of the low passenger seat and stood, smoothing The Dress as I did, and jamming Colette's small Jimmy Choo clutch under my arm. I took a deep breath and walked to the rear of the car, where Josh was waiting. He took me in appreciatively.

'You look incredible, Perfect Jean. I'm gonna have to keep my eye on the boys tonight. Especially Bones. He'll try it on, you watch.'

I smiled, thrilled he thought I looked good enough to tempt his friends. That was a kind of jealousy, right? You couldn't ask for more from an outfit: fear of being hit on by other males was the best possible compliment.

'Fancy a five-block pre-dinner stroll?' he asked, offering his arm.

'Love to,' I said, taking it. As we walked, I tried to squish down the mammoth knots of fear accumulating in my stomach. I would filch a drink right out of someone's hands if there wasn't one awaiting me the second I got in the door.

Finally arriving at a grand gargoyle-guarded hall, Josh subtly, gently, placed his arm behind my back and we walked into a foyer where what looked like several thousand people were milling and talking animatedly, schooners and champagne flutes in their hands.

I saw flashes of gold, aqua, pink, red and peacock blue in the crowd, all accompanied by masses of long, glossy hair and tanned (very) skin. I looked at my black dress and pale skin, and took a monstrously deep breath.

'Nice tie, Foxman. Where's your boyfriend?'

A rugged, good-looking blue-eyed guy with blond hair poked Josh in the chest.

'Thanks, Bones.' Josh opened Bones's suit jacket to reveal a white shirt and black waistcoat.

'You helping out the wait staff tonight?'

'Mate, get with the times; everyone's moved on from ties. You're livin' in the past.'

'Righto. Bones, this is Jean. Jean, Bones; real name Luke.'

Bones looked at me for the briefest moment, smiled and nodded a non-verbal hello. *He* was the one Josh had told me to watch out for? He seemed like he'd be more interested in jazzercise than hitting on me. Suddenly something over my shoulder caught Bones's eye.

'Wa*haaaay*, lookat Sharon!'

I turned to look for Sharon, seeing only a huge blond guy with brown eyes and tanned skin. He could've passed for a surfer if he were a quarter the size.

'G'day, boys.' He gave a big, goofy grin before settling his eyes on me.

'G'day there, I'm Pete.' He stuck out one of his giant paws.

'Pete, this is Jean. Jean, Pete; otherwise referred to as Sharon.'

'Should I ask why?' I queried, grinning.

Bones chimed in. ''Cos he's got tits like a lady, and he likes to dress up as one, too.'

Pete shrugged good-naturedly.

'We had a team bowls day a few months back,' explained Josh, 'and we all had to dress as something starting with S. Of course, Pete's logical interpretation was to come as a woman named Sharon.'

'And it's stuck,' said Pete/Sharon.

'Where's Kate?' Bones asked.

'She's coming, just having a ciggie.'

At that moment, a tiny blonde girl who could have passed for one of Pete's offspring appeared. She was seemingly bare-faced, save for some mascara, and her small frilly black dress made her look even smaller, if that were possible. The mechanics of the two of them doing, well, stuff, was brain-bending. He looked as though he could fold her up and pop her in his pocket.

'Hey, Bones, hi, Josh,' she said.

'Hi, Kate, you look lovely tonight . . . This is Jean.'

Kate smiled shyly at me and said hello, pressing into Pete's side. I knew immediately that we wouldn't be best friends, even though I was grateful that Pete had so generously offered his fiancée for me to play with, and that she was so small and non-scary-looking and un-Tess-like. After a few attempts at polite conversation it dawned on me that Kate either had a mouth full of peanut butter and couldn't speak, or simply preferred to remain mute. She was enormously agreeable in that frustrating 'What would you like to drink?'/'Whatever you're having' kind of way. I gave up when her answer to 'How long have you and Pete been together?' was 'Since school' and then another nuzzle into Pete's enormous chest.

'Do you know what this beer tastes like, boys?' Bones said as he drained his glass. 'More!' And he walked off to find a waiter. He was very fidgety, I thought, eyes always darting around the room, looking for something or someone more interesting. I couldn't help noticing how he openly checked out every girl who walked past. Every single one.

'Bones is single,' Josh explained. 'Actually, that's not entirely true. He has several hundred girls hanging around, but none that he'd ever bring to something like this, if that makes sense. Anyway, he hates these things, 'cos everyone's always partnered up.'

'Aha,' I said, smiling. Bones *was* very good-looking, I thought, watching him from afar. He looked a little bit like Matthew McConaughey. Without the Botox.

'Why do you call him Bones?'

'Oh, that. He has an obsession with girls' collarbones. A fetish, almost. First thing he notices about a chick.'

'I see.' I looked down to try to see mine. I had no idea whether it was nice or not. What constituted a nice collarbone, anyway? Protruding? Enveloped in flesh? Furnished with golden skin and silver chains?

We walked a few steps and melted into the crowd, the boys scooping beers and champagne for everyone off a moving tray. We sipped our drinks as Josh and Pete discussed their previous game. From his size and number of scars, I surmised that Pete did a lot of tackling. His ears appeared to have been nibbled on by someone with very small but powerful teeth. Kate, perhaps?

'Josh. How are you? Sorry to bother you but would you mind . . . um . . .' A smallish man – or perhaps that was just in contrast to the guys around me – hovered behind Josh with a football and a texta in his hands. That was weird. Why would he have a football —? I watched as Josh took the texta in one hand and rested the ball on his other arm.

'Who should I make it out to?'

'Oh, ah, Matthew, please. Thanks so much. This'll make his world. All the best for Saturday night.'

'Thanks, mate. Enjoy your night.'

Josh caught my expression.

'Does that happen a lot? People just walking up and presenting you with balls?'

He shrugged. 'Sometimes. Usually it's kids. But tonight's a members night, so it may happen a few more times, yeah.' He smiled awkwardly, apologetically. I loved how he was taking the time to explain everything in this strange new world to me, even if it did make me feel a bit like Cousin Betty from the country.

'They never want my autograph,' Pete said, with mock hurt. 'Only Josh's, 'cos he's pretty and scores tries.'

'Bullshiiiit,' said Josh, punching Pete playfully on the arm.

'Look alive,' Pete muttered, looking past me. 'Here comes the East German Police.'

I turned to look just as two women walked our way. One was wearing a blue empire-line floor-length dress and a lot of blonde hair. (I was pretty sure they were extensions, as the bottom five centimetres just sat there, lank and heavy.) Her boobs were the variety that screamed for attention: high, wide and, I imagined, quite expensive. To further draw attention to themselves, in case sheer volume wasn't enough, the boobs shimmered with some kind of glitter.

The brunette, who looked somehow familiar, had her hair in a high ponytail above a blunt fringe, and a similar empire-line dress, hers in a delicate silk fabric with an elegant brown-and-black pattern. She had a more modest boob offering, but there was still a definite focus on the general area. She was skinny but very nicely toned. Of course.

'Josh, how *aaare* you?'

Blonde kissed him on the cheek before stepping back to allow Brunette to grab his hand and take her turn. Suddenly I knew where I'd seen her before. She was Tess's friend from the after-match function! Neither looked at me as they closed in on Josh.

'Loooove your tie, it's just *gorge*,' said Blonde, lifting the hair sitting over her left boob as though it were rope, and slowly placing it behind her shoulder.

'Ryan was going to buy a pink tie. I should've made him – looks *so* hot,' Brunette said.

'Um, so, you both look, uh, nice,' Josh said, his eyes flicking over to me. I wondered how I had been pushed out of the circle without a single touch to my skin.

'This is Jean,' Josh said, finally receiving my mental text message.

'Hi,' Brunette said: a forced statement, her smile as tight as the skin on her friend's breasts.

'Hi.' My voice broke. Awesome. Josh snaked his arm over to me and pulled me in close to him. My heart must surely be visible, beating through my dress. They looked at me, then at Josh's arm, their beady eyes stripping me bare, their faces nursing incredulity at Josh's audacity.

'So, how did you two meet?' asked Brunette: the conversational equivalent of placing cheese in a steel trap.

'We met through Frank, actually,' Josh said confidently.

I took a long sip of my champagne, trying to swallow my nerves with the fizz. Come on, Josh, take us away from these women and their overpowering fragrance and aggressive décolletage.

'Never were one to move slow, were you, Josh?' said Brunette, her voice playful but tinged with venom, her eyes shooting invisible laser beams into Josh's.

He straightened up, his body language indicating he'd had enough. Sensing the tension, Blonde piped up.

'So, you hear about Patto and Scully?'

Josh squinted. 'No . . . ?'

'What'd they do now?' Pete said, his tone akin to that of a dad being confronted with more news on his naughty son.

'They've been canning on like mongrels since lunch. Patto cracked on to Coach's missus the minute he arrived, and Scully fell over while he was trying to piss straight at the urinal – and, of all the people who could've seen it happen, it was Henry Clifton.'

Josh's mouth had already framed itself into a disbelieving smile; now it flew open and he laughed with incredulity.

'Nooooo . . . you're shitting me.'

'Those two need their heads read, honestly.' Pete started looking around the room, presumably for one of the two booze bandits so that he could go and give them a stern talking to. I decided I liked Pete.

'Dickheads. When will you boys grow the hell up?' Brunette tsk-tsked and Blonde shook her head at Josh as if he were personally responsible for his team-mates' behaviour. 'I'm surprised Ryan wasn't part of this, to be honest,' she continued with disdain. She tipped her head back and swallowed the last of her champagne. 'I need a drink.'

The two women walked off in a haze of bronzer and attitude, all wiggling hips and hair flicks.

'I can't believe Patto's form. Scully, well, yes, but Patto . . .' Josh said as we walked, presumably towards the dining room. He looked back at Pete and Kate, who had been held up talking to a man who looked like he hadn't spoken to a Real Life human being for several years, and had to get out everything he wanted to say right now.

Josh went back and gently interrupted. 'Guys? I think they want us to be seated now.'

Pete dived on the cue. 'Oh, better move in then. Well, it's been nice chatting, Roger.'

I kept quiet as we walked into the function room, which was dark, and decorated with balloons and flower arrangements in the Bulls' signature royal blue. There was a stage with a huge screen behind it, the full set-up for a band, and a podium with stand and microphone.

'Sorry 'bout that,' Josh whispered. 'How twisted those two are – I can't even begin to tell you . . .' He shook his head.

'Who are they?'

He sighed. 'The brunette is Melinda – she dates Big Red (that's Ryan Redin). And the blonde is Morgan Simons – she's married to Phil Burnette. Melinda and Morgan own a spray-tan service together.'

Of course they do.

'Everyone calls them the Tandoori Twins.'

We found our table, right near the stage, and took our seats. There was a non-player couple already seated, who smiled and introduced themselves as Caitlin and Mark. Another polite older couple arrived at the table just as we sat; the room was filling up rapidly.

'Whasupp, Josha?'

I looked up to see a tall, latte-skinned woman with shiny black hair bending down to give Josh a big hug and kiss. Her hair was long and fell glamorously in a middle part. She was wearing a loose, muted goldy-grey shift dress and tan strappy heels. She looked gorgeous – Halle Berry meets Eva Mendes. Her words were veiled in a thick accent, which only added to the appeal.

'Hey, Paola, how are you?'

'So I got this crazy blister and its makin' me fuckin' crazy. I wanted to wear flat shoes, but choo know what Jimmy's like: *No way are you wearing sandals to a ball, you crazy bitch and rahrahrah* . . . Ooh, and who this pretty lady?'

She looked at me approvingly, giving a 'nice work' face to Josh. I could have kissed her, whoever she was. Someone nice – *there was someone nice here!*

'This is Jean. Jean, this is Paola. She's mad. And Colombian.'

'Choo don even *wanna* know how mad I am.' She bent down and gave me a kiss. It didn't seem too forward coming from her, somehow.

'Nice to meet you, Jean. Is it Jean? I don't wanna forget that. Maybe I'll call you Jeanie instead, like the little man in the lamps.'

I laughed. 'That's entirely fine by me.'

She stopped and stood up suddenly, staring at my neck.

'Honey, what *is* this necklace?'

I blushed, looking down at the piece I'd chosen to wear tonight. It featured several layers of heavy gold and black leather, entwined and twisted to make a kind of thick weave around my neck; it was one of my best pieces.

'Jeanie, this is 'mazing! Where you get this one?'

'Um, I made it, actually,' I said quietly.

'*Noooo!* You didn't! Is so beautiful. Chica, you is clever!'

I blushed again. Receiving Paola's praise made me feel like I was sitting in direct sunlight. She was so affectionate. And pretty. And enthusiastic! At school I'd had to work for years to get a compliment on my jewellery from one of the popular, pretty girls, yet here was beautiful Paola lobbing one at me within seconds of meeting me.

She looked around impatiently. 'Jesus, where's Jimmy? I don't even know which tables we're on.' (Please be on this one, I prayed. *Please.*) 'He's probably sucking up to the board of erectors . . .' Paola scanned the room impatiently. 'There he is, talkin' to a girl, as usual. I swear, I'm gonna break his balls one of these days —' She walked off to find Jimmy.

'She's cool,' I said to Josh, smiling. She was so natural and friendly compared with the other WAGs I'd met. She seemed genuine, like she didn't need to impress anyone, or make out as though she was some kind of terrifying alpha bitch who'd slash your tyres if you stopped to tie up your shoelaces.

'I knew you'd like Paola,' smiled Josh. 'Everyone does.'

'Is Jimmy a team-mate?'

'Captain. Nice guy. Head like a smashed crab but always attracts incredibly beautiful women. You'll see lots of ugly footballers, but no ugly girlfriends. Anyway, they've been together for years. She came over here for a holiday and met Jimmy, and never went home.'

'To Colombia?'

'New York, I think.'

'I hope they're on our table.'

Just then a quiet voice drifted in from behind.

'Josh, hi. Sorry to interrupt, but I was wondering if I could get a photo with you . . .' I looked up to see who the voice belonged to; it was a friendly-looking woman in her forties. She caught me looking up at her and shot me an apologetic smile. 'Sorry, love, you must get this all the time . . .'

I smiled at her as Josh stood for the photo. How strange it must be to have people constantly asking you for something, I thought. Just as that photo session finished, two pretty teenage girls asked for a turn. Josh obliged, only to be asked by a middle-aged man if he might be able to have a picture too. I watched Josh smile politely, and make small talk, and sign some caps and jerseys and balls, and wish each fan all the best. And I fell a little bit in love.

Add me to the long list of Josh Fox fans.

# ROUND 20
## Mean Girls vs New Friends

After an hour and a half spent chatting to a man whose company held the illustrious title of Australia's biggest exporter of shoelaces, and listening to people I had never heard of discussing a game I knew nothing about, and an entree and main involving two animals I did not eat, I needed some respite.

I excused myself with a whisper and, head down, made for the bathroom, hoping the Tandooris had already emptied their bladders. I pushed open the door and went straight into the only free cubicle of three. Two loud, tipsy voices emitted from the others.

'So, like, they pulled you over? And you'd been drinking! Shiiiit. Did you get done? For DYI?'

'It's DIY, stupid.'

Silence.

'Actually, I think it's DUI. Whatever. Look, I was totally over the limit, but I just, you know, did my little thing, and the police officer let me go!'

'You are *terrible*!'

Toilets were flushed, doors opened, taps run, clutches unzipped, compacts snapped open.

'So, you hear about Bones?'

'What now?'

'He's got some cougar who pays him thousands of dollars to text her pics of him naked.'

'Shut *uuup*!'

'True. Told Jess. Apparently he and this woman hooked up one night and she Facebooked him the next day, asking for a photo. Then she told him she'd give him a grand for each new photo he sends.'

'No way.'

'Then, like, a week later, he gets a cheque for a grand in the mail at the club, and a note saying there's more where that came from.'

'Shut up, shut *uuup*! Ohmygod, I would *so* send some slutty pics for a grand a pop!'

'He's sent a whole bunch now, as you can imagine. I hope she turns out to be an undercover journalist and prints them all in the papers.'

Both voices dissolved into loud laughter.

Anxiety suddenly washed over me. I flushed the toilet and nervously zipped up The Dress. *Please* couldn't they go? What, were they gonna re-do their whole faces? Well, I couldn't stay in here any longer. I took a deep breath and unlocked my cubicle.

Both girls were visibly relieved when they saw I was A Nobody. Both had blonde hair that had recently been on the receiving end of a high-powered hair-dryer. The taller one wore a slinky tube in canary yellow that only the most confident, tall and thin could hope to pull off. Her body, being devoid of all visible protrusions except for an enormous bust, filled out the dress perfectly. She had big brown eyes, gleaming tanned cheeks and masses of sultry eye makeup. She was the type of girl who makes men forget what they were talking to their wife about as they walk past her in the street; the type who might grace an *FHM* cover, with oiled-up skin, fake grease marks, a ripped white singlet, a wrench, denim cut-offs and a beefed-up car with its bonnet yawning for all to see its shiny metal teeth.

The other girl had a beauty that was less announced. Her hair, a tumbling mass of yellow gold, was both the thing that brought her attention and the veil that hid her from it. Her face was soft and pretty. Although it had been suitably hardened with grown-up makeup, her authentic, girl-next-door beauty shone through. She wore a short red cocktail dress that dripped with small beads and climaxed in a plunging V in the breast region.

They were mesmerising to watch, these girls. Terrifying to listen to, but mesmerising to watch.

'Seriously, can you imagine if she was setting him up?' Red Dress said with glee.

'He deserves it, for the way he treats chicks. What about that time *three* different girls came to the Girlfriends' Box saying they were his girlfriend. Unbelievable. Hey, gimme your concealer for a sec?'

I cleared my throat and edged towards the spare sink, which was decorated with half a M·A·C store. Yellow Dress checked me out briefly in the mirror before returning to her gloss application.

All of a sudden, I experienced a jolt of reality: these were the most popular girls at school, just all grown up. That's who became a footballer's girlfriend or wife. And I hadn't been one of those girls. I was one of the drifters, melting in and out of different groups (athletics, creatives, stoners). These girls had always been light-years away, socially. And now, just because of Josh, I thought I was capable of joining their highly glossed ranks? Who did I think I was kidding? Next I'd be trying to rumble lions with circus folk.

'Perfume?'

Yellow Dress took the bottle from Red, popping off the lid and spraying her long, tanned neck. I took a paper towel and dried my hands. Touching up *my* makeup would have to wait. I smiled with closed lips, put my head down and walked out, the sound of a fresh conversation erupting and bouncing off the tiled walls as the door swung shut behind me.

This wasn't my scene, I confirmed silently to myself; I was a wombat in WAG's clothing. And as much as I wanted to make some friends – desperately, in fact – I was pretty sure I didn't actually want to be friends with these girls.

'Hey, baby!' Paola was walking across the foyer, her hips swivelling just so, her boobs bouncing in the way a model requires multiple takes to perfect in a swimwear ad campaign. 'That's some good timing! Cigarette? I was *dying* in there. Honestly, every time I forget how fucking boring these nights is!'

I looked at Paola's happy face, and her short, pink, buffed nails holding out a slim cigarette. Since my epiphany in the ladies' regarding my non-popular-girl status, I'd forgotten about her and how nice she was. She was probably the only one like that, though. A rose between the thorns; a suntan amongst the sprays.

I frowned, wondering whether to have one. They usually made me cough and gave me a head-spin. But in the name of friendship, I guessed I could put those things aside. Seeing my face, Paola's brows scrunched up.

'You don't like?' She indicated the cigarette.

'No, no. It's just that, well, I don't really smoke. But I'll come out with you, if you don't mind.'

'Good one!' Her face changed instantly, lighting up with an enormous smile. 'I unnerstand why you don't smoke. I used to do it to keep me skinny, now I just do it 'cos of the habit. Jimmy hates it, but I don't complain about his musical arse so he can suck it up.' She whooped with laughter and started walking. I followed, smiling.

'So, how long you been with Josh?' Paola asked as she took a deep drag. She was the kind of woman who could persuade you to take up smoking just because she looked so glamorous doing it.

'Um, oh, not long at all. This is kind of, well, our second date, to be honest.'

She erupted into laughter. 'And he takes you *here*?' She shook her head. 'Baby, let me 'splain.' She lowered her voice and looked around. 'These nights? I'd rather set fire to my tits. They go forever, and you spend time on an outfit just to sit in the dark. Where is the dancing? The fun!'

She went on to tell me about an outrageously decadent party she went to on a boat in Croatia with Sean John and Naomi Campbell, back when she was modelling. I lapped up every detail, loving her accent, loving her stories, loving how she spoke to me as though we were already firm friends, just loving *her*.

Maybe I could stick this out a bit longer.

# ROUND 21
## The Footballer vs The DJ

I dialled Col. Again.

The shop was desperately slow, so I had spent the morning sketching some designs that I wanted to finally make this weekend. I had been inspired by some beautiful jewellery in a UK *Vogue* swimwear shoot, and planned to set Sunday aside to make the final pieces for Ingrid.

Finally, a pick-up.

'Jeeeeeeez, where've you *been*? I wanted to tell you about last night!'

Colette sighed on the other end of the phone. 'I was in a meeting, Jay, and while I'm sure they would've loved to have let me take your call, it just seemed somehow inappropriate to talk in the boardroom about my little sister's new cult.'

'Whatever. Anyway, so all the girls were wearing, like, really bright-coloured dresses, most of them maxi. It was like the theme was fruit salad, but Josh didn't pass on the memo.'

She laughed. 'Gorgeous. Were there lots of asymmetrical, jagged hemlines?'

'You bet. And lots of boobs. Boob town. Boobs *everywhere*. Mostly spiling over the top of strapless numbers that fell to just above the ankles.'

'Ohhh, the floor-length that isn't quite floor-length. *Always* a classy option. Perfect for showing off diamanté-encrusted silver shoes —'

'And there's this *stunning* South American girl, Paola, who I got along with really well – you'd like her, I reckon. Actually, everyone was very nice to me. Well, 'cept for these two bitches who are tight with Tess, but that's to be expected.'

'Oooh, do tell. Did the Wicked WAGs of the West shoot you some mad stink-eye from across the room?'

'Once or twice. Josh was adorable about it all: charming but laced with *fuck off*, y'know?'

'Impressive. So, what else? Did the cheerleaders dance? Was there a giant golden football on the stage?'

I decided not to tell her about the band dressed in Bulls jerseys, singing Meatloaf and Bruce Springsteen songs.

'The weirdest thing, Col, was people asking for autographs and photos with Josh every few minutes. Even when he was eating dinner. And these are, like, members, so not just street fans, but people who are regularly in contact with the players after the game and stuff.'

'He's a Local Hero, sis. Don't ever forget that. I mean, who cares about firemen and people who work with the homeless or save endangered wildlife? Footballers are men who *matter*.'

'You're a nong. Hey, wanna make pizzas tonight? I feel like I haven't seen you for ages, and we live in the same house.'

'Um, sure. Okay . . .'

'Don't sound *too* pumped.'

'No, it's just that, I was maybe going to dinner.'

'With who?'

'No one. Just, you know, the girls.'

'Oh. Well, maybe I can come?'

'Yeah, sure . . . Let me text you a bit later – tonight might not even happen. I gotta fly, Jay. Ciao, ciao.'

Click.

God, she was a weirdo sometimes.

I looked at the time. Barely twelve. But I was *starving*. I suddenly thought of Cameron; where had he been? Maybe we could get lunch. Or rather, maybe he could go get it and we could eat it here. I walked out onto the pavement and poked my head into his store. Electro-punk music was screeching at concert level, and a young, severely fashionised salesgirl dressed in an outfit that wouldn't have looked out of place at a 1983 New Order concert was singing along as she rearranged skinny-leg jeans on the sale table.

'Um, hi. Is Cameron in today?' I yelled to her.

She looked over, frowning, and shrugged. 'Might be in later, I think. Dunno.' She went back to her singing.

Helpful.

I walked back into the shop and picked up my phone. I'd text the little monkey, see if he was coming in anytime soon. Maybe he could get some Hong Hin Vietnamese rolls on the way. Yes! I would give blood for one of those chicken rolls. Cam and I often ate them and then watched each other as we both got jittery, headachy and hyper from the MSG. It was our twisted little game.

There was a new message waiting for me.

Thank u for coming last nite Jeanie. U looked amazing. Free tomrw? Luv 2 tk u 4 lunch. And wd u want tix 4 game sunday? x

He texted! He texted! He texted. Ahhh, he *texted*.

Tomorrow? Of course I could see him tomorrow! Hang on, tomorrow was meant to be a tracksuit-wearing, jewellery-making day. I'd promised myself I would dedicate the entire day to finishing my line. No ifs, no buts. *But* . . . this was Josh. Maybe I could see him at the end of the day, as a kind of reward for all my designing. Yes, that would be *perfect*.

My pleasure and thank you for inviting me. Love to see you tomorrow. Dinner?

Sadly will b in hotel w team b/c we are not 2 b trusted in real world by orselves – we mt get drunk n start fights or start doin meth.

Shit. Dinner was out. But I knew that if I said yes to lunch I wouldn't focus properly in the morning, and then wouldn't get any work done in the afternoon . . . Shit.

'Ange said you were searching frantically for me! *God,* why can't one day go past without women *hunting* me? I'm so *sick* of being treated like a piece of *meat!*'

Cameron stood at the door, gesticulating dramatically and generally carrying on like a pork chop. He was wearing gold trainers, his usual black skinny jeans, a white shirt and a bright chequered jumper. He looked obscenely, farcically trendy.

I smiled. 'Gimme one sec, just gotta send this text . . .'

Lunch sounds great. x

I would have to have some stern words with myself later. I was being very, very naughty giving priority to some guy over working on my designs. I turned to Cameron, a grin on my face. My phone beeped. I whipped around to check it.

Sweet! Pick u up at 1. feel free 2 wr same dress u wore last nite. x

I blushed.

Cameron, as usual, picked up on my every mood, move, thought and emotion.

'Don't tell me – that was your new boyfriend. Am I right? Was it him? Asking if you'll wear his championship ring? Or his jock's jacket? Or accompany him to the prom?'

I shrugged. 'Maybe, what's it to you?'

'Don't you feel like a bit of a groupie?'

'How am I a groupie? I didn't even know who he was when I met him. And actually, Cam, I find the footballer side of him a bit of a pain in the arse.'

'Ah, silly me. Groupies want a football hero but can't get one, whereas you have secured yourself one with incredible ease and efficiency. Sadly, that won't stop all his groupies from preying on him when you're not around.'

I shook my head. 'Whatever. The reason I was looking for you was to see if you wanted to have lunch, but now I think I'd rather eat solo.'

He walked over, a sooky expression on his face.

'Jay, it's okay to admit you've missed me and have been fretting about my safety and whereabouts. I'm here now. There's no need to be angry.'

I laughed despite myself. He was such a little shit.

'I can't take lunch till 1.30, so sit tight till then.'

'I'm ready to eat a T-shirt. I gotta eat *now*.'

'Have a snack.'

'No, I'm having lunch. Who cares – we can have lunch together another day.'

I started looking at the Japanese takeaway menu; I'd just order my usual teriyaki salmon and pick it up.

'Shit, it really is your way or the highway, isn't it?' Cameron shook his head.

'You know it.' I smiled smugly.

'Aren't you even going to ask where I've been all week?' he said, exasperation and hurt in his voice.

I put down the menu to look at him. 'Where?'

'Only performing in the National DJ Championships. But, you know, no big *deal* or anything.'

'Oh shit!' My hand flew to my mouth. 'Cam, I'm *so* sorry, I completely forgot to even wish you luck before you went! Ohhh, I am sorry. How did you go?'

'Too caught up knitting the other girlfriends' team scarves.'

I frowned.

'Okay, okay.' He took a deep breath, exhaling some nastiness as he did so. 'I came runner-up. Twister won. *Fuck* knows how – he scratches like a drunk and probably thinks Detroit is a breed of dog. And the tracks in his set – I know *all* of them, and they've already been done to death on the UK and New York scene. It just shits me, you know? They can't appreciate someone doing something original. I played the best set, researched for months, had it fuckin' perfect, and the crowd loved it 'cos it was something different. I mean, he played Armand Van Helden, for fuck's sake! Fucking loser.'

'I've never heard of — What's his name? Twister?'

'Oh, he's the "King of the Melbourne club scene"'. Cameron made quotation marks in the air with great sarcasm. 'Thing is, there *is* no Melbourne club scene.'

'Well, still, runner-up is very impressive. How many compete?'

''Bout thirty-five.'

'*Cam!* And this is a national competition? Runner-up is *awesome!* You've only been DJ-ing for two years, and you're already up there! I think you're missing the big picture here, maybe? That you should actually be very proud of yourself? And that you will probably get a whole heap of cool new gigs or even residencies because of this?'

His face was trying to smile and bask in some of the glow, but his cool exterior wouldn't permit it.

'Well, actually, the promoter at The Bow asked me to play the 11 a.m. set Friday and Saturdays . . .'

'The *Bow*? Isn't that the new big fancy club?'

His smile broke out, his head dropped and he actually scuffed his toe on the floor. For all of his tough guy-ness, he was really such a little kid. He so rarely let his guard down that I almost didn't want to speak, lest it shatter the spell.

He cleared his throat. 'Yeah, well Twister, he's the one with 25Gs worth of new DJ gear, not me. So even if he *was* shit before, it'll be pretty hard to be shit with all of that stuff.'

He tipped his imaginary hat and made to leave. 'Tomorrow: I'll take the noon slot and we'll get those falafel rolls from Habibi's, yes?'

His face was so hopeful and smiling that I hated to crack it. 'I'm not in tomorrow. Sorry, DJ Supastar.' And besides, Josh's already got that slot. 'But next week, yeah?'

His face fell ever so slightly. 'Okay, cool. Next week. Sure. Laters.'

And he was gone. Runner-up again.

# ROUND 22
## Wine vs WAGs

Tix in ur letterbox, c u after game Jeanie x

A giddy little shiver went down my spine. I *loved* knowing Josh had been at my house, popping small envelopes into my letterbox while I was upstairs, faffing about unawares. It was so romantic. Or something.

Mum had called a few hours earlier, and I had gushed about how much I liked Josh, and how wonderful he was, and how he was single-handedly ruining the stereotype of footballers being boozed-up pigs, sending salacious picture-messages to a groupie or buying cocaine with one hand while the other is stroking their girlfriend's hair. I tried not to think of Patto and Scully's behaviour at the ball the other night as I assured her of this.

I was stuck on what to wear. This WAG business was proving to be on a par with advanced trigonometry. I wished I had Paola's number so I could text her and ask what she'd be wearing to the game. I'd die if she wasn't there; she was the only one I knew, besides Tess and her evil wenchmen. Surely Paola would be there – her husband was the captain guy. She'd have to go, wouldn't she?

My ticket was for the Girlfriends' Box, where only the Wives And Girlfriends and their genetically gifted progeny were allowed to sit. I'd asked Josh if I could bring Col, or maybe sit with Kerrie, but he couldn't get any tickets for the members area, so it was either The Box or Ken the Irregular Armchair in our living room at home (the game was being televised). And I could tell Josh wanted me to come. So I would. Even though the thought of being in a confined area with all of the WAGs was only slightly less frightening than narrowly avoiding death by poison dart.

I had seen the pictures of Victoria Beckham and Cheryl Cole in *their* girlfriends' box, and distinctly remembered denim hotpants, hair extensions and five-inch heels. I screwed up my face and thought back to that first game I'd been to, trying to recall what the wives and girlfriends were wearing. All I remember seeing was slim, glamorous girls wearing very tight jeans, a brand of high heel more suited to a Saturday night than a Sunday afternoon, and *hair*. Lots of hair. Hair, I could do: I owned 23 kilometres of it, and right now, it was looking very . . . big. Col called it JBF hair – that is, Just Been Fucked. For *me*, this description suggested a style that looked like I'd just awoken and struggled to locate a utensil with which to separate large knotted sections of my hair; for Col, it suggested that I looked like I had just put out my post-coital cigarette and rear-ranged the pillows. She thought it was cool. Very Olsen twins. And as I couldn't be bothered washing it, it would have to do. I would choose to think of it as 'elegantly textured'.

I put on my trusty dark blue jeans and a white top with amazing layered sleeves that risked looking a *little* bit hippie-pregnancy-having-a-fat-day, but it was new and very much in fashion and I wanted to wear it. I wore a nude push-up bra and tugged the neck-line of the top a little to at least give my upper body some hint of shape. Shoes, as always, were the most difficult part of the out-fit, especially when one knew one was going to be on exhibit as a new specimen in a very exclusive zoo. There was no question about heels; I didn't want to show up there the only one in flat shoes, for everyone to look down on – literally – and snigger at. Plus, Tess had set very high standards for the role of Josh's Girlfriend, and while I wasn't competing (pitchforks were *so* hard to come by these days),

I still wanted to show them all that I could hold my own. Even when nursing a beer in one hand and a pie in the other.

I looked at my collection of heels. They all seemed inappropriate. Boring. Girly. Dull. To be honest, I was much happier in flats, despite wanting very much to be one of those sexy heel-wearing women you see in ads for shaving gels. I went and peered into Col's much more suitable – and sizeable – collection . . . ZING! Boots! *Boots* were what you wear to the football. I zipped up her sexy little black ankle boots and checked the time. I had twenty-seven minutes to do makeup, leave the house, drive to a stadium twenty minutes away and then find this Girlfriends' Box before kickoff. I'd never be accused of intelligence in a court of law.

At 2.39, after horrific traffic, a parking spot located somewhere near Indonesia and a frantic sprint halfway around the stadium in high-heeled boots a size too big, I walked into the box slowly, quietly, with my head on a Princess Diana angle, hoping that if I couldn't really see anyone, they couldn't really see me.

The box was actually a room. I wasn't sure exactly what I was expecting, but it was something much, much smaller than the wide expanse of grey carpet before me. This was a function room, capable of housing several hundred people. And there was nowhere to hide. There were about fifteen women and 465 children in here with me, the former with wine glasses, the latter with juice bottles, and all (children aside) in some variation of boots or heels. Phew. The first person I could make out was Melinda. She was wearing a very tight long-sleeved violet top – actually, make that *dress* – over black thigh-high boots. Her hair was in a high ponytail, her fringe relaxing perfectly on her forehead. *Wow.* Because she weighed less than my handbag, an outfit that could've pushed the skankometer through the roof actually looked incredibly sexy, in a Cindy Crawford way.

Morgan couldn't be too far away. I scanned to the other side of the 'box', which was located exactly halfway down the field and featured enormous ceiling-high windows and a sheltered balcony filled with seats. I noticed that several of the girls looked very young – nineteen, twenty – and seemed quite at home in jeans and jackets, opting for warmth over fashion and competitive styling. This gave me hope.

I scanned again: no Paola. Shit. Well, maybe she was just running late. She struck me as one of those people who perpetually run late. Okay, maybe Kate would be here; she was nice enough, and at least she'd remember me. Kate . . . Kate? There was no sign of her either.

God-friggin'-dammit! I felt like it was my first day at a new school. *Again!* Every time I found myself in a WAG situation it felt equally torturous and new. I gripped tightly onto my bag and eyed the wine. Should I? After nothing but toast and two Tim Tams all day, that might not be so clever.

'Hi there, you must be new. I'm Steph.'

A pretty, green-eyed girl in her early twenties stood smiling at me. She had unnaturally blonde hair, neatly brushed into a high ponytail, and a long fringe swept expertly to one side to frame her face. Her lashes were laden with several kilos of mascara, her face bronzed and her skin peppered with heavily concealed spots and set with thick powder. Her lips, and a few millimetres of skin around them, dripped with gloss. She was wearing dark jeans, knee-high tan boots and a low, tight white top. She liked her shiny things, I noticed: there were several silver and diamond bracelets on both wrists and a small suburb of impressive rocks and stones on her freckled, tanned hands, all of which attempted to thieve the focus from the huge gold chain sparkling around her neck, which stood out on her tanned skin like scratches on a new car.

'I go out with Mitch – Mitch Barry?' Her eyebrows leaped up as if to assist me in remembering who he was. But I could offer nothing except a blank stare and a smile. I loved how she said this name as though I knew the man attached to it. Seemingly, when you dated a footballer, it was assumed you knew stuff about the team you'd found yourself part of. Like who played in it.

'He's the boofhead with the number eleven on his jersey. Who's your guy?'

'Oh, um, my guy? Um,' I cleared my throat, 'um, Josh.'

'*Oooh!* Lucky girl!' She turned and yelled out to a black-haired woman a few feet behind her. 'Lou, come here and meet Josh's new bird!'

Ten women immediately snapped their heads to where we were standing. All I needed now was a glass box and my species name on a plaque. I managed a weak smile, while trying simultaneously to sink 156 centimetres into the ground.

Lou came over straight away. She was petite, in her late twenties or early thirties. She wore a black shirt, jeans and boots. Her skin was so tanned that her many freckles were barely visible, and her chest was in danger of being mistaken for expensive leather goods of some description. Her stunning hazel-yellow eyes were emphasised with black liner, and her lips were adorned with a bright pink lipstick that was as subtle as a nun in leather chaps.

'Hi, I'm Lou, married to Nick Freer. So, *Josh*, huh? Lucky you! He's an absolute *gorge*. Nice work getting a full-back, too – they're not as bunged up as our big guys, isn't that right, Stephy?'

'Too right!'

The two women burst into laughter (they were obviously firm friends), Lou slapping me lightly on the shoulder as she enjoyed her joke.

'I mean, lucky him too, of course. Look at this hair! Geez, wish I still had some when I see hair like yours.' She ran her long red nails (acrylics, surely) through her short black crop.

'Is this your first game? No offence, but you look like you could do with a drink, love. White or red?'

Lou was already heading for the small bar, wine glass in hand.

'Oh, um, white please. Thank you.'

Shit. White wine. White wine got me rapidly, messily drunk even when I had eaten my body weight in pasta. Lou was back in a moment.

'There you go, love. That'll help. I know we must seem like a pretty mad bunch, but you'll learn to love us. Well, most of us, anyway,' and she winked.

I took a sip of my wine; like a backpacker's kombi, it was cheap, heavy and yellow. I smiled warmly. I liked Lou. I liked Steph. I could do this, I thought triumphantly; I could be A Girlfriend. The velocity at which I oscillated between wanting to stay in and run from this world was dizzying.

'Game's on!' someone yelled. Immediately, everyone started grabbing coats, bags and children, and heading outside. Really? Outside? In this weather? Sensing my puzzlement, Steph spoke up.

'Get a better view out there. You're amongst the atmosphere, you see. Bit like watching it at home on the telly, in here.' I wondered how that could be, considering we had possibly the best view of the whole field, but nodded all the same.

To my relief, Melinda was already outside with Morgan. (How had I missed *her* coming in? She wore huge diamanté-speckled Dior sunglasses – it was cloudy and drizzling – and a puffy black jacket trimmed in fur. Her long blonde hair was attempting, unsuccessfully, to sit smoothly over the jacket's huge coned hood.)

To my further relief, Steph was at the table next to the bar, piling a plate high with sausage rolls and sandwiches. 'Share plate,' she said, by way of explanation. 'Quick, out we go! Come on . . . shit, what's your name? Sorry, darl!'

'Jean.'

'Jean. Nice, hun! Okay, out we go.'

I followed the two women and Lou's flaxen-haired toddler out the balcony door and into the last row of seats, grateful I had some 'friends' to sit with. But the second Lou sat down, she bounced back to her feet, screaming, 'Are you *kidding* me, ref? That was OUT!'

Catching my surprised expression, Steph laughed. 'Lou loves her footy. I love it too now. Nothing like sitting on the edge of your seat for a good match, and giving Mitch a big kiss after a win.' She took a sip of her wine and carefully moved some fringe out of her eyes. She couldn't be older than twenty-two, I decided.

'What do you do, Jean?'

'Oh, um, I just work in a boutique in town. You?'

'Still at uni. Should be studying now, actually – got an exam on Thursday. Doing a business/law degree at UTS. Two years to go. It's a real slut of a degree, pardon the language. I'm *so* over being a broke uni student . . .'

Business law. The sound of several stereotypes smashing rang in my ears.

Lou sat down, cursing and shaking her head. She looked at me, smiled and patted my thigh. 'Don't worry, you'll be the same way in a few games' time.'

But looking at the field, and at the players running into each other at high speed, to the accompaniment of sickening thuds, I just couldn't see it.

Tess was nowhere to be seen.

It was forty-five minutes into the after-match presentation, and surely too late for her to show now, but still my eyes swept the room like I was some kind of rookie CIA agent.

'Josh, great game.'

A salt-and-pepper-haired man in his fifties had manifested between Josh and me. Josh *had* had a great game – even I could tell: two tries and a hand in two others. He was 'on fire', as Lou and Steph had said.

'Thanks, Mr Clifton. Jean, this is Henry Clifton, the chairman of the board here at the Bulls.'

I know exactly who you are, I thought, as I smiled politely and sweetly. Your sperm created Tess, and your genes and job allowed her to get her hands on Josh. Which has created much stress in my life. So thank you for that.

'Do you think we need to rest Simon?' Mr Clifton said in a serious tone to Josh.

He had elected to pretend I didn't exist. Fair enough.

'Is his shoulder causing him pain on the field? He tells us he's fine, but I think that's horseshit. And if he's not going to play to his full potential, I want him off. Tell me honestly.'

Josh's eyes were full of panic. What could he say to that, exactly? I knew Simon was a friend.

'Um, well, he . . . he hasn't said anything to us about it being sore. And I know th—'

'His form, Josh, is not up to scratch. You know it. Do you think Edward is ready to play?'

Henry Clifton was a terrifying man. Tall and handsome with olive skin, and a dashing figure in a made-to-measure grey suit, he knew exactly who he was and what he wanted, and evidently had no tolerance for people who didn't speak and deal in emotionally void CEO shorthand. I wondered if he had always been like this with Josh, or if this was a post-Tess development.

'Willie, um, he seems fit – certainly the fittest he's been since the operation. But I'm not sure Simon will . . .'

'Will what?'

'Will give up his spot so readily, is all. I'm sure if Jimmy or Bones has words with him, he'll shape up . . .'

'Ultimately, it's not his choice. But I see your point.' Mr Clifton rocked on his feet and put his hands into his pockets before taking a step back. 'Enjoy your evening.' With a glance at me, and a nod at Josh, he was gone.

Josh exhaled loudly.

'Heavy.'

'So heavy! Is he always so . . . scary?'

'Yeah, kind of. But he's been good to me. Very good. Would you like another drink?'

I sensed the conversation was over.

'Actually, I might head off.'

'Really? You don't want to stay for another drink?'

*No*, silly! I'd rather go home and twist small fiddly pieces of silver into triangles and ovals. 'I would . . . but I gotta get home and do some work.'

'So disciplined. I'm impressed. I'm glad you came, Jeanie. I hope you had fun?'

I did have fun. In fact, I'd been having a rollicking time with Steph and Lou before Josh had finally emerged from the change-rooms, smelling like leather and grass and spices and looking far more handsome than was legal in his team suit. I found it bizarre that after rolling around in the mud all afternoon the boys had to don three-piece suits. It was as though they were proving that, despite recent appearances, they were actually grown-ups with well-paid careers. I was curious as to whether their testosterone levels were as easily transformed as their uniforms. Was is possible to be play-ing an intensely violent and aggressive sport one hour, and then be suited and civil and small-talky the next?

In any case, Josh – and, in fact, all of the players – looked very good. I found myself checking out Bones and another guy whose name I didn't know; judging by the way he dumped his training bag at Melinda's feet and gave her a quick kiss before going to drink with a congregation of suits, he must have been her boyfriend, Ryan.

I had never understood the appeal of footballers. But I was beginning to see why people were so fascinated by men who, at a rudimentary level, ran into each other for a small ball. They're alpha. Physically strong. Masculine. Rugged. Successful. Fit. Good-looking (for the most part). Some were famous and, I assumed, most fared well financially. And as I had witnessed, young boys wanted to be them, women wanted to be with them, and success-ful, grown men fell over themselves to befriend them. They were stars. At least in this city.

I watched Melinda watch Ryan walk away and noticed a tinge of anger in her eyes. It was subtle, but spoke volumes. The blonde she was with didn't seem to notice, holding her wine like it was an extension of her hand, waving it and spilling it freely as she spoke loudly at Melinda, who seemed to care very little about whatever it was she was saying, preferring instead to look over her shoulder at what her boyfriend was up to. I wondered where Morgan was; like a rap star walking into a club alone, Melinda seemed a little lost without her bitches.

I was a bit miffed that Josh hadn't asked me to go out with him and all the boys afterwards. Even though I wouldn't have gone. Apparently, it wasn't really a girlfriend-friendly zone, but Steph had explained that she always went out with the guys after the game because *someone* had to keep an eye on them. When I asked what she meant, she simply rolled her eyes and said, 'You knooooow.' After a bit more probing, I discovered she meant that if the boys were allowed to roam unfettered after a game – all wired up, plied with booze and hounded by groupies – trouble was inevitable. When I asked exactly what she meant by 'trouble', she was dismissive. 'Oh, you know, playing up on their girls, fights, that kind of stuff.'

Steph fancied herself as a kind of warden. She took great pride in being the girl who would put the drunk junior in a cab after he'd vomited all over the floor, or who reminded one of the boys that grabbing that blonde girl's arse was probably not appropriate, considering he had a fiancée.

I asked if Mitch minded her playing this role. She claimed he didn't, and that he didn't have a choice, because if she had to put up with his early starts and his being away all the time – which meant they could never drink during the week or watch 9 p.m. sessions at the movies – then post-game was the only chance they had to go out like a normal couple and be young and have fun. Plus, she liked to shoo away the 'Maddies', who, she explained, were groupies only worse, because they didn't want to date a footballer, they just wanted the bragging rights that came with having slept with one. Which meant that they would offer blowjobs in toilets without so much as the bat of an eyelash. All of which I found very interesting. And utterly horrifying.

Out of the corner of my eye, I caught Melinda staring at us, her face flushed with bitterness. What was *her* problem?

'Just *one* more drink?' Josh tried again. He was exceptionally hard to knock back, with his smiling blue eyes and floppy wet hair, all smiles and expectation, but I was tired and I needed to finish off a gothic-inspired cuff that I'd stayed up making till one o'clock this morning. I was determined to have my line ready for Ingrid by the end of the week; I had to stop making excuses, both to her and to myself, and get my stuff into the shop. Twice last week I'd sold dresses that simply cried out for one of my pieces to set them off. And twice I'd had nothing to offer the customer.

I shook my head. Josh took a deep breath and smiled.

'You're a little piece of work, you know that?'

'Excuse me, but are you two sold separately?' Bones had appeared from nowhere. And was clearly pissed. He sidled up to me and linked his arm through mine. His overfamiliarity didn't seem creepy, though; he was so charismatic and funny that it just worked. I could see how he wooed girl after girl.

'So, you'll probably want to buy me a drink after that awesome try I scored, won't you, Jean?'

I giggled, grateful he was being far friendlier than at the ball.

'Boys, we going or what?' The massive human I recognised as Melinda's boyfriend came up and hooked Josh around the neck with his left arm.

'Ryan, have you met Jean? Jean, this is Ryan. He protects me from 150-kilogram Tongans who run at me at 230 kilometres an hour.'

'Hi,' I smiled sweetly.

'G'day, Jean. Nice to meet you. So boys, how we gonna get to the Windy?'

'I can drive you guys, if you like,' I said. 'I'm parked a couple of light-years away but if you don't mind the walk . . .' As soon as the words were out of my mouth I wanted to hit 'recall'. I couldn't have Josh and Bones and God knows who else in Mary! Crappy little Mary with her dingy seats and *tape* player! Oh Jesus, and the back seat was putrid, littered with clothes and beads and fishing wire and metal and, oh, this was not good.

'It's settled, she's driving us,' Bones said as though we'd all agreed on this.

'Who's driving?' Melinda suddenly appeared next to Ryan.

'Jeanie in a bottle,' Bones said.

'Well, that's silly. I should just take you, seeing as though I'm coming.'

Ryan's face changed. He and Bones exchanged a look. A look that said, 'Fuck'.

'It was just gonna be the boys tonight, babe . . .'

'Oh really? Is that why Steph and Cassie are going, then? Because they're boys?'

Like a small truck hitting a brick wall, awkwardness crashed into the conversation. I decided I needed to get out of the way.

'Um, well, guys, if you have a lift, maybe I'll get going. Have fun!'

I took a few steps backwards and put my lemonade onto a small table behind me. Josh said, 'I'll walk you to the lifts,' and steered me gently towards the door.

'What was that about?' I asked once we were out of earshot.

'Captain Killjoy. Has to do anything Ryan does. Never lets him out of her line of vision. Like a schoolteacher merged with a sniper and a private investigator.'

'How come?'

'Insecure.'

'But she's gorgeous!'

Josh pursed his lips and shook his head.

'Footballers attract some strange girls. Some, well, they're lacking in the self-esteem department, so they hook up with a footballer and then they get approval from their girlfriends and workmates. It gives them some kind of identity. But unfortunately this usually means they place *way* too much emphasis on the relationship, and get all jealous and crazy. Put simply,' he said, kissing me on the lips, 'they're nowhere near as perfect as you.'

I smiled at him – at his insight, at his kiss, at the fact I was not territorial or angry or jealous and insecure about my boyfriend, like Melinda. I wondered how she had come to be like that. I couldn't imagine ever being like that with Josh.

'You should eat more cornflakes . . . you're not quite corny enough.'

He kissed me on the lips again.

'Thanks so much for inviting me to the game. I had fun. I really like Lou and Steph. I won't be so terrified next time you throw me into the ring.'

'I'll call you when I'm done. Maybe I can swing by later?' He pressed the lift buzzer.

A late-night rendezvous? How romantic. Who was this boy? And how on earth could footballers possibly get such filthy reputations?

I couldn't wait to tell Cameron how completely wrong he was about Josh.

'That'd be nice. I'm sure I'll be up late, so just call or text or whatever. Have fun!'

He leaned in and kissed me on the lips once more, before wrapping his arms around me and squeezing me tight. He let go just as the lift doors opened.

'Bye, sexy little Jeanie in a bottle.'

Bah, I thought, smiling to myself as the lift took me downstairs. Who needed wishes when you had a boy like Josh?

# ROUND 23
## The Enchantress vs The Press

My phone buzzed. It was Col and, since Ingrid wasn't around, I answered. She didn't even say hello.

'Have you seen the papers today?'

'Why? What's in there?'

'Um, so Josh and a few other Bulls guys are on the front page walking out of, um, a gentleman's club.'

'What's that?'

'A brothel. Anyway, they got kicked out 'cos one of them – *not* Josh – took photos on his mobile of some bird giving him a blowie, and she flipped out.'

I frowned, physically and mentally. That can't be right. Why would Josh go to a brothel?

'I'm gonna go get the paper . . .'

'Yeah, go buy it and call me back.'

I grabbed a dollar from the till, slammed the shop door shut and pinned it across the road to the convenience store. Where I saw a security-footage snap of Josh, Bones and some guy I didn't know walking out of a place called the Enchantress. The headline read: 'Bulls Players Kicked Out of Brothel!'

Subtle.

I studied the image: Josh was wearing the same thing he'd been wearing when he'd kissed me goodbye at the lift. Without warning, the smallest amount of vomit rushed up into my mouth. It tried to push through to my front teeth and I tasted the coffee

I'd had only an hour ago. I pushed it back down. Naughty vomit. Inappropriate. I paid for the paper and walked back to the shop to read all the details.

The story was basically the headline repeated in forty-six different ways: three Bulls players had been 'escorted' out of the Enchantress at 4 a.m. because one of them had paid for a room and some 'service', but had been picked up by security cameras trying to film it on his mobile phone. Which was not permitted. Obviously. From the photo, the offender appeared to be Bones. He was being aggressively steered off the premises by a man who was wasting a potential life of spoils and stardom as Mr Universe; Josh and the other player were simply trailing behind, glassy eyed, chuckling, obviously unaware they had starring roles on the CCTV.

I wasn't sure how to feel. I was disappointed, definitely. But was I justified in feeling upset? I mean, I probably deserved some kind of explanation, right? *Right?*

My phone chimed loudly with a new text. It was him.

Jeanie, am sure uv seen papers, just a beat up, uv nothing 2 worry about (Bones does!), will expln asap x

Do I write back? Am I cranky, or am I cool? Cranky or cool? What is the message I am trying to send here? I studied the photo again. Do I care that he went to a brothel? Yes, I was pretty sure I did. But if he weren't famous, I wouldn't even know that he'd been. Would I care then? Maybe ignorance *was* bliss . . .

Col called.

'Did you see it?'

'I did. He just texted, saying I had nothing to worry about and that he would call me soon.'

'Are you upset?'

'Not sure . . . I mean, yeah, he was at this "club". But I can't see him being there for *that*. Bones, the guy who got kicked out, it makes sense that he would do something like that, but I just feel like I can trust Josh, you know?'

'Honey. He was at a *brothel*!'

'Yes I *know* that, but I don't think we're both such bad judges of character that we missed the whole addicted-to-prostitutes vibe.'

'Well, okay, but he *is* a footballer, and we've all heard the stories . . .'

'God, not you too. You and Cam should start a bloody picket.'

I couldn't keep the defensiveness out of my voice. Why did everyone label Josh as 'A Footballer' and assume that he behaved in the same way as other Footballers? And why was I the only one who didn't understand that this was just 'the way it was' with them? Where had I been hiding when the email came around stating that all footballers were to be treated with extreme caution as they were likely to cheat, lie, have an orgy with fifteen groupies, and sell your firstborn to the leader of a drug cartel should you blink while making them breakfast. Josh had been nothing but a sweet, lovely, funny guy . . . but maybe that was all part of it. Maybe he *was* just A Footballer. I had no idea.

'Don't get shitty; I'm just saying don't wear blinkers.'

I took a deep sigh. 'I'll be speaking to him soon and I'm sure everything will be fine.'

It was Col's turn to sigh. 'Okay. I just hate the idea of my baby sis getting hurt, is all. And, you know, I guess my reptile brain kicks in when I see this sort of circus because of what happened with Eric . . .'

'I know you mean well, Col. I'll call you as soon as I've spoken with him.'

'Okay, okay. Love you, baby Jay.'

Bored and anxious with no Ingrid to chat to and far too many dull, just-looking-thanks customers, I spent hours willing Josh to call. Finally, mid-afternoon, his name lit up my mobile. I answered immediately.

'Hello?' I answered, even though he and I both knew his name was on my screen.

'Jeanie, hi. How's your day been?' He sounded exhausted. I imagine one would be after a 4 a.m. brothel visit and what was probably several hundred litres of beer. His tone threw me off; you can't be investigative with someone when they sound half-dead. It seems somehow unfair to probe people in that state, like trying to convince a small child to amuse themselves with an Excel spreadsheet.

'Not too bad . . . Should I ask about yours?'

He took a deep breath. 'I've had better. I'm sorry to call you so late in the day, but we got flogged at training, then we had a team meeting about the "incident" and — Jeanie, look, I realise how bad the papers seemed, but it was a massive beat-up. It's character assassination.'

I was silent, unsure of the appropriate response.

'We can't do *anything* – I mean, admittedly, what Bones did was insanity and he's an idiot. But that's hardly news. Plus, he's a grown adult paying for a legal service. But, his stupidity aside, we were just having a drink at the only place still serving at that hour, and now we all look like brothel-loving deviants. Because of that tool.' He sighed. 'Jeanie, could I pick you up and we could have dinner at my place? Mum and Dad are away, so you wouldn't have to do the parents-small-talk thing.'

'Does that mean they didn't see the papers today?'

'Oh no, they saw it. Dad was on the blower at seven this morning. They're only interstate.'

'Oh. They mad?'

'They were, but they've calmed down a bit now I've told them what went on. Mum texted me saying I was a – quote – *spectacular moron*. Anyway, I want to see your pretty face, tell you the whole fetid tale, and apologise for confusing a brothel for your place last night . . .'

I giggled.

'I've got a crisis meeting with my manager now until five or so. What if I pick you up straight from work?'

I watched my plans to go for a run and cook baked salmon with Col sail past me onto the street and under the wheels of a bus. 'Sure.'

Gee, way to play hardball when he's just been snapped exiting a brothel. Hang on, no. No. That's not how I'm going to play this. I had to stand my ground. These were early days; I didn't want him to think this was acceptable and that I would be cool and calm and accommodating if something like this happened again. I called back.

'Actually, I'll drive over around seven. I'm going for a run first.'

Silence. I bit my lip, waiting to see what he'd say.

'Oh, okay.'

'I'll see you at seven.'

'Seven it is. Thanks, Jeanie.'

I had nothing to worry about. I knew it. Josh was a good guy.

But as I put my phone back in my bag, a rush of terror gripped me: had I already become caught up in the WAG world, where something that might be a deal breaker in a regular relationship – evidence of visiting a brothel, say – is passed off as normal?

I had no one to ask, and no answers. More guesswork it would be, then.

# ROUND 24
## Neutral Faces vs Red Faces

Josh had exceptionally attractive feet: smooth and hairless with perfect little pink-and-white moons gleaming on the nails. They were far too attractive for a man, and a footballer at that. I wondered if he got pedicures. Or his toes waxed, maybe? I scrunched up my nose. Was that too feminine? Would I have a problem if he did? Or would we go off and have paraffin pedicures together one day in the future? My mind was so tired that it was diverting down very strange alleys.

'Can I get you some more water? Wine? A cigar?'

'No thanks.' I smiled politely. We'd finished our takeaway Thai and both of us realised that Josh couldn't put off his explanation any longer.

I sighed loudly to express my tiredness, and looked over to see whether Josh had picked up on my non-verbal fatigue indicator. He was leaning back into the corner of his enormous charcoal sofa, but his knees, feet and hands were all pointing towards me, perched daintily at the other end. I noticed that he used each opportunity – a readjustment of his jeans; reaching for his glass of water – to move a bit closer, without being obvious. All this eager body language indicated what he had so far been too reticent to physically do: touch me. Normally, within a few minutes of being near each other his arms would be languidly splayed over my shoulders or, if we were driving, his hand would be resting on my thigh. But it was as though he felt it was inappropriate to do any of that until he'd explained himself.

'Okay, so here we go.' He took in a deep breath. I released one.

'So you saw from my texts that I was, well, a little drunk last night. It became a bit of a big night – if by big you mean *massive* – and so the Black Elephant kicked us out 'cos they close at 3 a.m. But we were all still fired up and not ready to go home. You get like that after a game, *especially* after a win: your mind just won't settle down. And I'd taken a couple of Sudafed before the game, too. But it was a Sunday night, so our options were fairly limited . . .' Josh paused, as if waiting for me to confirm that I was listening.

'Uh-huh,' I said, smiling despite not meaning to. 'Go on.'

A reshuffle, and his arm now lay along the top of the sofa, stretching out towards me. My accidental smile widened.

'So the only place open at that time is the Enchantress, and because Bones likes a bit of a rub-and-tug, we set off there. And, Jeanie, before you ask, that's not my gear at all. Not for me. Ask Bones: they call me Monty Burns 'cos I'm so anal-retentive about germs, and I reckon those girls are full of them. I don't know how the boys do it.' He made a face of disgust.

I breathed a quiet sigh of relief. I liked that explanation. And I had noticed how neat and clean he and his car and his home were.

'So that aside, the Enchantress also has a bar. A normal bar. No strippers or lap dancing or topless beer wenches – just a bar. Of course, the friendly, football-loving journalists at the papers failed to mention that. We've been there plenty of times, but no one's ever cared before. Fuckin' Bones . . .'

'Mmm,' I said, nodding. 'Well, I know where *I'll* be heading next time I'm struggling to find a cold beer at 4 a.m.'

He smiled, glowing at me from the other end of the sofa, taking my joke as a sign that he wasn't in trouble.

'And so we're there, and Camel and I are at the bar drinking, and then this huge guy storms into the room where Bones is doing his thing, and there's yelling and the girl's screaming her head off, and then Bones is being dragged out, trying to do up his jeans, and then the clown who owns the joint starts doing his nut at us, and these security guys bloody come out of nowhere, and so we freak out and head for the door, and the big bastard pushes Bones out, like in the movies, and says, you know, something hero, like, "Don't let me see your face 'round here again!" And they took his BlackBerry so he wouldn't have the film. He's quite pissed about that, actually.'

'Well, I mean, he must've known he wasn't supposed to film her . . .'

'True. But that's Bones. He's a goose. And that, Jeanie, is what happened.' He nodded, his eyes tired and slightly hung over, but honest.

'I thought it would be far more salacious, actually.'

'I know! Jesus, we've had far crazier nights. I mean, not at brothels, of course – you know what I mean. But because of Bones's bloody obsession with prozzies and porn, we've all come off looking bad.'

I smiled.

'It's such a bloody nightmare,' he continued, shaking his head. 'The club is pissed, we're being *fined* for bringing the Bulls into disrepute, and my manager is worried about my Weety Snacks sponsorship.'

'What? But that's madness! Breakfast cereals and brothels are a perfect combination!'

He grinned at me. 'You're a little monkey, you are. Come 'ere —'

He reached over and grabbed my hands, pulling me into him, my lips onto his. We kissed for a few moments, then he suddenly opened his sparkling blue eyes, centimetres from mine.

'Is there anything else I can tell you to ease your mind about my brothel-tripping adventure?'

I shook my head and moved in for another kiss. His breath was sweet, lolly-like. He kissed me deeply, gently pulling me even closer, gracefully lifting me up onto his lap, my legs falling carelessly either side of him as he leaned back against the sofa's arm. As I kissed him back, I wrapped my legs around his torso. I could feel eighty-five per cent of my arse crack poking out of my jeans. I did not readjust.

His kisses became more intense; I pushed my hips closer towards him, so that I was almost straddling him, my hands travelling up to his hair, grabbing handfuls of it as our mouths swayed from side to side. His hands began wandering up under my top and onto my skin, massaging the small of my back. Within a few moments, he had masterfully unhooked my bra and gently started to lift my thin T-shirt. There was no mistaking where this was heading.

I pulled back from his lips and looked him in the eyes, slightly out of breath, my face flushed.

'Um, should we, maybe . . . ?' I looked towards his bedroom. I wasn't about to do the deed, for the first time, on his sofa. Aside from the fact that there were enormous glass windows and 894 down-lights spotlighting us, if we kept going the way we were, there'd be an awkward moment where I would have to ask about protection and he would have to scamper off to the bedroom, leaving me on the sofa, alone and naked. I preferred to avoid this moment.

Josh looked up at me with a devilish glint in his eye, his hair tousled, his olive skin showing faint traces of rosiness. 'You're right.'

He wrapped my legs around him and, steadying himself with one arm on the back of the sofa, stood up. He grabbed my bum with both hands and kissed me on the lips as he navigated his way around the coffee table and our leftover pad thai.

'Oooh, so strong,' I purred, gazing into his eyes as he began to walk towards the bedroom – which, knowing him, would be per-fectly neat, with the bed made and not only no dirty clothes on the floor, but clean ones in neat stacks ('casual', 'training', 'going out') on the ottoman. He laid me carefully on the bed, ripped off his hoodie and reached over to click on the bedside lamp. Instantly the dark room basked in a soft, romantic glow. Gosh he was *good*.

Now in just a white T-shirt and his jeans, he delicately arranged himself back on top of me, and began kissing my smiling lips into submission, stroking my hair and neck, his fingers soft, his kisses and breath soft, but something very not-soft pressing against my thigh. Not wanting to seem too forward, I decided to let him make the first proper move – the pants-off move. It was the first time and he was doing such a splendid job so far, why take over?

His hands moved down to undo my jeans. Again, his moves were like that of a well-oiled machine. I could view this quality in one of two ways: either he'd been with lots of women, or I was simply in for a wonderful time. I decided on the latter, not dwelling on the fact that these two options were not mutually exclusive.

Within one smooth, impassioned minute, Josh had expertly removed both our jeans, and my top and bra (which, thankfully, was a sexy little yellow-and-pink one I'd bought on the weekend and was already quite fond of, as opposed to the flesh-toned 'sensible' ones I usually wore). I lifted his T-shirt, pulling it up bit by bit, neither of us wanting to break the kissing for the few seconds it would take to get it over his head. And then it was skin on skin, two underpanted little things kissing fervently, trying to do everything slowly but wanting so badly to speed up and get to the Main Event. Sensing, from the way my back was arching up into him, that he was on the right track, he slid one hand down into my knickers, feeling instantly how ready I was for him.

'Take them off,' I whispered, unable to wait any longer. He did as he was told, following his hands down with his lips, kissing my chest and stomach on the way.

'Wait!' I said suddenly, remembering my brain, which appeared to have slipped out for a touch of shopping, leaving my groin in charge. 'You've got a . . . thing, right?'

He smiled and murmured a muffled 'of course' without taking his lips from mine. Then he leaned over me to his bedside drawer and pulled out the small foil packet. I wasn't sure I liked how available it was.

In a matter of seconds it was on, and it was *on*. I melted into him, the hit of pleasure travelling through me like a rush of adrenalin. He kissed my neck, my breasts, my lips, and I kissed him back deeply, taking my legs up to wrap around his lower back, gently guiding his pace with my ankles. Everything about this act seemed uncannily familiar – his body on top of mine, and the firmness of his muscular arms, stomach, thighs – as though we'd been doing this for years. And at the same time, it was an entirely new, glorious experience.

He looked me in the eyes; I looked back through my hair, which was strewn across my face, the pillow, my chest, and had to close my eyes. It was too intense. I'd never made eye contact during sex before; I didn't know why, I just hadn't felt connected enough to any of my boyfriends to be able to do so. Yet here I was with Josh, doing it the first time. Who *was* this man?

Keen to play and enticed to try new positions, I gently pushed up on his chest and made a tiny move to roll over. Sensing my desire, he smiled and pulled himself up to allow me to shift positions. As I rolled to my right, half-foetal, preparing to get up on all fours, he followed quickly – a little *too* quickly. One second he was above me, looking down onto my back, and the next I felt his weight shift to my right and his hand slide off my damp back. Then there was the sound of skin smacking floorboards.

Peering over the edge of the bed, I saw a very naked, very at-attention, very tangled Josh trying to clamber quickly back up. I couldn't help it; I exploded into laughter, burying my face in the pillow to stop the noise from filling the room. I heard him start to laugh too; it began self-consciously, slowly, but built up quickly to a full belly laugh. He collapsed on top of me, his chest pressed onto my back, and we both guffawed hysterically, the sweat and heat of our bodies merging, the idea of continuing what we had been doing just moments earlier now absurd.

'So, do you want a boyfriend?' he asked, panting ever so slightly and struggling to catch his breath after laughing so hard. 'A really hot, super-experienced Casanova-type who's a total hero in the sack and would never fall off the bed in the middle of the first time with a girl he really liked?'

I laughed, flipping over to lie underneath him, smiling, grateful that we had been able to laugh at the situation and diffuse any potential awkwardness.

'Yes,' I said, kissing him on the lips, 'I think that I do.'

# ROUND 25
## Bare-faced vs War Paint

Making new friendships was so much harder and more awkward now than at primary school, where the same sandwich spread was enough to ensure a lifelong bond and Best Friend necklace charms. But at least I was being invited to things now, like the party tonight for Steph's boyfriend, Mitch. I figured I was able to call Steph a friend by now. We'd taken the unspoken step of ensuring we sat next to each other at games, and I was grateful; it was much easier to walk into that box knowing I had someone to look out for and talk to. I wanted her number so that I could text her before the games to see if she would be going out afterwards – so that I could plan my outfit – but I was still too shy. It was ludicrous!

Paola was my favourite WAG. I felt lucky to be her friend, as though she were some kind of celebrity and she'd chosen *me* to join her on stage for a duet. I wasn't the only one: anywhere we went people were drawn to her, like drunk moths ambling towards a shining light. She was always kind, as well as glamorous, and she radiated fun. *And* funniness – most of the time unintentionally. But unfortunately, she was about as likely to attend functions or extra-curricular activities as an orang-utan was to see a burlesque show. It wasn't, she said, that she didn't *like* wasting her weekends watching football so much as she would rather sip on pesticide than spend any more time on football than was absolutely necessary.

I stopped daydreaming and looked down at my 'workbench', which, being the only desk space in our apartment, was a mess of metals, beads, wood, semiprecious stones and Col's 'For Rent' brochures. The photo of her on the back was always worth another look: she had straight, hairspray-soaked hair, bright red lipstick, a sludge-brown jacket that even Godfrey would be able to see was unflattering, and a painted-on smile that suggested she had just spied a reflection of herself. I found it endlessly amusing.

I checked the time; where the hell was she? She'd texted to say she was staying at Holly's last night but it was now 4.30 p.m. and no sign of her. It occurred to me that she was never around any more – always with Holly, or 'out' and tetchy about the details. Thankfully, Dave was so small she usually took him with her, otherwise the poor boy would have starved by now.

I'd begun to feel like a nagging housewife, asking her to check in and tell me where she was, or when she'd be home. It was my small-town mentality: in my mind, cities were flush with sexual deviants and serial killers, and I needed to know she was okay at all times. Col, on the other hand, was used to the big city and the lack of Hollywood-style abductions; it would take a news bulletin before she worried about my whereabouts.

As I twisted a small section of silver into a curl, I wondered again whether she'd started seeing someone and was keeping it from me. I couldn't imagine why she wouldn't tell me, especially since I was so pro her finding a new guy. Suddenly I lifted my head. I was going to have a snoop around her room. Yes! That's what little sisters did; it was in our terms of employment.

I pushed open her bedroom door. Her huge Balinese-style bed and matching dresser consumed most of the space. There were clothes strewn everywhere, making me want to retreat and forget about poking around – all too hard. I sighed and walked around the bed to her bedside table. I picked up a few papers, lifted some clothes off the floor, and noticed nothing.

I was about to walk out the door when something bright green in

Col's laundry basket caught my eye. I went over and picked it out. I knew what it was and what it meant even before I'd straightened it out: it was The T-shirt. Bright green save for a white image – of a rabbit trying to mount a pony – on the front. Eric used to wear it all the time, just because Col hated it so much. The only reason I knew about it was because he'd worn it to a family barbecue back home once when he and Col had stayed for the weekend. Eric had thought that wearing his 'animal love' T-shirt in a house of animal-lovers was hilarious.

Col was seeing Eric again.

That explained so much: the secrecy, the lies, the weekend absences . . . She was seeing Eric again and was so ashamed that she was hiding it from me. And probably everyone else, too. God, Mum would lose her shit if she found out. She haaaated Eric for what he did to her First Child to (Almost) Wed. Mum had been looking forward to one of us getting married since we'd landed on the delivery table.

Shaking my head in confusion, and wondering how I was going to broach this with Col, I put the T-shirt back and walked into my room. It would have to wait for now; I had to get moving, as Josh was picking me up in a cab at 6.30 for the party and, as usual, I had no idea what I should wear. I had a feeling the girls would all be very dressed up: flippy little dresses and heels and hair and tanned legs. But then part of me wondered whether, if I were to turn up like that, they would all be in jeans. In my defence, I did spend a moment grateful that the biggest dramas in my life concerned hemlines and self-tan, as opposed to war, cancer, survival.

Like a recipe from an obscure French provincial cookbook, my preparation was an intricate process requiring many steps and combining numerous ingredients, some – such as deep-red nail polish – that I had little experience with. But, like trying to create your first chocolate soufflé for a dinner party that was already forty-five minutes behind schedule and $82 over budget, when better to try new things out?

I applied a light self-tanner, which morphed me from clean-toilet-bowl white to slightly-dirty-bathroom-sink ivory; painstakingly ghd'd my hair pin-straight; and ironed a dress from the shop, which I'd decided to wear with my new wood-coloured heels.

As I stood in front of the mirror, it suddenly dawned on me that I was dressed purely for the benefit of the male eye. It was a shocking realisation. I used to scorn girls who tailored their whole look to make perving on them as effortless and luxurious as possible – and yet, here I was doing it. My entire outfit today, from my toes to my eyeliner, had been orchestrated to appeal to the gaze of the opposite sex; in my previous life, I dressed for myself – or, more accurately, for other women.

If I was brutally honest, it wasn't just Josh that I was dressing for; some part of me wanted the other Bulls boys to approve, to mutter amongst themselves that 'Fox's girl is hot', so that Josh felt like he was with a good-enough girl, and didn't think he needed to upgrade to a model or a TV presenter or a Tess Clifton. Deep down I wanted to feel that I was attractive enough to be his girlfriend; sadly, the only way I seemed to think I could do that was to dress in a way that vociferously announced that I had breasts, legs and lots of hair – the cornerstones of every Attractive Woman.

I thought I had more self-confidence than that, but clearly I had been labouring under an illusion. In a pre-Fox era, when I was single, or with Jeremy, a Saturday-night party would've called for a shift dress or a vintage flowing number. But now? Now I felt compelled to wear something tight, something new, something that announced I was worthy of dating A Footballer.

I reasoned that maybe I had changed because whenever I was out with Josh, people scrutinised me. And I knew what they wanted to see – or thought they should see – because the WAGs generously offered that information, gratis, every time I saw them. First they noticed Josh, and then (other women especially) their eyes would slide up and down me like a stripper working the pole: slowly and with intention. Almost like they *wanted* me to see them weighing me up. Like I was *supposed* to see. It was as though they were silently saying, 'Look, if you're gonna go round calling yourself Josh Fox's girlfriend, then you're going to be constantly inspected. It's part of the job, sugar. We don't like the fact you get to be his girlfriend, and we'd like to let you know it. So deal. Life could be worse: you could be *not* Josh Fox's girlfriend.'

Despite its insignificance in the big scheme of things, this scrutiny had quite an effect on me. Bare-faced was no longer an option, heels seemed necessary even for a Sunday-afternoon movie, and when I knew the other players or girlfriends were going to be around, my appearance effort soared from mono through to stereo with 360-degree surround sound and subwoofers. It was a fine art, looking 'pretty' and 'hot' without looking like you'd put in any kind of effort. Col was equally baffled and amused by Jean 2.0. But the other girlfriends had set the standard. Actually, they were worse. Or maybe that should be better, I couldn't tell.

When we'd had to pick up the boys from the airport last Sunday at 8.30 a.m., I'd popped on some 'dress' gym pants, trainers and a little singlet. Tinted moisturiser, lip gloss and a messy ponytail and I was off in Mary, thinking of nothing more than the prospect of a full day with Josh. But the other girls – most notably Melinda and Morgan, but even Steph – were heeled, jeaned and fully made-up. Massive Chanel and Dior sunglasses, and plenty of chatting in the pick-up zone – which meant tottering from one player's BMW to another's Audi – ensured that everyone noticed their efforts. And all before 9 a.m. on the Sabbath. It was a bloody circus.

Well, I thought, as I applied the finishing touches to my eye makeup and sprayed on some fragrance: hand me a spangly lycra leotard and swing me that trapeze.

# ROUND 26
## Groupies vs Jealousy

Josh paid the driver as Bones and I got out of the cab. I was around thirteen drinks behind the boys, but I was drunk by anyone's standards. Secretly I loved that it was just the three of us and that we'd left the rest of the party back at Mitch's. It seemed that within the football circle, it was impossible to do anything or make any decision unless twelve people were involved, so Bones had made an executive decision for us to bail and find fun elsewhere.

Bones was a fascinating beast. He'd suddenly decided we were to be best friends. I wondered whether Josh had had words, or whether he'd realised that I wasn't a Tess clone and didn't need a personality lobotomy.

I wasn't completely naive: I knew that Bones wanting to leave Mitch's translated to him wanting to find a piece of arse for the night. But I went along with it anyway. Steph was obviously staying at the party she had organised, and Paola and Jimmy promised to meet us later. They were lying.

'Yeeeew! Tonight's gonna be off – the – hook!' Bones kicked a Coke can that had jovially placed itself right near his foot, and shrugged his jacket back onto his shoulders. 'Hope you brought some Canadian currency, Real Deal, 'cos you just might end up in another country tomorrow morning.'

I laughed, shaking my head. Real Deal was Bones's nickname for me, which I loved. It was affectionate and, most importantly, it implied that he thought I was a good girl. Which implied that he liked me. Which implied that he would be telling Josh I was a keeper. All the girlfriends were keen for Bones's approval. They knew he had far too much sway over the boys when it came to keeping or kicking a girl. They also knew he was the kind of guy who would whisper in your fiancé's ear to sleep with the stripper on his bucks' night.

'Have a good night, mate. Cheers.' Josh finished paying the driver and came around the back of the cab.

'Oi, Bones, what's the guy's name who runs this joint again? Greek guy. Funny bastard.'

'Debbie.'

I laughed as I reapplied my lip gloss. Josh came in and swung his hand under my ribs, pulling me in for a kiss. He was 400 per cent more affectionate when he was drunk. I revelled in it.

'You're an idiot. C'mon, what is it?'

'*Greg*. His name is Greg. Stamp it onto your forehead, Fox. Greg—or—y,' as he spelled out each letter in the air with his finger.

'Ohmygod! It's *Josh Fox*!'

'And *Luke Dunn*!'

A group of nineteen-year-old girls stopped dead ten metres in front of us, and were doing the hand-over-mouth, bent at the waist, squealing thing most girls who recognised the boys seemed to do. I took in a deep breath, hoping to inhale some open-mindedness with the night air. There were five of them, each almost a clone of the others: long, expertly backcombed straight-ish hair, skinny jeans or tiny skirts and singlets, chunky open-toe heels and as much cleavage as could possibly be created and displayed without actually showing nipple. Apparently, Janome had a 'tart' setting.

'Can I get a photo with you?' The prettiest of the group, wearing an invisible 'Ringleader' nametag, approached us, looking Bones directly in the eye and holding out her phone.

'Saddle up, baby.' Bones pulled her in close, taking her phone and holding it up to get a picture of the two of them. Despite her excitement, she was very much in control when the shutter clicked. Her entire pose was engineered to ensure that the camera captured the perfect profile: head tilted down slightly and towards Bones, no teeth showing, commanding eyes. It almost looked as though he'd asked *her* for a photo and she'd reluctantly, finally, sexily relented. She'd score top marks at the Paris Hilton School of Photo Readiness.

As she reflected on how hot she looked in playback mode, Bones was swallowed up into a pool of the second-tier girls, who had slowly moved over to him, all giggling, their phones set to camera mode, lip gloss freshly applied, hair neatly flicked and a look of unbelievable expectancy twinkling in their eyes. Each of them seemed honestly to believe there was a chance Bones would decide that she was The One to drag him from the hell of being single, famous and wealthy into the splendour of a full-blown relationship. Their optimism was blinding.

Happy with how she looked, and thrilled she had a new Facebook profile picture – one that included Bones Dunn, no less – Skanky McSkank walked over to where Josh and I were standing, with Josh firmly in her sights. Her head was angled down, her enormous brown eyes coyly positioned to appear both innocent and promisingly promiscuous, and waves of hair framed her face.

'And now one with you? You're my favourite player, you know. Daddy reckons you're so gonna be in the Australian team.'

*Daddy?* And did she just bat her eyelids? I think she just batted her eyelids! It was as though my boyfriend was the soup and she was holding a big shiny spoon.

'Uh, sure.'

She didn't do the apology look. *I got no apology look!* Usually when people annoyed Josh for a photo – especially women – they at least gave me a squinty-eyed, closed-lipped little look that said, 'Sorry, I know this must happen a lot, I promise to be quick.' But not this one. She was pretending I wasn't even visible.

Josh gently untangled his arm from mine and shot me an expression that said: *I really don't want to do this. Sorry, babe.* Hmph. At least *he* knew to give the apology look. I smiled and nodded, trying not to indicate that internally I was huffing and puffing like a certain wolf faced with a certain house made of bricks. Eight-year-olds with player cards who interrupted us while we were buying the papers on a Sunday morning, I could do. Thirty-five-year-old shop assistants who took a moment out of being mum/wife/worker to be a star-struck groupie by requesting a photo when we were midway through lunch, no problem. Boozy middle-aged men who'd always wanted to be Josh barging into our conversation with the subtlety of a jackhammer when we were having a quiet drink, I could tolerate. But the bolshy, pretty young pretty things got to me.

There was just so much . . . *intention* dripping off them. And right in front of me! At the after-match party they would elbow me to get to Josh; one even spilled her drink on my top in her haste. Steph told me about a girl who had offered Mitch a handjob while she was standing on the other side of him at a club, and that it wasn't uncommon for groupies to work in tandem, playing off against each other to win over their prey – and then rewarding the player with a threesome anyway. Sickos.

And while I did trust Josh, I was pretty sure he didn't stand in the corner with an 'I Love Jean' T-shirt when he and the boys hit the town for a post-game drink. He was only human, after all. And having these women drape themselves all over him, and purr about how great a player he was – with dreams of dollar signs and magazine spreads dancing behind their shining eyes – well, it would be hard for any person in possession of a penis to resist. I tried to push the 'bad' thoughts from my mind and reassure myself that Josh wasn't like that.

I turned my head back to see how the photo shoot was going. In his intoxicated state Josh was, I felt, far too familiar with Skanky.

His arm dangled dangerously close to her boob and her head was actually leaning on his shoulder. I suddenly felt violently territorial. Why did his job mean that I had to stand by and watch other women – younger, hotter women with roughly eighty-nine times more self-confidence – snuggle into his neck? My job held no such side effect for him.

As she posed and giggled and said 'One more' to my boyfriend, I shifted my focus onto Bones, who was now piggy-backing one of the second-tiers while another two book-ended him, for a group shot. The girls were in heaven, apparently unable to believe that they were being touched by Luke Dunn, hero of the paddock and *The Times'* 2008 Hottest Man in Football.

'Josh! Josh Fox!' A trio of filthy drunk young men walking past had spied Josh and Skanky. 'How hot's his bird?' said one, not at all discreetly, clearly impressed at her perky 'n' pert cleavage/bum combination.

Skanky smiled wickedly at the compliment and planted a slow kiss on Josh's cheek. Josh, embarrassed, made to move away. But it wasn't *true* embarrassment, nor was it any indication that what she had done was a little inappropriate when his girlfriend was standing five steps away. By all means toot your horn a little, Josh, but do you have to lean on the fucking thing?

I'd had enough. I walked into the convenience store next to Bones's fan sandwich to buy something – anything. I tried to rationalise: why was I so upset by this girl? I had never, ever been the jealous or territorial type, and I was *hating* myself for feeling this way. After all, she was just a fan; *I was his girlfriend*. She'd be gone in a minute, and he would be back with me. He wanted to be with *me*, not her. I repeated this mantra several times, until I heard Josh calling my name from the door.

I poked my head out so he could see me.

'Over here,' I said, with a large, fake smile.

He walked over. 'Watcha doing, Jeanie?'

'Just buying some . . . gum,' I said, reaching for a pack off the shelf.

He cuddled me from behind and kissed me on the cheek.

'Do I have bad breath?'

No, but the last time I saw you, you seemed to be suffering from a human-sized lesion.

'Nope, just wanted to freshen up,' I said, pulling away, walking to the counter.

'Am I in trouble?' I heard from behind. I stopped dead, composing myself quickly, actively trying to create a genuine smile. I turned to him; his face seemed reconciled, like he knew this scenario well, and was expecting a tirade of jealousy and aggression. I was a little taken aback at how quickly he had assumed I was pissed off at him. Even though I kind of was.

'What? What for? No, of course not!' I smiled harder, turned and kept on walking to the counter, praying my mood would lift and return to the high it had been on before Sergeant Skanky and her Skankettes ruined my night. I really didn't want to be That Girl, that insecure, jealous girl who made a big deal out of a random groupie and then let it cause a fight and ruin the night. It was so far removed from the person I really was. I *wasn't* a jealous person. I *wasn't* insecure. Intellectually, I knew I had nothing to worry about; but emotionally, primitively, I was struggling. Of course, the alcohol didn't help.

'Ready?' I smiled. He walked towards me, hand outstretched to take mine. I gave it to him and we walked out of the shop, and, in my mind, into a fresh start for the night. Everything would be fine from now onwards.

Or not.

Bones and the groupies were finally pulling apart, with much yelling and carrying on.

'I'm texting you right now!' said Skanky, blowing him a kiss. 'Write back, okay?' Really? Bones had given her his number?

'Already have,' said Bones, kissing his mobile.

She threw her head back and laughed, her cronies taking their cue and laughing too.

'And we'll be at Salon later. *Come*. We'll have a fun time . . .' At this point, she winked at Josh. And I threw a javelin at her skull. And she fell to the ground, blood spilling into the drain.

'Try and stop us,' said Bones, watching as the girls finally turned a corner, a mass of hair and excited laughter and newly lit cigarettes.

'Man, I would *love* to sexually disappoint her later tonight.'

That was it. I couldn't stand by and listen any more.

'You're not really gonna call her, right?'

'Why not? She's hot, right, Josh?'

I looked at Josh, waiting for his response.

'You kidding, mate? She's loose as they come.'

Good answer.

'And what, you thought I was looking for a wife?' Bones laughed. 'I'll call her around two, if nothing better's shown up.'

He came over and punched me lightly on the arm.

'What's happening Real Deal, where we off to?'

'We're going to that club, remember? To see Debbie, the Greek?'

It dawned on me that no one was going to say anything to me about the whole Skanky McSkank episode. It was just a given that that stuff would happen. I started walking. Josh's arm crept around me protectively as we made our way down a narrow alley full of people lining up for small, seedy clubs.

'Does that happen a lot, what happened with those girls just now?'

'Couple of hundred times a day,' said Bones, holding his phone out in front of him, doing the one-eyed Cyclops text because he was so drunk.

'They're pretty, um — I mean, kissing you like that and stuff . . .'

'You got a kiss? You bastard!' Bones punched Josh in the back from behind.

Josh laughed and said, over his shoulder, 'Settle down, idiot. It was nothing.' But he said it in that way women say, 'Oh, this old thing?' when someone comments on their brand-new $800 dress.

'You've already got Jean, you don't need her too,' Bones said.

'She's all yours, Bones,' Josh responded, laughing.

'And if Josh wasn't here, baby, you would be, too.' Bones winked at me in an over-the-top manner and made a slimy face.

Suddenly we stopped out the front of a derelict-looking building. A queue snaked back from the doorway in the other direction as far as I could see.

'This is it. Wonder where Greg i—'

'Boyzzz!' A voice belonging to a man with terrifying eyebrows and wet-looking slicked-back hair boomed from the doorway. 'I thought you'd forgot where we were! We never see you any more!'

Greg weaved through bouncers and list bitches and door candy to where we stood, unclipping the rope for us as he did so.

'Greggy!' Bones vigorously shook his hand. 'You lost weight, mate? Been pumping iron? You're looking good. You wanna play for us next weekend?'

Greg liked that. He smiled and said modestly, 'I've been training a little. Won't ever be as buffed as you, though, will I, Bonesy?'

'Few will, Greg, few will,' Bones said, kissing each of his biceps in turn.

'How you been, Greg?' Josh shook his hand. 'I want you to meet my girlfriend, Jean.'

'G'day love, nice to meet you. Right, come through, you three. Take a balcony booth and order up – drinks are on Big G tonight.'

# ROUND 27
## The Rich vs The Hung-over

'Forgot to tell you, pumpkin head, we've got lunch today.'

I opened one eye, slowly, carefully, in case it caused me to explode. To label what I was feeling a hangover seemed somehow insufficient. My mouth tasted like wet socks, my brain featured a thumping bass line, and my stomach felt like it was on a dinghy in the high seas, slipping and sliding over waves of pain and nausea. I didn't have enough body to support all this hangover.

'What?'

We were in Josh's bed; I was facing the door, and he was behind me, spooning.

'I said' – he kissed my neck softly – 'we have a lunch on today.'

I opened my other eye, mistakenly believing that seeing clearly would help me understand the concept I had been presented with.

'Who . . . who with?'

'Mark Scott.'

'Mark who?'

He ran his fingers slowly up and down my thigh, clearly thinking about something other than the question.

'Mark *who*?'

He laughed. 'Mark Scott. He's a car dealer. Owns every second car dealership in this city. He's the one who upgraded me from a BMX to a BMW. Nice guy, worth gigabucks, but very normal and very generous. I think lunch is on his boat.'

I was blinking furiously, wondering how we were in this situation:

we were to have lunch with a car dealer on a Sunday, on a *boat*, when we'd been out till 3.30 a.m., and it had never crossed Josh's mind to tell me until now, at 10.49 a.m.

I sat up to lean on one elbow, gasping for breath like a geriatric faced with a long flight of stairs. 'I don— How come on a Sunday? Why didn't you mention it? What am I supposed to wear? Who's going to be there? Do we need to dress up? Oh God, I can't do this, not today . . .'

In my vulnerable, dusty state, each of my insecurities came tumbling out of my mouth, holding up signs saying, 'Oh, *hai*! We'd just like to announce that Jean is not perfect. In fact, she is just a scared little girl from the sticks who has been spending all of her salary on clothes and blow-dries in order to accommodate a lifestyle and mindset that does not come naturally to her!'

Josh tugged on my shoulder so that I half-rolled over to meet his gaze. Like waking up – or moving from this bed, ever – and showing him my grotty face was something I was remotely interested in. I resisted.

'Dooooon't, I've gotta clean myself up.'

I made a move to get out of bed and make the nudie dash to the bathroom, but his grip tightened and he forcefully, but playfully, rolled me right over. He was smiling, still looking perfect. Eyes clear, non-puffy. Not a hair out of place. It was hard to like him when he showed me up so badly. I furiously wiped under my eyes, trying to remove the remnants of a several-layered smoky eye and three kinds of liner.

'Still look good to me, baby. Little bit Twitchy the Tramp, but I quite like that. I do like to stop by the occasional brothel, after all.'

I laughed, shaking my head.

'Mark will love you, even if you wear Dad's beekeeper's outfit. It will just be a nice day out on the water. Easy. Wear whatever you like – just not those high heels.' He pointed to the offending pair splayed messily on his floor. 'You know, because I was going to ask if I could borrow them.'

I wasn't really listening; I had my own dialogue screaming through my head.

'It's not even that, I . . . I just feel so sick, and now we've gotta go on this boat and talk to people and —'

'It's just his family, I think. And girlfriend.'

'I've gotta get home, get dressed . . .'

Again, I made a move to get up, but was pulled back by a clearly toey Josh, who was now kissing my neck and moving down towards my chest.

'Relaaaax. I'll drive you in a little while.'


'So you're from the Gold Coast, huh, Jean? Got a few dealerships up there. They love their luxury cars, don't they?'

I laughed. 'If it's not canary yellow, it doesn't count.'

'Or mid-life-crisis red, of course.'

'Of course.'

Mark Scott was a small man, probably in his late fifties, with grey hair and some kind of allergy that made his skin look red and angry and like it was flaking off. It was very disconcerting. I didn't know where to look.

His girlfriend, Chelsea, was Nordic blonde, pale-skinned, busty, doe-eyed and roughly the age of a foetus. Each time I tried to make conversation with her, she blocked me unintentionally – 'Do you come out on the boat a lot?' 'Yup!' – and seemed far more interested in looking after Mark's children (from his previous marriage), who, in fairness, were much closer to her in age.

The three boys had been given a day with Dad, in order – I was guessing – to let their mum enjoy some uninterrupted rocking back and forth, and time to put away several bottles of Scotch. Despite there being *two* nannies *and* Chelsea to look after them, the boys still managed to cause complete chaos across the three levels of Mark's floating mansion. All their screaming was pushing my throbbing headache up towards the 'implode' rating, and their 'fun' game of stealing things out of my handbag was making me reconsider ever using my fallopian tubes. There was a special place in hell reserved for these children.

To compound my state, the wait staff constantly tried to get me to drink some alcohol.

'It's Vintage Krug,' they said, holding champagne up near my nose as I stood chatting to Mark.

'It's the *perfect* accompaniment to the lamb,' they warned, pouring me a glass of shiraz without asking if I wanted it.

'It's just fucking *rude* not to drink all of this expensive wine,' they said, silently, as they filled my water glass again.

'We should get you two to the beach house,' Mark said over a three-course banquet that, after no breakfast – and, in fact, just in general – was mind-blowing.

'They could stay in the shack,' offered Chelsea, feeding oysters to a dark-eyed four-year-old for whom they should have been marinated in Ritalin. I wondered whether she was trying to play mother to the boys, or just to be their 'pal'. They didn't seem to be buying either option.

'The shack?' Josh said, bemused.

Mark smiled. 'It's as much of a shack as this cruiser is a tinny.'

'We just had it all fitted out. It's beautiful,' Chelsea said, mopping up the little angel's deliberately tipped-over juice. *We?* Yes, I'm sure you put in a cool hundred thousand to see the new Italian kitchen installed.

'We'd love to. That's very kind of you both, thank you.' Josh was looking at me with excited eyes.

'Keys are yours whenever you two kids want a break. Just call

Danielle, she'll sort it out,' Mark said, gnawing his meat off the bone, the juice dribbling down his chin. I had to look away; my stomach was in a dark enough place already.

I couldn't help wondering whether Josh and I would be thrown the keys to the shack if he weren't a star footballer. If we'd be on this boat. If we would've been picked up in a shiny black Merc with a driver called Kingsley who opened the door for us to get in and out. Somehow I didn't think so.

I found it odd that rich, successful businessmen like Mark wanted to befriend Josh, to invite him to their houses and take him out for dinner. It was as if, despite everything they had achieved in their lives, deep down they just wanted to be sporting heroes; and, since they'd missed out, they wanted at least to enjoy the company of a hero, and to savour a voyeuristic insight into a life they wish they'd had.

What they didn't realise was that Josh wanted to be in *their* position. He'd told me that with his ten-year career-expiry date, the potential for injuries and the general uncertainty about Life After Football, the business side of things was a lot more reliable in terms of setting yourself up.

All of this just made me feel even worse for not spending more time on my jewellery. Here I was surrounded by people who had played for their country, or created whole empires selling lurid sports cars, and I was working in a clothes shop.

The problem was *time*. With Josh, I had no spare time. If it wasn't the game, it was dinner the night before the game, or the team barbecue the day after. If it wasn't a football thing, it was lunch on a rich guy's boat. I was staying at Josh's place more and more, and my life was revolving around his (inflexible) schedule. I was changing shifts and appointments so that we could be free at the same time. We were either Football Widows or Football Slaves, us girls. I vowed I would no longer mock women who gave up their careers to follow their men around the world for their sports. It would be near impossible to continue your relationship if you didn't.

I thought about the other girls. Steph was a part-time uni student. Lou was a full-time mum. Melinda and Morgan had their spray-tan business a couple of days a week. And Paola did the occasional modelling job. None of them were full-time career women, I realised. I sighed, sipping my coffee, bored with listening to Mark and Josh talk about shares, and desperately craving my bed and several hours of shhhhh. My mind drifted . . .

Maybe I should just enjoy the ride while I could; soak it up, and start off my jewellery business later. After all, it wasn't like it would be making me millions. Even though I loved it and would like to make a career of it, it was basically a glorified hobby. Putting it off a bit longer wouldn't hurt.

# ROUND 28
## Disclosure vs Hush-hush

Col put her hand on her hip and looked at me with that bored, pained expression she reserved for those times when I really annoyed her.

'I told you, shithead, I'm not seeing anyone. Why do you even have this idea in your head?'

'Um, maybe because you're *never* home any more?'

'And you *are*?'

'It's different. I have a boyfriend: Josh, remember him? I'm not hiding anything.'

'So what if I stay over at my friends' places? What's the big fricken' deal?'

'I don't know . . . I just don't believe you.'

'Whatever, Jean.'

'Oh yeah? Well, maybe Holly came into the shop yesterday and we had a good little chat.'

Kapow. I'd shot the first bullet. No turning back now.

Colette bristled and folded her arms, taking her weight off the kitchen bench.

'So?'

'She said that she's only seen you twice in the last couple of months. And yet, you claim to be staying at her place every weekend.'

'No I don't.'

'Uh, yeah, you do.'

'What is this, the Spanish fuckin' Inquisition? Who *cares*?'

'Jesus, Col. Calm down. I'm just curious, because if you've got a new boyfriend, well, I guess I'm wondering why you're not telling me about him —'

'But that's just it! I *don't* have a new boyfriend!'

'No.' I took a huge breath, terrified of what might happen next. 'Maybe it's an old one that you're revisiting instead . . .'

I held my breath, waiting for her to scream and throw the blender blade at my head. Nothing. Just her pupils moving wildly from one side of my face to the other in what appeared to be the initial stages of spontaneous combustion.

'Col, I saw Eric's T-shirt in your bedroom the other day. The one with the pony and the rabbit? The one he used to always wear?'

She looked at the floor, taking in a few deep breaths.

'Col?'

'*What?*' she exploded suddenly.

'Are you okay?'

She picked up her keys and put her handbag over her shoulder. 'I'm going.'

'But I was gonna give you a lift —'

'I'll get a cab.'

A furiously slammed door and she was gone.

I had my answer, but now wished I hadn't bothered asking the question. I stood there in the kitchen, rooted to the spot, feeling like pond scum.

Why did I execute it like that? If she *was* seeing Eric again, of course it would be hard for her to tell me. I mean, we'd spent months verbally slaying him, writing him off, wishing him bad luck, broken limbs, credit-card fraud and a stolen car. I'd promised that if I ever saw him again, I would spit in his face. Twice.

I didn't get it. She was so gutted and hurt by what he did to her that I couldn't imagine why she would go back there. What could he have possibly done to win her back, aside from commandeering a time-travel machine and undoing his infidelity? I really, really didn't get it. Cheating, in my eyes, was unforgivable.

At work, Ingrid was trawling through her own relationship woes. From what I could ascertain from a phone call she had with him, Justin was unnecessarily delaying his divorce, and she was a little bit upset about this, if by 'little' you mean 'enormously'. As she huffed and puffed and yelled at me, I tried to remember that she wasn't so much yelling at me as ranting and raving about Justin in code. It was obvious how much he frustrated her, and yet she stayed with him.

It baffled me that a successful, strong, sexy woman like Ingrid could allow herself to get into a romantic situation where she was settling not only for second-best, but a pretty shitty second-best at that. Justin was constantly cancelling on her at the last minute, or throwing her plans into chaos by inviting her away for the night with sixteen seconds notice, or just being generally the kind of rich, slick Playboy who makes me sick – and the kind that so many women fall for. Josh was smooth, but he was also genuine. I wouldn't have been attracted to him if he were all flash and dash, which was, apparently, precisely what Ingrid found so appealing in Justin. *Even though she could provide that flash for herself.* Perhaps she was just victim of a self-imposed pattern: her last boyfriend had also been a successful businessman – maybe that was her 'type' and it was all she knew, and all she wanted. And then, of course, there were those screaming ovaries . . .

Considering Ingrid and Col's relationships, I felt very lucky to have a boyfriend like Josh. Sure, there was the Tess stuff, and, well, the groupie stuff plagued me, if I was honest, but for the most part it was just easy and fun. He looked after me, made sure I was safe and happy, and even made up silly songs about my hair, or my eyes, or my 'moontan'. Whenever he called, I skipped a few breaths, whenever I knew I was going to see him at night, I looked forward to it all day. I even had him to thank for the fact that I finally had some friends down here. Paola was coming in to have lunch with me today; she needed a new dress, so she was going, she said, to 'hit two stones' and catch up with me as well.

'You know about her, right?' Paola looked at me over her sushi roll.

'Um, no?'

The conversation had drifted to the other girlfriends, as it usually did after a mutual bitch about the boys' crazy schedules, and how they went out too much, and how the club was retarded making them get up early for a recovery training session the morning after the game, when they should be allowed to sleep in, and then have a lazy weekend breakfast with their wives/girlfriends/kids. The WAGs deeply resented the post-game recovery session.

To the WAGs, the club represented The Enemy. I had only been around for three months, but I felt the fury. The club whored the boys out – especially Jimmy, Bones and Josh – to all kinds of events during their few precious moments off. They only gave them their weekly training schedule each Monday, so it was impossible to plan anything week to week because we never knew their availability until a few days before. Lou was having incredible difficulty planning her wedding because Nick was playing well and would probably get selected for the Australian team, meaning she would have to put off the wedding from October until January.

But right now, Paola wanted to talk about Melinda.

'She's been with half the team.'

My eyes, which I thought were already doing a pretty good job of being open, managed to find an extra fifty per cent.

'What do you mean "been with"?'

'Fucking them! What you think I mean?'

'Noooo. Really? But doesn't . . . I mean, wouldn't Ryan be a bit funny about being with a girl —'

'Half his team has fucked? You think so but he dossen care.'

I wanted to ask *who* she'd been with, but I was terrified Josh's name would come up. Sensing my curiosity, Paola slapped me gently on the wrist.

'Don't choo worry, Jeanie, your man never did. He's a good boy. I mean, he's had some fun, but you got nothing to worry 'bout.'

I smiled with relief. Hang on . . . what does 'had some fun' mean?

'But an even *better* rumours – and this one is crazy – is that Cassie's baby's daddy isn't Camel.'

Cassie was one of the girls who hung out with Melinda and Morgan, and as a result of this was perennially tanned. For these girls, tanning was less a skin colour than a way of life. Cassie was intensely blonde and attractive, but had a harsh face; it was as though, having granted her such a tremendous body, the Genetics Allocation Society had decided to give her a beak-like nose, and to place her eyes slightly too close together, just to even things out – to give other women a fighting chance.

Camel was one of the most aggressive players at the club, and if you didn't know this, his face – all beat up and scarred and bent out of shape – kindly offered this information free of charge. Cassie had been a finalist on *Big Brother*, which is how she'd met Camel – he was at the show's finale party and had commented on her spread in *FHM* magazine, in which, clad in a see-through white and gold bikini, she'd professed to championing the Bulls.

'Noooooooo! Get *out*! Who is it, then?'

'Like I say, it's just a rumours. But Jimmy, he knows I got a mouth, so he doesn't usually tell me things that isn't true. He told me not to tell anyone, of course. But he shoulda known better.'

She grinned and took a big sip of her miso as a full stop. I waited for the name of Cassie's controversial sperm-donation bank.

Paola looked me dead in the eyes. 'You can't say *anything*. Not to nobody. Okay?'

'Of course.'

'Ryan.'

'*Ryan?* Melinda's Ryan?'

'Mm-hmm. '*Paaaaarently* they had this big affairs, but she was with Camel the whole time, and he was with Melinda, and then when she was pregnant, she jus' played along and said it was Camel's.'

'*Nooo!*'

'He looks like Ryan. Same eyes, same nose . . . She gonna get found out, choo know. Camel's a dumbass, but he ain't *that* stoopid.'

'Does Ryan know?'

'Yup.'

'Melinda?'

'Jesus, girl! You crazy? What choo think?'

'So people really do that stuff? I thought that kind of scandal was reserved for TV shows about footballers, not Real Life.'

'Of course it happens! These people get some money and some fames and they think they're invisible!'

'Invincible.'

'They get cocky, Jeanie. Life is easy when you're a big star with time and cash, so they play with fire. They have to *make* excitement 'cos their life is too easy. Anyways, if Camel ever finds out, he'll kill Ryan. So don't say nothin', okay? News travels like the storm here, Jeanie.'

'Like lightning?'

'Why you gotta be like that? You know what I mean!'

I laughed. But inside I was trying to comprehend this world I'd found myself in. Where would Josh look for excitement if life with me became too boring?

# ROUND 29
## Secrets vs Solidarity

'Bloody Paola. She holds on to secrets with grease-covered hands.'

Josh had known about the Cassie/Camel scandal but hadn't told me. He found it highly amusing that Paola had spilled the beans, but failed to grasp my hysteria at the wickedness of the situation.

'But what about Camel? Does he know? Surely he must, if we all do.'

'Not necessarily. The club has this kind of . . . inbuilt protection mechanism. Scandals like this are usually kept private. You know, brothers protecting brothers.'

I imagined some kind of secret cult where the members all wore cloaks and masks and chanted, and nude women or fluffy lambs were brought in for sacrifice. I didn't like it.

'But, like, as a friend, don't you think you should tell him? Wouldn't you want to know if I was sexing your team-mate?'

'I'd hope you'd at least aim for my boss.'

'Okay then, your boss?'

Sweeping me up for a hug and a smothering kiss, he said, 'Honey, don't be silly. I would've been the one who set it up, for a pay rise.'

'But *wouldn't* you?' I wiggled free, not in the mood for hugs or jokes or topic avoidance.

'Jean, some things are better left unsaid. Jimmy's an idiot for telling Paola. I mean, imagine how bad this looks for the club. Last time something like this happened, it was the coach, and he ran off with one of the cheergirls. He's still with her – left his wife and kids for her. The media went ballistic, as you can imagine. The public thrive on scandal. Which is why that shot of us at the Enchantress made the front page. People love to tear us down once they've built us up.'

I shook my head, angry and disappointed at these stories. What was *wrong* with these men? Ruining their careers and families for some young thing with perky tits? Ryan had slept with his friend's girlfriend and got her knocked up, and had not even been man enough to remove himself from the microcosm. And he must go through each day with the evidence of his actions right before his eyes. How can he do it?

'Jean, baby, relax. Men will always be men. They'll always do stupid things and they'll always be found out. Don't get down about it.'

I looked into his eyes and sighed. Maybe I was taking it all too personally. Maybe I was angry about Col taking back her cheating ex. Maybe I was just scared that Josh was too good-looking and too famous not to be tempted by the same kind of opportunity that caused someone to leave his wife and kids for a cheergirl. And maybe I was angry that I wasn't nearly exciting or attractive enough to prevent him from giving in to such temptation.

'Ooh, someone's got a fat fly in their soup.'

Cameron walked beside me on the busy footpath of Lloyd Street, head tipped back, trying to get the last of his milkshake. A simple white T-shirt, a V-neck striped vest and dark jeans: he looked cool and preppy and, to my surprise, kind of handsome. Had his hair grown a little since I'd seen him last? Did he have some colour? I couldn't put my finger on it.

'Celebrity Footballer boyfriend causing you grief? Told you he would. You didn't listen.'

All thoughts of Cam being attractive – gone.

'If you're gonna pick up that bone and drag it along with you, you can piss off.'

I walked into the bank, allowing the door to close behind me. I took a number and sat on the communal lounge the bank had installed to make waiting for a teller feel less like teeth-pulling. Through the window, I watched as Cam threw his milkshake carton in the bin. Then he followed me into the bank, his head cocked to the side, eyes squinted, one finger pointed towards me.

'What have you done to your hair?'

My hand flew to my hair. I'd had $200 worth of caramel highlights put though, and was now sporting the kind of sun-kissed shade J. Lo herself would approve of.

'Got some highlights.'

I'd decided my brown hair was dull, common. I'd needed something more glamorous; all the girls had colour in their hair. Most were blonde, and it always seemed to look more exciting than plain old brunette.

He frowned, shaking his head, taking a seat next to me.

'You're turning into one of *them*.'

'And what's that supposed to mean?' My eyes were flashing, daring him to say what I already knew was coming, because maybe, on some level, I was terrified it was true.

'A WAG, of course. Look at you. All tanned and bloody blonde.'

'It's just a few highlights, Jesus —'

'And you've lost weight, you know. You look like a bloody stick with hair. Don't know why you think that's sexy. Look like a bloody broom.'

'Fuck off, Cam.'

I had lost a little weight, actually. I'd become more conscious of what I ate, and had been taking Dave for runs, as opposed to half-arsed walks. If I was honest, I felt I needed to look good to make Josh look good. The expectation was always there, lingering in the back of my mind, warning me that People were watching, weighing me up, making sure I was good enough for him. I knew the non-verbal transaction by heart now: people see Josh, their eyes flash with recognition and then fly over to me. Up. Down. Up. Back to Josh. Flicker between the two of us. Then back to me. Make internal summation that Josh could do better – should have an actress or a model on his arm, not this pale-faced little imp. Continue on way.

My morphing into a textbook WAG hadn't blown into a fully fledged issue yet, but I was aware that it might at any second. The day I wore heels and full makeup to the airport at 7.30 a.m. would be the day I had gone too far. That, or the day I succumbed to acrylic nails.

'Touchy, aren't we? Must be all that starving yourself. Makes people terribly cranky, you know, starvation. Just ask an Ethiopian.'

'Actually, I could quite go a chicken wrap. Why don't you go buy me one, if you're so worried I'm fading away?'

'Get it yourself.'

'Pleeeeease? Please Cam? It's three shops down, and I'll be stuck in this queue for ages. I'll give you the money.'

I saw his eyes soften. He sighed, and his head dropped to one side. He was adorable when he lost the tough-guy, teasing-brother shit. I grinned, took a tenner from my wallet, and held it out to him.

'Thanks, Cam. Feel free to pick yourself up something pretty with the change, won't you?'

'When are you going to repay me for all of the kindness I have bestowed upon you? You realise you owe me, don't you?'

I scribbled 'I Owe You. Signed, Jean Bennett' on the back of my ticket and held it out with the money.

'There: documentation. Happy?'

'Very,' he said, taking the note and money from my hand as I beamed triumphantly.

'I'll make you pay one day, you wait.' He looked me in the eyes, nodding, smiling mischievously.

'Whatevs. Chop chop with that chicken wrap already.'

With his back to me as he walked towards the door, Cam let his jeans slide so that all of his boxers and half of his thighs showed. I laughed hysterically as the bored, distracted bankers frowned disapprovingly. As much of a pain in the arse as he was, Cam did make me laugh.

# ROUND 30
## Rage vs Reprieve

Laughing at his impersonation of Dave trying to get a back scratch, I pushed Josh off me and stood up to make us some tea. He was staying over – a rarity – so I was trying to make him feel accommodated and looked after, in the hope of tricking him into doing it more often. I was sick of staying at his house because it usually meant him dropping me home – still half-asleep and in a bra-less T-shirt, tracksuit bottoms and barefoot combo – at 6.30 a.m. on his way to training. Aside from the uncomfortableness of it all, I always seemed to run into gung-ho joggers on the pavement outside my place; they'd look at me unpleasantly, all iPodded and judgemental.

As I turned the kettle on, I heard Col's key in the door. I inhaled sharply: I hadn't seen her since we'd had the fight about Eric the other morning and I knew she was pissed at me, because she hadn't called or texted once. Our only communication had been two rudimentary notes about Dave being fed.

Walking into the living area, she spotted Josh first.

'Oh, hey, footyhead. How are you?'

I could hear Josh getting up to greet her with a kiss. Such good manners, I thought, simultaneously pleased with my perfect boyfriend and excellent Suzy Homemaker tea-presentation skills. As they made small talk, I waited to see whether Col would come into the kitchen on the way to her room, or walk straight past.

'Hey, Jay.'

I turned to see her standing at the kitchen entrance. She looked tired and a little washed out.

'Oh, hey, Col. Want some tea?'

My voice was high, nervous; a failed attempt at playing it cool and normal.

'Nah, I'm good thanks. I'm beat – going to bed.'

And she was gone.

I turned back to the kettle, fuming. What the fuck was she on about? How long did she want to carry on like this? When were we going to have a grown-up conversation? I stood there, huffing and puffing and thinking about how uncool it was of her to keep on acting as if nothing had happened – or, rather, as if something had, but she was too busy to talk about it with her sister, her own sister who had come down to live with her after Eric ripped her heart out.

That was it. I slammed down the teaspoon I'd been gripping with white knuckles and walked to her bedroom door. I was just about to knock when I heard her on the phone, crying.

'I jus— I can't do this,' she was saying, through tears. 'It's too hard, and it's not worth it to try again . . . Oh, sure, yeah, well that's because you were the one who fucked everything up, not the one who had to sit by and have it happen to them —'

Must be Eric. Had to be Eric.

'*HOW* CAN I BE FUCKING SURE? TELL ME *HOW!*'

Whoa.

She was sniffing, sobbing. I so wanted to bust in and give her a big hug and tell her everything was going to be okay, but first she needed to hang up that phone and *get the fuck away from Eric*. For good.

'Oh, it's all so easy for you to say, isn't it? Just rolls off the tongue, like all the other lies.' Her tone was dripping with anger, spite, hurt, betrayal. Poor Col. She was clearly tormented at the idea of being back with Eric, but at the same time she really wanted it. My anger began to dissipate and I just felt incredibly sad for her. How dare he, I thought. How dare he break her heart, ruin her plans for the wedding and the rest of her life, and then, just months later, try to come snivelling back? Without so much as a bunch of flowers or a poem? He had more hide than an Easter egg.

'Jeanie? You okay?'

Shit, Josh. I tiptoed back out to the living room and smiled at him lying on the sofa, watching a re-run of *Girls of the Playboy Mansion*.

I shook my head. 'Honestly . . .'

'What? I watch it for the classy fashion!'

I went back into the kitchen and made two teas. I considered making one for Col and leaving it at her door, but had a feeling she might be on that phone call for a while yet. Like, maybe a month or two. I *had* to speak to her about all of this. I was pretty sure I wasn't the only one she'd been hiding her romantic re-run from, and she clearly needed some support. I felt like a right bitch for the way, the other morning, I'd announced that I knew she was back with Eric. *Bad* sister.

As I set the teas down on the coffee table, my face must have shown my torment.

'You okay, baby?'

Josh sat up and kissed me on the cheek.

'Yep, fine. Just tired.'

I offered a weak smile. I really wanted to explain the whole situation to him, but it would have been a selfish act for me to reveal all of my sister's problems to my boyfriend just because I was bursting with the need to speak to someone about it.

'You sure?'

I looked at him sitting there: legs apart, hair everywhere, steaming hot tea just centimetres from his face, his eyes directed at me but his whole concentration taken up with gauging how likely he was to burn his tongue if he took a sip. Suddenly, more than ever, I wanted to tell him I loved him.

It had been on the tip of my tongue for two months, but I wasn't sure whether it was premature. And besides, the guy was meant to say it first. Preferably with skywriting. It was killing me, though. I *did* love him. I did. And I wanted to be able to say it.

I kept half-saying it, starting off recklessly then reshaping my sentence urgently before it finished: 'I love . . . the way you cuddle me all night,' I would say. 'I love . . . it when you do that little crinkly dimple thing with your eyes,' I'd say, feeling deflated, like I'd been given the most glorious mansion in the world but no keys to get inside. It wouldn't be long now, I thought. He loved me. He just had to find the right way to say it.

'I'm sure.'

# ROUND 31
## Resurfacing Exes vs Reassurances

Mike Scott had given us the keys for his beach house for the night, and every single one of my cells was vibrating with excitement.

The boys had played last night – a win, but Captain Jimmy had suffered a broken ankle, which had dramatically mattified the victory's shine. I'd never seen anyone respond as fast as Paola had. One second we were refilling our wine glasses for the third time, and laughing about Paola's sheer, nipple-revealing top; the next, Lou was yelling: 'Paola, quick! Jimmy's done himself an injury!'

Paola, instantly sober, had dumped her glass and bolted outside. Her eyes were wide open, trying to make sense of the situation down on the field. Two trainers were crouched beside Jimmy, who was writhing around in pain, clutching his ankle. There was dead silence in the box as everyone paid their respects to Paola's fallen hero.

'Come on, Jimmy, get up, *get up!*' Paola was wringing her hands, bouncing up and down on her heels.

'They should have a phone number, you know – a number of someone we can call when this shit happens. This is a joke!' Steph said angrily.

'Darl, I've got Doc's number from when Camel did his shoulder – here, dial this,' said Cassie, all trench coat and hair, nursing Ryan's progeny on her lap while scrolling through the contacts on her pink-skinned iPhone. Paola was right: little Flynn did look like a miniature Ryan. All those hits must have affected Camel's vision.

'He looks like he's in real pain there. Sorry, hun, but I reckon it's a break,' offered Lou, perhaps unhelpfully.

'How can I know if he's okay? *Fuck!* Where do I going?' Paola asked with urgency and irritation, before reverting to her native tongue and rambling through what I'm guessing was a long string of swear words.

From inside the box, and without the commentators to guide us, it was hard to tell what was going on. But when Jimmy failed to get up after two minutes and the little stretcher cart raced onto the field, Paola couldn't wait any longer.

'I going down.' She grabbed her coat and bag, and tore off before I could ask if she wanted me to come.

She'd called me later to say that initially they hadn't allowed her into the dressing sheds. However, once she started screaming – in a mix of Colombian and English – that she was as good as Jimmy's wife and for them to let her the fuck in right now, they'd been frightened enough to open the sacred Players' Entrance door for her. None of the girls had ever been into the sheds before. She was an intrepid trailblazer, a fearless South American pioneer who wouldn't take no for an answer.

What she'd found was a delirious, distressed Jimmy, and a calm, slow-speaking doctor who had assessed that his ankle was broken in two places, and was sending him to hospital immediately.

'How long will I be out?' Jimmy had slurred.

'I can't say for sure, but maybe three, four months,' the doctor had said.

'*Fuuuuuuuuuck!*' Jimmy had said.

Despite their leader being in the emergency ward, the rest of the boys had gone out to celebrate a massive win over their arch-enemies. Jimmy would've wanted it that way, Ryan had said solemnly. (You fathered Camel's child, I thought.) The coach had told them explicitly not to go out because it was a short week and they played again in five days. But they'd gone anyway.

I'd gone home after one drink in the members lounge, to pack for our night away. I'd taken a cab to the game, because Josh had told me to drive his car home and then pick him up in it in the morning on the way to the beach. I was very nervous about driving his big fancy BMW, but didn't let on.

The thrill of walking to Josh's big, sleek car in the car park, getting into the driver's seat, not being able to figure out where the lights were, and turning on the windscreen wipers instead of the indicator, had been immense. Driving my boyfriend's expensive car – even if it wasn't yet from one beauty appointment to the next, sashaying around in stilettos, or dripping with rocks and lip gloss – I finally felt like a proper WAG. With a strange kind of detachment, I wondered if I would ever really become one of those girls.

I flicked my hair at the lights. I checked myself out in the mirrors. Guys in the car next to me checked me out. It felt goooooood. I could get used to this, I thought.

It struck me why women who went out with high-profile men found it hard to break out of the cycle and go out with a 'regular' guy. How quickly you could become used to this lifestyle: being treated as though you were 'special'; walking around and having people notice you; enjoying free meals; getting invited to red-carpet events; and getting let off parking fines. To leave all that behind and date a plumber would inevitably feel like deprivation.

Please God, don't let me become like that, I prayed, trying not to notice that I had already dipped one toe into the pool: suddenly I could see the appeal of spending a lot of money on a car, even though I'd always said I'd rather go overseas for six months than buy a silly car. Seemed I was getting used to the Good Life. Must be careful, I warned myself quietly, like a detoxer in a room full of pastries. Don't want to end up an UltraWAG.

UltraWAGs were the worst of all the WAGs. I preferred the High-school Sweethearts, like Kate and Morgan and Lou. Then there were the Have Their Own Profile girls, like Cassie, a *Big Brother* graduate and cable TV weather girl, and Trisha, a gorgeous Filipino who hosted a kids' music show. Next there were the Whatever WAGs, like Paola, who just carried on with their lives, and often, their kids, and couldn't give a rat's arse about the whole football thing. If anything, they found it to be a hindrance. And finally, there were the UltraWAGs. These were the WAGs who loved being photographed, and basked in their boyfriend's spotlight, and went to as many events and did as many magazine spreads as possible.

Of course, there were some crossovers: Steph was a mix of Whatever WAG and UltraWAG, and Melinda *acted* as though she was a High-school Sweetheart, when really she was a total UltraWAG. I liked to think I was a Whatever WAG, but I knew I nursed UltraWAG tendencies. I reasoned that my motive for being photographed at events with Josh, though, was so that all the groupies and footy moles would back off – even though I knew that to them, a girlfriend or wife was about as much of a deterrent as foil on a chocolate bar to a girl with PMS.

No, I thought to myself sternly: I mustn't get caught up in it. I must maintain a sweet, the-simple-life-is-the-life-for-me attitude. I was determined to remain the girl who didn't view herself as above anyone else just because she had a boyfriend who played football and was in the papers all the time.

But, when I thought about it, even Paola insisted on an Audi and complained when she had to drink cheap wine. Meh. It was a slippery slope, but my shoes had grip. I'd be fine.

Early the next morning, I knocked on Josh's door, even though I had his house keys along with his car keys. I felt sexy in my white 'beach-house' dress and tan heels. I'd applied self-tanner last night and blow-dried my hair, and felt very Jennifer Aniston.

I knocked again, this time with force. No answer. I wondered if he could still be out. The boys often stayed out til past 6 a.m., but it was now 8.30; surely he wasn't still at some rank bar, or at Bones's place playing poker and talking shit. A small tennis ball of anxiety formed in my stomach. The idea of Bones and Josh out all night then ending up back at Bones's *without* Bones bringing back girls seemed unlikely. I thought of all the groupies who approached Josh when I was there and then considered the volume who might pounce when I wasn't.

No, I was being silly. Josh wouldn't do anything. I took a deep breath and reminded myself of some very simple facts: I had his car, and was off to a five-million-dollar beach house with him for the weekend. Perspective, Jean, perspective.

Anyway, Josh had told me that we'd leave for the coast before nine, so surely he wouldn't have stayed out that late. After all, it was a three-hour drive, and I didn't think he'd be making (letting) me drive. My mouth scrunched over to one side as I wondered what to do. I decided to get over it and open the door. Ten minutes was enough.

I unlocked the door to the living room/kitchenette to find a mass of sofa pillows on the floor, an enormous blanket draped over the sofa and glasses everywhere. It smelled of smoke and spilled beer. It seemed the boys did go back to someone's place last night, only it wasn't Bones's.

I walked through the mess to Josh's bedroom. The door was closed. I opened it a crack and was knocked back by the smell of breath laced with multiple forms of alcohol. Holding mine, I walked to the vertical blinds and flipped them open. Finally, the lump under the sheets moved.

'Foxy? Wakey wakey, hands off snakey . . .'

He sat up, hair a mess, eyes bleary and bloodshot.

'Wha'? Oh, Jeeeanie.' He rubbed his eyes. 'You look pretty.'

I perched on the edge of the bed as he lay back down on the pillow, groaning.

'What time is it?'

'Well, we're supposed to be leaving in five minutes. But I'm guessing that won't be happening.'

He groaned. 'Never – drinking – again.' He looked at the empty beer bottles on his bedside table. 'Or entertaining.'

I laughed. 'Can you maybe start with a shower? You stink. Bad.'

His eyes rested on me, a smile spreading over his face. Then he quickly grabbed my waist and pulled me down to him. I squealed, trying to avoid his breath, even though the stench appeared to be emitting from each of his several million pores.

'No!' I pulled back and jumped up. 'Get yourself together, Foxman! Let's hit the road.'

'I'll be fresh as a daisy in four minutes.'

'Have you packed?'

'No, but what is there to pack? I'm telling you, I'll be ready and in the car in four minutes.'

'*Course* you will.'

I walked back to the living room and began picking up glasses. I knew Kerrie would clean the whole place while we were gone – Josh was such a spoiled little shit – but thought I should at least make an effort while I was waiting.

The cordless phone rang.

'Can you get that? It's probably just Mum,' Josh yelled from the bedroom. I heard the shower come on.

'So you made it home, huh?' a young woman's voice purred down the phone line.

'Um, hello?'

'Oh . . . Where's Josh?'

187

'He's just in the shower. Can I ask who's calling?'

'It's Tess. And I'm guessing that's Jean.'

In an instant, my entire physiological state shifted. The back of my neck prickled with heat, my mouth went dry and my stomach felt as though it had just been at the receiving end of a very large medicine ball. I had no words.

'Well, tell him I called. He knows why.'

Click.

What – the – fuck – was – that? Why was Tess calling this early? Why was she calling his home phone? Why was she calling *at all*? Why was she beginning conversations with, 'So you made it home'? Why was Josh still speaking to her? And how often? I sat down on the arm of the sofa, trying to make sense of the situation.

Okay, she called him. She was insane and Josh could be entirely innocent. I shouldn't jump to conclusions. I needed to play it smart; Paola had coached me on the subject. She didn't want me to end up like some of the girls, who knew their boys fooled around on them but weren't prepared to sacrifice their lifestyle for the sake of a one-off (or four-off) indiscretion. You're better off single, Paola had said.

I cleaned up a little more, then walked into the bedroom. His hair dripping wet, Josh was wearing nothing but undies. Mustn't be swayed by how toned his abs and back are, or that he has the best arms I've ever seen. *Stay on task*, Jean.

'So, have a big night last night?'

'Mmmm.'

Right. Helpful.

'Just the boys?'

'Mm-hmm.' He was putting his jeans on, doing them up, answering absent-mindedly. Eventually sensing the anxiety streaming out of me, like sunlight under a curtain, he stopped and looked up.

'What's up? Ohhh, *I* know, you're hungry! You've got your food mood on. Don't worry: we're stopping for bacon and egg rolls as soon as we get around the corner.'

I unfolded my arms, putting my left hand on my hip, and leaving the right to furiously finger-comb my hair, fiddle with it, and finally tuck it behind my ear.

'No good? I think there's cereal in the kitchen. Sniff the milk first, though, it might —'

I sighed. How could I go about this elegantly?

'So, it wasn't your mum on the phone.'

He rolled on some deodorant. 'No?'

'No, actually. It was Tess.'

He looked up, startled.

'Why would *she* be ringing here?'

'Um, I believe it was to check if you made it home okay.'

My voice was calm, but my eyes sparkled with anger.

'Jeanie —' He walked towards me, still shirtless, his eyes saying: *This isn't what it looks like.*

'I did run into Tess last night at Parc. We all did – she was there with some friends.' He moved towards me, taking one of my elbows in each of his hands. 'Jeanie . . . baby . . . I know this looks bad, but I have no idea why she would call here and say something like that. She shouldn't be calling here at all.'

Ah yes, but she *did*. And maybe she *does*. All *the time*.

I looked him directly in his red slits of eyes, speaking slowly and with extended pronunciation. 'Why would she call and check on you, if you just ran into her?'

There was a schoolmarm tinge to my voice, but I couldn't help it. Terror that I had been lied to in a revolting fashion was beginning to wash over me. Josh stepped back and sat on the bed, looking up at me and sighing deeply again. A sigh of submission. *I knew it.*

'Jeanie, I don't know what to say. I saw her at Parc, we were all drunk, everyone was there. We were in this sectioned-off private area because we weren't meant to be out drinking last night; she was there because of some fashion show. She was actually being quite normal and friendly so we chatted for a little bit. That's all. You know how I feel about her.'

Oh really? Awesome. Tell me, was it on a cosy lounge in a dark corner? Was there a jazz band playing smooth grooves as you drank martinis and talked about the Good 'Ol Times?

'Jeanie . . . are you okay?'

All of my fears about Josh getting back with Tess were bubbling up, frothing out of my mouth with incredible force. I felt sick knowing they'd been out together, drunk, sprinkling Jiffy firelighters onto old flames, while I'd been at home sleeping soundly. I couldn't look at him. I walked out to the kitchenette for a glass of water. I had no idea what to do. Get over it and enjoy our weekend away? Push it with Josh a little further so that I felt entirely at ease about the situation? Or was I scared that if I did that, I might discover that I *wasn't* at ease with it at all, that this might be the end of us? It didn't bear thinking about.

He *had* explained it all with no hesitation, and hadn't been shifty about anything. If he'd been defensive or made excuses, then I would have the right to be shitty, but I had nothing to arc up over except for the fact that she'd called his house. He didn't call *her;* she called *him.*

I skolled my water and sighed. Okay, Tess was the problem, not Josh. I knew that, and I had to be careful not to tar him with the same brush just because of some phone call she'd made. I had to trust him. Otherwise I was just setting myself up for a whole lot of torture and overanalysis.

Josh walked into the living room, fully dressed, hands in pockets, his eyes locked onto mine.

'Jeanie? I understand how this must look from your end. I do. But I am telling you, 100 per cent, that this is nothing. She called up, she shouldn't have. Yes, I saw her last night, but that will happen from time to time when I'm with the boys, because she's still friends with the Tandooris an—'

'And she wants to see you and flirt with you and make you see what you're missing out on.'

'Whatever her reasons are, they're *her* reasons, and she can do what she likes' – he walked towards me – 'because I'm with you now. And I only want to be with you. And we're going to go to this sweet-arse beach house and have a romantic weekend.' He wrapped his arms around me. 'And we're going to forget all about her.'

I looked up at him for a few seconds. His eyes, bleary as they were, were very reassuring.

'You need eye drops. And your breath still stinks.'

He kissed me on the forehead and smiled.

'That's my girl.'

# ROUND 32
## Blonde vs Brunette

'This place reminds me so much of Santorini.'

'Really? When did you go?'

'Never. But I reckon it would look like this. Don't you?'

I laughed. We were sitting side by side in a small cove, dipping our feet into a rock pool and looking out over the ocean. Behind us the cliffs were smattered with oversized mansions, all of which were probably occupied seven per cent of the year by wealthy families or couples who thought nothing of spending five million on a summer beach house. We were staying in one of the biggest. It was tough.

'Probably.'

'You know, I get time off at the end of the year. Maybe we should go over there and see if it *does* look like this . . .'

I snapped my head to look at him. He had one brow raised and was grinning excitedly, searching for a mirror of his enthusiasm in my eyes.

'Don't you think, Jeanie? You and me and a couple million Greeks, enjoying the sun and eating tzatziki for a week or two?'

'Are you serious?'

I had a feeling he was. It would slot right into the express lane we had created for this relationship. We'd only been together three months and already we were taking weekends away and fighting over ex-girlfriends. Why not begin planning trips overseas?

"Course I am. I can think of no person I'd prefer to travel with.

Except maybe The Fonze.' He took my hand and kissed it. 'Mmm, sunscreen.'

I smiled. 'I'd love to go away with you, Josh.'

I wanted to go now, in fact. I wanted to be like the girls in the movies who got unashamedly, unapologetically swept up in romance, and forgot about Real Life and responsibility and rent, and it all worked out perfectly. And when I thought about it, it seemed I was on my way. Pretty much my whole life had been taken over by a sly little Fox and a pack of Bulls.

'You're not throwing big plans out only to retract them later and leave me high and dry, are you? What if I go and learn how to smash plates, and then you cancel the trip?' I complemented this with a cheeky grin, but deep down I meant it. I was worried Josh was going to startle himself any minute now, realise that he'd accidentally found himself in another long-term relationship, and bolt for the hills. He always threw long-term plans out there – we'll hike here, we'll camp there, we'll spend New Year's here – and as we were still in the short term, I had no idea whether he was: a) Full of horseshit; or b) Legitimately besotted and wanting to make several football-playing, jewellery-designing progeny in the next couple of years.

'I'm red-banding, Jeanie, I know that. But I'm happy. *Really* happy. Life is easy with you. I'm playing my best football. Things are good. I wasted my last relationship for . . . well, for lots of reasons. But this time it's different. So I want to enjoy it. You know?' He stopped speaking and began tracing my jaw line with his hand before starting again. 'You've come in and changed everything, Perfect Jeanie. I've fallen into another relationship, and I wasn't meant to. After Tess, I thought that I needed some time to be young and single, and to tool around with Bones for a bit. But you came along and stuffed it all up.'

I laughed, mentally pinching myself at what had just fallen from his lips. This was the first time he'd said anything like this, and I was greedy for more.

'No wonder Bones didn't warm to me right away. I bowled in and ruined his plans,' I said.

'Don't worry about him; he'll be single till he's eighty, anyway. And he loves you now; you know that. Loves you a little too much, actually . . .'

'I'm not young and hot and dumb enough for Bones, we both know that.'

'True. Anyone over twenty-one is category D to him.'

'Category D?'

'Never mind. So we'll go away? I want to see more of Europe. Sucks, playing here in the winter. You can never travel when the rest of the world is enjoying summer. All my mates – my non-footy mates, like Aaron and Damon – they all piss off to France and Italy for weeks and I'm stuck here.'

'But if the season ends in October, that won't be so bad, will it?'

'Yeah, I guess. Just annoying. I'd like to go and play over there eventually. Maybe France. Or England. Can make a looooot of money over there in a pretty short time. And you get all set up: the big house, the nice car, a job for Jeanie . . .'

Again. He'd done it *again*: more long-term plans with me included. I had no idea whether he meant them and I should allow myself to get excited, or whether he said this to all his girlfriends. Or whether Greece was originally planned with Tess in mind.

*Tess*. I quickly installed my mental stop sign. This was a trick Colette had taught me to avoid going over and over something in my mind. Her therapist, Billy, had taught it to her when she'd gone through the Eric debacle. He had also advised her to listen to CDs of Buddhist chants as she drove, which provided a very entertaining background track to her traffic Tourette's ('Oh, would you learn to fucking DRIVE?') But the stop sign worked, I thought. And I should know: I'd planted 200 of them today since Tess's phone call.

'Sounds amazing. How much longer are you signed to play for the Bulls?'

'One more year. Thing is, they've just bought a new full-back, Jez Norton, who's the full-back for Australia, so I'm not sure what will happen . . .'

'They can do that? But you're an amazing full-back. The club loves you. Why would they do that?'

'At the end of the day, the club wants the best possible players for their money. And Jared, well, he's the best. So they bought him. There's no loyalty when it comes to how long you've played for the club, or what you've achieved for them. It's business. I get it.'

'But where does that leave you?'

He shrugged. 'I'll find a new club. My manager is on the case now. We'll probably have a pretty fair idea of who wants me soon. I want to be signed up as quickly as possible; nothing worse than playing with an uncertain future, watching all the money go to other players while your manager tries to lock you into a contract. I'd even take a release if they'd give me one – start next season at a new club.'

'Won't the Bulls try to keep you?' I didn't like this idea of a new club. He could be forced to move interstate, or even overseas.

'I don't think they can afford me. They've bought Jared from the Thundercats, and this massive Pommy forward, Martin, and a couple of younger players too. That doesn't leave much money in the kitty for me.'

'But . . . but aren't you upset? That your own club won't bid for you? Haven't you been there for ages?'

'Five years.' He was quiet for a moment. 'It's not a great feeling, to be honest. But like I said, it's business.'

I sat there frowning at how disloyal these football clubs were.

'It's okay, Jeanie. This is how it is these days. I just want to get it sorted so I can focus on playing good footy.'

He bent his head and kissed me tenderly on the lips. I kissed him back before leaning my head on his shoulder and snuggling into him.

'Have you gone blonder?' he suddenly asked.

I had gone even lighter, thanks to Steph's persistence. I now had more blonde than brunette in my hair. It was very beachy, I thought, and very attention-grabbing. Never before had I had so many looks and lecherous whistles from labourers and drunk men. Col said I was starting to look like a page-three girl, minus the tits. (At least she and I were talking again. It was stilted, overly polite, and there was an enormous elephant sitting in the corner, playing Sudoku and waiting for us to acknowledge it. But at least we were talking.)

'I have. You like?'

"Snice. But I like you best dark, I think.'

I immediately put my hand through my hair. *He didn't like it?* But I'd done it for *him*! To look more . . . more like I thought he would like me to be! More like Tess! More like the other girlfriends. More like the girls Bones liked.

'You don't like it?'

He kissed me on the head. 'It's nice.'

I tensed up a little and he felt it.

'Jeanie, you know I think you look beautiful. I just prefer your natural colour, is all. Doesn't mean I don't *like* the blonde, just means I *prefer* the dark.' He wrapped his arms around me and shook me playfully. 'Are you cranky? Don't be cranky; you look great. Honestly, you do. Come on, lighten up. Ha! Geddit? Okay, do I need to clean the slate? Do I? 'Cos I'll do it. I will.'

He stood up and in one swift move jumped into the rock pool. His shorts saturated, he turned to face me before launching into song:

*Jean, Jeanie, with your blonde hair,*

*Jean, Jeanie, you make all men stare!'*

I laughed, shaking my head. He splashed about in the water, pointing at me like a fool.

'You smiled! Clean slate! Clean slate!'

I kept smiling, but inside I was angry at myself for dying my hair a colour that I didn't like, for a guy who preferred my natural colour. I looked down at my tight jeans and expensive wrap top that scooped low, and cursed myself again. Why was I changing how I dressed and looked when I didn't even like it, and perhaps Josh didn't like it either? Who exactly was I trying to impress?

He sat down and turned to look at me, one arm around my back, one covering my hands in my lap.

'I love you, Perfect Jean.'

He'd said it. *Finally.* Jesus, talk about a build-up! For months I'd been trying to subliminally coax those three words from his lips so that I might tell him I loved *him* – and then he springs it on me in a bloody rock pool.

I returned and held his gaze, and simply said what I'd been dying to for so long.

'I love you, too.'

# ROUND 33
## Emasculation vs Eric

After three, maybe twelve, hours of gridlocked freeway traffic, I arrived home and dumped my bag on the floor behind the sofa.

'I'm hoooo-oome,' I called out to no one.

I walked into the kitchen and opened the fridge, hopeful of seeing a large plate of strawberries, or a giant slice of chocolate cake. Instead, the offerings of the Kelvinator Gods consisted of cheese, half a bottle of wine, yoghurt and some Thai leftovers from last week. Yummy.

Suddenly I heard voices from Col's bedroom. I pricked my ears and lifted my head. There was definitely a male voice. Noooo, surely not. Could she really have invited Eric into our home? Oh, this was too much. Especially since he was the reason we'd been acting like third cousins for the last few weeks. I couldn't help myself: I walked out into the living room for better hearing. It sounded nasty – a fight of some kind. Figures. He did cheat on her with his ex a few months before they were due to WED.

I tiptoed over to her door to see whether I could make out what they were fighting over. There were muffled strains of Eric defending himself (I imagine he was getting quite used to that by now). I could hear Col bellowing about something, and the words 'disrespect' and 'trying' came up several times. Eric's voice suddenly became a lot clearer, and closer. Oh shit, he was at the do—

'Jean! What are you doing?' A shirtless, red-faced Eric confronted me.

'Jean's here?'

Col walked over to the door, wearing only a singlet and knickers. Gross. They'd been sexing. Hope she wore protection. Who knows what that filthy man had been up to.

'Um, I just got home, and I was —'

'You were listening to us, weren't you, you little shit.'

Her voice wasn't angry; more defeatist. The elephant in the corner stamped its foot in celebration.

Eric, who looked like he'd been working out recently, and possibly taken some kind of sojourn to Barbados, looked to Colette for help. She offered none.

'Go, just go,' she said with a wave of her hand, walking past me to the bathroom, where she slammed the door.

Eric picked up his jumper and shoes and walked into the living room, where his keys and wallet sat on the dining table. I stood in the hallway just outside, arms folded, waiting to give him some fierce stink-eye before he left. He put on his shoes, shirt and watch, and picked up his keys, finally raising his head to meet my steely gaze.

'Jean —'

'Yes?' I cut him off with my pert response. *Yes*, I wanted to say. *How may I help you and your wandering penis?*

'I'm so sorry for all the hurt I've caused your sister and your family.'

With that he turned, opened the front door and walked out.

Oooh, dramatic. Cue 'To Be Continued' across the bottom of the screen. I heard the bathroom door open and Colette emitting a sad little sigh.

'Thought you'd stay at boofhead's tonight.'

'No, he has an early start, and I needed to wash my hair . . .'

'Of course. The new flaxen locks must be pristine at all times.'

I chose not to bite. She was like a baby's teething toy, ready for a nibble 24/7.

'So, um, wanna talk about the guy that just left?'

She sighed again and shook her head, walking out to the living room, collapsing onto the sofa in a cross-legged position as she grabbed a pillow and jammed it in her lap.

'There's a lot about this situation you're not going to understand, or like. But if you can be an adult, and deal with that, and not lose your shit at me, or judge me, then sure. Let's talk.'

'Col, I'm not judging you. I'm just protective of you. Surely you can see that? To me, Eric symbol—'

'I know all of that, Jay. I do. And that's exactly what I don't want to hear.'

'Truth hurts.'

'Okay, I'll change that to: exactly what I don't *need* to hear.'

I sat down on Ken the Irregular Armchair and sighed too.

'Okay. Go. I'm an open vein to your verbal insulin.'

'First of all, I'm not back with Eric.'

'You're just sleeping with him? Even better.'

'Can you relax? Fuck, Jay – this isn't easy, you know.'

Finally, a crack in her feisty veneer. Her eyes showed both hurt and sincerity. I decided to shut up and let her speak.

'Okay, okay, no more from me. Go.'

'A while back, 'bout the time you met Josh, Eric started emailing me, explaining things – but this time without all the insincerity and bullshit. He'd been seeing a counsellor, and had started meditating. And he'd moved out of his mum's, who, as we all know, thinks I'm not good enough for her precious fucking son, and apart from having a moustache and the breath of a rotting carcass, is a brainwashing bitch. Anyway, he sounded like he actually understood why he did what he did.'

'Which was?'

'Well – and this won't come as a surprise to *you* – he cheated on me with Lily for lots of reasons, but the main one was because I

was . . . well, I was emasculating him. I was too bossy and too asser-
tive and too masculine. A ball-breaker. Squared.'

She stopped, waiting for me to laugh, or guffaw, or hold up a sign
saying 'Bingo!' But I didn't. So she went on.

'You know, I took *total* charge of the wedding, and I was earn-
ing more than him because he got dropped to part-time, and I was
always tired and exhausted and yelling at him, and refusing his help
whenever he offered it because I thought I could do it better. And,
well, I guess instead of talking to me about it, 'cos he was scared of
me, he ran into Lily's arms, because she's a wimpy little pixie who
would never strip him of feeling like the man in the relationship.'

It took everything in me not to blurt out: *Didn't mean he had to
fuck her!*

'And so, you know, I started to think about my behaviour, and how
I act in relationships, and' – a lone tear had snuck out of her left eye
and she wiped it away – 'I saw that he was right. That I wasn't being a
good partner, that I had become a bitch who had it her way or no way.
And, you know, in the bedroom . . . well, there were big issues there,
because, I mean, we weren't really having sex, and I would get insecure thinking it was because he wasn't attracted to me, when really it
was because I was so masculine to him.' She sniffed and wiped some
more escaped tears. 'The last thing he wanted to do was make love to
a woman who made him feel like he was worthless.'

'Col —'

'And, you know, I just think that maybe if I hadn't of acted like
that, or he had told me what I was doing, and I had changed, none
of this would've ever happened. And things would be how they
were, and I'd be getting married in a couple of months, you know?
I'd still be getting married . . .'

She started to sob openly, wiping her eyes and pushing her curls
behind her ears and shaking her head, and I watched her and my
heart broke for her.

I got up and moved over to sit beside my sister. My poor sister, who had been through so much heartbreak over the past six months, and who was now blaming it all on herself. I put both arms around her small, jerking frame and cuddled her.

'Oh, Col, you can't blame yourself. Col, I'm so sorry . . .'

She finally let her head rest on my shoulder and returned the cuddle, and we sat there, me crying silently for her hurt, her sobbing and sniffing and not saying anything for a few minutes, until she moved forwards, sniffing loudly, conclusively, and gathered her hair up into a bun using a band from her wrist. I sat back against the sofa and waited for her to collect herself, not wanting to say anything, but finally – finally – to just listen to her, which I now realised I hadn't been doing at a time when she needed me to do it the most.

She sniffed and wiped the mascara from under her eyes.

'He's still a fucking fuckface for cheating.'

I burst into laughter.

'Men, huh? They cheat if you're too clingy, and they cheat if you're too independent. How the fuck are we meant to get it right?'

I couldn't help pondering what she'd said, and wondering where I sat on the clingy–independent scale with Josh. I hoped it was somewhere in the middle.

'So, what's happening with you two now, then? I mean, after those emails, and him explaining everything, all his reasons for doing —'

'Well, when I realised he actually had some valid points, and that I couldn't go on putting all of the blame for what happened onto him, I started writing back. And it was so cathartic, to finally speak to him – well, on email – and to explain everything that made me that way back then – how I felt I should just do everything because it was easier, and that it irritated me that the Incredible Bearded Mother still had so much sway over him, and that he listened to her more than his wife-to-be . . . And, Jay, I can't quite explain it, but after writing back and forth for weeks – and I'm talking deep, heavy, three-page emails – we started to realise that we still loved each other.'

'Why didn't you tell me any of this?'

She turned her head to look at me, her eyes big and sad and red.

'After all the "If I ever see him again I will cut off his balls and use them as a yoyo" talk? I was embarrassed, Jay! It feels like I'm betraying myself, and the goddamn sisterhood, to fall back in love with a cheat. I knew you would lecture me, and Mum too, and I just didn't want to deal with that. Plus, like I said, we're not back together, we're still working things out, so why bother getting everyone frothing for no reason, you know?'

'I'm sorry. I'm so sorry . . . I've been so caught up with Josh and my own life that I didn't even consider how hard this must be for you. What was the fight about just before? Is everything okay?'

She sighed before standing up and walking towards the kitchen.

'We've got a lot of creases to iron out – put it that way. 'Cos even if I *was* a bitch, he still fucked another woman, and that's not easy to live with.'

# ROUND 34

## Trouser Snakes vs Jewellery-making

'Ball-breaker. Absolute ball-breaker.'

As we sat around a balcony table at the pub where Paola liked to eat before matches, she and Lou were commenting on Melinda's more elegant personality traits. Steph and I listened with amusement.

'And I'm sorry, but if you gonna wear some tiny leetle skirts to the futball in the winter, don't sit outside and say, "Iss cooold, iss so cooold."'

'I know! Oh, and did you hear her giving it to Morgan last week? Told her to go back and sit in her original seat because the boys were losing and it was *bad luck* for her to keep moving around!'

'True?' I asked in disbelief, and then surprise at the fact I had just replaced 'really?' with 'true?', which was one of Lou's favourites and, to my mind, had always been slightly bogan.

Lou went on, nodding, wearing her signature 'amazing but true' expression: brows up, lips pursed.

'I feel sorry for Ryan, the poor bastard. What about that time he passed out in the back of a cab, so the cabbie dropped him off on some random street, and he fell asleep in the grass, and she thought he deliberately didn't answer his phone all night and was cheating on her, so she threw all his shit into their pool and then leaked it to the bloody papers!'

No wonder Melinda and Tess got along, I thought to myself.

'She makes the rest of us look like angels,' said Paola, trying to get the attention of the waiter to order another bottle of wine.

'Ahh, God bless the mad bitch,' said Lou, shaking her head and taking a sip from her glass.

I'd noticed the phrase 'God bless her' was thrown around a lot amongst the girls. It always followed a session about someone, as though it wiped clean all the gossiping that preceded it. By saying 'God bless her', you were absolving yourself: *See? Even though I just performed verbal terrorism, I'm not a bad person.*

'So, Lou, those sexy knickers you buy work?'

Lou rolled her eyes. 'He fell asleep on the lounge.'

'Kidding me!' Paola said, outraged. 'Everyone thinks that this boys, oh, they so fiiiit, and oh, they so seeexy and so maaaanly, but really they is just granpas!'

Steph and I giggled. I took a sip of my white wine, which had been ordered by Paola because the other two whites available tasted like 'the cat's pissing'.

'Although to be fair,' Lou said to the table, 'I'm not exactly gagging for it most of the time. Wait till you lot have kids – I'm always so buggered; last thing I want to do is shake my tits in the hope of a quickie. Nick's never around anyway, so by the time he comes home, plays Hollywood Dad and undoes all the good work I've done in just twenty minutes of couch-jumping and ice-cream, I'd rather *kick* him in the dick than put it in my mouth.'

We laughed, shaking our heads. Why did Steph so badly want the ring and the kids, I wondered? Didn't sound that enticing to me. Lou seemed to be basically raising their kids alone; Nick was always away or training.

'Jimmy's lucky to make it till nine,' said Paola. 'And he's tired, always so tired. Especially with his ankle. Actually, comes to think of it, during the off-season he won't leaves me alone, but when he's playin', *forget* it.'

'And of course the last thing they wanna do is make love after a day of running around and beating each other up, 'cos they don't have the energy,' said Lou. 'But they gotta service their women sometimes, or we start looking to the mailman! Ain't that right, girls?'

Steph cleared her throat.

'Actually, um, Mitch . . . Mitch goes okay.'

There were 0.06 seconds of silence before Paola erupted.

'Ooooh-hoo-*hooo*! Look at choo! All smug 'cos you gettin' lucky!' she teased.

Like grenadine flowing into a tequila sunrise, a deep shade of red poured into Steph's face. *Please don't ask me next, please don't ask me next*, I willed. I really don't want to discuss my sex life. I don't.

'What about you, Jeanie in a bottle? How's Foxy?'

I couldn't have been more uncomfortable if Paola had asked me to slip on a pair of underpants that had been smothered in a coat of honey and then dipped into a nest of small, angry fire ants.

'Everything's fine with us,' I said, burying my face in my wine, hoping the conversation would be drowned by the liquid trickling into my mouth. But when I emerged, the three girls were staring at me with the kind of expectation that should follow a sentence like, 'Did I ever tell you about the time I slept with David Beckham?'

'Fine? Or fantastic?' Lou said.

'Come on, Jeanie. Everyone's been dying to know how Josh goes.'

'Yeah, come on, Jean.' Even Steph was joining in now.

'Guys, I'm not gonna talk about Josh like that.'

'Oh, don' be so boring,' snorted Paola. 'We're all friends here. All go through same shits. It's bonding.' She grinned at me, raising her brows up and down quickly.

I looked around at the girls; I guess she was right. I wanted to feel like I was one of them. And they'd all said something about *their* men. I looked around at each of them before speaking.

'Put it this way' – I paused – 'I've trained him up nicely.'

'*Woooooooo!*'

Paola whooped and hollered, Lou clapped and cheered, and Steph laughed and whistled. All three of them were looking at me with a cocktail of shock, glee and awe. I was giddy with the thrill of being accepted, of being naughty, of sharing secrets I wasn't supposed to with a group of women who possessed a special connection.

'*Hombre loco, mi amor,*' Paola yelled. '*Hazme el amor!*'

We all laughed, even though we had no idea what she was saying. It sounded funny. Anything she said did.

'Can you believe that came out of *her* mouth?' Lou said to Steph, pointing at me and shaking her head.

Once they had all settled down, Paola said, 'Ahhh, choo two are still on the funnymoon. Let's ask her again in a year, huh, chicas?' She had one eyebrow raised knowingly.

Lou agreed, nodding as she took in a huge gulp of wine. 'Zatlee. It's always all-night marathons and "How can I please you?" in the early days.'

'Well, Mitch and I have been together for two years, and we're just fi—'

'There she goes again. Would you listen to the little bragger?' Lou shook her head disbelievingly and we all laughed again.

Paola stood up to go the ladies', and I took in her leather bomber jacket, intricately wrapped grey scarf and tight black jeans. She'd had her hair cut dramatically and was now the proud owner of a chin-length bob and a chunky fringe, which amplified her already incredible beauty by roughly 768 per cent. Her natural loveliness and effortless chic made me long for my brown hair and cute vintage dresses and colourful tops, which I'd somehow managed to completely phase out in favour of a wardrobe of low-cut tops and jeans.

'Hey, *love* those earrings. Where they from?' Steph asked me, taking one of my earrings in her fingers to examine it. They were round drop earrings with gold and white enamel, and tiny wooden beads.

'These? I, um, I made them, actually.'

'Noooo, get out! Really?'

'What?' piped up Lou, putting away her phone and picking up her wine again. 'What's she saying now? More penis stories?'

'No, no. She *made* these earrings – can you believe it?'

Lou squinted in the general direction of my ears.

'I'm rubbish without my glasses. Hold your hair up for a second?'

I did, feeling silly. These were old earrings; I could do so much better now.

'Whoa, they're *gorge*! Actually, Jean, you always wear really glitz jewellery, doesn't she, Steph?'

Steph nodded, looking at her own glittering hands.

'I looooove jewellery. Mitch says I spend too much money on it, but it's my thing, y'know? I'm more a classic girl-girl, though, with diamonds and stuff. I don't know how to wear all that trendy stuff like you wear, Jean. You always have cool bracelets and necklaces. It really suits you.'

'D'you sell it?' Lou was getting drunk; her eyes were slightly glazed and her sentences impatient and loud. Her lipstick had faded, leaving a harsh perimeter of flamingo-pink lip liner around the outer edges of her mouth.

'Um, no. Well, I used to, back home. But I've been a bit of a slack-arse since I've been down here.'

'What, like at markets and stuff?'

'A couple of boutiques. It worked well with the kind of beachy vibe up there. Not sure how it would do down here.'

Oh, goody: I'd just invented another excuse as to why I had stopped making any pieces. That one was a corker – right up there with it being winter, and the fact that Ingrid probably wouldn't let me put my collection on the counter. I had become The Excusinator.

But Steph wasn't letting me off the hook. 'That's silly! Of course they'd sell here. Do you make, like, formal stuff? I'm always after nice stuff for these black-tie things that come up – stuff that can dress up a plain black dress, you know?'

'Who's dressing up?'

Paola had arrived back from the ladies', freshly glossed and bronzed. Now Lou stood up, noisily pushing back her chair with her legs. 'I gotta pee.'

'I was asking if Jean could make jewellery for a black dress I have. Did you know she makes jewellery? Look at those earrings – she *made* them!'

'You shoulda seen the ones chiquita wore to the ball the other week. She's one clever little monkey.' Paola turned her face to mine. 'I've been meaning to ask if you could make me ones like you had on that night. You know I'm good for the cash.'

I laughed.

'Not before she makes *me* some earrings; I asked first,' Steph said.

I couldn't believe that Steph and Paola were fighting over buying some jewellery from me. I'd forgotten that women actually liked what I made; it had been so long since I'd sold anything and had that feedback from the buyer that inspires you to keep making more. I felt the rush of excitement that had initially stirred me to want to sell my pieces in the boutique.

Paolo's skin tone would look amazing with some dark woods and ivory and gold; and Steph, being a blonde, tanned, silver-wearing girl wanting to wear black, should be wearing silvers and turquoise and maybe a pop of orange to lift things and keep them from looking cheap and market-jewellery like.

'So, are we on?' Paola was unscrewing a fresh bottle of semillon.

'Yes. Yes we are. Give me two weeks.'

'For both of us?'

'Of course.'

'What you charge, Jeanie? 'Cos if it's Cartier prices, we may have a problem. I don't wanna have to go back to the pole to pay for my *joyas . . .*'

I grinned. 'Nothing. If you like them, and wear them, that's enough payment for me.'

Steph rolled her eyes – 'No freakin' way!' – and Paola shook her head.

'No, I'm serious. If you like them, and you want to buy more, well okay. But I don't want the pressure of having to do it for money first time round.'

They looked at each other. Paola shrugged. 'Hokay. Choo mad, you know that? Don't you know how much our boys earn?'

Steph laughed uproariously, slapping her knee and holding her stomach. Lou, who had returned from the bathroom with freshly applied lipstick and far too much blush, sat down messily and immediately filled her glass with the chilled wine.

'Wass so funny?'

# ROUND 35
## Fermented Grapes vs Coffee Dates

As we strutted with purpose into the stadium, two wines off shit-faced, we saw a gaggle of girls our own age smoking against the small fence that formed the perimeter of the stadium complex. Each was wearing a Bulls scarf or jersey with tight jeans, and criminal amounts of makeup.

These were the Bay Nine Girls: too knowledgeable about the game to be labelled groupies, too butch ever to be considered serious girlfriend material. They were forever velcro-ing onto the boys at pubs, the members' post-match party, or anywhere else they could weasel themselves in. The WAGs didn't view them as a threat, just an annoyance, like the pushy mums who demanded autographs when you were quietly eating poached eggs at a cafe, or the shopping-centre clowns who eyed off Josh from 100 metres, only to wait until we passed before yelling out, 'Fox is a wanker!'

The Bay Niners gave us squinty elevator stares as we walked past them through the VIP entrance, their beady kohl-rimmed eyes taking us in, hating us and who we were and that we were allowed to have sex with men who they knew *so* much more about – like how many rep games they'd played for Australia, and what the catastrophic result of that misjudged hospital pass in Round 6 was, and how many kilograms they bench-pressed at the gym.

Paola spied them staring at us as we were having our tickets checked. 'Oh, look,' she said gaily, 'it's the Bay Niners! Wave, everyone!'

Steph and Lou waved and smiled condescendingly, regally, but

I couldn't do it. I was too new to the game to start acting like I deserved to be in it.

Being a Friday-night game, a clan of hardworking teenage baby-sitters had been employed across the city to give the girls a night off, and everyone had put a little more effort into their appearance in case they went out afterwards. Feeling bad for Col's Eric situation, I'd asked if she'd like to come with me to the game, but she said she'd rather polish up our fridge magnets than spend an evening with a bunch of glorified cheerleaders, so I left it.

In the Girlfriends' Box, Melinda and Cassie were sitting side by side, slurping away on red wine, talking loudly and gesticulating with the passion of Italians. I wondered how Cassie did it without batting a guilty little eyelid. I was pretty sure that if Melinda found out about Cassie and Ryan, and little Ryan junior, she would be the type to throw punches. And vases. And lawsuits.

Cassie had balls. Big, brazen, not-entirely-admirable balls. I wondered where Morgan was. Maybe she'd finally had enough of being talked down to by Melinda and had elected to watch the game with her family instead of the WAGs.

The game, now almost over, seemed to me to have gone for around three minutes. The Bulls had had such a massive lead, from so early on, that none of the girls bothered to pay much attention, preferring instead to gossip and chat and drink litres of nasty ries-ling, which, for some reason – probably one involving us already being soaked in alcohol – didn't taste half as bad as usual. Cassie was an exception: Ryan had made a couple of whopping errors, including somehow scoring a try for the other team, and she was as pissed off and self-flagellating as if she'd committed the errors herself. It fascinated me to watch how quickly and completely some of the girls clicked into the emotion appropriate to however their boy was playing. It was as though by knowing their boyfriend was going to be angry with himself for a bad game, and accommodating that by being sombre and empathetic when he came up from the change-rooms, they were indicating not only how connected they were to their man, and what a bond they had, and how much they 'got' him, but also that they very much understood the specific brand of theatre that was required of a WAG post-match. It was absolutely intentional, this public show of solidarity, especially in the company of groupies. I thought about how I behaved around Josh after a game and realised that I was guilty of this very conduct: beaming and full of praise when he'd played well, and quiet and serious when I knew he would be unhappy with his performance.

Paola, of course, bucked this trend, preferring not to indulge Jimmy's wallowing when he was down, and instead cheering him up and reminding him of the Bigger Picture. Her approach made sense to me intellectually, but I wasn't nearly confident enough to risk Josh feeling like I wasn't being supportive when he needed me. He might think it patronising if I were to dismiss his moods with frivolous talk about it being *only one game* or the fact that *the team won and that's what counts*. It was confusing, because my natural instinct was always to try to cheer someone up if they were in a sulk, but in the football world it seemed you had to stand by your man, mimicking his mood and demonstrating a united stand.

'We've *wooon*, let's have some *fuuun*, we've *woooon*, now we can *ruuuun*!' Steph was sitting in her seat, wiggling and dancing and trying to get us to go up to the members bar for drinks. Her theory was that as there were only eight minutes to go, and the Bulls were five tries in front, we had already won and should commence the next stage of drinking immediately. She was also desperate for a cigarette, as was Paola.

But Lou tried to thwart us. 'Are you lot for real? This is the last game before the semi-finals, and you know the Lions are famous for coming back strong at the end, and you want to just leave? Oh, I'm sure the boys would *love* to hear that . . .'

'Oh, look!' said Paola. 'She's got her dick on again.'

Steph burst into laughter, gathering up our coats and bags to indicate that we were leaving. 'Lou, we're gonna go straight to the members'; there are TVs there. Why don't you come with us?'

I felt torn. I didn't want to look like one of the girls who came just to chat and drink without paying any attention to the game – even though that's generally what I did. And I *did* want to watch Josh, who, as far as my distracted, bleary eyes could tell, seemed to be playing well, although it all went so much faster and was so much harder to follow when you were drunk that if he asked me anything about the game, the best I would be able to offer was that they were definitely wearing blue this evening, and there was a *lot* of grass involved. Meh, they'd definitely win, all I would need to say was congrats. I decided to go with the girls.

Lou waved us away without looking at us. So we got our stuff and, giggling while we tried to avoid the looks from the other girls, schlepped through the box and out to the lifts.

'How can Lou see the football when she can't even see where to use her lipstick?' Paola asked.

'We *have* to tell her to get rid of that colour – it's *so* wrong,' said Steph.

'It's her thing. She can wear what she likes,' said Paola, flourishing her unlit cigarette. 'We don't tease you 'bout your love affair with the spray-tans gun.'

I stifled a laugh.

'Oh, says the bloody native,' said Steph. 'It's all right for you, the skinny model with the permanent tan!'

'Chiquita, don hate me cause I'm pretty and popular.'

Paola winked at Steph and pushed open the door to the car park, where the two of them could finally suck on the little white sticks they had been dreaming of.

An hour later, the members bar was heaving. As the Bulls had now secured a spot in the semi-finals, everyone was in a hyper-charged, alcohol-fuelled frenzy. Even Melinda was caught smiling occasionally.

'Oh, look! It's Petey Pissy Pants,' said Steph, her eyes glazed and her cheeks flushed as she took in Josh, who was walking towards us carrying three vodkas.

'WHO?' yelled an especially jovial Josh over the noise of 150 drunk football fans, players and partners.

'NEVER MIND. WHERE'S MITCH?'

'ZAT THE BAR!'

Steph performed a wobbly curtsy and turned to go and find her man, leaving Josh and me to kiss hello. As always, his enormous training bag was with him: carried on his shoulder and then dumped at his feet wherever he decided to halt. I felt compelled to offer a few generic comments, since this was all I could manage, on the game.

'Baby, you played so well.' (Guess and hope that he didn't actually let in three tries.) 'Congratulations on the win.' (Foolproof.) 'How exciting about the semi-finals!' (Show I know what's going on.) 'Are you pumped?' (Put it back on to him.)

'Thanks, my li'l Jeanie . . .' He had a bemused smile on his face. 'You've had a bit to drink, haven't you?' He smiled at me lov-ingly – not reprimanding, just stating the obvious.

'Ummmm . . . a little.'

He wrapped his arms around me, looked me directly in the eyes and kissed me on the nose.

'You're even cuter when you're drunk. Must remember to take advantage of you later on.'

'How can you take advantage of me if I want to do it?'

'Ah, but you don't know what "it" is yet.'

He smiled mischievously and, keeping his eyes locked on mine, removed Bones's hand from his arse.

'So I like to gently caress his buns. What of it?' Bones complained. I laughed as he pecked me on the cheek.

'Real Deal . . . looking good. You know that once you're sick of Fox you can come my way, right? Don't worry, I'll forgive you for dating one of the rookies in the team before coming to see what it's like to be with a *real* man.'

I shook my head and smiled the teeth-free smile reserved specifically for the lame sexual innuendo Bones poured all over every conversation.

'Look at her, Fox. She can't even argue, because I just slapped her with what smart people like me call infallible logic.'

I groaned. 'I prefer my men to have had less than 900 sexual partners.'

'I'm sure there's millions of women out there who would love to be number 901,' he said. 'I just gotta make sure she's drunk enough that she can't see how much less attractive I am than Josh.'

'See, what you don't understand is that that stuff right there – that whole self-deprecation thing you just did? Way more attractive than talking yourself up.'

He ignored me, clearly on a roll. 'What about your sister? She's hot. She single?'

'Um, yeah, no, she's, um, no . . .'

'It's all right, plenty more birds in the park. Oh! Almost forgot why I came over to talk to Barbie and Ken. The Tessticle is here.'

# ROUND 36
## Confrontation vs Inebriation

Even through my haze of sickly-sweet wine and the covers band and the sound of the pokies and the excited buzz of what felt like 5000 people, Tess's name stood out like the rumblings of diarrhoea when stuck in a traffic jam.

Josh grabbed my hand immediately. 'No biggie, we'll just make sure we don't bump into her.' He looked at me for confirmation that this was okay. 'You cool, Jeanie?'

'Totally.' I smiled at him, hoping it provided a mask adequate enough to hide the anxiety I felt knowing that she was in the room. *Why?* Why would she come here? She had no reason. Okay, so her dad was the boss and it was a huge game. But aside from that, no reason whatsoever.

Josh kissed me quickly on the lips and looked towards the bar.

'How about I get us a drink? Bones, can you try not to sexually harass my girlfriend for a few minutes?'

'I can't make any promises . . .'

As Josh disappeared into the sea of people, Paola sidled up next to me.

'Where you been hiding? Oh, you're being slimed on by Bones. Thank Gods I'm here to save you.'

'Do I have *no* other personality traits apart from sleaziness?' Bones asked, shaking his head.

'Of course you do, Bones. *Una golfa.*' She grinned and poked him in the chest.

'Don't *Spanish* me! You know I hate that. What did you say?'

'Paola, do you need to go to the ladies'?' I asked.

'Yes, let's. Bones, you wanna come touch up your makeup?'

'What did you call me, Scarface?'

'Ciao!'

As we wove our way through the crowd, my eyes raked the sea of heads for Tess's blonde hair. It shouldn't be too hard to spot, what with the devil horns peeking out. I spotted Cassie laughing hysterically at something a handsome young guy with a shaved head was saying, and Steph talking very flirtatiously to a man who was not Mitch. Seems we were all as drunk and messy as each other.

Just as we were about to reach the toilets, I heard a screech.

'Paola!'

'Janet! Get *out*! What you doin' here? Oooh, we miss you, baby!'

Paola was suddenly wrapped in the tanned arms of a toffee-blonde with huge brown eyes and an enormous Joker-style smile.

'Janet, this here is Jeanie; Jeanie, Janet. Janet used to be the marketing girl for the club, but then she went and had some *bebés*.'

'Hi, Janet. Nice to meet you.'

'You too.' She smiled at me and then quickly went back to Paola, elegantly pulling her out of the thoroughfare to engage her in a conversation about nappies and sleep deprivation. Sensing this might go on for a while, I excused myself and walked through to the toilets.

And a queue.

And a Tess.

She was applying some glimmering pink Chanel lip gloss to her already reflective lips, and looking closely at herself in the mirror. She was wearing incredibly tight, faded jeans, tan ankle boots, a white singlet and what had to be a cashmere scarf. Her hair was huge, bouncy, positively weavetastical. She looked toned, tanned, slim and so TV-ready it made me want to vomit.

'M'linda! You done or what?' Tess shouted at one of the cubicles.

A muffled voice emerged. 'Nearly. Jesus, relax!'

As Tess turned back to her reflection, she caught sight of me leaning against the back wall, head down, trying desperately to activate my camouflage button. She froze, mid-gloss. I looked to the door behind me, praying that I could either pass through it, Casper-style, or that Paola would sense my need for help and barge in. Then I looked to the two girls in front of me to see if they might be of any assistance, but they were so busy talking about their bikini waxer that I could've turned into a giant mango and they wouldn't have noticed. There was no escape.

'Jeeeeean, how lovely to see you. How *are* you?'

Tess's tone was menacingly syrupy, tinged with condescension and saturated in faux friendliness – not dissimilar to the tone used by Hollywood-movie serial killers as they stroked their victims' necks with a large knife.

'You must be so happy with how the Bulls played tonight, particularly Josh. I mean, what a game he had!'

I nodded slowly, wondering where she was heading with this.

'It's fantastic that his ankle held out, isn't it?'

She smiled at me and started rifling through her bag for something. Most likely her phone, to tell Lucifer that she was on her way back down.

What ankle? What was she on about?

'Of course, he's had niggling Achilles tendonitis for years but, I mean, what bad luck to have had a flare-up this week.'

I crossed my arms. What flare-up? And how would she know, anyway?

'Shame you couldn't join us for coffee on Tuesday, but Josh said you were busy . . .'

Shocked into speechlessness, I had no reply. And then someone came in to save the day! Only it was the wrong person. And she didn't so much save as slaughter.

'Oh, it's *Jean*!' said Melinda, strutting out of the cubicle to the sink. 'I was wondering who you were talking to.'

'I was just telling her what a great catch-up Josh and I had the other day.'

'Oh, yeah' – she cleared her throat – 'that's right.'

Melinda wouldn't look at me as she spoke, inferring the possibility that she wasn't *entirely* malevolent, but I didn't feel like sticking around to see more proof, or to hear what would fall from Tess's mouth next. I turned around and pulled the door open. It didn't move. I noticed the 'Push' sign and changed my tactic, already hearing in my head Melinda and Tess's patronising laughter.

I was back in the pulsing crowd, which included a boyfriend who was seeing his ex on the side, and was a world that, to my mind, was *completely fucked up*. My hatred for Tess was now on a subatomic level. My anger with Josh wasn't far behind.

I saw Paola still talking teething and 3 a.m. wake-ups with Janet, which infuriated me even more. With the grape-fuelled devil in me, I realised that the only thing to do right now was to leave. And so, with tunnel vision and deliberate steps, I walked out of the club, onto the street and into a waiting cab.

Josh could ask *Tess* where I'd gone.

# ROUND 37
## Angry Anderson vs Apologies

I woke up with a head that had apparently been infiltrated by a small marching band and a vague recollection of something not great happening last night. I switched on my phone and heard the tinkle of several messages come through.

Where r u? Been looking evrywr! Call me

And the second.

Jean, worried abt u, answr ur phone!

And the third:

No 1 nos where u r! uv just disappeared, pls call me so i know ur ok!!

Goodness! So many exclamation marks, Josh!!!
And from Steph:

Hun, where r u?

Nothing from Paola, which came as no surprise as she was entirely techspastic.

Next, the voicemails:

'Jeanie? Jeanie?' came Josh's voice over hundreds of others, all speaking at foghorn level. 'Are you there?' Then Bones's voice in the background: 'Did she answer?' 'Nah, man, I think it's message bank,' from Josh, then click.

Twenty minutes later: 'Jeanie? Where'd you go? I've been looking all over for you. Call me soon as you get this, okay?'

And once more: 'Jean.' A lot quieter now, with a bit of an echo. Was he in the bathroom? 'I spoke to Melinda. I'm coming over. Listen for the front door, okay?'

I frowned. Did I really sleep through his knocking? I *was* pretty drunk . . . but surely Col would've heard? Maybe she was at Eric's pretending to not be in love with him.

I chucked my hair into a low plait, noticing all the roots coming through as I did so, and opened my bedroom door. It was dead quiet. I walked past Col's room – she wasn't home – and into the living room. I sat down on Ken the Irregular Armchair and thought about what had happened last night. Had I overreacted? It might be that Tess was just making things up again. Or maybe not. Which meant that Tess and Josh *had* been seeing each other, and that Josh had omitted to tell me. I wondered how many times they'd caught up, and whether there was more to her call two weeks back when she'd rung his house.

Hearing my phone blare from the bedroom, I raced in at breakneck speed, my head pounding with each step, and grabbed it off the bed. It was *him*.

'Hello?' I sounded rough. Like I had a deeply entrenched cigarette addiction. And possibly an Adam's apple.

'*Jean!* Jesus, I thought something terrible had happened to you!'
'I'm fine.'

'I'm so relieved! I was at your door at 1 a.m. this morning, you know. Were you there? I was knocking and tapping on windows for a solid hour . . . Look, I've just finished training; I'll have a shower and be right over, okay?'

'Okay.'

'See you soon, Jeanie.'

Click.

I arranged my legs on the sofa to hide any thigh dimples and hit rewind on the CD again. Where the hell was he? It had been well over an hour, and my mind was going into overdrive. Plus I hadn't eaten because my stomach felt a little too unsettled, which made me even more fidgety. I had dressed deliberately in little shorts I knew he loved, and a soft grey singlet, and done my hair half-up, half-down, which was his favourite style. I wasn't sure why I'd done these things, except that I always felt compelled to look 'sexy' these days. Even when emotionally wounded and a little bit LIVID.

A knock at the door. I jumped up, nerves shooting through me as though they had just consumed several shots of Turkish coffee. Opening the door, I tried to maintain my best pissed-off face, but as soon as I saw his concerned blue eyes, his wet hair and his freshly shaved jaw, I had to bite my lip and turn my head to keep from smiling. He was gorgeous and I was screwed.

He pulled a delicate bouquet of flowers from behind his back. They were freesias – my favourite. He remembered! And I had told him that, what, months ago, fleetingly, at that engagement party. I scrunched my mouth to one side to hold back the tenacious smile that was pushing through.

'This is why I'm late.'

'Flowers only come when men have done something wrong,' I shot back, turning and walking purposefully to the sofa.

Following me, he placed the freesias on the coffee table and sat down on the arm of the sofa, sighing. 'Jeanie, Melinda told me what happened last night.'

'I thought, you know, being pro-Tess, she would've kept that little performance to herself.'

'Well, she didn't. She's actually a decent girl underneath all the theatrics. Tess . . . well, Tess kind of screwed her up, to be honest.'

So, he clearly knew Tess was a psycho and *still* he met with her for coffee, at the risk of me finding out! He took his hands out of his pockets and placed one on each thigh.

'Jeanie, I did have coffee with Tess last week, but it's not what you think. And the reason I didn't tell you is because the circumstances didn't even cross my mind as being inappropriate. I was at the physio for my ankle, and there's a cafe next door. I was with Ryan, having a coffee and waiting for the doc, and she was there too, because she has a bad back from an old horse-riding accident. I put her onto my doc years back. Anyway, she came over and sat down with Ryan and me, and asked why we were there, so I told her about my ankle —'

'Why didn't you tell *me* about your ankle?'

'Jeanie, it wasn't intentional! It was a short week, with a Sunday and then a Friday game, and I was just so busy. I wasn't *not* telling you, I just . . . it didn't cross my mind. Anyway, look, I know what she's like, and that she made it out to sound like we'd arranged to meet and I confided in her. But that's horseshit. It was incidental, and I left for my appointment, seriously, not ten minutes later.'

I digested what he was saying. Whenever I thought I had a genuine reason to be shitty with him, he came back with a very logical, reasonable explanation, leaving me feeling ridiculous.

'She happened to be there at the same time as me, that's all. Jeanie, you have to remember that there were some good reasons I broke up with Tess. Her lying and her insecurity and this . . . this schoolgirl bullshit. Trust me, this is not the first time she's played tricks. Not by a long shot. And, you know, that's a big part of why I love you. You'd never pull something like this – it wouldn't even cross your mind to do such a thing. You couldn't be more different from Tess.'

I exhaled slowly, taking in all he had said. Really, there was nothing wrong with what *he'd* done. It annoyed me, but it wasn't criminal. Tess, on the other hand . . .

'So why the flowers?'

'Because I can see how it might have looked to you. And because Tess is . . . well, she's not my *responsibility*, but it's because of my past with her that you're upset. Plus, you're my girl; I should be buying you your favourite flowers more often.' He smiled, looking straight into my tired, red eyes, and moved artfully from the arm onto the sofa. Then a bit closer.

I looked back at him, falling unwillingly into those deep blue pools. But then a spear of anger disrupted the stillness.

'Why does Tess . . . why does she *do* these things? That's what I don't understand. Is she trying to get you back? To split us up? I don't know what's going on. I've never been in a situation like this before.'

He said nothing, thinking about what I'd said.

'I mean, how would you like it if my ex was calling me, or holing you up and making out like we still had something going?'

I looked closely into his eyes, my pupils darting back and forth between his, hoping he saw that I wasn't *angry* with him, just needing his support. He moved over so that he was sitting right next to me, and took my hands in his, his dark eyebrows knitted with concern.

'Tess is a problem, Jeanie, I know that. You've been an angel through all of this, and on top of having just moved here, and having to fall into the whole footy world . . . Even when you have the right to lose your shit, you're still so graceful.'

A tear dropped from my eye. When he said it like that, it occurred to me that I had indeed been tossed into quite the motley little universe.

'So you'll be happy to know I called Tess and told her to cut it out.'

I frowned and dropped my hands from his.

'You called her?'

'Yeah . . . that no good?'

Was I meant to feel okay about that? Even if his call was to tell Tess that she needed to stop tormenting me? Was I becoming hyper-sensitive and super-paranoid? Where was the fucking rule book!

'S'fine.'

His face furrowed in confusion.

'You sure?'

I stood up. 'Yep, it's all good. Hey, um, I gotta get ready for work. Thanks for the flowers.'

'Jean, wait —'

'Josh, I'm fine. I'll be fine. I'm just hung-over and tired.'

I tried to submerge the rockmelon-sized lump in my throat and keep my cool. But I was so far from cool that there weren't enough frequent-flyer points in the world to get from cool to me. Surely it was far too early in the relationship to be feeling so jealous, so inse-cure, so distressed.

'Have I done something wrong? I thought you'd be happy I called her to tell her off.'

'Josh, it's fine, I'm fine. Really!' I smiled, walked to the front door and held it open. Frowning, bewildered, he followed me.

'Well, okay then. So you'll call me later? After work?'

Still offering a feeble smile, I nodded and looked down.

'I love you, Jeanie.' He kissed me gently on the forehead and walked out.

I closed the door and burst into tears.

# ROUND 38
## Disbelief vs Denial

'Wow. I've never seen you look so un-hot.'

Cam was leaning against the counter, performing mouth gymnastics with a toothpick. He got all brave when Ingrid wasn't around, staying in the shop for up to an hour at a time, annoying and baiting me and flirting with customers.

'Shut up, Cam.'

'Seriously, you look even worse than that day after you and Colette went to that benefit thing and ended up doing karaoke till 5 a.m., and you accidentally wore your top inside-out, and you had that *mega* zit on your —'

I stopped folding T-shirts and turned to face him.

'Shut *up*, Cam.'

'Maybe you shouldn't drink so much when you know you have to work. Makes you ugly and full of gnarly lady rage.'

'I knew I was only doing twelve till five, so I thought I would be fine. And anyway, I was home by midnight.'

'Why so aggro, then?'

I shook my head and a mixture of lethargy, anger and upset kicked me in the throat for the fifty-sixth time that day.

'I'm fine,' I said irritably. 'Anyway, shouldn't you be in your *own* shop?'

'I'm on my break.'

'Well, take it then. Why do you have to come and annoy me?'

''Cos it's fun to pick on people when they're hung-over.'

227

'Seriously, Cam, beat it. I'm not in the mood.'

Silence. Maybe he had finally got the message.

'Is it ape trouble? Sorry – boy trouble?'

'You know, Cam, you haven't even met the guy. Can't you lay off him for once?'

'What'd he do? Grab one of the cheerleaders on the arse? Forget to include you in his post-game speech?'

That was it. I spun around and glared at Cam, a T-shirt scrunched up in one of my white-with-rage fists.

'You know, as much as you'd like to think life is simple and all a big joke when you go out with a footballer, it's actually a *total* head screw. It's like being on another planet, and I don't feel like I fit in most of the time, and on top of that, there are some really fucked-up people who make it very clear they don't want me to be there. Okay? So yeah, it's *boy trouble*. You happy?'

His face had dropped with each word I'd spat out. I managed to extract the scrunched-up T-shirt from my hand and refold it before storming over to the counter. Cam turned to face me, hardly daring to say a word.

'Jay . . .'

'Cam. Just go. Please?'

He paused, tapping one finger lightly on the glass counter as I entered the codes for the T-shirts into the computer.

'I'm sorry, Jay; I had no idea. I'm sorry. Usually . . . usually you just throw it right back.'

'Well, today I'm not in the mood. Sorry to ruin your fun.'

'Can I ask what happened?'

I looked at him.

His brown eyes, usually flickering with playfulness, were concerned, unsmiling, full of kindness.

'Jay, what's wrong?'

I locked eyes with him for the briefest moment, but had to look away. It was too intense. It was unsettling to see him like this; it made me feel uncomfortable in an 'Interesting . . . You've never been attractive to me before this moment, yet now I find myself looking away so as to avoid eye contact with you' kind of way.

I cleared my throat. I was clearly not thinking straight. I was overtired and dusty from eighty-three glasses of economically sound riesling. Cam and I had become close and usually had no problems discussing dating stuff, but talking about Josh was different. Partly because I was in love with Josh, and partly because Cam had made paying out on him a sport, which put me on the defensive as soon as his name came up.

I sighed, defeated. 'It's not him, it's his ex.'

Cam's ears pricked up. 'What about her?'

'She bailed me up last night, and made out that her and Josh were still hanging out.'

'Are they?'

He had moved down to my eye level, with his elbows on the counter, and was looking at me closely. I'd never noticed before how long his lashes were; they were incredible. Camel-esque.

'Well no, but . . .'

'But what?'

'Well, they did, but it was accidental.'

He raised one eyebrow then guffawed. 'What, as in he fell on top of her in a club?'

'No! Nothing like that. Look, he explained it all, and it's all fine, I just . . . I don't know, I don't like that they have a past, and that Tess is utterly insane and purposefully tries to get me riled up. And, you know, he wouldn't be having coffee with her in the first place and not telling me about it, innocent as it may have been, if he was truly over her. Would he.'

To say Cam looked unimpressed would not even be approaching the truth; he looked as though I'd just told him I'd walked in on Tess and Josh screwing, and had believed Josh when he'd told me they were only performing an ancient Hindu sheet-cleaning ritual.

'You're fuckin' kidding me.' More disbelieving air-exhalation noises. 'He's lying about seeing her?'

'No, no. Well, *yes*, but it's not what you think . . . Forget it. It's fine.'

I dismissed the situation with my hand, as if the gesture would physically make Cam forget what we were talking about and start ribbing me about my plaits again.

'Uh, no. It's not.' He shook his head, his eyes bulging with anger and disbelief. 'You like this guy – God knows why, but you do – and he's *so* fuckin' lucky to have you. I mean, any guy would kill to have a girl like you, Jean – you're one in a goddamn million. He doesn't even understand what he's got, and then he lies to you? And he's seeing Tess on the side?'

Pause. Rewind. *What?* Any guy would kill to have a girl like me? From which crevice did that fall? Cam's job was to pay me out, not shower me with compliments. I quickly installed my mental stop sign to avoid thinking about what Col and Ingrid had always said about him having a 'thing' for me. He was just Cam. Annoying, panama-wearing, musk-eating Cam.

'Cam, I think you're overreacting a little. You don't know the full story.' I started to clean up the credit-card receipts in a terribly busy and efficient manner, to symbolise that this conversation was over.

Sensing he may have tiptoed over the invisible boundary of *The Jean and Cam Show*, he stood up, bunching his mouth over to one side in thought.

'Jean, just promise me one thing.'

'Mmm?' I was far too busy performing Visa Receipt Management to give him a proper answer.

'That you won't get so caught up in that whole world that you forget how you deserve to be treated. You said yourself that it's all a headscrew. Well, that shit can be contagious, believe me, and you're far too smart and far too beautiful to fall into that kind of cesspit.'

I absorbed Cam's sincerity and his wisdom, not daring to look at his face, instead continuing to stare at the small pile of paper in front of me. When I finally looked up, he was standing there with his hands jammed into his preposterous neon pockets. It was endearing, I decided, the way he was being so protective. Yes, protective – that's the way I would mentally classify today's behaviour. *Protective*, like any brother or male friend would be.

'Sure thing, Cam. Will get it tattooed onto my wrist so I don't forget.'

He shook his head, disappointed. 'You're a loser,' he said, only he didn't smile like he usually did when he signed off with an insult. Before I could say anything else, he turned and walked out, the chain from his wallet swinging against his jeans pocket the only thing to puncture the silence.

I looked at the spot where he'd stood and tried to make sense of what had just happened. And how my perception of him had been quietly disarranged.

# ROUND 39
## Accolades vs Anger

'Geez, Louise, would you *look* at these *earrings*!'

I was sitting with the girls in Cassie's backyard, where Cassie was hosting a barbecue for Camel's birthday, and handing out the pieces I had made for the girls. Cassie was doing her best impersonation of 'casual', in tall wedges, tiny white shorts and a tight blue singlet. Her blonde hair smacked of mousse and upside-down flips, and her bronzer application was neither stingy nor precise.

I hadn't wanted to come. Col and Eric were hosting a small lunch for their closest friends, to announce gently that they were giving things another chance, and I had really, really wanted to be there for Col. But they hadn't told me about it until this morning, figuring there was no chance I would be booked up on a Sunday. Fools! In the football world, Sunday is the busiest day of the week. If it's not a game, it's an airport drop-off followed by shopping with the girls, or an airport pick-up followed by lunch and a movie with Josh, or a club barbecue.

I tried to not see little non-Camel junior running around, with Ryan's mushroomy nose and wide, flat forehead, and I tried hard not to look at Cassie, Ryan, Melinda or Camel in general, lest my eyes give something away, like the fact that Cassie had been sperminated by the wrong man.

As per the *Australian Barbecue Rule Book*, the men were unable to move further than two metres from the barbecue for fear that a mystery sniper would pierce their skulls with a white-hot laser. They stood there in their uniform of thongs or trainers, sunglasses, long baggy shorts and colourful tight T-shirts, beer in hand, muttering about footy and ribbing each other constantly. Meanwhile, the host and her helper (in this case, Cassie's mum Jan, a rotund woman in a floaty pink-and-white kaftan, who looked like she should be writing romance novels in a boudoir somewhere instead of handing out burnt sausages) ran inside and out with food offerings, stopping only to ensure everyone had some form of liquid in their hand at all times.

The ringless, childless girls were grouped together, wedged (the perfect barbecue shoes: height without spikes), blow-dried and glossed, drinking and smoking and talking about shopping and how *amazing* Melinda's new tanning product was, while the drool-covered, dummy-wielding mums and their small human troops occupied another, much larger, table and talked about outrageous day-care prices and which four-wheel-drive was the best and how Yogalates was *really* helping them get their core strength back, as they broke off small sections of bread roll for their children. There were no wedges here, just sandals or ballet slippers, jeans, singlets and the standard enormous black sunglasses.

As usual, Paola, Steph, Lou and I sat together. Since Toiletgate, I had refused to look Melinda in the eyes – a shift that was scarcely of note, since we never really spoke anyway, but in my head was an extremely defiant move. Steph had cautiously mentioned earlier today that Tess and Melinda had gone around telling anyone who would listen that Josh and I were on the rocks after I'd fled the post-match party, and recounting the toilet showdown as a wonderfully entertaining anecdote. I hated the fact that Tess was able to orchestrate people's opinions of my relationship with Josh and nothing could be done about it. Steph had then gone on to tell an epic story involving finding a text from some 'slut called Ashley' in Mitch's phone last week, and the war that ensued. Mitch swore she had only texted *his* phone because she was having it on with Simon Willis, and Simon didn't want his girlfriend to see the texts in *his* phone, so the idea was that Ashley would text Mitch's phone instead. I was stunned by the amount of thought that had gone into the boys' plan, disgusted with both Mitch and Simon, and shocked at how not-shocked Lou and Paola were at the story. Apparently, this kind of behaviour was neither new nor cause for uproar. Steph had eventually taken Mitch's word for it, but only on the basis that he gave her 'total access to his phone' whenever she wanted it. I could offer nothing but frowns and disbelieving headshakes.

As Steph dispensed her anecdotal outrage, I snuck a look at Melinda, who had her usual sour face on. I wanted her to know she was a bitch, and that while I'd always known that, I now had an actual experience to justify my knowledge. She clearly resented me being here, and was working with Tess to ensure I was rattled. The worst part was that it was working.

I felt tougher with my squad. I no longer felt like the New Girl, especially since Brett Langton had shuffled a new girlfriend – Amber – into the fold. I looked at her, glued to his side, quietly trying to extract some conversation from Kate just as I had once done, and made a mental note to go and speak to her as soon as I'd handed out my goods. How things had changed in the past five months, I thought; I was now the lifeguard instead of the swimmer.

I watched on as Lou inspected her new earrings, trying not to look as though I cared too much about her reaction. I'd spent almost three full days making each girl's gift, which was twice as long as it should've taken. But I so badly wanted them to be perfect, and for the girls to like them, and to actually wear them instead of saying they liked them but never taking them out of their little plastic baggy again, that I'd laboured over every tiny detail and colour and bead choice for far too long.

'So you like them?' I asked, nervously.

Lou looked me dead in the eyes, every inch of her face indicating that I had one hand under the table, delicately pulling her leg.

'Are you for *real*? You're an absolute *star*, babe; these are *hot*!' As they so often were, Lou's sentences were riddled with italics. 'I'm gonna put 'em on now. Paola, hold this.' Lou thrust her plastic wine glass into Paola's free hand and started unwinding the huge diamond stud in her left ear.

'You sure you want to do that? You don't want to lose your studs . . .'

'Pfffft, don't be silly. Your earrings will look *heeeaps* better.'

I wasn't so sure about that. The earrings I'd made her were Aztec-inspired turquoise, wood and fuchsia stacks with a beautiful gold drop at the bottom. They were better suited to a breezy white summery dress and a deep suntan, or a black ankle-length halter-neck dress and tan sandals, than her caramel top and black jeans. But if she wanted to wear them now, so be it.

'Huh? *Huh*?' Once she had them in, she turned each side of her head to Paola, Steph and me, eyebrows raised expectantly, lips pouting playfully.

'Ummmmmm, they're kind of the best earrings I've *ever* seen,' said Steph, who until now had been texting away on her phone, stopping only to sip her red wine. She always opted for red if possible; she claimed it was medicinal, whereas white shouldn't just be called 'leg-opener', but 'leg-widener', given the number of kilojoules hiding between the fermented grape juice. Steph had a thing about her weight, even though she had a sexy, swimsuit-modelly figure. She would be struggling to fill a size ten, but she was obsessed with being smaller, and was always slurping on protein shakes or green tea, and skipping lunch to go to the gym.

Paola clapped. 'Okay, bored of her. Mine, please!'

Trying to play down how overjoyed I was that my earrings were a success, I handed Paola her parcel. She began to rip open the paper and then, catching a glimpse of her necklace, stopped.

'*¡Querido! Guapísima! Muchas gracias!*'

We laughed; Paola always slipped into Spanish when she was excited. It sounded wonderful rolling off her tongue: sexy and romantic, and as if she were featuring in a foreign movie with Penélope Cruz or the girl from that Adam Sandler movie about the adorable Spanish nanny.

She unwrapped the necklace carefully, letting all the adornments glide out of the bag slowly so that nothing tangled. It was a three-tiered piece, with dark wood, muted gold and long, oval ivory beads. It was African-inspired. (There was no chance I was going to create something South American-looking – who'd give cowboy boots to a Texan?) As she placed it around her neck – she was wearing a delicate, low, white V-neck singlet, which would work quite well – I insisted on doing it up. I'd spent a lot of time on the clasp because of Paola's new short hair – when she wore the necklace, it would be seen – and with three separate chains all linking back to one clasp, it had been an absolute bitch to make. I did it up and moved around to see it on her.

'Baby, choove outdone yourself.'

Steph had her hand on her chest and was shaking her head. 'Jean, that is *sooooo* nice. Honestly, it's *just* beautiful.'

Lou stood back and took in the whole look. Taking her cue, Paola struck a pose. With her amazing figure, smooth olive skin, toned arms and perfect breasts, my necklace did look amazing. I'd never seen any of my work look so good. Of course, being a model, it was her job to make stuff look good. But still, I felt proud.

'Jimmy! Look what Jeanie made me!' Paola yelled.

Jimmy was a few metres away, talking to Josh. He looked over and nodded, surprised.

'You made that, Jeanie? Jesus, that's pretty good.'

'She's extremely clever, my little Jeanie,' replied Josh, looking at me, his blue eyes impressed and proud simultaneously.

Josh and I had had a strange week after the Tess thing last weekend. We'd talked it all over the night after my weird conversation with Cam, and I was glad, but something still felt unsettled within me. Josh had soothed me and reassured me that there was nothing going on with Tess, but I couldn't ignore my gut, hard as I tried.

I found myself listening in on his phone conversations. I bristled when he sent a text at 10.32 p.m. And I quizzed the girls on the boys' schedules, so that I could catch him out if he said he was somewhere other than what the Bulls had laid out for him. Without even realising it was happening, I was becoming one of Those Girlfriends: paranoid, distrustful, interrogative. Everything I thought I would never be. And I hated it. My role in any romantic script had always been that of the cool, carefree, easygoing girlfriend. But that was before I was going out with a celebrity footballer with a loopy ex-girlfriend.

As it was the lead-up to the semi-finals, the papers were full of 'Foxy'. He and his chiselled abs appeared in a 'Hottest Footballers of the Season' celebration, which stated, along with his height (181 cm), weight (96 kg) and favourite movie (*The Departed*), that he was single. I seethed about this in silence, not wanting to give him the satisfaction of seeing me care about something as silly as what a national newspaper said about my boyfriend's relationship status – as he apparently wasn't in a relationship, and thus I didn't exist anyway, HOW COULD I BE ANGRY ABOUT IT?

It was exhausting, this finals business. All Mum, Godfrey, *anyone* wanted to talk about was footy; even Ingrid had started to care. Obviously, along with the other girls, I was really looking forward to the season being over. Lou was pumped because . . . well, she would finally get pumped, as she put it. Paola was excited because she and Jimmy were flying to New York for a white Christmas. And Steph was off to Thailand for two weeks with Mitch. They weren't alone: around eight other Bulls couples were going to Thailand or

Bali for their break. The reasoning seemed to be that these places were close and cheap enough to offer a solid five-star holiday (and a solid tan) during which a girl could unwind with her footballer boyfriend after he had spent the last eleven months training for or playing a sport about which she cared very little but which dominated every aspect of her life, and during which – hopefully – she might acquire a large diamond set in a platinum ring. Steph was convinced she would be coming home with said diamond.

I believed this to be a dangerous expectation, considering neither she nor Mitch had blown out as many as twenty-three candles on a cake yet. But Steph was convinced it was going to happen. She'd seen a brochure for a jewellers on Mitch's desk, which was apparently all the proof she needed.

Me, I was just looking forward to having time with Josh without the third wheel in our relationship: football. He still maintained that we'd be going to Greece, but everyone else seemed to think he would be picked to play for Australia in the test series, in which case we wouldn't be going anywhere until the Christmas break, which consisted of ten days, at least five of which Ingrid would expect me to work. I was beginning to see the appeal of a quick flight to Denpasar.

'May I see mine now, Jean?' Steph was clapping excitedly in her chair, her newly bleached silver-ash-blonde hair bouncing around her face, as Paola and Lou discussed the merits of artisan wooden jewellery over 'plain old platinum and diamonds'.

I pulled her earrings from my bag. They were delicate drops of thin silver circles intermingled with large, round chocolate-brown and tangerine glass beads that I'd picked up at an antique shop and that I'd been saving for myself; but, wanting to really impress the girls, I'd sacrificed the beads.

Steph gasped.

'Oh – my – *God*. Ohhh! Goody! Goodygoody! I was *so* hoping you'd done silver for me, and you *did*! Oh, I love them. Look, guys, look at mine, aren't they just *glitz*?'

Paola looked at Steph's earrings for a moment, then, shaking her head, looked to me. 'Choo know what happens next, right?' She had one brow raised and one hand on her tiny hip.

I shook my head.

'Choo get your leetle arse home, and choo make a whole bunch more like these, and choo start selling them in that shop. For *big* monies!'

I smiled, blushing. And, half-listening to Steph and Lou carry on – '. . . would pay good money for these, you know . . . can *never* find nice jewellery for, like, night-time, and I don't like that cheap costume stuff . . . don't mind *some* of the stuff in Sportsgirl . . . would look *so* nice with that white dress of yours . . . ' – I began to think that maybe I would.

# ROUND 40
## Scar Tissue vs Wedding Dates

'Think I might just stay home tonight, actually, babe,' I said, yawning.

Josh and I were out the front of my place in his new gunmetal-grey Range Rover. Mike ensured he had a fresh car every few months; with so few kilometres on them, they could still be sold as new. As the engine quietly purred, Josh looked at me curiously.

'Jeanie, what's wrong?'

'Nothing,' I answered in a fashion that implied there were sixty-seven things wrong but I was playing that fun game often played by people owning ovaries where he had to guess one of them before I would admit to it.

He sighed. 'You're not still upset about Tess, are you?'

'No, no, no. Don't be silly. I'm fine. Just tired.'

He paused, still staring at me, me still staring directly ahead.

I was about as good a liar as I was a footballer. He saw straight through me immediately, reaching over to grab my hand and pulling me around to face him.

When I looked at him, I couldn't place quite what I felt. It was a mixture of wanting a little more from him, but knowing he was doing all he could to reassure me. I was angry with myself that I was letting Tess get to me. And if I was brutally, pathetically honest with myself, Cam had confused me. *Had* I changed? Did I deserve better? Was I starting to get tangled up in the cars and the parties and Josh's fame, failing to see the smoke and mirrors that enveloped it? Was Josh just an avenue to an easy lifestyle, and actually more

trouble than he was worth? I'd never had so many issues and insecurities in my relationships with regular, non-spotlight guys.

I was also pissed that I hadn't been with Col today. Plus, the talk
at the barbecue had all but confirmed Josh would get picked for
Australia and be away for two months. Like a cheap polyester skirt,
everything seemed to be slowly unravelling.

'Jeanie, something's up, I know it is . . . Can you please let me
know what's going on up there?'

I gulped, trying to avoid his eyes. Impossible. And as soon as I
glimpsed them, all wide and gentle and concerned, I felt the lump
in my throat rise. Oh, this was absurd. I had no reason to cry. I had
to get out of this car or who knows what would fall from my lips.
Someone had taken over my ship, and I had a feeling it might be
Captain PMS.

'Josh, everything is fine, really. I just had a big week staying up to
work on those pieces for the girls and —'

'They were amazing, my Jeanie. You're so incredibly talented.
Maybe now you've seen how much the girls loved them, you'll be
inspired to make more?'

And what was *that* supposed to mean? If it hadn't been for him
and this stupid football world, I would've had a whole collection in
the shop by now! Inwardly huffing and puffing, I resolved to calmly
remove myself from the car and then go about my blow-up, alone.

'I think I should go. I'm . . . tired and snarky. See you tomorrow,
'kay?'

I looked at him fleetingly. Bad idea. His expression – with his
eyes aimed at the gearstick, and his brows bunched up in confusion – was one of unease and sadness. I kissed him quickly on the
lips, then opened the door and got out. It wasn't till I reached the
front door that I heard him speed off.

I walked in to find the Happy Couple on the sofa. My, how quickly things can change, I thought, recalling a time not long ago when it was Col who would return home to an occupied sofa.

Eric stood quickly when I walked in, straightening himself up and pulling his shirt back into place.

'Hey, WAG-hag,' Col said absently.

'Hey, Col, hey, Eric.'

'Hi, Jean. How was your barbie?'

'Yeah, it was okay.'

I put my bag down on the dining table and took off my – Col's – leather jacket.

'How did it go today?' I said to anyone who felt like answering.

Col, who now had her head resting on Eric's lap, looked up at him, her smile gooey, her face soft. He returned her gaze with a knowing smile, and began playing with a rogue curl that had fallen onto his wrist.

'It went really, really well,' she said finally.

Eric carefully lifted her head and stood up again, excusing himself to go to the bathroom. Col propped her head on her hand and looked at me.

'You look fug. What's up your arse?'

I slapped on a fake smile and shook my head. 'Nothing. So, tell me about today. I'm so sorry I missed it . . .'

'Price I pay for having a sister who'd rather hang with thugs and their trophy wives.'

I bit my tongue. I found that comment incredibly inflammatory, even though it was just Col being Col, but I didn't want a fight.

'So,' I said through gritted teeth, 'who came?'

'Oh, you know, Holly and the girls, Lucas and Adrian and a few other of Eric's deadshit friends. Pretty much everyone who already knew we were back together, whether we'd told them or they'd figured it out for themselves.'

'Oh. Oh well. I'm glad you had a nice time with all your friends. I'm sure they're all very happy for you – for you both.'

I went to my room but Col followed me, pushing the door closed behind us.

'Jay?' she said quietly.

I sat down on the bed. What now? I was irritable and wanted only a shower and sleep.

'I know this Eric thing is weird for you.'

'Mm-hmmm . . .'

'You're not the only one freaking out, trust me. But I wanted you to know that it's just a trial. We're taking things slowly. You know, a lot of shit went down when we split, and there's a good chance we won't be able to get past it. Me, especially. I mean, you've seen us – one day we're all loved up; the next, I want to tear his fucking arms out.'

I smiled. I had to admit I was relieved.

'I think that's a good idea, Col. Really good. I would hate for —'

'I know, I know, for me to get hurt again. And that's why I love you. Even though you ate all the bread, and used my ghd and left it on and could've burned the whole joint down.'

'But I wa—'

'Shoosh. Don't care, whatever. Go to bed, snarkyarse; see you in the morning.'

With that, she kissed me on the cheek, spun on her heel and went back to the sofa and her trial boyfriend.

# ROUND 41

## Misguided Jealousies vs
## The Twinklings of Truth

According to Godfrey, I was in danger.

'Where can you go from here? Any man after Josh can only suffer at the hands of what it was like to be with a professional football star. Your standard of living will be stratospheric!'

I laughed as Mum tore the phone from his hands.

'Now, you know I'll be down next weekend? I'm showing the princess on Saturday, which means we can all spend some time together Sunday. I'd like to get the full story on this Eric situation with both of you there. I don't know that Colette's telling me the full story.' ZING! So she *did* know about them being back together. I decided not to ask her thoughts on it. Now wasn't the right time, as I was likely to plant several verbal spears into Eric. 'Oooh! Maybe we can do some shopping!' she continued with glee. Mum loved to shop in the Big City; there so many more animal prints on offer.

Oh shit. Hang on, Sunday was the day I was going to be at Morgan's for her Semi-final Spa-palloza, where all the WAGs were going to have manis and pedis and champagne and massages and blow-dries before heading off to the game in limos. I couldn't help wondering what we'd do if the Bulls got into the grand final. Caviar facials and golden helicopters?

Actually, I didn't mind Morgan. She was being quite nice to me these days. Paola said it was because she had fallen out with Tess, so was free to befriend me now. She'd been through a bitch of a time lately: Phil had been busted cheating on her – publicly, because the nineteen-year-old he'd cheated with (in the pokies room at an inter-state nightclub, no less) had gone to the papers – and the media scrutiny of the 'perfect glamour couple' had been heavy. Phil had bought Morgan pistachio-sized diamond earrings to make up for it, but apparently didn't need to, as she was unfaltering in her support for him. Which I found a bit bizarre. She was telling anyone who'd listen that the girl in question was a filthy little slut and had slept with half the players in the comp, and wouldn't have said a word to the press if Phil had bothered to put her in a cab afterwards.

I understood why she was upset, but I found Morgan's venom towards the girl a little unsettling, considering it was her long-term boyfriend who was as much at fault – perhaps even more so, con-sidering his age and the fact that he had a live-in girlfriend. And yet there she was, snuggling up to him at breakfast in the social pages of the Sunday papers. Paola was convinced Morgan was a fool, and that Phil had been playing up for years, but even she couldn't get through to her. Morgan was simply not prepared to end her relationship over this indiscretion. I'd wondered if maybe she might be pregnant, and needed to keep the relationship for that reason, but the way she put away champagne after the match ruled out that idea.

I guess it just came down to what you were willing to put up with as a WAG. I was certain that in the same situation I would break up with Josh straight away. Cheating is not okay in my books; I don't care how famous you are. And the arrogance of doing it in a night-club, with people all around, spoke volumes about how invincible some of the boys thought they were, not to mention how much they drank on a big night out. Phil was a pig.

Mum was still waiting for an answer on shopping. I would have to find a way to do both. I was sure I could manage it: I'd just sneak off from Morgan's for an hour or two.

The first twinkling of summer air had drifted in and work was revolting: furiously busy, boxes upon boxes of new stock, and lots and lots of customers looking for formal dresses for the races, or flippy, flirty dresses for parties. Finally able to sneak out for a bite at 2.30, I walked next door, exhausted and starving, to see if Cam was around and wanted to come with me.

I saw him as soon as I walked into the store, serving a gorgeous little thing with icy-blue eyes and a sweet little blue dress, waistcoat, sandals and a tangle of string necklaces and bracelets. He was laughing and smiling with her as he rang up a denim belt miscast as a skirt. She flicked her hair from side to side, smiling coyly; he leaned forward on the counter, his eyes gripping hers, making her laugh, flirting with Olympic-style skill and prowess.

I stood in the bikini section, pretending to fondle an eighties-style one-piece but unable to tear my eyes away from Cam and pretty Little Miss Waistcoat. I watched as he wrote down what was probably *not* his grandma's Mars Bar cookie recipe and held it out to his little doe-eyed princess. Who took it. And smiled. And flicked her hair cutely before closing her tan leather vintage handbag and picking up her shopping. *Ooh*, look at *me*, I'm so cool with my eclectic jewellery and totally alternative waistcoat and op-shop bag.

Watching her walk out, I wasn't sure what stunned me more: my malice, or the effect that seeing her and Cam carrying on had had on me. I collected myself quickly and walked purposefully towards the counter, watching Cam watching her walk away.

'Love at first purchase?'

Cam's head whipped around to me.

'Where'd you spring from?' His face was flushed with being-bustedness.

'She was cute. Reckon she'll call?'

A smile spread slowly over his face. It was spicy. I didn't like it.

'Yeah, actually. We're gonna go and see Dreamer play next week,' he said, with feigned insouciance. 'She comes in every now and then. Ava, her name is.'

'She legal yet?'

He looked at me. 'Yes, she's twenty-three, actually.'

'Ooooh, he already knows her age. Must be love. I'm sure – if she can lift her arm, with all of those bangles – she'll call.' He raised one eyebrow. I bulldozed on, unable to stop. 'But are your star signs compatible, that's the *real* question. Actually, does she like house music? *That's* the real question.'

He continued to look at me with an expression I couldn't quite figure out – but I think it might have been a sibling of disgust's.

'What's your go?'

'What?' I said, smiling in what I hoped was a totally normal fashion.

'You're being all twisted and bitchy.'

'No I'm not. I'm just screwing with you.' I folded my arms.

'Whatever.' He turned around and started tinkering with the cash register.

'You're incredible, you really are. You can tease and terrorise me whenever you like, but the *moment* the tables are turned, you get all defensive.'

'There's a difference between teasing and being a bitch.' He still had his back to me.

'Ex*cuse* me?'

'Well, you don't even know her, and you're being gnarly. You know, you actually sounded just like a jealous gir—'

'Go on.' My voice was slow and saturated with barely disguised fury.

'Nothing. Forget it. Why'd you come in, anyway?'

'Never mind.' I shook my head in disbelief, spun around and walked out of the shop. He could have his silly little Ava. What did it matter to me? I didn't care. *So* didn't care. Couldn't care less than if a giant care extractor had come along and extracted every last ounce of the stuff from my body. I walked out of the shop in a huff and started towards the revolting sandwich shop on the corner. It would have to do. Just as I reached it, I ran into Col and, of all people, Frank.

'*Frank!* Hi! God, haven't seen you for ages!' We kissed on the cheek and smiled genuinely at each other. I adored Frank, he was such a winner.

'I know. Bet you miss your handsome brother-in-law, huh?'

I laughed. Same old Frank.

'Very much. Josh does too – what's with all the travel?'

Frank had received a promotion a few months ago and now seemed to travel non-stop, both interstate and throughout Asia.

'I'm too good at my job, so they make me train people all over the place. It's tough being lauded as some kind of idol. The pressure is intense, but someone has to do it, right Col?'

Uh-oh, he still looked at her like that. Poor Frank. I wondered if he had any idea about Eric or if he still thought he had a chance with her.

'So, what are you two doing?' The curiosity was oozing from my pores.

'Oh, you know, Frank and I ran into each other. At my office. *At my desk.*' Col shot Frank a wry smile. 'And now he's accompanying me to the bank because he was' – she made quotation marks with her fingers – 'heading that way anyway.' Despite her sarcasm, she was smiling.

'Ahhh, I see . . .' I said, not really seeing at all. I wondered if they had caught up before and Col had failed to tell me, but figured it was probably more a case of Frank being obsessed with her and having another shot at the title.

'Okay, well, I'd love to stay and chat but I'm *starving* and—'

'Fine by me, Jay. I'm happy to have Col all to myself. Even if that does make her nervous because she knows deep down she wants to kiss me passionately and may not be able to control herself.'

Col rolled her eyes and I stifled a laugh.

'I've told Frank that I'm off the market but he —'

'Yeah, and with the ex! Jay, how did you let this happen?' Frank's expression had become one of disbelief.

'Um . . .' I looked to Col for help.

'If Jay'd had her way, there would be no ex. Trust me.'

'*See?*' Frank said emphatically. 'Your sister sees the error of your ways!'

'Frank? Please drop it. I told you before, Eric and I are just giving things a go. Jesus, I'm not *marrying* the guy.'

'Well, you know what they say – if you go backwards, you fall over . . .'

'Frank, I know what I'm doing, okay? As I explained before, if I don't do this, I'll always wonder what could've been, and I don't want to live that life. Now, can we drop it? Please?'

I saw Col's eyes flash with irritation and decided now would be a really awesome time to leave.

'Hey, so, Frank, I'll see you at the game, right? How are you going to get to the stadium? I could give you a lift, if you like . . . God, you know what? We can sort that out later, I gotta eat and get back to the shop. See ya, Frank. Later, Col!'

I blew them a kiss and dashed off, wondering very much where their heated little conversation would end up. I had to commend Frank's impressive persistence, but I had a feeling that even he couldn't penetrate Col's steely resolve. Very few things could.

# ROUND 42
## The Past vs The Future

'See that column over there – that big yellow thing?' We were sitting on a flat boulder, overlooking the city from a perspective I'd never imagined existed. It was incredible – almost worth the forty-five minutes of steep climbing in gripless shoes that it took to get up here – and I loved that Josh had insisted we do this together, especially in such an important week for him, in the lead-up to the semi-final. Feeling included, feeling like a priority when everyone wanted a piece of him was, I was embarrassed to admit, both blissful and a bit of an ego trip.

'About five years ago, some mates and I came up here and got completely ripped. And we all swore that column was Homer Simpson, and I think we laughed for about twelve hours about it. Can you see how it kind of looks like him, with the shirt and the . . .?'

He looked at me, excited, eyebrows raised, finger extended towards the yellow mass in the distance, and I laughed, shaking my head.

'Noooooot really, I'm afraid.'

'Well, next time you take a couple of hits from a huge skull-shaped bong, come up here and try again.'

'Of course. That's if I can get up here with all the chip sandwiches and Mars Bars I'd need to sustain my munchies.'

He looked into my eyes, smiling, and planted a kiss on my lips.

'What was that for?'

'What, I'm not allowed to kiss my girl?'

He was beaming at me, and knowing what an anxious week this

was for him, it was enormously comforting to see him so calm and happy. I admired his chilled-out state of mind – he was always calm under fire. It was sexy, I thought.

Having never paid attention to football previously, I'd been unaware of the whopping media focus and intense build-up leading into the finals. It was bordering on ridiculous. Every day the headlines screamed about what the boys ate for breakfast, whether any of them had been spotted anywhere 'inappropriate' leading up to the game or, God forbid, having a drink. There were photos of Nick, Lou and the kids wearing Bulls jerseys, posing cheesily in their backyard, and – my personal favourite – a photographic trip down memory lane for Josh Fox, from his first game at five years of age to his shirtless Men of League calendar shots. It was nuts.

'You know, Jean Bennet,' he said, leaning in and kissing me again, 'I shouldn't be up here with you. Not only is it dangerous physically – I could trip and injure myself – but we're meant to resist all "temptation" before the semi. Coach's rule. The thing is, you look very tempting in that little singlet . . .'

I kissed him in return, passionately, forcefully, then pulled back and looked him dead in the eyes, gripping the collar of his polo shirt.

'Let's do it. Right here. Come on.' Josh's eyes flashed, seemingly unable to comprehend what I was suggesting. 'What, are you shy? Scared your coach will find out?' I watched his face as his brain clicked and whirred with the possibility being presented to him. 'Come on, over there behind those trees.' I stood up, dusted off my shorts and held a hand out to him.

'Really? Jean . . . are you sure about this?'

'Course! I've always wanted to make love propped up against a whopping great eucalypt —' I couldn't play the game any longer; laughter tumbled from my mouth.

'Ohhh Foxy, the look on your face,' I said, catching my breath.

'Honestly, you love to play the Casanova, but when push comes to shove . . .' I climbed onto his back, piggyback-style, and kissed him on the cheek. It felt good, *so* good to be playful and fun with him again.

He grabbed my wrists from around his chest and kissed them. 'Ohhhh, you're a little piece of work. 'Swat I love about you. So easy, so fun . . . so low-maintenance.'

'That makes me sound like I don't shower or brush my hair.'

'You know what I mean.'

I peeled myself from his back and came to sit close by his side on the rock again. He wrapped his arm around me.

'With you, it's never hard. And that's how it should be, you know? I always have fun with you. You prop me up, give me some perspective away from footy and all of that stuff. I think – and I'm sorry to bring her up – but with Tess, I think I was confusing "hard" with "passionate", and assuming that because our relationship required so much work, it must've meant we really loved each other, because we were always working so hard to keep it alive. But being with you, I can see how wrong I was.'

I turned to face him, smiling. He came out with some very emotionally evolved stuff for a guy. Impressive.

'I suppose if I'm dead honest,' he continued, 'with Tess there was an element of showmanship, too. I felt like I had to have this girlfriend who was . . . over-the-top flashy and, well, I guess high-profile, because that's what you're meant to do when you're a footy guy, you know? I even remember my manager pushing it, saying that it would help my profile, and that it looked great for the club because of her dad being Henry, and the media loved a power couple, and . . . *maaaaan*.' He stopped and shook his head. 'It's pretty twisted, Jeanie. Like, okay, the perks and everything are great, and I'm grateful for that stuff, but none of it comes free. There is so much arse-kissing and shit talk that comes with it, and when you're young, and you're suddenly thrown all this money and everyone knows your name, it can be hard to remember that no one actually cares about who *you* are, who you *really* are, they just want a piece of who they think you are, or who they want you to be, because it makes them sound cool to know a footballer.'

Sensing he was on a roll, I stayed quiet.

'And I see it happening to the young boys coming through, you know, and part of me wants to shake them, and sometimes I try to guide them a little bit. But in the end, it's their lesson to learn. It's just fucked, though, when you see them living this David Beckham-style life, which they can't really afford, and playing the local hero, and then cut to ten years later, when they're too old for first-grade and they've spent all their cash and no one wants to know them any more. I'm just lucky I had Dad and Frank there when I was younger, because I was heading for that end *real* fast.'

Josh had never opened up to this extent; I wasn't quite sure how to respond. I decided that my only job was listening. That, I could do.

'Anyway, enough about that. Past-life stuff. Point is, I'm glad I'm out of all that shit, and being with such an honest, down-to-earth girl makes me realise just *how* glad.'

He took my hand and kissed it. He was so touchy-feely-kissy tonight! Maybe it was the fresh air – I needed to bottle some of it. And to wear this singlet more often.

'Well, I'm glad you're happy. And that you avoided a rock-star demise. It's funny, I can't imagine you being all flashy party guy —'

'Jean, if you'd met me a few years back, you would've thought I was a complete tool. Mainly because I was. You wouldn't have given me the time of day.'

'Hmmm. Well, if you say so . . . Hey, any word on your contract stuff?'

On top of the semi-final, Josh's head was full of decisions to make about his future, and I knew it was stressing him out. And despite having roughly as much clue about football as did a piece of furniture, I felt privileged to be able to let him bounce ideas off me. Though of course, whenever the conversation arose, it made me nervous and a little bit sick to think of him changing clubs, states or even countries. Now he sighed.

'Well, yes and no. It's all coming down to the length of the contracts being put up – there've been some good offers from local clubs, but they're all two-year deals. We've even had a couple from the UK and France, which is pretty cool. As I said at Mike's, the last thing you want is to be coming off contract at twenty-nine – that's footballer suicide. No one wants to buy someone that old, and if they do it's for fuck-all money. So that's where we're at: trying to push for a four-year deal, because I need the security. I'm happy to play the last couple of years by ear, but not now. I've got two mortgages to pay off plus, you know, I want to come out of football comfortable, set up, not needing to find a job straight away to support my family . . . or whatever.'

I tried not to think about being part of that family, instead concentrating on other aspects of what he'd just said.

'A Real Life job – imagine that. What would you do, do you think?'

'Well, I started an industrial engineering degree at uni before I began playing first-grade. I only have one-and-a-half semesters under my belt, but I think I'm going to try and finish it by correspondence. My uncle's a partner in this big aviation engineering firm, and he's going to let me come and do some work experience. He reckons I should chuck the degree and get on-the-job training, but I don't know. I don't think it's the kind of field where you can dismiss all the science and theory, and I kind of like learning about all that stuff, anyway.'

'You're a nerd. You're actually a complete nerd. And yet, you've got everyone fooled into thinking you're some big jock . . .'

He dropped his head and smiled self-effacingly, all but scuffing the ground with his shoe.

'Nahh, I just enjoy it, is all. Love all the puzzle-solving. I feel like since being a footy player, I've been utilising about thirty per cent of my brain's potential, and I can't wait to get into it, to be honest.'

As Josh spoke of this pull he felt towards career #2, something swelled inside me. After all, it was explicitly clear in the football world that playing wasn't for ever, and when one of the Bulls boys, Andy Nash, had suffered a horrific, career-ending neck injury a few games back, it had served as a bit of a wake-up call to everyone, Josh included.

Lou and Steph constantly ruminated over what Nick and Mitch could possibly do after football. Nick had done cabinet-making before he went into first-grade, but Lou didn't think a bit of wood-work was going to be enough to support their family, especially in the comfortable lifestyle they currently enjoyed. Steph was convinced that Mitch would buy a pub somewhere semi-rural, like so many ex-footballers did, and expect her to move there with him while he acted as owner/manager/all-round nice guy. On her happiness scale, this situation would rate just below being told her brand-new Volkswagon Golf had been decimated by an out-of-control semitrailer. She was a city gal, and she wasn't moving to 'no shit-hick town to have ten kids while he drinks every night'. When I thought about it, the girls' slant was undeniably negative – and not only when they were talking about the future, either. I guess it was a pretty intense life, being a WAG, and especially after a few years of it. I wondered if – when – I would become jaded. I could definitely see how it might happen.

I wasn't sure whether I would be around when Josh finally gave up his football career and morphed into Mr Engineer, but as I looked at him sitting there – gorgeous, smart, insightful and, astonishingly, choosing to be with *me* when he could have any girl he wanted snuggling into his side, taking in this magnificent view – I couldn't help hoping I would.

# ROUND 43
## Footballers' Wives vs
## Family Matters

'That is the most *lushest* shade. I want that one too . . .'

Steph was looking at the plum varnish dancing on my finger-nails, her head tilted to one side, her extremely low and tight pink top overflowing with boob. She was wearing too much makeup, as usual, and I had to consciously stop my hand from blending in her blush, which had spread lazily over the entire side of her face.

We were sitting in Morgan's lounge: tiled and neutral-toned to interior-decorator perfection, with an enormous flatscreen TV dominating one entire wall and weekly magazines fanned over the glass coffee table. It was the Semi-final Spa-palloza and all the girls were dressed as though they were about to walk into a bar, with tight jeans or skirts, low-cut tops (more breast on offer than Charcoal Charlie's front window), four-inch heels and tanned, toned legs.

I'd gone with tight black pants that were pretending to be jeans, Col's new black skyscraper heels and a sexy, J. Lo-y top in peach. I felt way cooler, taller and skinnier than ever before, thanks to the height of the shoes. Freshly highlighted, straightened hair with a sexy centre part, simple gold hoops, a touch of self-tanned cleavage and a whole lot of arse completed the look. I felt like Cheryl Cole – or her sister, at least. It was a good feeling.

We were having our nails done, sipping on champagne and peach nectar, and listening to sugary R'n'B. All around us the other WAGs were talking loudly, ducking outside for ciggies, gossiping, constantly toying with their hair, checking their phones, texting, and squealing with apparent excitement about the game. Melinda claimed that she was so anxious she hadn't slept, while Cassie was talking up the benefits of Valium and bourbon to soothe the nerves the night before a big match.

I had slept fine. After my little moment with Cam the previous week, I'd vowed to get things back on track with Josh. And that was all going swimmingly now. Cam was a little arsehole and that would be the last time I allowed anything he had to say to get under my skin. He could take his Ava and shove it.

Happily, Josh had been incredibly receptive to the 'old Jean' resurfacing, and with our hike as the highlight, we'd had a great week – well, as much of it as we'd been able to spend together, given Josh's schedule. He was in excellent spirits: excited but calm, optimistic about a win.

Paola was running late, and Lou's babysitter had cancelled so she was not coming at all. Thank God for Steph – I felt slightly like I was at the wrong party, with Melinda, Morgan, Cassie and co. running the show. That said, Morgan was making a real effort to include me, playing the ultimate hostess, and constantly – tipsily – reminding us that we were all entitled to fifty per cent off their spray-tans. I couldn't be sure, but I think she'd had another several kilos of hair attached to her head, as well as going for a triple spray-tan and man-aging to find the lowest jeans in Sydney. Her tanned, freckled chest was merely a backdrop to her enormous breasts, which sat cosily in a Wheels & Dollbaby black-and-pink bustier, waving merrily to all those who laid eyes on them.

I felt my phone buzz and tried to retrieve it from my handbag with-out jeopardising my still-wet nails. When I finally answered, it was Col.

'Are you still coming? Mum and I are waiting.'

Oh fuck. Fuck, fuck, *fuck*! I looked at the time and was sud-denly, sharply sober. I was meant to be meeting them at Patterson Avenue, forty-five minutes away, for our catch-up and shopping trip. Because I had left for the hairdresser's at eight that morning, I hadn't seen Mum or Col and had missed the vital reminder conversation. I stood up and walked out of the dining room for some quiet.

'Um, well . . . Shit, Col, I —'

'Tell me you're not still with the cheerleaders?' her voice was incredulous. I could hear Mum parroting her question in the background.

'Yes, but I'm leaving right now —'

'Have you been drinking?'

I mentally counted: three drinks. That qualified as a yes.

'I'll just jump in a cab – easy.'

'Oh yeah, 'cos you've got fifty dollars to spare on a cab ride after pumping your entire salary into your hair. Tell me, how did you *think* you were going to get here?'

I had no answer. I listened to Col explain to Mum what was happening, feeling a deep, wide hole forming in my gut. 'No, she's still there . . . she's been drinking so she can't . . . wouldn't be able to find it anyway, she can barely find her way home from work . . . No Mum, don't worry about it . . .' Then she was back in my ear.

'You know what, Jay? You've really taken this WAG shit too far.'

'What are you on about —'

'I mean, you'd clearly rather hang out with a bunch of vacuous blow-up dolls, and talk about nails and hair and your totally awesome footballer boyfriends, than with your mum, so good one, sis. Hope it's worth it. You fit better and better into that world every day.'

Click.

I closed my mouth, shocked, listening to the tone of being hung up on. I thought of Mum – all excited about spending the afternoon with her girls, who she hadn't seen for months, shopping, and stopping for coffee and cake and gossip – and how I'd let her down. I sat on one of Cassie's gold-and-white dining chairs, the guilt rolling over me in waves.

Hang on, maybe I *would* take a cab. Maybe I would surprise them and show up! I looked at the time on my mobile. It was already nearly 2.30; by the time I got there it'd be three, and with the game starting at five . . . I couldn't do both. I had to choose.

Cassie walked in on her way to the bathroom and spotted me sitting there, fighting back tears.

'Hun! Are you okay?' She came over and kneeled next to me, her hand on her knee. 'What's happened?'

I shook my head, looking into her huge eyes framed with coat upon coat of mascara and black liner. I thought about her hiding her secret from Camel all these years, and the fear of him finding out and leaving her, and the guilt she must feel on a daily basis for that one mistake . . .

'Nothing, Cassie. I'm fine. It's just that, well, I was meant to meet my sister and Mum somewhere and I forgot, and they're pissed at me.'

The look in her eyes softened.

'Is that it? *God*, hun, I thought someone had carked it!' She laughed hysterically. 'They'll get over it. Just make it up to them with some flowers – does the trick every time. I use Fantasia, they're *amazing*.' She winked and stood up. She was right, I thought. I had made a mistake and I was in trouble, but they would get over it.

'What *you* need is a daiquiri!' Cassie clapped her hands and looked at me for a nod of agreement and the unspoken sign that should I accept this frozen beverage, I would stop moping and move on and be fun again.

I managed a weak smile. 'You're right.'

She clapped her hands even faster and yipped, skipping off towards the kitchen. She stopped just before walking in and turned to me.

'By the way, hun, *love* your hair blonde. Looks *so* much hotter.'

# ROUND 44

## Mad Monday vs Mobile Phone Lunacy

'What are you looking at?'

I was propped on one elbow, staring at a just-waking-up Josh.

'Just enjoying the view while I have it.'

'Oh. Very funny.' He smiled and closed his eyes again. 'Why are you even up? It's too early . . .' He frowned and groaned, covering his head with the pillow.

'Awww, we a little bit hung-over, mate? Hey? Little bit sick? Little bit dusty? Little bit under the weather?' I prodded him annoyingly in the bum as I spoke.

'Mmm. Someone must have slipped me a bad ice-cube.'

I laughed. 'Come on, dirtboy, get up. It's ten and you've got Bones's party to get to.'

As the boys had lost last night's semi-final, it was now Mad Monday, which meant they would drink and drink and drink for as many days as their bodies would allow them. The girls *hated* Mad Monday because their boys disappeared for several days, with no phone contact, no regard for personal hygiene and no desire for sobriety.

Steph was particularly opposed to it because Mitch was a horrendous drunk, and was often found passed out in a park or bus shelter. Last year he'd ended up at the bottom of a slippery slide with no ID, no shirt, no phone and no keys, asking for creaming soda. And none of the boys had even noticed he was missing! Lou was similarly disenchanted, as Nick had a penchant for taking copious amounts of whatever drug he could lay his hands on, and she worried he would end up at a brothel, or on a plane to Vegas, or dead in a gutter somewhere. And Cassie, somewhat ironically, hated Mad Monday because she said it was when the boys were most likely to play up with the swarm of faithful groupies who had followed them from bar to bar all season.

As it was my first Mad Monday, I didn't know quite what to expect. But I couldn't imagine Josh would simply not contact me for days, and I knew he didn't do drugs, so I wasn't too concerned. Josh said that in order to hide from the media and the public, they usually hung out at one of the boy's places, or a filthy local pub that no one but a few dirty old barflies frequented.

'Already? But we just went to bed . . .'

He was only millimetres from the truth; we'd all had a very, *very* big night commiserating that the Bulls wouldn't be in the grand final. I'd never seen grown men become so emotional: some had cried and others had simply gone mute, but most had just drowned their sorrows in glass after glass of vodka.

Despite the loss, it had been a good night; I'd stayed out until an hour usually reserved for paperboys and tai chi types, and Josh had stumbled in at 8 a.m. Paola and Jimmy had come, even though Jimmy was in a foul mood for most of the night – partly because his team wouldn't be playing in the grand final, and partly because his injury had proven to be even worse than first thought, and after two months of pain, he was in for another three. Paola's way of dealing with this was to pull up her little black dress and flash her butt whenever she walked past him, and to throw ice-cubes at him when she was dancing.

After a lot of whingeing, and approximately 400 calls and texts from Bones and the others, Josh dragged himself into the shower, claiming he'd only be drinking lemonade today. I lay there wondering how they could start drinking again having finished only a few hours prior, if that. Bones clearly hadn't slept; according to his last text, he was currently playing Wii in the nude, to the enjoyment of ten or so grown men.

When Josh emerged from the shower, it was clear that he was in awful shape, hung-over as hell and feeling sick in the gut. I'd give him till tonight, tops. Maybe we'd even be able to see a 9 p.m. movie, I thought happily.

By Tuesday afternoon I was flirting with madness. I had not seen or heard from Josh since dropping him at Bones's yesterday. Steph had told me that even if you're going *nuts*, the golden rule is not to call the boys on Mad Monday. She said that last year Bones had dropped Alistair McDoherty's phone into a glass of beer because his girlfriend was calling him too much. Bones was a turd, I had decided. But I was obedient. I'd written a few texts, but saved them as drafts and sent none. I didn't want to be The Girl Who Didn't Know The Rules.

I looked at my phone for what felt like the third time in half an hour: still nothing. I put it on silent and left it out the back of the shop in the storeroom so that I wouldn't be tempted to keep checking. After two solid hours of no looking, I rewarded myself with a peek, *positive* he would've made contact. But he hadn't, and I went all psycho again and brought the phone back out to the counter. I hated this archaic, insipid game!

Have you heard from Mitch yet??

Maybe Steph had heard from her man – who would obviously be with my man – and then I would know he was still breathing and not nude, wrapped in packing tape and tied to a bus stop on Market Street with 'Beware Fox – I will steal your chickens!' written on his torso. With people like Bones and Camel around, I just couldn't be sure, especially with thirty-six hours of drinking tucked messily under their belts.

No!!! u?? If i don't hear frm hm soon i'm dumpin him! srsly, they r unblvble . . . let me now if u hr frm Josh xox

Fuckit. There was no point asking Paola, as Jimmy wasn't drinking because of his injury, and Lou had only allowed Nick to go if he came home by the time she woke up, because now that they had kids, she was allowed to make excellent rules like that.

Being Tuesday, the shop was agonisingly slow. And of course Cam was a shithead, so I didn't want to talk to him. And Col was still pissed at me from Sunday, even though I had totally made it up to Mum yesterday morning, so I had way too much time to think about my silent phone.

Driving home, my concern and worry for Josh started to liquefy into anger. It was now 6.30 and he still hadn't called or texted. So much for 'not being up for a big one' and 'getting older now' and 'can't go too hard in case I get picked for the Australian team and have to go into camp'. What a load of bullshit! He was just like the rest of them: a little caveman who had to do whatever his equally Neanderthal companions were doing.

I thumped the radio button to off, to give my rage more room. I needed to think, to analyse, to wonder how I would play it when he finally did call. Probably, I decided, I would let it ring out for the first 600 times. Then, when I did answer, I would sound as though I were incredibly busy and hadn't even *noticed* he hadn't called, because it was entirely normal for your boyfriend not to call for several days, and I was having too fabulous a time to care about what he and the Great Apes were doing.

Arriving home, I was faced with an emptiness that further compounded my off feeling. I was so hoping Col would be home, so that we could take Dave for a walk and she could listen to my whingeing and bitching about Josh and the boys. But as she was still being gnarly, she wouldn't be interested anyway, let alone home.

Suddenly – triumphantly – I knew what had to be done. I would order something fatty and exquisite from a carbohydrate service provider, and I would sit at the desk and I would make jewellery, dammit! *Lots* of jewellery: incredible, delightful, sexy, expensive jewellery. Enough was enough. Josh did whatever he needed to or wanted to for his career, and I just fell into place around it, like foam squishing into a box to cushion an expensive vase. I was sick of not putting the same kind of dedication into *my* career.

# ROUND 45
## The Wonder WAGs vs The Sleazy Exes

I woke with a start, feeling my eyes open abruptly like I was some kind of possessed child in a horror movie. There was no reason I should be awake this early. It wasn't even entirely light outside, and I hadn't gone to bed until 2.24 a.m., because I hadn't allowed myself to sleep until I had ten finished pieces for Ingrid. (During this undertaking, I had accidentally consumed a twelve-pack of Freddo Frogs, which further inhibited sleep.) I had finally fallen into bed woozy with pride, mentally drained and lazily hissing at Josh.

I looked at my phone. It spat back an empty screen. I added another 500 to the number of calls I wouldn't be answering when Josh finally decided that I deserved a call. I tried to go back to sleep. I was weary and cranky and in no shape to serve those customers who insisted they were two sizes smaller than they were, even if it meant that the alluring roll of fat around their gut was pushed up to create a kind of third horizontal boob. Into the bargain, it was Wednesday, the day the uni students got their government payments. The more fashionable of them usually shuffled into the shop and blew their rent on a new top. They knew that looking good earned them astronomical tips at whichever seedy bar they worked in, and so an expensive new top was actually an economically sound investment. I had to agree, and did so enthusiastically – all the way to the till. Finally, I decided to get up and treat myself to breakfast at Cafe 78 before work. Hotcakes and espresso would get me on track.

I sat in the back corner of the cafe, still an hour too early to open the shop, and pulled out my final pieces of jewellery – three sets of earrings and a cuff. How could I best present them to Ingrid? She was all about presentation. She checked her lips in the mirror every forty seconds or so, constantly scanned the racks for rogue coathangers jutting out, and was relentlessly telling me I should dye my hair back to brown – and cut it, too. Of course, she did so in such a subtle fashion that sometimes I struggled to catch her point: 'Look at Victoria Beckham,' she'd say. 'The fashion world only started to take her seriously when she got that bob. As for the pixie – it confirmed her as a style icon. Do you think Marc Jacobs would've touched her with a fifty-foot pole if she'd still had that disgusting, too-long blonde mess? Not a chance.'

Yes, I had to make sure my jewellery looked good. Better than good – *amazing*. It had to be the accessory equivalent of Kate Moss in a ball gown: cool, glamorous, sexy and emanating some form of enchanting wish-I-had-that aura. And a name. I still didn't have a bloody name for my label . . . well, except for *my* name. Maybe that would do. Jean was a good name – certainly not 'common', which was Ingrid's worst possible insult.

As I sat there tinkering with my pieces, I felt someone's eyes on me. Probably the owner of the cafe, the filthy swine. He ran the place with his wife and was constantly belittling her in front of customers, saying things like, 'I'd trade in five of my wife for one of you!' as he served me, apparently thinking that I would find that a turn-on, and not at all inappropriate in front of his long-suffering, schnitzel-frying wife. But when I looked up, it was Cam. He was over by the counter and his outfit was feverishly cool – but with less silly than usual. It was a nice change. He looked cute. I smiled a closed-lipped smile and dropped my eyes. For some reason, I suddenly felt shy. He didn't come over, so I continued with my work, trying to concentrate.

'Hotcakes, huh? Did I forget your birthday?'

Cam stood over me now, his arms folded, one hand gripping a coffee cup, the other some toast in a white paper bag. It would be Vegemite and banana and it would be wrong as, but he ate the same disgusting combination every day.

'Nope. Just needed a pep-up.'

'Rough night?'

'Bit of a late one, yeah.'

'Three-thirty?'

'No, two. Why, do I look that bad?'

'No, just wanted to slip in to the conversation what time I finished DJ-ing at the Nursery last night.'

I smiled, shaking my head. 'You're a loser.'

'Shyah, if being a world-class DJ who substitutes his addiction to buying vinyl with a shitty job in a shitty shop and still manages to get his arse to work on time is loserish.'

'You ain't saving the world, Cam. "Last Night a DJ Saved My Life" wasn't literal, you know.'

He smiled. 'So hard-core, so early . . . So, you wanna pay Mr Kobisan a visit at lunch?'

*A lunch plan?* Things were back to normal! Thank God for that. That teeny speck of normality might just make my day.

'Only if you snort wasabi again.'

'Of course. No better intermission for your day than burning nostrils and hospital-grade headaches.'

I laughed at the memory of last time: of the pain (Cam) and the hilarity (me).

'See you 'ron, Tiffany & Co.' He smiled and walked out. And a couple of hundred kilos fell from my shoulders.

At 4.56 p.m. precisely, Josh called. I'd wished for this for so long that when it finally happened, I almost didn't believe it. It had been days since I'd heard from him, and when I saw his name flash up, I felt like another couple might be in store, only this time I would hold the keys to the torture chamber.

I let it ring out, arms folded, angrily squinting at it vibrating on the counter as though it were an old friend who had drained my bank account years ago and was now asking for forgiveness. He could wait; I was busy.

And I was. I was serving Morgan and her sister, Heidi. I had grown quite fond of Morgan after spending the day and night with her on Sunday. Yes, she was 'darl' this and 'hun' that, and her tan was not dissimilar to the colour of a cigarette butt, and she *always* wore heels, and all of it was ridiculous – but that was her. And she thought it was fabulous. So who was I to argue?

She and her sister, who surely couldn't have been older than fifteen, had walked in a few minutes ago.

'Hun! Cass told me you worked here. *Looove* this shop! How good is it, Heids?'

Heidi, who was already pawing through the new stock, nodded. She sported a similar shade of white-blonde hair to Morgan's, backcombed into loose submission; a white terry-towelling dress tracksuit; and nails that were long, square and boasting the fat strip of neon white across the top that was so popular with the Bulls girls. She was quietly drifting down the same aesthetic canal as her older sis, and the direction seemed to suit her just fine.

'So, how'd Josh pull up?' Morgan folded her arms, her huge diamanté 'M' keyring and BMW key still clutched in her Barbie-pink-nailed left hand. I didn't know what to say; I didn't want to admit that we hadn't spoken in days, but couldn't offer any information as to his state, as all I really knew was that he was still breathing.

'Um, well, to be —'

'Still drinking, huh? The younger ones, they go *sooo* hard, and the others try to keep up. You'll be looking after him for days, you watch.'

Not bloody likely, I thought. He could sleep in a lake of his own vomit for all I cared.

'You heard about Melinda and Ryan, right?'

'No?'

'She can be *such* an idiot sometimes. It's Tess, you know. Tess makes her that way.'

'What? What happened?'

Morgan picked up a section of blonde rope-like extensions and, placing it behind her shoulder, looked around to check that Heidi was out of earshot.

'So Mad Monday's dick time, right? None of us are meant to be there, 'cos it's about the boys letting their hair down and blahdy-blahblah. I'm very serious about the fact that I don't call Phil; I just let him get on with it – it's better that way. I've had yeeeears of Phil carrying on like a pork chop for a few days at the end of the season and it took me a long time to get it, but now I know the best thing is to just pretend like he doesn't even exist for a few days.' A look of ice passed across her eyes. 'That said, he knows what will happen if he plays up . . .'

And then, in a split second, the iciness was gone and she was back to rambling excitedly. I didn't know whether to be impressed at her grace and the liberty she had bestowed upon Phil the Pig, or to think of her as a fool for imagining a proven cheat wouldn't fall prey to temptation. That said, it sounded very much like the boys were quite isolated from the general public, so maybe Morgan knew there was little chance of mischief.

'So *anyway*, Melinda goes out drinking with Tess last night (they're bloody alcos, I swear – I mean, it's a *Mon*day . . .) and of course – and I don't mean any disrespect here – Tess still has it for Josh. You knew that, right?'

I gulped. I hated that it was assumed knowledge that Josh's ex-girlfriend still thought she had a chance with him. And I hated that Morgan delivered the information like that, as if because everyone – even me – knew about it, then it must somehow be acceptable.

I took a breath in and out. 'Yeah, I mean, there have been a few incidents . . .'

'You mean like the Facebook one and the —'

'What Facebook one?'

'Oh. You don't know?'

I tried to read her tone: was she selfishly unloading things she knew would upset me, or genuinely filling me in?

'Oh, it was, like, aaages ago. Tess sent a message to all of us saying that, oh . . . whadshesaaay? That you were a mole and a boyfriend-stealer and not to be trusted and all that sort of shit. You didn't know about that?'

My heartbeat was set to Formula One speed. Morgan picked up on it; her tone was disbelieving, her facial expression confused. Clearly I was the only one who didn't know about this little political campaign of Tess's. Why wouldn't Josh have told me? Was he protecting Tess's reputation? Or protecting me? I cleared my throat, attempting to get rid of some of the rage and hurt at the same time.

'So, um, what did Melinda and Tess do last night? You were saying something about the —'

'Oh yeah, right. So they got pissed at Mojito's and then they knew the boys would be at Scruffy O'Leary's, so they thought it would be funny to go and surprise them.' Morgan saw my expression. 'I know. Could she *be* more desperate?' She tilted her head, her eyes and mouth clicking into 'serious' mode. 'Hun, um, don't know if you know, but I fell out with Tess a few months back. Mel doesn't see it, but once Tess does her over like she did me, she will. So don't, like, hold back. She's a *total* bitch. She told everyone I was stealing money and clothes from her!'

That sounded like a spectacular story, but it would have to wait for another time. I was focused on last night.

'So what happened when they got there?'

'Well, Ryan went off his nut, right, cause he was so pissed off that Mel would show up, and they had this massive barney and she started abusing him, saying he was the father of Cassie's baby and all *kinds* of crazy shit, and he *lost* it, and kind of pushed her out of the way to get past her, so she went and called the police and asked for a restraining order – how did you *not* hear about any of this? – anyway, and then she got all the locks changed on their place first-thing yesterday and so he's, like, locked out: no clothes, no nothing. She even blocked him from their joint account.'

'Man. That's heavy.' I wondered whether Morgan knew about Cassie and Ryan but thought I didn't, or whether she genuinely didn't.

'I *know*. Now, darl, Phil did say Tess was giving it a good nudge with Josh, but he was *so* drunk – all sloppy and gross – that he couldn't even talk.'

Morgan looked at me, watching the blood drain from my face, and her expression softly morphed from that of Animated Gossip to Caring Friend.

'He could barely speak, hun. I don't think he was in any state to play up . . . not that he would anyway, of course.'

I wasn't hearing her. The idea of Tess placing her serial-killer paws all over my boyfriend – my drunk mess of a boyfriend – was winding me up further by the second. What kind of woman did that? Why did she find it impossible to leave Josh alone? She was one nuclear accident off being a supervillain.

'I don't get it. Is there some kind of bond between those two? Why does Tess do this?' I couldn't believe I was asking Morgan – of all people – for advice.

Morgan paused in thought, her head tipped on an angle.

'They were one of those on–off couples who fought heaps and

then made up and it went on for, like, two years. But honestly? He's off her, hun. He was off her before they even split. Devastated her. Made her nuts.' She looked into my angry, sad little eyes, searching for the right thing to say. 'He loves *you*, hun. Anyone can see that. He's heaps different now.'

Tears sprang to my eyes.

'Ohhh, hun. Come 'ere.' Morgan stepped forward and gave me a hug, patting my back, her shimmery bronzer re-colouring my white top. I gulped back tears ferociously, catching sight of Heidi staring at us, confused, from the accessories wall. Morgan pulled back after a few seconds, holding me by the shoulders and staring me in the face.

'Now, you can't blame him for her behaviour, you know that, right? If there's one thing I've learned, it's that you can't go off at your man every time some little tart wants a piece of him. You can't live that way. You gotta be smart, be strong. So, you forget about Tess, and just make sure you go home and look after your man. He's had a big season and a big drink, and he'll need you to look after him.'

I had to stop myself from searching for a sticky green tentacle, because Morgan was clearly from another universe. Steph and I were ready to tear strips off our boys, but Morgan was on her way home to pop on a nurse's outfit and give Phil the Pig a sponge bath.

'Do . . . do you know if . . . do you think he and Tess are still in touch? She called his house the other week —'

She shook her head. 'Oh, she'd do her best, that's for sure. But Fox wouldn't be that stupid.'

In the next ten seconds, I thought about everything she'd said. And I knew what I had to do.

'Morgan, could I ask you a favour?'

# ROUND 46
## Hazy Memories vs Lazy Eyewitnesses

I sat in Mary, my thumb gently resting on the green call button of my phone, wondering what I was going to say when I heard 'Hello'.

I hit call..

'Hello?'

I cleared my throat. 'Tess. It's Jean.' My voice was shaky, weak.

Silence. Then, 'What do you want?'

As expected, more ice than on one of Jay-Z's necklaces.

'To know why you can't leave Josh alone —'

'Is that what you think this is? That *I'm* chasing *him*?' She tried to laugh wildly, but it was forced and scratchy.

'I don't understand. You could have any guy you wanted —'

'Well, Josh's got you fooled, hasn't he? Making you think I'm the crazy ex-girlfriend who can't move on. Jean, let me tell you something. The bottom line is I've been at the Bulls my whole life and I'm not going anywhere. Josh waltzes in a few years ago and now I'm the one who has to go? Just because we broke up? You're kidding yourself.'

'Tess, I don't care if you're at the games. I care that you're calling his house, and falling all over him on Mad Monday, and making out that you had a coffee date with him, and —'

She forced another laugh. 'Ever heard that expression "It takes two to tango"? Ever wonder why we keep "bumping" into each other? Look, you can choose to think it's all me, or you can take your blinkers off. I know what he's like – why do you think we broke up all the time? He's incapable of monogamy. Can't help himself. He's no better than Bones.'

Momentarily stunned, I quickly gulped and regrouped. No! She was not going to hornswoggle me with her verbal sorcery.

'All right, well, explain the Facebook thing. And the stealing his phone and texting me as if it were him. How is *that* normal behaviour? Why should I believe *anything* you say?'

'Don't believe me then. Just don't come crying to me when you realise what a fool you were.'

Because you'd be the first person I'd turn to, idiot. A rush of strength surged through me.

'If you're done with your supervillain threats, maybe you could answer my questions?'

'Sweetheart, I don't owe you anything. Don't call again.'

Click.

If I was confused before, I was now the square root of confused. She had this way of speaking – this patronising tone, this all-knowing intonation – that made me doubt everything I knew and start believing her lies again.

'Uuuurgh!' I shook my head and arms, trying to shake off these feelings of paranoia and anger and uncertainty. I was calling Josh. I didn't want to be in *The Ball and the Beautiful* any more.

'Hello, my little Jeanie . . .' His voice was soft, sleepy, cute. He was in Baby Fox mode, my favourite.

'Hi. You at home?' Mine was hard, sharp.

'Mm-hmmm. I tried to call you before . . . I miss you, baby. When can I see you?'

'Well, I could come over now. I'm just leaving work.'

'Mmmm, yes please. Can we lie in bed and watch a movie?'

Not likely. 'See you soon.'

'Jeanie? Can you bring me some Powerade? The blue one? And

maybe some KFC? I haven't eaten anything for days . . . so hungry, babe.'

'Kay. Bye.' I hung up.

I reapplied my blush and gloss while waiting for his food. Luckily, I was wearing a nice little shirtdress. In fact, I had dressed nicely every day since Monday, foolishly thinking that I might see my boyfriend at the tail end of one of those days. I'd managed, with the help of some dry shampoo and a lot of flat-ironing, to keep my blow-dry going since Sunday. And even my paltry spray-tan – Morgan had watered down the lotion so I wouldn't look orange – had hung in there with some careful towel-drying and lots of gradual self-tanner.

Still forced to wait, I looked carefully at the ends of my hair; they were gruesome. I missed having glossy brown hair. Now I had expensive, brittle hair with roots that grew like some form of mutant bacteria, and my length – which used to be my best asset – was now my biggest downfall. Something needed to be done. I was over being blonde. Sure, it got me more attention, but of what calibre? And Josh, who I had essentially done it for, didn't even bloody like it. And these push-up bras could use a rest, too – I felt like my ribs were constantly being squeezed by a G-clamp. What – who – had I become? I could hardly remember the Jean who lived a simple life on the Gold Coast. Clearly my brain had erased the tape to make room for all the new information that had streamed in since moving down here: infidelity, scandal, psychotic ex-girlfriends, what a line break is . . .

I knocked on Josh's door, using the side path so I didn't have to chat to his parents. I was struggling to balance a bag of grease, fat and salt, and two bottles of disgusting-looking blue drink. I was wondering how long I could wait before asking about Tess. It wasn't going to be long: I was about as good at hiding my anger as I was at lifting large trucks and throwing them.

Josh came to the door with a towel around his waist, his hair dripping wet. He'd lost weight over the last few days. Well yes, that does happen when you go on a vodka diet.

'Little Jeanie, my angel . . .'

He leaned down and kissed me, his breath tinged with the pungent scent of alcohol, his normally shining blue eyes scribbled with red and enclosed behind puffy lids. I kissed him with my lips closed, and started to make my way inside.

'What's up, baby? In a rush?'

'Your breath is gross.'

I could hear him breathing onto his wrist, trying to smell it.

'But I brushed my teeth. Twice!'

He grabbed me from behind as I placed 'dinner' onto his breakfast bar. He nuzzled into my neck, swaying from side to side.

'So, what have you been doing for the past week?'

'Ohhhh, baby, don't be like that. It was only a day.'

'Nudging three, actually. Anyway, whatever. Did you have fun?' I was clanging plates and glasses and cutlery, dishing up food without care or precision. He spun me around to face him and gave me a gooey, loving smile.

'Baby, don't be mad. I'm here with you now – you've got me all to yourself.'

I frowned. 'I don't care that you drank yourself stupid for almost three days —'

'I got home last night and slept for fifteen hours . . .' He was still smiling. Usually it would have melted me, but I had all kinds of wrath bubbling through my arteries; no smile could win me over.

'Whatever, I don't care. I just . . . it's just that —'

'I'm sorry I didn't call. I told you I probably wouldn't. We . . . well, the boys, they kind of . . . We're banned fro—'

'Banned? Honestly.'

'Ah, Mad Monday – nothing makes a girl happier . . .' He was shaking his head, trying to hold back another smile.

'Yep. In fact, it makes *some* girls so happy they go and join in the drinking.'

He looked at me blankly, a small frown spreading across his face.

'Okay, you've lost me.'

'Ummmmm, Tess?'

The small frown made way for an XXL version. 'Tess what?'

I gave an exasperated sigh. 'Are you for real.'

There was no inflection at the end of my sentence because it was less a question than rhetoric swathed in sarcasm. I went back to dishing up the food.

'Baby, help me out here.'

'Okay. I know you hate the Girlfriends' United Front and all the *he-said-she-said*, but Morgan told me your ex-girlfriend was sitting on your lap as you all drank merrily on Monday night. That help?'

As he had exhausted his frowning capabilities, he had to settle for slightly scrunching up his cheeks and nose to signify his confusion.

'I don't remember seeing Tess . . .'

'How convenient,' I mumbled.

'What?'

His tone was three parts confusion, one part annoyance; the sweet, sleepy, hung-over guy was two seconds from taking his Powerade and collapsing on the sofa to watch WWF wrestling.

'Why would I let that happen? Babe, that never happened.'

'Only it did, Josh! Everyone saw it!'

Morgan had told me not to say that. She had in fact told me not to bring up the subject at all, let alone scream at him over it. If this conversation was an exam, I'd just earned myself an F.

Josh shook his head rapidly, his face still scrunched up. 'Where? Where is this coming from?'

I folded my arms. 'I called Tess. I needed the truth.'

'The *truth*?' He spat out the words. Oh shit, I'd gone too far.

I knew I'd gone too far. 'You called *her* for the *truth*? That's like giving a kleptomaniac a trench coat and asking them to not steal anything! That girl isn't *capable* of the truth!'

'Well, what am I *supposed* to do? Morgan told me that Melinda and Tess showed up at Scruffy O'Leary's, and that Tess was all over you, so rather than just take it as the truth, I thought I would ask Tess about it. Actually try and figure out if it was even worth raising with you. Did you know about her little Facebook campaign, by the way?'

He looked at me, confused, startled.

'Anyway, she basically told me that I was being naive to think that you weren't part of whatever the hell it is that you two still have going.'

He shook his head. 'Babe, I love you, but how silly do you have to be to take her word over mine? Especially when you stand there yourself, telling me all of the crazy shit she's done! And yes, okay, I knew about the Facebook thing – Bones told me – but why would I offer that information to you, my new girlfriend, who I was trying to impress and not scare off with the antics of my ex?' He looked at me as though I was the poor stupid kid who just didn't get the message.

'Well then, why . . . why do you still have coffees with her and let her sit on your lap?' A tear of exasperation, confusion and anger dribbled down my face. Tess may have got under my skin, but Josh was currently branding it with hot irons. On top of that, I was so angry at myself for trying to do all the right things, and be all the right things, and look the right way, and be this perfect WAG creature for Josh, when all he does is go back to Tess *anyway*! I was such a *fool*.

He spoke slowly and calmly. 'Jeanie, I don't know how I can make you see that you have nothing to worry about. I know Tess a lot better than you, and I know what she's doing. She hates you – hates all that you represent, hates how happy we are – and she's trying to cause irreversible damage. And now she's winning, because we're fighting, and you don't trust me, and that's just what she wants!' He took a step back to lean against the doorframe, his face disbelieving, his eyes aimed at the floorboards.

'Can you honestly tell me you don't remember seeing her Monday, and her sitting on your lap?'

'*No!*' Josh looked at me as if I was insane. Which was probably very attractive to him, since his track record indicated that to be his 'type'. 'No, babe, I don't remember. I'm telling you the truth.'

I gulped back more tears, wondering whether to believe him or to believe Tess; this dilemma was becoming the fun game that was going to decide whether we stayed together or not.

'Look, let's call her. Come on, let's get it from the horse's mouth. I want you to see what she's up to. On speaker.' Josh grabbed his phone and started pressing buttons.

'What are you do— '

'Hello?'

'Tess, it's Josh. I'm standing here with Jean —'

'Oh p*lease!* I have nothing to say to you two fre—'

'I'M STANDING here with Jean, who tells me we were seen together at Scruffy's on Monday night. Would you care to confirm either way?'

'Listen, I've got my own problems. I don't need your relationship bullshi—'

'Just answer the question, would you? I didn't see you Monday. Can you tell Jean you're lying, so we can all move on?' His voice was stern, warning.

Tess shrieked with laughter. 'Oh yeah, sure thing, Josh. I wasn't there, and neither was that little groupie in the denim shorts you seemed so fond of. No, I wasn't there. I didn't see Bones jump over the bar and start serving drinks, I didn't see Melinda slap Ryan in front of everyone, and I didn't see Camel rip off one of your sleeves.'

'You're lying.'

'Am I? Well, why don't you tell Jean how you got vodka and cran-berry all over your jeans. 'Cos we all know you don't drink that. Or why don't you stage a speakerphone attack on Bones instead, and ask why he didn't do anything to stop me from sitting on your lap for a goo—'

'That'll do me.' I picked up my keys and bag and walked towards the front door.

'*Jean!* I was drunk. I was so, so drunk. I'm sorry, I don't remember anything! I honestly do not remember any of that . . .'

I turned as I got to the door. 'Alcohol is the cheapest and least courageous of all excuses. Spare me.'

'Jean . . . *Jean!*'

I slammed the door behind me, swearing like a pirate, stomp-ing like a soldier and sobbing like the freshly heartbroken. Fucking cockhead fucking liar arsehole! I shuddered with anger. I didn't want to contemplate what else I didn't know about those two. What sordid story their in-boxes and sent items might reveal. What Bones might be able to tell me. What Melinda might know. Would I see something in the papers about Josh's drunken antics? And *who was the little tart in the denim shorts?*

I didn't know what the next move was. I believed Josh when he said he was so drunk he didn't know what he was doing, but since when was that an acceptable excuse? Tess and Josh still had some sick link and I was bored with trying to pretend that they didn't.

# ROUND 47
## The Foliage vs The Fury

With red, swollen eyes that were about as covert as a T-bone in a tofu shop, I made my way to work in Mary. I'd had an atrocious night's sleep, kicking and crumpling and cursing Tess and Josh.

I blamed Colette, of course – for if it weren't for her having met Frank, I would never have met stupid Josh again in the first place. And to cap it all off, now, in my time of need, she was still carrying on and being all pissy at me because I missed the shopping trip, and was basically living at Eric's. I'd really needed her last night, after getting home from Josh's, but she wasn't there and her phone was going straight to voicemail, and that only made me more gnarly. She'd even taken Dave, just to ensure I was *really* alone. Nice.

Being a Thursday, the universal payday, it was going to be busy in the shop today. I didn't mind; at least it would keep my mind off things. Ingrid was in one of her usual foul moods – Justin still hadn't divorced his wife, surprise, surprise – and she was getting to the end of her tether. That particular tether end must be quite worn, I thought. But at least her bad-mood goggles stopped her from prying.

We barely had time to slam down our coffees before the rush began, and I barely had time to realise it was lunchtime and I was hungry before Cam sauntered in to enquire as to the state of my food intake in recent hours.

'You know what I could really go for?' he said, casting aside platitudes and diving straight into cuisine gabble, despite the fact that there were customers around. 'Some fish and some salad and those yam chips they do up at Something Fishy. Don't you reckon?'

I looked at him – his tanned, gently freckled face smattered with facial hair and framed by perfect, thick eyebrows grinning at me from across the shop floor – and realised how happy I was to see him. I heard giggling and looked over at the sale rack to see two young MySpace types with Nicole Richie-style headbands and too much foundation looking shyly at Cam and then looking away. I looked at him again. It occurred to me that they thought he was good-looking. To me – and even though I knew he was – this was strange. He was, after all, just Cam.

Regaining my concentration, I walked him outside so that I didn't have to belt out my lunch preferences across the store.

'That sounds excellent,' I said, trying to stop the wind from whipping my hair across my freshly lacquered lips. 'But I want normal chips. I need full grease.'

He peered into my eyes. 'Whoa, you do too. How much did you put away last night, Jay? You look *rough*.'

I put one hand on my hip and tilted my head. 'Thanks. Can always rely on you to pump me up when I'm feeling like shit.'

'Shouldn't've got smashed on a school night, then. Should leave that stuff to the pros.'

'You mean alcos? Like you?'

'You got it. Now, let me guess. You can't leave because Ingrid is here and so, yet again, I am the carrier pigeon, and, yet again, we eat like slaves in the back room, even though it's a glorious day out here.'

A delivery guy with a funky smell and the kind of hair that may not have seen a shower head for many weeks raced past into the shop with a colossal bunch of pink, white and red roses. Cam raised his eyebrows.

'Ingrid's non-boyfriend sucking up,' I said knowingly. Justin was always weaselling off Ingrid's shit-list with lush foliage.

A few seconds later, Billygoat Gruff was back at the door, flowers still in hand.

'You Jean Bennett?'

I looked at Cam as I said, 'Yes, that's me.'

'Sign, please.'

I signed his little electronic notepad and took the enormous bunch of flowers. Billy vanished as quickly as he'd arrived.

I knew who they were from. The same man who had been calling and texting all last night and this morning. Tess's number-one guy. I flipped the card over.

*Each petal is an apology . . . I love you, Jean x*

'What'd he do this time?' Cam's eyes had cooled; his tone was low.

I cleared my throat, gulping back the golf ball snaking its way up.

'Long story. It's his ex, basically. Won't leave him alone.'

'Why does that deserve kiss-arse flowers?'

'I'll tell you later. Do you need money for lunch? It's my turn, isn't it?' Nursing my roses, I walked quickly back into the shop to get money. I didn't want to discuss Josh with Cam any more. But when I came out, Cam had already left. When he finally returned, half an hour later, holding paper bags and plastic containers, I tucked twenty-five dollars into his shirt pocket before even allowing him to dump the food.

'That took so fuckin' long . . . The girl who serves there is on smack, I'm telling you. Slow as shit and concentration of a goldfish. Don't have time to eat with you now, but you finish at six, right? We're going for a drink.'

'But, I think —'

'Jean, shut it. You're not seeing him tonight. What message would that send – that he dispatches flowers and everything's okay? Man up, ladybird.'

I stood there frowning, watching as he walked out. He was always such a little hurricane, blowing in and unsettling things and making me doubt myself. But I had a feeling he was right about this one. I took out my phone to text Josh one of the six drafts that I'd already scripted in my head to thank him for the flowers, but there was already a message from him.

Jeanie can we pls talk? 2nite? I need 2 speak 2 u. This is crazy . . . xx

No.

Sorry, Josh, but I was busy tonight. Just *thinking* that response confirmed that it was the right thing to do. But I would write back later. I wasn't callous by nature, and his flowers were breathtaking – they deserved a thank you . . . right?

Cam's suggestion that we have a drink was splendid. Jesus, did I need a drink. This week had been rougher than a sandpaper sandwich.

# ROUND 48
## Schemers vs Naivety

'And how he'd park in the no-stopping out the front and call you to come out and see him, just so everyone could see you, and him, and the car, and put it all together that he was pretty much the world's biggest hero, ever.'

I drained my vanilla vodka, mint, lime and soda. It was one of Cam's poncy DJ drinks and was frighteningly easy to knock back. I was at that point of the evening when each drink went down like water, but none was. Some actual water would be an awesome idea in terms of Hangover Management, but I knew I was as likely to follow through on that as I was on leaving 'after the next drink'.

'And then, and *then*, when he called *you*, thinking that *you* would put in a good word for him, when *you* were the one who wrote the break-up email *for* me . . . !'

We dissolved into hysterics again. Dean the Deadshit was an endless source of amusement for us. He was the only man this side of *Happy Days* who still used pistol fingers as a farewell. He also thought his rule of 'No panties in the Porsche' was both hilarious and sexy, somehow failing to see both the potential risks: the first pertaining to hygiene, the second to face-slapping.

Cam was facing the bar, leaning every which way on his stool like some form of deranged jungle chimp as he tried to make eye contact with the bruiser manning it. As we had only put away six drinks each in two-and-a-half hours, we were desperately in need of another, or there was a chance neither of us would get to vomit tonight.

'That man is ignoring us.'

I swung my head around to try my luck at catching his eye, but tired of it after two seconds. 'Jus' *go* over there and buy them. Here's some money. Catch!'

I threw a twenty-dollar note at Cam; it floated elegantly to the carpet near the feet of my stool. He jumped off his stool and bent down to get it, resting his hand on my knee for balance. As he came up, he smacked the back of his head on our tiny bar table. It made a sickening crack.

'FUCK! Are you okay?' I covered my mouth in horror.

He ducked back down and reversed out before rising. He was rubbing his head with the hand holding the note; his other hand was still resting on my knee. He smiled a goofy grin.

'Can't break steel, baby.'

'Bet there's a bump – one of those instant ones, like in Daffy Duck. Come 'ere, lemme feel.' I pulled him in close by tugging his T-shirt and ran my hand over his shaved head. 'Can't feel anything. Dr Jean says take two Panadol and see a real doctor if pain persists.'

Cam was standing so close to me that I could smell his aftershave. It was spicy and woody, like cloves and amber and pepper and cinnamon. I took it in, closing my eyes briefly and forgetting to pretend I wasn't . . .

I opened my eyes to see Cam watching me intently, his brown eyes just inches from mine, boring through me. I could see his breath rise and fall under his T-shirt, I could smell his skin, and I could feel something enormously unfamiliar flicker and spark in the air between us. I coughed and let go of him.

'Well, there's no blood and no bump, which means you can still go and get the drinks. Garn.'

His eyes lingered on me for a second longer before he turned slowly and walked to the bar. My heart was doing funny things: it felt like it was going too fast, then too slow. This isn't right. I felt my phone buzz in my back pocket, where I had kept it in case Josh called or texted, which he had not done since I'd got the guilts and sent him a text (saturated in industrial-strength icicles) to thank him for the flowers.

I pulled the phone out of my tight-tight-tight black jeans and clumsily unlocked the screen. It was just before nine. The night was young. A zygote, in fact. Cam had suggested karaoke before he had to DJ at 11.30, and I thought that could just be the best idea ever. Nothing like tonelessly warbling through 'Cherish' to cheer a girl up.

The message was from Josh.

Am glad u liked them. I guess ur busy 2nite. Can I see u tmrw? I can pick u up 4 lunch? need 2 talk 2 u, explain . . . xx

I sighed, locked the screen and put the phone back into my pocket just as Cam returned with two strange red drinks and two small shot glasses that appeared to be on fire.

'What the —'

'Alcohol-free. All of them. Promise.'

'Cam, I know as a DJ your tolerance for alcohol exceeds even the most hardened hobo's, but I will fall off this stool if I drink those.'

'Y'sure?'

'Yes! And *stop* trying to get me smashed. It's *soooo* transparent.' I meant this in our usual joking way, but once the words were out of my mouth, I realised it could have other connotations.

'You did it yourself by ordering those margaritas first up.'

'Pfft.'

'You sure you don't want one?'

I nodded clumsily.

He sank the two shots in a row and chased with the vodka. I took a sip of my vodka and wondered when I would be able to get my mitts on some kind of kebab.

'So, Michael J. Fox text you yet?'

'As a matter of fact, yes.' I was relieved to be able to answer in the affirmative.

'Whatcha gonna do?'

I sighed. 'I dunno. 'Smessy. I – we – love each other but, well, Tess is always going to be a big, fat, bitchy, psychopathic roadblock. And I need to be able to trust him, y'know?'

'Tess is a piece of work, that's for sure.'

I laughed. 'You say that like you know her.'

Cam cleared his throat. 'Look, Jay, I gotta be honest. From everything you've told me, he's just not over Tess. I know how boys work, how they play these things so that they *look* like the innocent party. And, I'm sorry, Jay, but he's not over her. Anyone can see that.'

'Caaaaam, lay ooooooff.' I closed my eyes and shook my head. He was so predictable with his anti-Josh shit.

'No, I mean it. You've had problem after problem with him – and her. I told you footballers were hard work. It's not like Real Life, Jay; it's very, very different. And I've watched you change to try and fit into it, and look where it's landed you.'

'Where? What have I become? A junkie? A thief? A prozzi? I dyed my hair and have had some fitting-in issues but, God, you act like I got a tit job and started doing coke every night.'

'Whatever. The point is, he's fooling around with his ex.'

'He not "fooling around" with her. They're just . . . he was . . . they . . . urgh! What does it matter? You've hated him from day one.'

He ignored me, clearly on a roll. 'Jay, relationships should be *fun*. Fun and easy. You and your sister – I don't know what's wrong with you two, but you get yourselves into these fucked-up relationships where there's always drama. Shouldn't be that way. You're amazing, gorgeous girls and you could be living this great life with great guys who worship you, you know? "Hard" isn't code for "romantic", Jay.'

He took a long sip of his drink and I thought about what he'd said, twiddling my straw through the maze of ice-cubes and lime in my drink. After a few quiet minutes, I knew exactly what I had to do.

'Let's sing!'

# ROUND 49
## The Best Friend vs The Boyfriend

We stood out on the street in the warm night air, watching full cab after full cab zoom past us unsympathetically.

'Come on, Cabbie Bradshaw, hail us a ride, would you?'

'You're the local! You should know all the tricks.'

'But I don't have boobs and long legs, and we all know that, after beaded seat covers, boobs and long legs are a cab driver's biggest weakness.'

I bent at the knees and pushed my shoulders and upper arms in so that what little cleavage I had was pushed together in a comically OTT fashion.

'Scuse me, officer, but is this some kind of *bust*?' I purred in my best Jessica Rabbit voice.

'Jean?'

I turned around to see Morgan and Phil, both licking gelato in cones.

'Morgan, *hi*!'

Phil's face was crumpled in confusion; Morgan's less so but she was still clearly wondering why I was offering up my boobs to a good-looking guy who wasn't Josh Fox.

'Hi, hun . . . what're you up to? Who's your friend? Where's Josh?'

The corpses of sensitivity and subtlety sat on the ground below Morgan's staccato interrogation.

'I'm Josh's cousin.' Cam stepped forward and put his arm around me. 'I'm minding Jeanie tonight. I like to play sport. With my feet.

And balls. Especially with balls. I *love* playing with balls.'

I elbowed him hard in the ribs.

'This is my friend, Cam; Cam, this is Morgan and Phil.'

Cam curtsied, Phil squinted, Morgan frowned.

'So you're *not* Josh's cousin?'

'No, he's not. He was being an idiot.'

'Hey, have we met before?' Phil asked Cam.

Cam shook his head. 'Not a chance.'

'But you look familiar. I'm sure we've met somewhere . . .'

'Cam works in that shop on —'

'TAXI!'

Cam's two-finger whistle pierced the air and brakes screeched.

'Come on, Jay; Whitney Houston waits for no man.'

Cam tugged my arm and pulled me backwards. I giggled, crashing into him. The look on Morgan's face was a blend of astonishment and puzzlement; Phil's was more one of confusion and suspicion.

"Sall good, guys, I'll 'splain later. Bye! Enjoy your ice-cream!'

And then we were in the cab, laughing and pulling away from the curb, the ramifications of what had just happened as far away as my fifth birthday.

Because we'd both slid in from the footpath, and Cam had only gone as far as the middle of the seat, we were squished together: two naughty kids wreaking havoc and thrilled to be on their way to more booze. Cam's whole left side was against me and our shoulders overlapped slightly.

Cam, being a DJ, couldn't go thirty seconds without music.

'Driver – some music, please? Preferably something either in the death-metal or symphonic-orchestra categories. Many kind thanks.'

The driver wordlessly jabbed on the radio and the car filled with the strains of Marvin Gaye.

'Niiiiiice. This will put us in the mood perfectly,' I said, tapping my hands to the beat, looking out the window on my left at the passing traffic.

'I *beg* your pardon?' said Cam.

'I said it will *put us in the mood perfectly*,' I enunciated, still looking out the window and enjoying Marvin's soulful trills and tremors.

'For what?'

'For karaoke, of cour—' As I said this, I swung my head round to give him the 'You're an idiot' face I sent his way 200 times a day, and was met by his face, which was already positioned to meet mine. We looked at each other, our matching brown eyes perfectly level, our lips perfectly level, and when Cam moved his face towards me ever so delicately, I moved in to meet him, allowing our lips to meet.

He kissed me softly, all lips and gentleness. I kissed him back. He kissed me again; I kissed him back. He opened his mouth ever so slightly, and I mirrored his move, allowing his lips to delicately cover mine, and feeling my breath rise sharply. He placed his right hand onto the left side of my face, caressing me tenderly, lovingly. Then, pulling away ever so slightly, he looked deep into my eyes.

'You can*not* know how long I have waited to do that.' Cam exhaled, smiling, rubbing his thumb up and down my cheek, searching my eyes for something – perhaps a similar sentiment, perhaps shock, perhaps uncomfortableness.

I closed my eyes and moved in for more of his kisses. It felt right, as though, after years of searching for a set of misplaced keys, I had finally found them. I took my right hand up behind his neck and stroked the back of his head as we kissed, pulling him into me, wanting to kiss him deeper, trying to extract more of him with each kiss. Taking his cue from me, he took his left hand and snaked it behind my back, lifting me up and over to him, his fingers tracing my —

'$23.25. Machine not working, cash only.'

The physical light came on and, with it, the metaphysical. I was drunk, in the back of a smelly cab, making out with Cam. The first two I had prior references for, but the third was entirely foreign. I pulled back as if bitten, and quickly, avoiding eye contact, reached into my handbag for my purse. I was trying to catch my breath and not look at Cam, hoping that by the time I located some money, a large pin would have materialised and pricked the bubble holding all the OMFG that was suffocating this cab.

'Thanks, mate.'

I looked up to see Cam handing over a fifty, looking at me for some kind of clue as to how he should act now, and what he was allowed to say. He looked utterly terrified. Which, for some reason, I found adorable. My face cracked into a huge smile, which I tried to hide by looking down and winding my hair up and back into a high, dishevelled bun.

'Uh, Jean?'

'Mm?'

'You kiss good.'

I exhaled. There he was: the same old Cam with a syringe full of comedy at the ready. I was grateful and relieved. I was confused about what had just occurred and stunned to consider what might have happened if the cab ride had been any longer.

I wasn't in the mood for karaoke any more. Kissing a guy who wasn't Josh was weird enough without then being forced to sit in a small neon booth with him, drinking sake and singing Billy Joel songs as if nothing had happened. I needed to go home and get out a big magical calculator and figure out what the hell had happened tonight.

'Cam, I might . . . I might go on home, actually.'

'Why? How come? Noooo. You wanted to sing! You had your Blondie lyrics ready to go!' He looked shattered.

'Yeah, but then, well . . . ' I smiled.

'Please get out of taxi now,' said the driver.

'Just a second, buddy, she might keep driving. Just hang tight?'

293

He turned to me. 'Shit, Jay, I don't want to end the night like this . . .' He grabbed my left hand and looked me square in the eyes. 'Jean, I'm sorry for doing that . . . but I don't regret it. Not one bit. I haven't . . . fucked up things between us, have I?'

I looked into his eyes, wondering how everything can change between two people when they simply press their lips together. I scrunched my forehead in thought; I had no idea whether he had ruined things. The thoughts running through my head about asking him to drive me home so we could kiss some more kind of inferred he hadn't, but deep down I had no idea, full stop. Plus, I was as responsible for what had happened as he was.

'To borrow a line from the antichrist, it takes two to tango. Look, I'll see you tomorrow, 'kay? It's cool, we're cool. Totally cool.'

I gave his face a meaningful last look, trying to figure out how it was that just minutes ago I was attached to it. He exhaled, picking up his change from the little plastic money tray.

'You seem to have made up your mind.' He paused, searching for something in my eyes. 'G'night, Jeanie.' He leaned in boldly and kissed me on the lips, gave a sad little smile, swivelled and got out of the cab, looking at me once more before closing the door.

'Fifteen Arlington Avenue, please driver.'

We sped off and I put my head in my hands. I was drunk, I was a cheat, and I was more confused than the Chief of Confusion on the confusingest day of the year.

# ROUND 50
## The Pot vs The Kettle

I sat at the shop counter the next morning eating a toasted cheese-and-ham sandwich. The filling scalded my tongue, making each bite more painful than the last. I didn't care. I was so, so hungry. I hadn't eaten since lunchtime yesterday, which was likely one of the reasons I'd ended up kissing Cam in a cab, the other being that I had consumed enough alcohol to power a small boat.

Ingrid wouldn't be in till midday because she and Justin had ducked off to a vineyard yesterday afternoon, which was handy, because as it stood, I had been given a valuable insight into how death may feel, and being in a relatively cold state, I needed a few hours of warming up before seeing her. I planned on showing her my 'collection' this afternoon, in the hope that I could start selling it tomorrow. It was hiding out the back, under a big scarf. I needed a stand, I'd realised. 'So you do,' my brain had said in response to such a difficult puzzle. 'But I hate you right now. Figure it out yourself.'

I allowed my mind to coast lazily back to the feeling I'd had when I was kissing Cam: how right it felt, how perfectly compatible it seemed we were . . . I wondered where the hell it had all come from. And was it *purely* alcohol-fuelled? I quietly admitted to myself that I was excited about seeing him again today.

I looked at my phone. I was yet to reply to Josh's text about seeing him tonight. There was no way I could see him; I was so hung-over and confused. There was a large, deep hole inside my stomach that came from the realisation I'd cheated on him. I'd *given* it to him for letting Tess sit on his lap, and then I'd gone and pashed on with a guy in the back of a cab.

Had I done it out of spite, perhaps, to get him back for dragging Tess and her golden hair and perfect skin into our relationship, and refusing to leave her in the past? If that *was* the reason, it was not only *real* twisted, it was entirely subconscious, because I don't remember thinking about any of that at the time. I just remember feeling it was the natural thing to do.

More coffee. *Urgently.* I popped the 'Back in seven-and-a-half minutes' sign on the door and walked the block to Spresso. When I entered, it was to find Cam spinning around from the counter, all shiny-eyes and joke-cracky with the blush-inducing Italian barista, holding two coffees in a tray in one hand and his wallet in the other. He was glowing like a 100-watter, and was wearing a particularly silly outfit: gold trainers, white jeans and a pink T-shirt that had the outline of a giant rat on it. The look was completed by a black beanie. Of course.

I dropped my head, blushing, and walked towards the counter. Fuck. How, at this exact second, was Cam here? Was it A Sign? As our eyes connected, furious, nervous thoughts raced through me, and the small amount of saliva that had kindly graced my mouth this morning vanished. How would this go? Would this be weird? Would I feel like jumping into his arms and kissing him passionately? Or would he just be . . . Cam?

'JB, good morning, *good morning!* I was just on my way to see you and deliver you a soy chai when I thought you might have already had a coffee, y'see, 'cos, well, I figured you might've needed it today, and I know you can't have two 'cos you go loco, so I wen—'

I smiled at him shyly. 'You know me too well.' Then I laughed because he was bumbling, speaking too quickly – could he be nervous?

He sidled up beside me, facing the door, and looked me in the eyes. 'Shall we walk together? Talk about that nice pash we had last night?'

'*Cam!*' I hissed, looking around, ducking out of the door before him. '*Jesus.* Shut up, would you?'

'Hey, hey, little lady, calm down.'

'Well, what do you expect? You can't just say shit like that. I still have a *boyfriend*, you know.'

'You can have a new one, if you like. He's got great fashion sense; spins a mean turntable.'

'Cam, that's not funny.'

We walked slowly, silently. I had my arms folded and was deep in thought.

He sighed. 'Sorry, sorry. Just trying to normalise things.'

As we waited to cross the street, I looked at him standing there, trying his best to play it tough when I knew that inside he surely had to be just as unsettled as I was.

'Oh! I made you something.' Cam thrust the tray at me and pulled out a CD in a plastic sleeve from his back pocket. He held it out, smiling, proud as punch.

'What's this?' I said, a bemused look on my face.

In all the time I'd known him, Cam had always promised me this mix and that compilation, but had never actually delivered. Now, I tried to hide my astonishment and be gracious.

'I made it for you this morning when I got home. Just, y'know, some nice music that I think you'd like. Some Cinematic Orchestra, some Sweetback, some of the less suicidal Bon Iver stuff . . .'

I held the CD in my hand, smiling so hard it hurt my cheeks, enjoying every second of how vulnerable and shy the King of Smart-arse had suddenly become.

'Uh, Cam? This is a *mixtape*. You made me a mixtape?'

'*First* of all, it's obviously a mixCD, not a mixtape, and second, it's not like I, you know, sat there thinking of your eyes and your hair and your lips and your smile and how amazing last night was when I was making it or anything . . .'

There were no cars blocking us from crossing the street, but we stood rooted to our spot. He looked at me, hands jammed in his pockets, waiting for my reaction. Despite having had less than four minutes' sleep, he was still very handsome. His big brown eyes were a little rough around the rims, but the feeling behind them was luminescent.

I stood there looking at him, amazed and flattered that he was both so thoughtful and so honest about his feelings. My heart was having a severe identity crisis. Until yesterday, its papers were signed by one Josh Fox. Now, within the space of twelve hours, a yellow Post-it had been stuck over Josh's name, with one suggestive little word: *Cam?*

I thought about all the times Col and Ingrid had said that Cam and I were the perfect grotty little couple, and all the times I'd rejected the notion, saying he was more like a brother or a best mate – we had too much fun together for it ever to be romantic. But maybe that was the whole point – relationships were meant to be fun.

I smiled at him. 'Thanks, Cam. That's very special. No one has ever made me a mixCD before. Thank you.'

'The last track is a secret track, but you'll understand why I put it on there when you hear it.'

He reached out and plucked his coffee from the tray, leaving my chai unbalanced and alone. How fitting.

'So, lunch? Maybe?'

'Cam, I . . . I don't know. I've got to see Josh at some point . . .'

I looked down as I said Josh's name.

'Of course. Maybe just call Tess instead of calling him direct.'

'Not funny, Cam.'

He started walking across the road, smiling cheekily back at me.

I followed him, walking slowly, wondering why the idea of Tess and Josh still seared through me, even with all of these new Cam developments. Bit rich, really. I needed to see Josh. I needed to see him and I needed to sort this out once and for all. It wasn't fair for me to do this to him.

My phone buzzed. Ohmygod. *It was going to be Josh*. And it was going to be A Sign. I pulled out my phone and looked at the text.

It was Col.

Home 2night? We need 2 talk.

Well, she sounded to be in a terrific mood. There'd almost definitely be cupcakes and balloons awaiting my arrival . . . Pah, I'd write back to her later; I had some thinking to do.

# ROUND 51
## Mixtapes vs Mix-ups

I dropped my keys *again*. Stooping to pick them up, I realised I was stomach-turningly, three-swallows-per-second nervous. I was terrified Josh would be able to tell I had kissed another man, that there would be something different about me somehow. I'd felt the same way when I'd faced Mum the morning after I'd lost my virginity; I was convinced she'd be able to tell just by looking at me.

I reasoned for the zillionth time that the Tess stuff was the bigger issue here and that, really, this talk was going to happen anyway. Whether or not I'd sucked face with Cam in the back of a cab. And then accidentally started feeling things for him that were entirely foreign and really, *really strange*. Especially when the secret song on his mixtape was 'Hold You In My Arms' by Ray LaMontagne. He knew how much I loved that song.

I shook the thoughts of Cam out of my head. They were inappropriate. I was here to speak to my boyfriend, who I loved; after all, it was only days ago that I was in tears over his conduct with his ex-girlfriend.

I knocked gently on his door. I had to go to his place because he was waiting for a delivery of some computer software or something, he said. It was far from neutral territory, but I was hardly in a position to start throwing my weight around; I'd done enough of that in the cab last night. Josh opened the door and it was as though I was seeing a long-lost friend. At once, the tears I didn't even know I was holding in gushed forth.

'Oh, Jeanie, baby, come here.'

He came out onto the step and embraced me in a heart-warming, soul-melting hug, pulling me in tight, letting me cry and sob and sniff without saying a word, just holding me and stroking the hair that snaked down my back. Finally, I wiped my nose and eyes and pulled away. He looked a little perplexed, unsure of what had just happened but more than willing to try to understand. He was all big blue eyes and concern and comfort.

'Shall we go inside?'

I nodded, wiping my eyes and sniffing every two seconds. He would have no idea why I was so upset. The last time he had seen me I was crying, sure, but they were angry, banging-head-against-the-wall tears caused by rage at Tess and his lying about her. These were obviously another brand of salty eye water.

I walked into his living room and sat down on the sofa.

'Would you like a tea? White with half, right?'

I nodded and smiled. 'Yes, please.' I loved that he took the trouble to remember little things like that. I looked around the apartment. It smelled of artificial lemons – the kind that are mixed in with skin-burning chemical agents – and, as usual, was clean and tidy. How was it that Josh and Cam were the same age, and that I got along with each of them so well, and yet they were polar opposites?

I wondered what would come of today's talk. I was feeling confused as to what outcome I wanted. Had my mind been clouded by Cam's eleventh-hour affections, or did I genuinely want to break up with Josh? And would it be fair to break up with Josh, citing Tess as the problem, when clearly Cam revealing his feelings to me, and me revealing my tonsils to Cam, had a role to play too? In fact, *confused* was a gross understatement.

I tried to transport my head back to when I'd left this apartment a few days ago, to capture those feelings, but all I felt was guilt. When I thought of Tess and her twisted plans, some of the feeling came back, but not enough to make me remember how to conduct – or even to open – this conversation. I decided Josh could get the ball rolling. Ironically, he thought he was the wrongdoer in the room, and I could sense he had prepared for quite A Talk.

Finally done making the tea, he came over and sat in the lounge chair to my right, placing both mugs neatly on coasters on the coffee table.

'So, um, how's work?'

'Fine, fine,' I said, a little too quickly.

He exhaled, positioning himself so that he completely faced me: legs, arms, head, everything.

'Jean, I want to apologise again. Thinking back, I see how many times Tess upset you during our time together, and I see now that I wasn't nearly the boyfriend I should've been. I should've been telling her to stay away from you. I should have been protecting you. But I didn't. I let you down. Everything I love about you – all of the things that make you so great, so real – Tess started to destroy. This whole stupid football world has started to change who you are, through no fault of your own, and that is the last thing, the *last* thing, I want.'

He looked at me, eyes searching for some kind of response, but I could offer none. I needed to see where he was going with this before I said anything.

'And . . . just back on Tess again for a moment. Well, if I'm completely honest, I guess on some level I was protecting myself from Tess's father, because I know what he's like, and what she is capable of making him do, and, you know, I was hoping they might re-sign me, so I didn't want to rock the boat . . . And look, Jean, I . . . I have to come clean, I have to.' He took in a huge breath, shaking his head as he did. I was rooted to my chair, mind tripping over itself trying to imagine what he might say next. 'I . . . well, you may know that in the past Tess and I were on and off, always putting each other through hell, and, well, I was largely responsible for that. I wasn't a saint and I did a lot of things I regret. I've changed now – you've made me want to be a good man, a better man, but I am to blame for why Tess is the way she is. Well, partly to blame, anyway; she was always a bit . . . unstable. But I guess on some level I felt that breaking up with her was unfair, in the sense that I had done some things that were unfair, and made her insecure and extremely territorial. And, of course, meeting you, which was completely unexpected, just compounded how bad I felt leaving her. So, I kind of . . . you could say I maintained some form of friendship with her, if only to lessen the guilt I felt about what I'd done.' His head was hanging low, but he lifted his eyes to peer cautiously into mine. He was clearly terrified of my reaction.

My eyes instantly pooled with more liquid. It was true; Tess wasn't lying. She was crazy, but she wasn't a liar. All this time he had been in contact with her, fuelling her mad thoughts of them getting back together . . . Hang on, *were* they mad thoughts?

'Did . . . did you do that with the thought that maybe you two would get back together?'

He shook his head, exhaling a seemingly inexhaustible supply of air.

'Jesus, no. Jean, I love *you*. I have *no* wish to be back with Tess. What I have with her is more like . . . being a carer. She needs help, she really does, and I didn't want her doing anything stupid, largely – selfishly – because I felt I might be to blame. So I didn't shut her out of my life.'

I gulped. Everything he said was so heartfelt, so honest, so hard to dispute. I didn't like that they were still in touch, but I believed him when he said there was nothing going on that I needed to worry about. I actually felt sorry for Tess more than anything. Because whether he knew it or not, Josh was still dangling a carrot in front of her by being her friend, or 'carer', or whatever he wanted to label it.

'Jean?'

I sniffed, picking up my tea and warming my hands with it.

'I understand, Josh. I can see why you did it.'

'And?'

'No and.'

'No and?'

'Well, I mean, you lied to me about the extent of your contact.' As I said these words, a small guilt bomb marked 'Cam' exploded in my head, forcing me to change tack. 'But I trust you, and there's nothing really else to say.'

'Hang on, so what are you saying?'

I sipped the tea. It was scalding hot and I recoiled. Josh leaned over and gently took the mug from me, placing it back on the table. I had no idea what to do next. My own guilt was making it impossible for me to breathe, let alone be legitimately angry with him, even though Tess hadn't been lying when she'd bullied me all those times, and I felt like a fool for believing Josh. I looked at him now. He couldn't be sitting any closer if he tried, despite being on another piece of furniture. I took a deep breath.

'Josh, I think I need some space to think about all this.'

There. I hadn't lied, I had just omitted. And he would have to understand, after what he'd just told me, that I would need some space. I had a head full of directions and no map.

To my surprise, he let out a massive sigh of relief and grinned.

'*Space?* Space I can do. Oh, Jeanie, I was so sure you were going to call it all off. I was convinced, and I was so hoping you would be understanding, even though I know I did wrong. But there was no cruelty or deceit intended, and there is absolutely nothing going on with Tess and me. I couldn't be less attracted to her. That's over – no more. She's gone. It's you, Jean. All you from now on. And you have some space, by all means. But, just so we're clear, y'know, *I* don't need any. I'll just wait until you're ready.'

I blinked a few times, trying to comprehend what had just

happened. He was totally cool with a break, and I would just call him when I was ready? This was unprecedented. I felt worse with everything he said. It was as though he knew I'd done something wrong and was now ensuring he did everything in his power to be the World's Best Boyfriend. (*Now comes with English Breakfast Tea-making skills!*)

This was crazy. I had to get out of here. The world had flipped upside down.

# ROUND 52
## Infatuation vs Deception

As Ingrid seemed to have forgotten she actually owned a shop, I'd taken the liberty of setting up my jewellery stand without her approval. I decided to just see what she said next time she came in, which, judging by current patterns, would be sometime around the third millennium.

I knew what she'd been doing, of course: faffing about with Justin. It was hard for me to understand how such a successful, together woman could just lose herself in a relationship like this, especially when he was still dicking her around with the whole 'I'll get divorced soon, baby' line. And yet there she was, going away to Melbourne with him on his business trips, staying in hotels with him, coming into the shop later and later, and taking long lunches. If she were my employee and not my boss, I'd fire her arse.

Grateful for the distraction from a head full of Josh and Cam, I had spent last night creating a jewellery stand. It was made from thin gold and silver wire, and was cross-hatched with collapsible support on both sides of the base. I'd come up with a 'logo' from my name, which I'd had printed onto black, in gold type. It was small, subtle, lower-case, discreet. I was very happy with it. At least *something* in my life was working right now, I thought.

I couldn't wait for a customer to see my designs, but as the rain was coming down on a diagonal slant, I'd be waiting a while. I thought of going next door to get Cam and show him, but I was uneasy at the thought of seeing him again. Instead, I sat down at the counter and rested my head in my hand. Whether anything came of that kiss or not, things would never be the same between us again. Just the idea of him made my insides go a little woozy, as though my arteries and veins had given up on blood and oxygen, and started carting around rum instead. I was nervous about what the universe had in store for me; clearly she had an entirely perverted sense of humour.

I heard my phone chime in with a text message. I wondered if it might be Josh, even though he'd assured me yesterday that he wouldn't contact me and would wait for me to make the first move . . . and here I was with a gooey little smile, listening to a mixtape made by Cam.

When I got out my phone, there were two animated envelopes awaiting me; the first was from Cam.

Stop thinking about me so much, I can hear it from in here.

I broke into a huge smile. God, he knew all the right things to do and say, didn't he? Little shit.

The second message was from a number I didn't recognise.

Hun, call me asap when u get this. Morg xo

My hands flew to my mouth and I gasped. Shit! I just remembered that I'd seen her and Phil the Pig the night I was with Cam! When I was drunk and falling all over a guy who wasn't my boyfriend. Uh-oh. And Phil and Josh were quite tight, too. Oh, shit. And here I was thinking my filthy little indiscretion would be safely tucked inside the cab driver's shirt pocket, never to be released.

I looked around: no customers, no sign of Ingrid. I dialled Morgan's number.

'All Year Tan, this is Morgan. HowmayIhelpyooo?'

'Hey, Morgan. It's Jean.'

'Jean! Oh my *God*, have I got some goss for *you*. Wait a tick, hun.'

I heard her muffle the phone receiver and talk a customer through the pre-spray-tanning requirements before coming back to our conversation.

'So, how did you pull up yesterday? You were pretty smashed Thursday night, darl, weren't you?'

I tried to giggle with her, but was too curious and scared to make a good go of it.

'Hahaha, yeah. I've felt better, that's for sure . . .'

'So anyway, get *this*. Phil was doing his *nut* over that guy you were with when we ran into you, right, as in like, where he knew him from? But he figured it out and you'll *never* guess!'

I gulped. Please let her say he knows him from the shop.

'He's that guy Tess has been seeing!'

I blinked, as though lubricating my eyes would help me to understand what Morgan had just said.

'I mean, you know Tess and I fell out but, God, I can't seem to avoid the silly cow. Anyway, so yeah, Phil has met him with Tess once before, at some cafe down at St Marks, and then I think I saw them at that club where her sister works, the Nursery? Back when we were still friends and she didn't carve me up to other people behind my back. Can you believe she was actually telling people we dilute our lotion? I mean, *every*one knows Summer Tan are the ones who dilute. Honestly, I don't know how Melinda is still friends with her . . .'

I wished my brain had a record button. I needed to hear that again. And again. And again. Because it wasn't making sense. *None of it made sense*.

'Anyway, thought you should know, 'cos I didn't know if you knew, and I know the troubles you're having with Tess and the whole Josh thing – well, everyone does, but that's the Bulls for you, no one's business is private. Speaking of which, Melinda and Ryan are, like, *so* over, and apparently Cassie and Camel are too, since Melinda went and told Camel that his baby was actually not even *his*, even though she doesn't have any proof whatsoever, which I think is a bitchy move if ever there was one, but she swears it's true, and I guess if you look at Flynn, you can kind of see —'

'Morgan, do you know for sure they were together? Tess and Cameron?'

'Well, unless kissing and cuddling is what friends do, ummm, yeah. That's why I thought it was so weird seeing *you* with him, because I know you and Tess don't get on, and if he's with Tess, well, I wouldn't be saying too much to him about anything, if you know what I me—'

'And how long ago did you see them?' I wondered whether Morgan could hear my heart hammering through the phone.

'Phil saw them last week, I think . . . You sound real confused, darl, and I was *sure* you didn't know, that's why I got your number off Lou, because I thought you should be careful, hun, you know?'

'I . . . I didn't know that, no. Thanks, thanks so much for the call, Morgan. I have a customer, I'll have to go.'

'Anytime, hun. I would never tell you something 'less I thought it was important, and I just had a feeling that this was, for some reason. You know, people can say what they like about us WAGs, but we stick by each other when it counts.'

'Thanks, Morgan, really. I'll see you soon.'

'Bye, darl. Come in for a spray this arvo, if you like; bit of colour always makes me feel better.'

I placed my phone on the counter in front of me. Then I placed my elbows either side of it and massaged my temples with my middle fingers. My eyes roamed as though I had just injected two kilos of speed; my brain raced at a pace that suggested three. Could this really be happening? No, no it just couldn't. It was too much. I felt like I was in some twisted thriller starring Halle Berry or Clive Owen.

How did Cam even *know* Tess? My mind flew back to the first time I'd mentioned Josh. Oh shit, he did know her. He'd straight-away mentioned that he knew her because her little sister worked at the Nursery.

So Cam obviously knew who Tess was, but did Tess know who Cam was? Did she know his connection to me? I couldn't see why else she would go for him. Sure, he was good-looking, but he was no F1 driver. And why wouldn't Cam tell me he was seeing Tess? And if he was seeing Tess, or whatever it was that they had going on, why would he make a move on me, and make me a mixtape, and be so fucking headfuckingly *keen*?

It was too screwed up for my brain to compute. I needed to speak to Cam so that he could tell me none of it was true.

# ROUND 53
## Friend vs Foe

I felt light.

I felt heavy.

I was going to fall over.

I grabbed at the doorframe and steadied myself. I peered through the racks of bright hoodies and deconstructed denim by obscure Swedish designers and I searched for Cameron Riley, because I was pretty sure that I urgently needed to cause him grievous bodily harm. But first I had to lure him next door.

I walked towards the counter, trembling. He was standing there, nodding to the music, typing on the computer, yelling over his right shoulder to one of his minions.

'Ssst!'

His head swivelled in my direction. Upon seeing me, a huge smile lit up his face, and his eyes shone with familiarity and fondness.

'Come next door for a sec?' I lifted my brows and gave what I hoped was a seductive, encouraging smile. He raised his brows mischievously before making a 'gimme two' hand signal.

I went back to the boutique, closed the door, hung the 'Back in seven-and-a-half minutes' sign, and waited. I felt each second pass, because with each came a new thought about what Tess and Cam could possibly have in common aside from myself and Josh, which led to another far more sinister thought, and another, and another, and my knuckles clenched and unclenched, and I told myself to stay calm and not to explode straight away, because I needed to extract as much information as possible from Cam before screaming at him and scaring him off.

I hoped that Morgan had it wrong, I truly did, but my gut told me she did not have it wrong, and in fact it was *me* who had it all so incredibly, mind-blowingly WRONG.

Finally, after several ice ages had passed, Cam's familiar head poked around the corner. He noted the sign on the door as he came in, and looked at me curiously.

'I don't know what you're up to, Jean Bennett, but I think I like where it's heading, you devilish little crumpet.'

I smiled and beckoned him over.

'I just wanted to ask what you were doing tonight,' I said, standing behind the counter, offering a smile that stopped at the lips.

'Did you now?' he said, walking closer, hands snugly in his jeans pockets, nodding his head. 'That was all?'

'And a little chat. You've got a few minutes for me, surely?'

He gave me a suspicious look. 'You've been drinking, haven't you? You're being all weird and flirty.'

'Well, there is one other thing —'

'I *knew* it!' he said, one finger wiggling at me meaningfully. 'Mary's got another flat, hasn't she?'

'No, actually, it's not about Mary. It's actually . . . it's actually about Tess.'

I watched his face change, but in the most miniscule fashion. If I wasn't loaded with ammunition, I would have missed the signs altogether: the sparkle in his eyes shutting down, the smiling lips slowly shrinking.

'What's she done now?' he asked in a singsong tone that was riddled with derision and non-verbal head-shaking. 'I thought you and Fox were done, anyway. Why do you still let her get to you?' He spoke dismissively, dotting the end of each sentence with disgust.

'It's not about *me* and Tess, though. Or even Josh and Tess. Is it, Cam?'

He looked at me, daring me to keep travelling down this path.

'How long have you been seeing her, Cam?'

He blinked twice, fast. 'Don't know what you're on about.'

'Um, I think you do.'

He made a snorting, guffawing sound and scuffed his foot. 'What are you on about? Jesus, you're as crazy as her now.'

'Am I? You sure? Nothing you need to tell me?'

'About *what?*' he spat.

'About how people saw you and Tess making out at the Nursery? And how a friend saw you guys down at St Marks?'

I had him. I had him and he knew it. His breathing had quick-ened and was now streaming through his nostrils as if he were an angry bull about to charge. His face, which I had previously thought so adorable, and so handsome, was now shrouded in rage and ugli-ness. He shook his head; the movement was tiny and accompanied by pursed lips and squinting eyes.

'You wouldn't understand.'

'What, that you have some kind of relationship with my boyfriend's ex-girlfriend who you have *counselled* me about, and then – and *then* – knowing how upset I was about Tess and Josh still hanging out, you put the moves on me, while at the same time you were actually fucking *her?*' I had to stop and take in a few breaths after such a huge sentence. 'Cam, you know what? You're right, I don't understand. *Please* enlighten me.'

He was gritting his teeth, staring at me with a quiet fury I could feel boring through my skin.

'I have never fucked her, as you so elegantly put it.'

'Whatever. Look me in the eye and tell me what I just said isn't true. You can't, can you?'

He breathed out and glanced sideways before looking to the ground.

'It's not what you think.'

'Then *what is it?*'

'Look, I met her through her sister one night. She was blind drunk. You'd only just started seeing Josh, and even though she was being 100 per cent DJ candy, spilling her drinks all over my equipment, all she spoke about was Josh fucking Fox. So, I put two and two together, and I got her number.'

'Go on.'

'I called her for a coffee a few days later. She couldn't even remember who I was – she was a fucking bitch, actually – but when I mentioned your name . . . well, she agreed to come along.'

The pit in my stomach widened by another four or five kilometres. My mobile rang on the counter in front of me – it was Mum. She'd have to wait, I thought, as I pressed the 'silent' button.

Cam shifted his weight to the other foot, visibly uncomfortable at having to verbalise what he'd done.

'All right, you know what? I'm just gonna put it all on the table. Fuck it. I'm fucked now, anyway. Jean, you never knew this, and I don't expect it'll account for much now, but pretty much the moment I met you, I . . .' He shook his head, looking down. 'I can't see how you never saw it. Everyone else managed to. You were, you *are*, an amazing girl. Everything I ever wanted – you're cool, you're funny, you're gorgeous, we have fun together . . . But I knew that you didn't think of me like that. And once Josh came onto the scene, I knew I didn't have a chance. The classic fucking high-school scenario all over again: dickhead jock gets the girl, loser arty type ends up alone, pining over the dream girl he'll never get blahblahfuckinblah.'

He took a breath and looked at me for any kind of sign that what he'd just admitted had softened me. I gave him nothing.

'Anyway, so I figured that Tess's all screwed up over Josh dumping her and I'm pissed because he's got my girl . . . so why don't we work together?'

'Work together how?' I hissed.

'Work together to . . . to split you two up.'

Tears sprang to my eyes. 'You would *do* that? Even though you could see how happy I was?'

He shook his head. 'How *happy* you were? Give me a break, Jean. You were complaining about him all the time – how it was all so hard, and how he was letting you down, and, well, Tess had already made her little sicko stamp on the relationship; all I had to do was keep encouraging her, really. And when you'd had enough,' he dropped his head, his voice now just above a whisper, 'I just had to let you know how I felt.'

A lone tear fell from my right eye; I immediately wiped it away and sniffed myself upright. He was *not* going to see me cry.

'Jean, look . . . Okay, it's outrageously fucked up, I know that. But what happened the other night in the cab *happened*. Don't deny it didn't feel right – you can't. I felt it, I saw it, it was meant to b—'

'Don't. Just *don't*.'

I turned my head and wiped a small band of escapee tears.

'Sometimes,' his voice was soft, 'people do crazy shit for love, Jay.'

'Get out. Get out of here.'

Like guitar strings being tightened, his voice shifted from soft and harmonious to hard and sharp.

'You know, Jean, I did you a favour. Tess and Josh are never gonna be over; they speak all the time. Okay, yeah, I guess I played you, but he was lying to your *face*.'

'I *know* that, he *told* me that, he *admitted* they speak, because she's a nutcase who'll probably jump off a fucking cliff if they don't! You do *not* compare what you did to what he has done. How *dare* you! You're *scum*. You make me *sick,* you know that? I can't believe that I was your friend and you did that to me. But most of all, I can't believe that for one second I actually *felt* something for you.'

He stared at me, unused to seeing me in such a frenzy.

'I said get OUT!' I didn't so much speak my words as chew them up and spit them at him. The tears were falling, the fury was flowing and he needed to take my advice or I was likely to throw a punch, or a cash register. He gave me one final look before turning to leave – a look of bitterness and disappointment. He walked to the door and, as he had done so many times before, stopped and turned to have the last word.

He looked at me menacingly. 'Oh, and just so you know, Tess will be telling Josh about our little moment in the cab, if she hasn't already. So if you thought you could go running back to your big hero footy guy, think again. Wheels were in motion well before you wised up, Jean.'

His angry eyes were mailbox slits, his words delivered in a foam of barely contained rage. He walked out and slammed the door.

As calmly as possible, I pulled my cardigan off the back of my stool, kneeled down behind the counter and, into its soft wool, screamed as loudly as my small, shaking body would allow.

# ROUND 54
## Wake-up Calls vs Selfishness

I felt hollow, raw, angry, helpless, agitated, lost and cruelly alone. I sat at home on the sofa, clutching a pillow, crying, crying, crying. I was in shock more than anything. I'd come horribly unstuck, losing it all because I stupidly thought it was all mine to begin with. Oh, it was all so *eeeasy*! Why, I'd simply freeze Josh until I decided if I wanted Cam, and *then*, once I'd decided who better suited me, well, I'd just let one kick the other into the gutter. A flawless plan! God, and I had the audacity to call Bones a player, and judge Cassie, and look down on Eric . . .

I heard the key turn in the door. I quickly wiped my eyes, sniffed, smoothed my hair and straightened up. I wanted so badly to tell Col everything that had happened, but I was worried she'd have no time, and even less sympathy, for her weasel of a sister. I realised with a sharp stab that I'd never even responded to her text about needing a chat the other night, because I'd needed to speak to Josh. Awesome. Way to fortify my plea.

She walked in, dumping her coat and bag and keys on the dining table.

'Oh, look who's home.' Her voice was tinged with disdain.

'Hey.' I sniffed.

'Are you crying?' She walked over to face me, eyes squinting, head on an angle, and it was confirmed that, yes, I was indeed crying.

'Jay, what *happened*?' Col immediately kneeled down in front of me and snapped into caring-big-sister mode. I must have looked pretty bad for her to drop the resentment without so much as a snipe. I shook my head, trying to keep the tears in.

'It's . . . it's okay. I've been such a . . . a cow to you lately . . . I'm f-f-fine.'

'Shut up, loser. What happened?'

I looked into her eyes, loving her for being Col. Technically, we weren't even speaking at the moment, yet here she was being kind and understanding.

'It's such a mess. I've ruined e-e-everything. Cam' – the sobbing kicked in – 'see, because, I just found out that Cam and Tess were together and they were trying to break Josh and me up, but I didn't know that until after I kissed Cam, and —'

'Hang on, whoa, whoa, whoa. You kissed *Cam*? Tess? *What?*' Her face was alert with shock and confusion. It didn't occur to me until this point just how far apart we had drifted; she didn't even know that Josh and I were having troubles with Tess in the first place.

I took her through the whole miserable scenario, being sure to play up the suspense and drama of the Tess-and-Cam reveal, and marginally downplay the part where I semi-dumped Josh. I was rewarded with *Noooooooo*'s and *You're fucking kidding me*'s in all the right spots, until there was nothing left to say and nothing left to do but for me to get up for some more tissues, because the measly collective I had clutched onto in my time of need looked as though they'd been through the claws of a playful labrador.

Collapsing back onto the sofa while Col remained on the floor – one arm resting on the sofa, propping up her head, deep in thought – I wondered what advice would finally spill from my sister's mouth. I knew it would be as blunt as a caveman's club, and probably delivered in a similarly fitting fashion, but I'd be grateful for *any* kind of guidance.

'So, Cam admitted that he and Tess were together?'

'Yep. Remember I told you he said that she'd already told Josh

we kissed? Which means they must've spoken today or yesterday.'
I shook my head, taking a new tissue to once more clear the banks
of the Great River of Snot.

'What a fuckin' little schemer. I mean, we all knew he liked you,
but I wouldn't have guessed he'd do something like this. That said,
they're kind of suited, Cam and Tess. Sickos. They could psycho-
logically torture each other happily without ruining anyone else's
lives – buying each other straitjackets for Christmas, Hannibal face
masks for Valentine's Day . . .'

I managed one of those noises that sits midway between crying
and laughing.

Col shook her head. 'And I thought *I* had relationship issues . . .'

'How . . . how is that all going, Col? The trial?'

She twirled a chunky curl with her left hand and shrugged.

'It's okay, I guess. I'm not sure, to be honest, if I will ever be able
to trust him fully. I really wish I could, but there's some serious scar
tissue there I just can't seem to get past, no matter how much he
tells me he's changed and he'll never do it again. But, you know, I
guess everyone deserves a second chance – we're all human and
yada yada yada – so I promised myself I will give it at least a few
months before I cut the cord once and for all. Who knows what'll
happen . . .'

There was a soft silence.

'Col, I'm . . . I'm so sorry for not being there for you. And not
just at your barbecue and shopping with Mum that day – although
I really am sorry about that – but emotionally, you know, the whole
bit. I've been so caught up in my own world and myself, and I know
this can't be easy for you after what happened with Eric, and yet, I've
just completely abandoned you. I'm an arsehole, Col. I apologise.'

'You'll hear no argument here: you *are* an arsehole.' She looked up
at me, a tinge of sadness in her eyes. 'I know I play tough bitch, but
I've really needed you lately. And it's partly my fault for not telling

you that. But, I don't know, I thought sisters were just supposed to feel it in their waters or whatever.'

I didn't expect that. But I did deserve it. Fresh tears, direct from the Non-relationship sector of my brain, filled my eyes.

'Don't get all upset. Just be a grown-up, Jean, and accept that not everyone's going to love you all the time. Especially if you let them down. I'll forgive you, but sometimes you gotta take your blinkers off and be a bit more sensitive to the people you love, and what they might be going through.'

I nodded, gulping back my tears and wondering how I hadn't fallen between the cracks of the sofa, seeing as I now felt around 1.6 centimetres tall.

'And did you even know BillyJeanSkyBelle was sick?'

'What?'

'She's got cancer.'

I felt as though I'd been punched in the stomach.

'She's got *cancer*? But she's only young? And so healthy. You couldn't find a more loved, better-looked-after cat . . . '

'Yeah, well, cancer's indiscriminate, Jay.' More tears, this time from the Guilt and Sadness sector, came forward to offer their wares. 'Mum told me last week. She said she'd tried to call you but you never called her back. Surprise, surprise . . . ' She punctuated her sentence with a bitchy raised eyebrow.

But I was oblivious to Col's conversational thorns; my thoughts were with Mum. BillyJeanSkyBelle was like her third child; she'd be a mess. I was disgusted with myself for not calling her back, and not realising she was upset. How did I go from living with her, seeing her every day, to not even finding the time to call her back?

Col exhaled loudly. 'Don't get all angsty and suicidal. Just make sure you call her tonight.' She got up, stretching out her legs, and then sat on the edge of the sofa, looking at me.

'Rough day, huh?' she smiled.

I placed my head in my hands and shook my head. 'The worst.'
My words were muffled, my heart broken up like some kind of
infographic pie chart into all the areas of my life I had screwed up
and needed urgently to rectify.

'So, what you gonna do about Josh?'

I took my hands away, folding them across my chest.

'Don't think there's anything I can do.'

'I agree. You should give up.' I looked up at her, bewildered. She
had a mischievous smile pasted on her face. 'Of *course* you don't
give up, idiot. You love him, right? If you think about it, he really
hasn't done anything wrong. Poor bastard. Look, he's a bit dumb,
done some silly things, but he adores you, and he's a good man.
You both made mistakes but, God, it's not like you fucked his best
friend, or he had a gang bang in the dunnies with a bunch of groupies – you'll both get over it. What was that I was just saying about
everyone deserving a second chance?'

My face was focused on Col but my mind was already out the
door. She was right. This was ridiculous. We'd been set up and it
wasn't fair. Josh would understand, of course he would! He loved
me, and I loved him, and this was just a big, ugly, garlicky hiccup.
I'd tell him everything, and we'd get back on track and things would
be wonderful again.

# The Preliminary Final

I called Josh again. No answer. Maybe he was in the shower, or at the gym or something. It was 11 a.m., so even if he'd gone out and had a big night, he should be awake by now. Time for a text.

Foxy, can we talk? Please call me when you get this x

Two hours passed; no reply. Steph called, but I let it ring out. Her voicemail was so sweet, so protective – asking if I was okay because Mitch had mentioned that Josh and I were having troubles, and could she do anything – that it almost brought me to tears. It didn't even bother me how fast word was spreading – right now I was grateful for support and offers of shoulders.

But no call from Josh. I turned my phone on and off to check that it was still working, and called it from the shop, just to double-check. It was working. I tried calling once more – nothing. He would now have six missed calls from Little Jeanie, which was how he'd saved me into his phone (along with a smiley picture of me from our weekend at the beach house). I'd tried to call three times last night, after my chat with Colette, filled with hope and intention and resolution, but he hadn't answered. I'd called Mum first, and had an hour-long catch-up, peppered with apologies (mine), dismissals of apologies (hers) and tears for BillyJeanSkyeBelle (hers and mine).

I needed to get some feedback, some reassurance from Col. I was losing my mind trying to relocate my heart.

Col, he's still not answering . . . ☹

I stared out at the street. I wondered if Cameron Fuckstick was next door. I hoped he was, and that someone had poisoned his coffee and he was currently writhing about on their stupid polished-concrete floor in agony.

As I leaned miserably on the counter, it suddenly occurred to me that my jewellery stand was gone. Oh, Ingrid was *unbelievable*, she really was. I'd briefly shown it to her yesterday, when I was a complete mess, and sure, maybe I couldn't muster the enthusiasm the occasion deserved, but even so, why would she take it down so callously the moment I left? She'd told me she was impressed, and that the pieces I'd made were perfect now that the weather was warmer and we'd had a rash of light, flowing 'Hippy Luxe' dresses and tops come through. Said she would probably even sell some of it last night! Told me I was talented, even! And then she'd gone and taken it away – probably jammed it out the back with those ugly ruffled skirts not one person had bought. She was a bitch, a deadset bitch. I'd worked *so* hard on that stuff.

My phone lit up, vibrating and chiming with expectation. What if it was Josh? No, Col.

J, don't 4get he knos u kissed cam . . . prbly v v hurt

Of course. For all I knew, Tess had painted an outrageously salacious picture of what happened between Cam and me, and Josh was sitting there looking at my name flash up, thinking: *Fuck off, you filthy little tramp. Why don't you go hang out with your DJ mate?*

I felt nauseas, jittery, panicked. I hated to think of Josh thinking so ill of me that he'd just write me off, wipe his hands of me, without even allowing me to explain myself. I couldn't bear it. I needed to see him. It was an emergency. The longer he thought badly of me, the more people who'd find out and the harder it would be to convince him things weren't as they seemed. My breath was short, sharp, fretful, like I'd just come up for air after being underwater those few seconds too long.

Col, I feel sick. What should I do?? He must hate me.

This time, she was quicker to respond.

I guess u need 2 trk him down. Wd he b @ his house?

She was right. I needed to confront him, this, everything. I needed to ask him for forgiveness, and explain the extent of Tess and Cam's meddling. I went out the back to get my bag and re-do my makeup. Where the fuck was Ingrid? Couldn't she come into work before 3 p.m., just once? Too bad. I would call her and tell her it was an emergency and I had to go.

I heard the electric alert signal that someone had entered the shop. Dammit, not now! I came out to see a girl of about my age, dressed in tight faded blue jeans, a cool little red blouse, and muted silver ballet slippers. She had a brown bob with a sharp fringe, and winged eyes masterfully lined with liquid liner. Wow. That kind of liner perfection was impossible.

Her eyes were scanning the counter anxiously.

'Hi.' I tried for a relatively cheerful tone. 'Can I help you?'

She looked up, eyes wide, sparkling, smile beaming.

'Hi! I'm just wondering if that big cuff is still for sale? I'm hoping it hasn't been sold, but I didn't get paid until today, and the woman – the other woman, with the dark hair? – she said she couldn't put it aside because someone else already said they were coming back for it . . .'

I looked at her, frowning.

'Which cuff was it, sorry?'

'Um, it was kind of gold and black, with, like, leaves and —'

'Birds?'

'Yeah, that's the one!'

She was talking about my cuff, that *I* made. She wanted to buy it – she'd come all the way back with her money. Pride and excitement tried to push their way into my cerebral cortex, but anxiety and panic had already set up camp there so territorially that they had to settle for perching on a small rock until it was their turn.

'Um, I'm really sorry, but I don't know where it is . . .'

'Where what is?'

The First Lady of Fashion had strolled in, looking impossibly thin and glamorous, still wearing her enormous black sunglasses and holding a coffee.

'Oh, hi!' said Fringey. 'I came in last night? I was hoping to buy that black and gold cuff with the —'

'Yes, I remember. Unfortunately I sold that one. I'm really sorry, I had no idea those pieces would sell out in one day' – she shot me a look which, although I'd never seen it before, I guessed was the Ingrid equivalent of a high-five – 'but the designer should be delivering a new collection within the next few weeks.'

Fringey scrunched up her nose. 'Oh, shaaaaame. I really liked it. Can I put my name down, maybe, so I don't miss out next round?'

'Of course. Jean here would be happy to take down your details.'

I looked at Ingrid, my hands shaking, asking with my eyes if this was really happening. She nodded, smiled and winked.

'Okay, so it's Hannah Atkins, A-T-K-I-N-S, and my email is Hannah at Gloss, G-L-O-S-S . . .'

I heard her but wasn't listening. I wrote down the letters and numbers she told me, but there was a good chance I'd written them in Sanskrit. Once she had gone, I turned to face Ingrid.

'What just happened?'

'What? It's fairly simple: your collection sold out. In one day. *Half* a day. What's there to be confused about? It's no big deal.'

There was a mischievous smile etched onto her perfectly made-up face.

I smacked my hands onto my cheeks in disbelief.

'Really?'

'Really. Congratulations, Jean.'

And then Ingrid did something so foreign to her that I almost forgot how I was supposed to respond: she came in for a kiss on the cheek and a hug. It was awkward and it was over quickly, and I was grateful that it was, but still, *affection*! Who knew she was even capable of such a thing.

She reached into her Hermès shopping tote and pulled out a bottle of Veuve Clicquot champagne, wrapped with a big bow.

'This is for you and your new career as a world-famous jewellery queen.'

'Ingrid, you shouldn't have! Thank you.'

Today was fucking ludicrous. Here I was thinking she had taken my work out the back because it made the shop look cheap when, in fact, it had completely sold out and she was pleased. It occurred to me that I hadn't priced any of the pieces; I was going to let Ingrid do that.

'What did you end up selling them for?'

'I started at, what was it, $75 for the earrings and went up to $150 for the necklace. Could've gone higher, easily. Silly, really. Never mind, there's always next time. There's a nice little envelope for you under the till.'

I was in shock: people were prepared to pay $150 for one of *my* necklaces?

'Ingrid, thank you . . .'

She smiled genuinely and began to scan the racks for protruding hangers. I took a deep breath.

'Um, Ingrid, I have a favour to ask. There's . . . we . . . I can't go into it right now, but I messed up with Josh and he thin—'

'Go.'

'Really?'

'Yes. Come back later, if you can.'

I picked up my bag and phone, and smiled at the strange, kind version of Ingrid standing before me. Was she real? I didn't have time just now to find out.

'Don't forget your fizz. Maybe you two can drink it as you're making up.'

She held out the champagne, winking.

*If* we made up, I thought.

# The Semi-final

He wasn't home. Even his parents seemed to be out. I called his mobile and his home phone – nothing. I considered switching off my caller ID and calling again, but would need to wait, as he'd surely figure out my tactic if I did that straight after my other calls.

I sat on his front step and thought about what I should do. What I *could* do. The season was over, there was no training – he could be anywhere. I racked my brains – had he mentioned anything about what he was doing this week? – but came up with nothing. I stared at my lifeless phone, wishing with all my might for him to call.

*I* knew who to call – Paola! I'd been meaning to call and tell her all this for days. I was mindful that she may have already heard, but figured she would have called by now if she had. Steph and Lou were both away, but because of complications with Jimmy's injury, he and Paola had had to postpone their trip to NYC. Paola was understandably thrilled.

On multiple occasions I'd heard the girls talk about how hard it was to cope with injuries – not only physically, but emotionally. The boys turned into surly, miserable lumps. Lou was particularly enraged that the club always made the boys get any lingering injuries operated on as soon as the season was over so that the off-season was spent recuperating rather than having fun or travelling. She thought it was a ploy to make sure the boys didn't party too much.

I dialled Paola, praying she would answer.

'Shut *up*!'

Bingo.

'I was gonna call you today! You musta got my ESPN!'

'ESP?'

'Whatever. Now, chica, you got some things you wanna tell me? Huh? Here I am thinking you this sweet little girls and turns out choo haves *two* men!'

I cleared my throat. 'Um, well, why don't you go first? Tell me what you've heard. Sounds entertaining.'

She laughed. 'Jeanie, genie, 'sokay, no judgements from me.'

'What have you heard?' The familiar feelings of nervousness and illness swooped back into my stomach.

'Well, the first one I heard is that you and Josh are over. This one true? I told Jimmy it can't be; you two are in love! Did this really happens?'

I took a deep breath and filled her in on every sordid detail. Artic-ulating it somehow made it sound even worse than it was, as though I was describing another girl – another awful, stupid little girl who any third-party observer could tell had made a categorical error. I momentarily wished I was back with Mum and Godfrey, pottering along, living an easy life. Hell, I'd even give Jeremy another chance, just so long as life could be simple and easy again.

'Oh, chica. It's a sad story. But I'm sure wherever Josh is – actual-lys, I know where he is, he's in the Gold Coasts with Bones – he's not happy, and he's missing you.'

I tried not to think about what a single Josh and a single Bones could be getting up to on the Gold Coast, where girls preyed on footballers like the Japanese preyed on whales. I shuddered. Any money he was taking 'revenge'. I wanted to find Tess and place an iron set to linen on her hand for several minutes as I gave her a piece of my furious, spinning mind.

'*Honey*, this is movies stuff! What choo gon do?'

Missing its cue by a few seconds, the golf ball in my throat quickly scooted up to somewhere near the back of my mouth.

'That's why I'm calling you . . . I have no idea. I've been trying to call Josh, but he's not taking my calls, and I even went to his house, but obviously he's not home 'cos he's off having jacuzzis with Bones and a bunch of eighteen-year-olds . . .'

I could hear her take a gulp of whatever it was she'd been sipping throughout the phone call.

'What you need to do is 'splain everything, like you did to me. He'll be angry but he will see your view. What choo *really* need is Tess to tell everything.'

'What does she care? She's wanted me gone from day one. I bet they get back together again now . . .'

I heard the sound of liquid being rapidly expelled from a mouth without any warning or intention. Then some muffled expletives (no doubt) in Spanish, before Paola was back in my ear.

'Are you *kidding*? After these trick she's played?'

'But *he* doesn't know that!'

'Then you *tells* him!'

'*How*? He won't answer my calls.'

There was a thoughtful silence, and another mouthful taken.

'Jus' shows up.'

'Where?'

'Friday night! It's presentation night! He has to be there. Just shows up and talk to him.'

Presentation night. Of course. In all the drama, I'd forgotten it was this Friday. I had bought an incredible olive-green floor-length dress and made a special pair of earrings for it, too. I'd even helped Cassie choose a dress from the shop, to prevent her from looking like one of the girls who accompanied rappers to nightclubs in film clips, which is the effect her original choice would've had.

'Isn't that kind of stalking?'

'*Noooo!* Maybe. Chica, you gotta tells him what happened. You can't let it finish like this. I won't let you.'

I started blabbering, nervous at the idea of what she was suggesting, and quietly delighted at how protective and supportive she was being. I had to hand it to them; the WAGs had really stepped up to the plate in my time of need.

'But . . . what if he takes Tess? He might take Tess instead of me. Everyone takes partners, right? What would stop him from taking her? In his eyes —'

'Jeanie, it's *perfect*! I'll tell Jimmy we will pick up Josh, and then when we getting close, you'll be waiting there, and I'll walk away with Jimmy, and you grab Josh and tell this story.'

Paola sounded very satisfied with her plan.

'Just ambush him?'

'You tells me another way that is better.'

She had a point. Even in Spanglish, she had a point.

# The Grand Final

I sprayed on some more Chanel Coco Mademoiselle, which Josh had bought for me duty-free when he flew to New Zealand last month, and checked my makeup for the eighteenth time in as many seconds. I'd deliberately done Josh's favourite look: a string of winged brown eye-liner along the lash line, à la Audrey Hepburn, and lots of mascara. Fresh, glowing cheeks, lots of gloss and my newly dyed, shiny, mahogany hair blow-dried to soft, bouncy perfection, and I was as Jean as I could be. The hair had been done in an attempt to show him that I was still the same girl he fell in love with, that I hadn't really changed. I had had far too much time over the past few days to think about what a different person I had become since meeting Josh, and most of it was pretty unsavoury.

My outfit was going to be wrong, no matter what I wore. Everyone would be in full glamouflage: Jimmy would be suited up, Paola would be wearing a beautiful gown and Josh would be sporting one of his made-to-measure Zegna suits (probably the dark blue one – I'd been to the fitting with him). In the end, under Col's guidance, I'd gone with a cute little flippy floral dress that I thought made me look cute and harmless: the sartorial version of a small, fluffy kitten.

Was Tess going to be with them? I wanted to know *now*. It was killing me waiting here, parked near the club like some kind of deranged, gypped prowler spying on her ex-boyfriend. Good lord! It suddenly occurred to me how Tess I was being, waiting here to

332

ensnare Josh. No – mental stop sign. I mustn't think like that. This was different, it was definitely different.

Jesus, it was 6.35 and Paola still hadn't texted me —

My phone vibrated in my hand.

FOX TRAVLS SOLO

Paola's inability to text in anything other than screaming caps did little for my nerves. And only 0.003 per cent of my anxiety dissipated knowing that Josh was sans lady friend. I wouldn't have known what to do if he'd brought someone different, replaced me in the time it takes to send a text message. But if it had been Tess . . . well, that might actually have worked out okay, provided I had Cameron hiding behind a nearby tree, willing to come out and bully Tess into telling the truth – a scenario only slightly less feasible than Paris Hilton tapping on my window to ask for directions.

I felt my phone vibrate again.

ABT ARIVE U HV DO THIS B STROG ! !

'Be strog' indeed. My heart started pounding along at sprint pace, my breath shortened, my palms became damp and clammy. I had parked right near the entrance to the club. It was a no-stopping zone but there was no option. I at least needed the shelter of Mary.

I saw Jimmy's Audi pulling up and I dropped my head. Because obviously that would make me invisible, and Mary too. He was lining up to park in the disabled spot. Bit cheeky, I thought, but then I guess he *was* temporarily disabled.

I saw Josh get out on the driver's side and Paola's long legs leap out like lightning. She bolted around the back of the car, incredible peachy-tan dress falling elegantly around her, as her eyes darted about furiously for me. I waved and she saw me. She motioned for me to get out quickly, and then retrieved Jimmy's crutches from the boot.

I took a deep breath and stepped out of Mary. I shook out my clammy hands and tried to focus on the speech I had mentally prepared over the last few days, but it had vanished.

Josh stood on the pavement, facing Jimmy's parked car. He looked incredible: tanned and healthy and striking in a beautiful dark grey suit with an open-necked stormcloud-blue shirt. He hadn't seen me; head down, he was fiddling with a cufflink. The evening sun framed his silhouette, making him look as regal, holy and untouchable as he was – at least to me, right now. He waited for Jimmy and Paola, then accompanied them towards the front doors of the club, which had been tarted up with several enormous potted palm trees and a deep Bulls-blue carpet.

I walked towards Josh, moving gingerly but quickly to make sure he didn't disappear inside before I could reach him. I was five steps off the entry when the sound of Paola and Jimmy cursing penetrated my tunnel vision; they were squabbling, lovingly, over Paola's inability to pull Jimmy and his crutches along effectively. Quickly, Paola looked over at me and gave me the thumbs-up. Jimmy followed her gaze and gave me a strange look: it was neither disdainful nor encouraging, but just, *Oh, there you are*. I got the message: I'd messed with his 'brother'. Jimmy's contempt made my nerves triple. My fight-or-flight instinct smacked me fair in the head.

I couldn't do it. There was no way. The timing was wrong. I made to turn around and get back into Mary when Josh looked up and saw me. For the faintest second I saw something in his eyes that resembled affection. Then, as fast as it appeared, it disappeared, and all I could see was repulsion. I walked quickly towards him. It was now or never. I was going down fighting.

But he threw the first verbal punch.

'I have nothing to say to you, Jean.' He began to follow Jimmy and Paola into the club.

'Josh, I gave you six months of my life. Please may I have as many minutes?'

He stopped, jamming one hand into his pocket. Even the back of him was beautiful. He scuffed his foot twice and then turned, squinting into the sun.

'Start speaking.'

He was so cold. Everything about him screamed that he would rather be lying under the footpath than standing on it with me. I saw Morgan and Phil come round a corner and walk towards me, Josh, and the entrance to the Bulls presentation night. What the *hell* was I thinking coming here? I wanted to melt into the earth, Wicked Witch of the West-style. Morgan was wearing what could only be described as a long gold tube, with a huge slit up the left leg that broached on inappropriate, and gold bejewelled heels with straps that wrapped around her legs to just below her knees. Her hair was coiled on top of her head and her ears bore enormous gold hoops. She looked so . . . snaky.

Morgan shot me a look that said good luck. I didn't look at Phil. They disappeared inside and I resumed the most awkward conversation in history.

I took a step back, hoping Josh would follow my lead and move away from the entrance, but he stood rigid.

'Josh, please allow me to explain.' I took the biggest breath my lungs could cope with and began. 'You've not answered one call or text; you've not even bothered to ask me what the truth is.'

He laughed a nasty laugh. 'Well, you said you wanted space, Jean.'

I glared at him. 'I know what Tess has told you, but perhaps you might like to know what she did to get things to where they were.'

'Oh, here we go. It's all Tess's fault again. I suppose she was the one who made you get it on with your little retail mate?'

'Well, kind of, yeah.'

He chortled. 'Give me a break.'

'Did you know she'd been *seeing* him? That she had been for months, and that the two of them had been trying to break us up? Did she happen to mention *that* when she was dragging my name through the mud?'

'Save it, Sherlock. I don't have time for this.'

I was astounded by his arctic manner. I'd only ever known him to be warm, funny, engaging, wonderful. But bugger it; it wasn't ending like this. I'd made an utter dick of myself standing out here in a sundress while everyone else arrived in black tie and I was going to get my point across, dammit.

'Well, *make* time for it. Yes, I was drunk, and I kissed Cameron. But you must be able to see that that would not have happened if there were not some serious problems in our relationship already. Tess had interfered so much and driven a wedge so far between us that I was angry. And when Cameron *pretended* to be the sympathetic ear, I took it.'

'Am I supposed to clap?'

'Josh, I'm asking for forgiveness. Whether you grant that or not is up to you, but please just hear me out first.'

He sighed dramatically and folded his arms.

'Josh, please don't forget that *I was very upset with you*. As far as I knew, you'd been doing me wrong for months with Tess, and yes, I now see that you were a pawn in her game, but the only reason Cam even made a fucking move on me was because Tess had *told* him to, because she had spoken to *you*, and you had told her that things looked like being over with me. So because she wants you back so bad, and always has, and because Cam had a thing for me, the scene was set for those two to prey on my vulnerability the minute things weren't sunshiney between us, for the simple purpose of going back to you and telling you what I did, so that we would break up for *good*!'

I was crying now, trying to catch my breath after my dramatic soliloquy, with all my carefully applied makeup sliding down my face. Finally, I saw a glimmer of kindness in Josh's eyes. He sighed again and shifted his weight to the other foot.

'How do you know all of this? That they were together?'

I wiped my eyes carefully, hoping I didn't look like a junkie or a vampire. Another couple walked past us and into the club; I didn't recognise them, but both took an appallingly tactless look at us before going in. I can only imagine how rapidly the gossip about our little scene would be infiltrating the pre-ball drinks inside.

'Morgan and Phil saw Cam and me when we were out, and they recognised him from seeing him with Tess. So I confronted Cameron, and it all came out.'

He looked away from me and shook his head before speaking quietly. 'When Tess told me what you did, I was so angry, and so disbelieving, but she would not let up. It was like her wish had finally been granted, and she didn't care that I was hurt or upset. She couldn't understand that I didn't want to jump into bed with her.'

A wave of intense anger and jealousy rose within me. A visual of Josh and Tess in bed crept into my mind without permission and made me physically ill with rage. I now had some idea of what Josh must be feeling about Cam and me.

Josh finally looked back at me. 'She's lost the plot.'

I raised my brows as if to say, no shit.

'I'm angry, Jean, of course I am. But I guess I have to take some responsibility for her, for how this may all have unfolded.'

Sensing an opportunity, I jumped in.

'I'm so deeply sorry for what I did, Josh. But . . . we can try to work things out. I mean, if she's gone out of our lives . . . And Cam – you don't need to worry about Cam, he's dead to me, I —'

He was shaking his head. 'I don't know, Jean.'

I didn't know what he didn't know, but I figured that if I stayed quiet it would come out. I'd said more than enough. I wondered if one kiss in the back of a cab had ruined my chances at happiness with Josh. Didn't I get *any* points for honesty and begging for forgiveness and stalking him in a dramatic Romantic Comedy way?

He looked at me, his mouth flat, his eyes full of something unidentifiable – maybe anger, maybe sadness, maybe defeat.

'Jean, it's too late . . .'

Something fell somewhere far away – a Boeing 747, perhaps – and I felt the shock ripple through me. That sentence, *it was the wrong one*. That was not what he was supposed to say! I had tried to prepare for the fact that he might not want to give it another chance, but I now saw in high-definition that that was like trying to prepare for a flood with a pair of floaties.

'What do you mean?' I asked, my voice barely above a whisper.

He took a step towards me. 'This isn't the place or the time . . . I have to go.'

'We're leaving it like this? That's all you have to say to me?'

I hated how desperate and small I sounded, but in the race between my head and my heart, my heart had just been given a pair of rocket boots. I saw Ryan arrive, without Cassie, and I pretended not to see him. He made moves to come over, but, sensing the situation, put his head down and walked inside.

'No, Jean, it's not that black and white —'

'Oh, I think it is, actually. I'm damaged goods now, aren't I? I have one kiss and I'm fucking Satan. Well, that's just fine. You seem to have made up your mind, and if you can't see yourself forgiving me for one mistake, even though your ex-girlfriend was the whole reason *any* of this happened, and we had an *excellent* relationship apart from that, well then fuck, Josh, I love you, but I'm not going to stand around and —'

He stepped closer, took my hands gently and looked at me with his huge blue eyes.

'Jean, Jesus! Get a grip. That's not what I meant. I've . . .' He took in a breath and exhaled it slowly, never once dropping contact with my teary, miserable eyes. 'Look, I've signed a contract to play in France.'

I stopped. Stopped crying, stopped fuming, stopped breathing.

'You've *what*?' I whispered, my vocal chords only barely indicating that I was still alive and functioning normally.

'You knew I was looking for a new contract. Well, a French club came through with an offer I couldn't refuse. Mark Scott had a contact over there, and we had a couple of emails and conference calls. I'll earn in two years what it would take me ten to earn here, and I don't have ten years left in me.'

I swallowed in an attempt to create some saliva so that I might speak.

'When . . . when do you go?'

He looked down. 'I have to leave next week. The season has already started there and they need a full-back pretty bad.'

I looked down, trying to take in his words. He was leaving the club, the country, me.

'Jean, I know – it's full-on. But, well, let's just say Henry's not so much releasing me from my contract a year early as kicking me out. And after what happened between you and me, and with the money on offer, all signs pointed to yes, you know?' He seemed to be waiting for a response. Failing to get one, he kept going. 'You must be able to see my reasoning, Jean? It wasn't an easy decision, but I honestly felt there was nothing left here for me. I had a few days with Bones, just fishing and drinking and talking it over with him, and I feel like it's right.'

I looked up into his eyes, searching for any sign that this wasn't really happening. Nope, it was definitely happening. His eyes, gigantic and glassy, were not the eyes of someone who was about to slap his knee and tell me he was yanking my crank.

'I just thought that —' I faltered. What was the point? He was leaving anyway. Why spill any more guts than necessary on the pavement? No point. Messy. Stupid. 'I had no idea you were seriously considering France. I thought it would be, you know, Queensland, or Melbourne at the worst. But you're right. It all makes sense . . .'

I tried to smile at him, to show him I was happy for him. It didn't work. Instead I was rewarded with a fresh batch of tears. My tear suppliers were such dedicated workers.

He looked straight back at me, engulfing my gaze with his eyes, as if trying to say a thousand things with them that he couldn't say with words. He gulped and took in an epic breath, the kind you exhale through your lips after you've made them into a small tunnel.

'I know this might sound crazy, Jean, but maybe . . . maybe you could come with me?'

# Acknowledgements

Thank you to Rachel, Nicci, Kirsten and the tireless team at el Penguino Inc for indulging me with a title, book and cover that I am both proud of and delighted with. Thank you to Tara and Pippa for all your help and hand holdiness. Thank you to Mum, Dad and the whole dingin' family for being so proud and supportive. Thank you Meowbert for sitting two millimetres from my keyboard at all times, your big ridiculous eyes watching me adoringly as I thumped keys. (You *can* read this, right?) Thank you to all my cherished, ever-encouraging friends (especially Donk) for not dismissing me altogether as a Fun Young Person even though I've had my laptop on IV drip for 878 years. Thank you to Craig and the NRL for granting me access and insight into the football world – I, quite literally, couldn't have written this without you. Finally and most importantly, thank you to all the 'WAGs' – cricket, soccer, football, surfing, golf – I've had the pleasure of meeting/eating pies with over the years. It's a weird, wild little ride being the partner of a professional athlete and I admire and salute your strength and sisterhood. (Important Caps Locky Sidenote: The gnarly WAGs in this book are FICTIONAL. Can't have a good story without villains.) Special mention must go to Renee, who managed to make a beefed-up Holden and a State of Origin jersey look elegant, and Marie, not only the most gorgeous girl to ever grace a grandstand, but one of the most beautiful human beings I've ever had the joy and privilege of knowing.

ALSO BY ZOË FOSTER BLAKE

# Air Kisses

**If the devil wears Prada, then God wears La Mer.**

'Everyone knows that a beauty editor's headshot has to be
a masterpiece of shiny, bouncy hair, lacquered lips, twinkling eyes,
and well-blended eye shadow so that the readers believe that the
woman instructing them on bronzer application actually knows how
to apply bronzer. I looked at my headshot again. Gross. In a way,
it was symbolic: I was always going to be the girl with unblended
foundation and a wobbly trail of liquid eyeliner. In fact, the more
I thought about it, it was an absolute farce that I was advising women
on how to look perfect. But somehow, somehow, I had managed
to hoodwink everyone into thinking I had a clue about this beauty
thing. Until now, anyway.'

'Air Kisses *has launched Zoë Foster as a stylish, witty author
of chick-lit.*' SYDNEY MORNING HERALD

'Air Kisses *is written in such a sexy way that it's difficult to put
down . . . Clever and cheeky.*' SUN-HERALD

'*Its wit-strewn pages will give you a smile from ear to ear.*'
SUNDAY AGE

# the Younger Man

## He was only supposed to be a bit of fun . . .

When Abby enjoys a memorable night with a delicious 22-year-old, she easily waves him out of her life the next morning. She doesn't have time for these sorts of distractions. And he's only 22, after all! A child. But the charming young Marcus isn't going to let her get away that easily. He knows what he wants and takes it upon himself to prove that age is irrelevant where the heart is concerned. Abby, though, isn't convinced. She feels certain she should be with someone her own age, someone more impressive, someone more . . . settled. Surely nothing can ever come of this relationship?

*'Charming, witty and oh-so addictive . . .*
*A great read that will have you yelling, "I know*
*exactly what she means!" over and over.'*
**WOMAN'S DAY**